The ROYAL
Station Master's
Daughters *in* Love

Ellee Seymour is a journalist and PR professional living near Cambridge. *The Royal Station Master's Daughters* was her debut novel. Ellee was inspired to write it after meeting Brian Heath, the great grandson of Harry Saward, who was the royal station master at Wolferton for forty years from 1884 to 1924 and who the novel is based on.

Also by Ellee Seymour:
The Royal Station Master's Daughters
The Royal Station Master's Daughters at War

The ROYAL
Station Master's
Daughters *in* Love

ELLEE SEYMOUR

ZAFFRE

First published in the UK in 2024 by
ZAFFRE
An imprint of The Zaffre Publishing Group
A Bonnier Books UK Company
4th Floor, Victoria House, Bloomsbury Square, London, England, WC1B 4DA
Owned by Bonnier Books
Sveavägen 56, Stockholm, Sweden

A CIP catalogue record for this book is
available from the British Library.

ISBN: 978-1-83877-684-8

Also available as an ebook

1 3 5 7 9 10 8 6 4 2

Typeset by IDSUK (Data Connection) Ltd
Printed and bound in Great Britain by Clays Ltd, Elcograf S.p.A.

Zaffre is an imprint of Bonnier Books UK
www.bonnierbooks.co.uk

Dedicated to my darling grandson George.
May you enjoy a lifetime of peace and love

The living owe it to those who no longer can speak to tell their story for them

Czesław Miłosz, Nobel Prize winning poet and author

Chapter One

October 1919

'Come along, Rosie. Get a move on. The train will be 'ere in a minute and we can't miss it, else we'll be on the streets tonight.'

Kitty Willow had just set foot on the platform at the royal station, Wolferton, with her six fatherless children, their clammy hands gripping tightly to each other, frightened expressions on their faces. Kitty bit her lip and her dove-grey eyes looked away as shame engulfed her at the way she'd spoken to her daughter.

A young girl's voice whimpered, 'I'm scared, Ma. I want to go home.'

Kitty's tone softened. 'I didn't mean to shout, Rosie. We just need to get a move on. We're leaving 'ere, there's nought I can do to stop it.'

Rosie puffed out her cheeks and threw a doll she had been clutching onto the ground, pulling a defiant face.

A wave of emotion swamped Kitty. She wiped away a tear with the sleeve of her dark blue dress and crouched down to comfort her four-year-old daughter, dropping her bags at her feet. 'I'm sorry, Rosie. Please forgive yer ma for upsetting

1

yer. We 'ave to go, we don't 'ave any choice. Everything will be all right.'

She surveyed Rosie's own doll-like features with a sinking feeling in the pit of her stomach. Her porcelain skin and her peacock-blue eyes were framed by a mass of tumbling golden curls. Rosie's bottom lip quivered and her cheeks were puffed out and reddened. She sniffled and opened her mouth as if to bawl, but her eldest sister quickly stepped forward.

'Shush, Rosie,' Victoria cajoled, bending down to pick up the doll that Rosie had tossed aside on the platform. It was Rosie's favourite and she smoothed it carefully with her fingers. 'You can see Ma is upset. None of this is her fault and we must be good for her.'

Rosie snatched the doll from her sister and pressed it tightly against her chest. Her bottom lip wobbled as she wailed, 'I don't wanna go away. Why can't we stay 'ere?'

Kitty stretched her arms out to her daughter. Rosie stuck her nose in the air and turned the other way, sucking hard on her thumb and resting her cheek on her doll. Her reaction cut through Kitty's core like a sharpened blade and she winced, knowing she was the cause of her daughter's unhappiness.

Kitty could hardly blame Rosie for being upset. She was, after all, taking her children away from the only home they had ever known, here on the royal Sandringham Estate, leaving their friends behind, to start a new life with strangers who, like her, had fallen on hard times.

At thirty-one, with fine flaxen hair, milky skin and a heart-shaped face, she could only see one dark day after another, and a pitiful life that relied on the charity of others. She com-

2

forted herself with the thought that at least they would all be together and have a roof over their heads. With the chilly autumnal days and darker nights setting in, she had no choice but to accept whatever refuge was offered.

Kitty had intended to show a brave face as the family prepared to leave their cottage on the grounds of Appleton House on the Sandringham Estate where they had lived while she was in the employ of Queen Maud of Norway, Queen Alexandra's daughter. Notice to quit the tied cottage was served on her as her husband was still missing and unaccounted for almost a year after the end of the war, and the home was now needed for a new estate worker and his family.

In truth, she wasn't sure she was a widow; she didn't know if her husband was dead or alive. Frank Willow had vanished while fighting in the ill-fated Gallipoli campaign in August 1915 when he was serving along with the Sandringham Company. Like many other comrades from the royal estate who had signed up, his fate was unknown. He was *missing presumed dead*. With no body or witness accounts to prove he had died, she clung to the hope that he was still alive somewhere. She vowed that unless she heard otherwise from the War Office, she would never wear widow's weeds.

Inhaling a deep breath, Kitty pledged, *Whatever the future holds, I promise that my children will make something of their lives and never face being turfed out of their homes again.*

Rosie tugged at her mother's skirt. She lifted her face up, her bottom lip trembling, 'I'm sorry, Ma.'

Kitty embraced her daughter. 'You sweet child. It's me who should say sorry. I promise that all will end well, one day. We must have faith and believe our fortunes will improve. Until then, we must keep our heads down and get on the best we can. Do you think you can do that?'

Rosie nodded seriously. 'I will, Ma, I promise I will be a good girl. Will I be able to keep me princess doll and cuddle her when I feel sad?'

'Yes, of course you can,' Kitty replied softly. She took the doll from Rosie and tipped it upside down which turned its clothing inside out. 'See, she's happy now. Can you give me a nice big smile too?'

Rosie's face broke into a wide grin. The next moment she pulled a sad face to match the different mood on the doll's face as she flipped it inside out again. The doll had two heads; a smiley countenance was painted on one side which matched her pink floral dress with pearl buttons, but when turned inside out the doll had a sad expression and was dressed in a green costume edged with dainty white lace. It was Rosie's most treasured toy and had been given to her by Queen Maud on her fourth birthday.

Victoria pointed ahead. 'The train is coming now. It's time to go. Rosie, remember what I said, try to be good, for Ma's sake.'

Victoria caught her mother's grateful expression. Her eldest daughter was a replica of herself at thirteen years old, having the same heart-shaped face, milky skin, flaxen hair and dove-grey eyes. She had the kindest heart and was always willing to lend Kitty a hand when she was tired looking after the children, sensing it intuitively without being asked.

'*Thank you*,' Kitty mouthed gratefully to Victoria, as she ushered her brothers and sisters onto the train clutching their

4

few possessions. Victoria was aided by her twelve-year-old brother, Pip, who was taller than her and gangly, with spindly arms and legs. He now assumed the protective role of man of the house without complaint, though sadly they had no home of their own – for now.

Kitty bit her lip. A wave of nostalgia fluttered inside her as her eyes scanned the station for one final look. Royalty from all over Europe had stepped onto the platform where Kitty and her family now stood and she had considered it a privilege to work for them. There was no red carpet laid out today for a royal visit to Sandringham House, just two miles away.

From the corner of her eye she spotted the affable royal station master, Harry Saward, talking to three lady passengers with their young children further along the platform. Two of the women wore black armbands and were dabbing their eyes with lace-edged handkerchiefs. She caught Harry looking in her direction, his eyebrows raised, and their eyes met briefly.

She would forever be grateful to Harry and his wife, Sarah, and their daughters Jessie, Beatrice and Ada, for their immense support during her husband's disappearance. Jessie was particularly close to Rosie, she was like a second mother to her and had packed the children a bag of sweets and chocolates to take with them when they met the previous day to say farewell.

Rosie had been a playmate for Ada's son, Leslie, who was a year older, and enjoyed teasing her. If one of her children had a minor ailment, Beatrice, a nurse, would willingly offer her advice. Sarah had been like a mother to her and handed Kitty a fruitcake for the family to take away baked by their housekeeper, Betty.

Kitty had also become close to Maria Saward, the royal station master's step-sister, after her meeting through their work for the royal family, and Maria's young son, Joey, had adored the happy company of her children.

The porter was piling bags onto a trolley for an elderly couple who were in a carriage ahead of them. Her stomach knotted at the happy memories, the friendships and good life she was leaving behind.

She inhaled deeply, took one final glance of the station and picked up her bags, vowing only to return when she could hold her head up and feel no shame.

'Kitty!' cried a breathless voice, as she was about to board the train.

Kitty screwed up her eyes. She was incredulous. 'Maria? What are you doing here?'

Maria panted, holding onto her sides. She waited a moment to catch her breath. 'I was hoping to catch you before you left. I have something for yer. 'Ere, take this, it's for you and the little 'uns.'

'What is it?' she asked, eyeing the purse that had been thrust into her hand.

'It's a little something to keep yer going. The mothers from the baby group 'eld a collection for yer, and some others chipped in too when word about it got out. There's just over eight pounds.'

Kitty's heart thumped, her eyes moist. 'But, but . . . I can't take it.'

'You can and you must. We only wish it were more. I'll stay in touch with yer, Kitty, if yer don't mind. I promise, this isn't goodbye.'

6

Kitty hugged Maria, her throat thick with sobs. 'Make sure you do, Maria Saward. Will yer thank everyone for me.'

Harry suddenly appeared at her side. 'I wanted to say farewell. We are all so sorry to see you go, Kitty. I want to wish you the best and I promise I will let you know if I should hear any news about Frank. Everyone is doing their best to discover what happened to him. We'll never give up.'

Kitty dabbed her eyes with a handkerchief. 'Thank yer, Mr Saward. Someone must know what 'appened. I'm grateful for everything you and yer family have done for us.'

He thrust a brown envelope into her hand. 'God be with you all, Kitty.'

Kitty's voice wobbled. She stared at the envelope in her hand. 'But Maria has already given me some money. I can't take any more. It's too much.'

'Yes, you can, and you must,' Maria and Harry replied in unison, as the station master pressed her hand firmly around the envelope.

Kitty paused. 'I'll never forget yer kindness and I promise if I should have need to use it, I'll pay back every farthing.'

Kitty leapt aboard the train and joined her family in their third class compartment.

∞

A moment later, a fair-haired man in his late thirties with a moustache suddenly dashed onto the platform, his face flustered. He wiped his brow. 'Thank goodness, I've just made it.'

Jessie Saward, the station master's eldest daughter, rushed alongside beside the man, her sweetheart, Jack Hawkins, her eyes sad.

7

The royal messenger drew her towards him and enveloped her in his arms. She clung to him for a brief, but sweet kiss, feeling his heart beat with hers as one, not knowing when she would see him again after he embarked on his latest secret assignment. When Jack pulled away, he mouthed, 'I apologise that our time together was fleeting, but remember this, I love you, Jessie. I will see you again as soon as my duty permits. Goodbye for now, my sweetheart.'

Jessie, who suffered from a hearing affliction, read his lips and replied, 'I love you too, Jack Hawkins. Come back soon.'

Jessie knew once the train was out of sight her insides would be knotted; their partings, caused by his duty to the King, left a deep well of emptiness inside her. Her toffee hair was pinned up neatly and her violet eyes watched him take his seat towards the front in the first class compartment. *Is this how their lives would always be*, she asked herself pessimistically, twisting her hands in front of her.

The guard blew his whistle and raised his flag to announce the train's imminent departure. She felt a pang when the engine departed and she caught sight of the sad faces of Kitty's children glued to the window of their compartment as the black belching engine set off, rumbling along the line, a ribbon of steam trailing overhead until they were no longer in sight.

∞

Maria, Harry and Jessie were not alone in viewing Kitty's departure. Queen Alexandra was peering through the curtains in her royal retiring room on the platform and observed Kitty and her family, her curiosity roused by the commotion

8

Rosie had made. She had a keen interest in families living on the royal estate and her face was etched with concern as she turned to the station master's wife who was attending to her.

Wearing her favourite styled high-neck blouse with a pearl choker at the throat, a cleverly disguised wig of curly hair piled high on her head, she asked, 'That poor woman, Mrs Saward. I couldn't help but notice her struggling with all those children. Her face is familiar, but I can't quite recall her name. Do you know who she might be?'

'Yes, I do, Your Majesty,' replied Sarah, having witnessed the heart-breaking scene herself. 'That's the poor Willow family. I'm afraid they've had notice to leave their cottage at Appleton House. Her Frank was a gardener there and is one of the Sandringham Company still unaccounted for in Gallipoli.'

Sarah's last few words were spoken in a hushed tone. But the Dowager Queen understood only too well the meaning behind them.

'Poor woman. Yes, now I recall seeing her at Appleton House when I stopped by to visit my daughter, Maud. Do you know where they are going?'

'To the workhouse, ma'am.'

Now in her seventy-first year, the Queen Mother's shoulders shivered as she contemplated the thought. 'The workhouse? That's just too awful.'

She pondered for a moment. 'Please keep this to yourself, Mrs Saward, but I believe we might have news soon from Gallipoli. I am waiting to hear any day from the army chaplain who has just returned from a visit there seeking information. It's been far too long coming, and I have been trying so very hard on their behalf. I shall press him for news of Frank Willow. Everyone has tried so hard, but to no avail.'

'I know that, ma'am. We are all anxious to know the fate of the King's men.'

Queen Alexandra straightened her back and arched her long neck. 'How they manage to carry on, day after day, without knowing is beyond me.'

'They have no choice,' muttered Mrs Saward under her breath.

The remark went unheard by Queen Alexandra who had hearing difficulties. 'I would very much like to help Mrs Willow, if there is any way I can. I will give it some thought and discuss her situation with Maud. She is arriving tomorrow and I am sure will be concerned about the family's unfortunate situation too. Please keep me informed.'

'Yes, ma'am, of course. Kitty and her family were very well liked by Queen Maud, I am told.'

The Dowager Queen pressed a hand to her chest. 'While I still have breath in my feeble body I vow to discover the truth and help these unfortunate women whose lives have been ruined by that terrible war.'

Chapter Two

Joey was running rings around Betty when Maria stepped into the kitchen at the station master's house. Her four-year-old son dived behind a chair and Harry's good-natured housekeeper made pretend she could not see him.

'I 'ope he ain't been too much trouble. Thank yer for keeping an eye on 'im, Betty. I would 'ave been 'ere earlier, only I stopped off at the station to see Kitty.' Maria's eyes were downcast.

'Joey? Trouble? I have no idea what you are talking about,' chortled Betty in a loud mocking voice.

In a serious tone, she added, while filling the kettle with water, 'Tell me, how did it go at the station? Do you have time for a cuppa?'

Maria nodded meekly. 'I'd like that. It was very sad, I could see Kitty 'ad been crying and little Rosie was upset. How will they manage?'

Joey suddenly leapt in front of her. 'Boo! Yer couldn't see me, could yer, Ma?'

'Joey Saward! You 'ad me fooled there,' Maria retorted, ruffling Joey's dark hair between her fingers.

'Why was Rosie upset?' he asked.

Maria pondered before answering. Leslie, Joey and Rosie had been close playmates, and enjoyed running through the woods and having teddy bear picnics.

'Rosie and 'er family 'ave 'ad to move away to a new 'ome, but they're not far away. Once they've settled in, we can visit them.'

The answer seemed to satisfy Joey and Betty and Maria exchanged relieved glances. Joey hungrily devoured a slice of gingerbread the housekeeper offered.

Maria smiled appreciatively. 'You do spoil 'im. What would I do without yer, Betty?'

'I won't lie, I do get breathless and my back aches when I bend. But I keep pressing on. I fear if I stop, that will be it.'

Maria stirred the tea and sat alongside Joey, who was licking his fingers. He slid off his chair and picked up an abacus to play with, flicking the wooden rainbow-coloured counting beads from one side to the other and saying the numbers out loud.

Betty rubbed her back, wincing, and flopped into a chair. She had been housekeeper for Harry and his wife Sarah for twenty-five years and was regarded as one of the family. The creases that criss-crossed her kindly face were a sign of her milestone seventieth birthday that had passed the month before.

Maria rose from her chair as Ada and Jessie entered the room, accompanied by five-year-old Leslie.

Harry and Sarah joined them a moment later. Their expressions were subdued as there was only one topic of discussion – Kitty's and her family's distressing departure.

Jessie's melancholic feelings about Jack's departure were forgotten as she inhaled a deep, pained breath. 'I was delayed with Jack and didn't get the chance to say farewell to Kitty. I hope she will forgive me.'

At twenty-nine, she was the eldest of the station master's daughters and had become accomplished at reading lips since suffering hearing loss in one ear caused by a virus as a child. The words that slipped from her father's lips were too awful to believe and the concern etched across his face confirmed what he said.

She asserted, 'We can't abandon them to the workhouse. Kitty is our friend and I have a deep fondness for her children, especially Victoria who has the sweetest nature. I shall help Kitty and her family in any way I can.'

There was a chorus of consensual agreement. 'They do not know it, but they are not abandoned. Queen Alexandra saw the family depart and expressed concern. She has the family's interest close to her heart and she is a woman of her word.'

Ada, the youngest of the daughters at twenty-seven, agreed. 'I'm sure Beatrice will want to do something about it too,' she stated, referring to the middle sister, a nurse at Hillington Hall, a stately home used now for the rehabilitation of soldiers injured during the war. Beatrice had inherited her mother's dark features while both her sisters were fairer, like their father.

Maria was twenty years old, eleven years younger than Kitty, and had brown eyes, thick long auburn hair and a curvy figure. She became close friends after Kitty called in at the Big House, as Sandringham House is referred by locals. She was on an errand from Appleton House where she worked, one mile away, and while chatting Maria discovered Kitty's daughter Rosie was four years old, six months younger than Joey. Their friendship grew and Joey, being an only child, would beg Maria for them to visit Kitty as he enjoyed the company of other children.

He'd watch in fascination as Pip flicked his penknife open, picked up a piece of wood, and chipped away at it until it resembled a shape, usually an animal. The two women confided in each other about their work and lives and Kitty's situation made Maria realise that she too could have ended up in the workhouse, if it hadn't been for the kindness of Harry and his family.

Only four years ago when Maria and her mother, Ruth, faced the prospect of being homeless and destitute, they turned up out of the blue in Wolferton seeking help from Harry Saward. It had been a shock for the Sawards to discover that Maria was, in fact, Harry's step-sister, despite their thirty-eight year age difference, and she was step-aunt to Jessie, Beatrice and Ada, and much younger than them.

Harry's father, Willie, had been the station master at Audley End in Essex where Harry grew up, and had fathered ten children. After his wife died he remarried at the age of seventy-one, which set tongues wagging, especially as he wed his housekeeper, Ruth, who was only twenty-eight years old. They had three further children, Maria, Freddie and Archie, but when Willie died, his new family found themselves without a roof over their heads and turfed out of their cottage in his name.

Later, Maria could barely believe her good fortune when she was offered a position at Sandringham House, starting off as a pot washer, where she was only too willing to roll up her sleeves and do what was asked of her. She was determined to make the Saward family proud of her and prove her worth and was overjoyed when she became a maid in Queen Alexandra's rooms.

To complete her happiness, Maria had found love with Eddie Herring, a porter at the station, who she was engaged to marry. He adored Joey and she knew she wanted to spend the rest of her life with him, but, when he returned after the war, she could see he was not the same man; he was unable to face his old job and the constant loud noises from the engines.

Jessie pressed her hand on Maria's arm. 'Are you all right, Maria? You seem deep in your own thoughts.'

Maria's brows furrowed. 'I can't 'elp thinking that could 'ave been me and my family forced to live in the workhouse, if it weren't for your family.'

Jessie replied, 'Oh, I'm sure it wouldn't have come to that, Maria.'

'Are you? It could easily have been us.'

Joey tugged at his mother's sleeve. 'What's a workhouse, Ma?'

There was an awkward pause in the room. 'I'll tell you on our way 'ome. It's time we left,' Maria replied softly, rising to leave.

The mood was sombre as Maria bade her farewells. She turned to glance back at the grand mock Tudor station master's house when she reached the end of the path.

Joey asked, 'If Uncle Harry is the station master and this is his 'ouse, does that mean this is a workhouse, seeing as 'e works 'ere?'

15

Maria's eyes narrowed as she tried to make sense of Joey's question. When she realised what he was saying, she knelt down and took his small hands in hers. 'I see what yer mean, Joey. But, no, this ain't a workhouse, even though it's an 'ouse that comes with the job. Kitty 'as gone to a different kind of workhouse, I'm afraid. It's very big 'cause lots of people live in it, but it ain't grand like this. It's for poor people with no 'omes of their own.'

Joey pondered for a moment and put his arms around Maria's neck. 'It sounds 'orrible. I'd like to be a station master one day and live in a big 'ouse like Uncle Harry.'

Chapter Three

Nine miles south-west of Wolferton, in the busy port and market town of King's Lynn, Kitty and her family stood apprehensively in front of two towering iron gates.

'I'm scared, Ma. I don't like it here.' Rosie's voice quaked as she raised her eyes upwards towards the grey sky and blinked at the dark forbidding building behind the gate. Kitty felt a catch in her throat as she wondered how her country-loving children would cope in these dismal surroundings, unaccustomed to streets lined by tall industrial buildings with smoking chimneys and black sooted walls.

Kitty's heart drummed. She struggled to find words of comfort, engulfed by feelings of hopelessness. Her stomach churned as she took in the small windows which were dimly lit and stretched up four floors, offering no hope of comfort within.

Her attention switched to three women dressed identically in grey dresses, white aprons and mob caps scurrying across the yard carrying baskets of laundry, their faces masked with misery.

She watched as they walked quickly past the front door-step, keeping their eyes in front, and saw a severe-looking woman standing there with her arms folded across her chest watching their every move. She had a cold and austere manner and held her head high in a way that indicated she held a position of some authority. In the distance a church clock chimed five times. Kitty sighed with relief, thankful they had arrived punctually.

The workhouse was situated on the edge of the town, close to the busy docks frequented by sailors and dock workers who loaded and unloaded their cargoes, as well as a catchment of unsavoury characters who patronised raucous inns on the waterfront. Kitty suddenly noticed with alarm that a group of rowdy men were edging their way unsteadily towards them and were soon within spitting distance. Their smell preceded a couple of the men as they approached, the heady odour of their unwashed bodies wafting in the air. They paused and sidled up to Victoria, eyeing her up and down with interest. Her natural good looks, porcelain skin and oval-shaped eyes attracted admiring glances and it was clear to see Victoria had inherited her mother's good looks.

Kitty recoiled, her face plastered with fright. Pip stepped forward and thrust his chest out. Kitty feared a confrontation as she spotted Pip slip his right hand into his jacket pocket where he kept his penknife, and sensed he was about to warn him off, when the men sniggered, and wobbled off laughing.

One of them, however, the youngest of the group, in his early twenties, edged closer and fixed a crooked smile on Victoria's stricken face, showing his blackened teeth, his face almost touching hers. His dark eyes lingered on her face and he removed his cap and nodded slightly, his intense stare penetrating through her, before he turned tail and joined the others.

Victoria let out a distressed cry and covered her face with her hands. The ominous encounter made the children fretful. With the men out of sight, Victoria calmed herself and the children huddled around Kitty. She gently stroked their faces and tried her best to soothe them. This was a world far removed from the they lived in with their beloved father Appleton. There they could roam freely in the parkland and woods and merrily traipse along glorious country lanes lined with hedgerows and lace-topped cow parsley, playing chase with their young friends, Joey and Leslie, with a song in their hearts. There were no pretty cottages here with flower-filled gardens, no trees reaching up to the clouds, only a building that sent a shiver down your spine.

No mother could be prouder of her children. Victoria had a good head for arithmetic. She was a bright child who enjoyed school and was told she could one day be a school teacher. Pip (short for Philip, but nobody called him that unless they were cross) was brave and protective and good with his hands, like his father. His ten-year-old russet-haired brother, Laurie, looked up to Pip. Billy, aged eight, fumbled for his penny whistle in his trouser pocket, which he couldn't resist pressing between his lips. Iris, seven years old, and a tomboy, was happier playing with her brothers rather than dolls, despite Rosie's best efforts to persuade her to join her dolls' tea parties. Rosie was the baby of the family, born within weeks of her father's departure, a father she had never seen, other than in a photograph wearing his khaki army uniform.

Another daughter, Lily, had been born dead between Iris and Rosie and Frank had tenderly suggested they have another child to help Kitty recover from her grief of losing Lily.

Rosie's birth had been long and painful, lasting more than a day and night, and Kitty prayed that she would not suffer another stillbirth. The midwife called the doctor earlier this time as she could see that once again the baby was the wrong way around in her womb. The doctor skilfully turned her around and Rosie was born crying and kicking. It saddened Kitty that Frank had never met his gutsy daughter who was determined to enter the world and she wondered if Rosie's clinginess was due to not having met her father and sensing the family's sadness at his loss.

Kitty clung onto the hope that one day Rosie would see her father in the flesh, and not just in a photograph. She prayed that he might somehow have survived the fierce and bitter onslaught in Gallipoli, a battle their men had been poorly prepared for. All sorts of possibilities passed through her mind, and the one that seemed most likely was that he might have lost his memory and was languishing in a hospital somewhere overseas. One day his memory might return. Miracles did happen. With no body or knowledge of his whereabouts, Frank could not officially be declared dead. It meant she was unable to receive the widow's pension, paltry as it was and slow to be processed.

Frank had started at Sandringham as a gardener and quickly learnt the Latin names of every plant, which greatly impressed the head gardener. Having a strong, muscular build, he'd lent his hand as a woodman too when needed, when trees were blown down in a howling gale. He'd salvaged some wood and shown Pip how to cut carefully into it to create an animal, and Pip showed he had talent and flair.

Frank was an apprentice gardener at the Big House when his eyes first lit up on seeing Kitty scurrying past the bothy where he slept on the estate, on her way to work there as a maid. She was seventeen, one year younger than him, and they were completely smitten with each other. They wed within six months, and Victoria was born the following year.

Kitty brushed away her wistful thoughts of past happy days with Frank, twisting the wedding ring on her finger. The children were still whimpering and clinging to her skirt. She had been so preoccupied with her own thoughts that she hadn't seen a figure approach and the iron gates creak open. A woman's voice boomed sharply, 'You must be Mrs Willow. We've been expecting you and your brood.'

Rosie whined and hid behind her mother's skirt as they entered the courtyard and stepped towards the woman, the same one who had been standing on the front doorstep. She walked around Kitty and poked Rosie on the shoulder. 'We have ways of dealing with those who make themselves the centre of attention. We put them in a dark cellar with rats and other vermin that find their way to us from the port. Do I make myself clear? Would you like me to inform Mr Mumbles how ungrateful you are? Our guardian won't take kindly to hearing this.'

Kitty intervened sharply. 'Please accept me apology . . . Miss, Mrs . . . ?'

'It's Miss Feathers to you.'

Kitty's knees shook and she was tempted to turn and run far away from the hostility that faced them, the deep unpleasantness they were confronted with that her children had never encountered before.

She forced a brave face and brushed aside the voice in her head that asked how they could have sunk so low that they were forced to live among lunatics and paupers, regarded as the pariahs of society.

She was brought back to the present when she heard the woman's voice demanding, 'Did you hear what I said, Mrs Willow. We don't have daydreamers here. Are you coming in, or not?'

'Er, yes, Miss Feathers. I do apologise.'

Rosie's sobs became louder. Miss Feathers pointed a long bony finger in her direction. 'Do tell that child to stop its whimpering. I've made it plain we don't stand for any of that nonsense here.'

'My Rosie, she is a good girl, Miss Feathers. She's just . . . well, scared. I promise yer she's a good girl. She's just homesick.'

'This is her home now, so she had best get used to it, and learn to show her appreciation. There's plenty more that would like her bed. She can count this as her final warning. We don't tolerate bad behaviour here. Now follow me.'

Miss Feathers turned swiftly, her black skirt swishing as she swirled around. The children exchanged nervous glances, tightly gripping hands to draw comfort from each other, too afraid to speak. Kitty summoned all the inner strength she could muster and gently shepherded her children along. Rosie held onto her hand, sucking on her thumb and burying her face in her princess doll.

22

A scrawny-looking elderly man appeared from nowhere and closed the gates without a backward glance at the forlorn Willow family as they trundled across the yard and round the side of the building, entering through the back door.

Poor sods, he muttered under his breath, stooping as he turned the key in the gate, shaking it to make sure it was locked.

∽

Kitty's cheeks burned as she entered the workhouse. Before she could stop herself, the words tumbled from her mouth. 'I'm so sorry Frank, I 'ave failed you. If only you . . .'

Victoria overheard them and took her mother's hand in hers. 'That's not true, Ma. Wherever he is, I'm sure Pa knows yer doing yer best for us. Like yer said, this isn't going to be our forever 'ome, it's just for now.'

Kitty wiped her moist eyes with her sleeve. 'I'm sorry, Victoria. What kind of ma am I to sniffle like this? You're putting me to shame with your wise words, when it's me who should be consoling you.'

Victoria whispered, well out of Miss Feathers' hearing, 'What 'ave yer done with the money you were given? Is it safe, Ma? You don't think they'll take it away, do you?'

Kitty muttered behind her hand, 'Over my dead body.'

Kitty had concealed the money in a grey stocking and placed it in the bottom of her case. She had counted twelve pounds, eight shillings and some coppers in the two envelopes.

Kitty observed that Miss Feathers was a formidable and austere woman, tall, in her mid-forties with sharp features, her dark hair streaked with white. She introduced herself as

23

the superintendent in charge of women inmates, answerable to the workhouse guardian, Mr Mumbles. Kitty noticed that Miss Feathers' lips curved up at the corners when she mentioned his name.

It was a momentary change as her eyes reverted to a steely gaze. She surveyed Kitty from top to toe over the rim of her round spectacles. Kitty had retained a shapely figure and smooth skin, her face glowed with goodness and love for her children. She held her head high, refusing to show signs of weakness.

They came to a stop at the top of the staircase. As Kitty feared, it was announced that the family would be split up. She had prepared her children that this might happen, leaving it until as late as possible on the train to tell them, knowing how upset they would be.

Kitty hugged the children, squeezing them tightly, before she was led away, with other staff members suddenly appearing from nowhere to accompany the children to their dormitories. As Kitty was about to turn the corner, Rosie's shrieks were still ringing in her ears.

She let out a stifled cry and turned to run towards her daughter, but was restrained by Miss Feathers, who put her arm out to stop her.

Within seconds Rosie's cries had halted. Kitty fretted whether force had been used to silence her child. Miss Feathers ignored her protestations and ushered Kitty along a corridor where she opened a door and indicated to her to enter the room. It was furnished with bench seating on either side of narrow tables. She gasped as she stared at the expressionless faces of the women seated there. Some of them glanced up as she entered, staring at her curiously from the corner of their eyes, nudging each other and pointing at her. She noticed some had peculiar features, their mouths and eyes distorted. Others ignored her, sitting slumped on the bench, staring blankly into space. A couple of the women who appeared to be more alert were sewing. It looked like they were embroidering initials onto the corners of white handkerchiefs.

'This is the women's common room,' Miss Feathers informed her brusquely, stepping through the length of the room which led into another room at the far end. Kitty followed Miss Feathers into the adjoining room; reading her name on a brass plaque on the door. It was sparsely furnished with a small desk and a bookcase that bulged in the middle with large ledgers. Without warning, Miss Feathers snatched the two bags from Kitty and handed them to a woman hovering nearby. 'You won't be needing these while yer 'ere.'

'But, they're our possessions. What are you going to do with them?' Kitty protested.

'They'll go into storage. There's no room for sentiment while you're here. You will wear the garments we provide. Is that understood?'

Kitty's lip wobbled. 'You will keep them safe, won't yer, only . . .'

She twisted her fingers in front of her, knowing she couldn't mention the money in her case as drawing attention to it would result in it disappearing.

She bit her lip, taking the grey dress and white apron that had been handed to her.

'Thank you, Miss Feathers.'

Miss Feathers wrote Kitty's personal details in a large ledger. Kitty was asked to sign her name in it agreeing that her two cases were being placed in their storeroom. She could see no point in arguing and duly signed.

The superintendent slammed the ledger shut, rose and opened the door. She spotted one of the inmates coming out of the common room and raised her arm, indicating for her to come over. A woman entered the office with Miss Feathers and Kitty recognised her as one of the women who had been sewing.

Miss Feathers instructed, 'This is Milly and she will show you where to change. You will sleep in the bed next to hers, and work alongside her in the laundry. Tea will be served in ten minutes.'

'Thank you, Miss Feathers. Before I go, can you tell me, where are my children? Can I see them? I want to know they are being taken care of.'

'You have brought them here to be under our care and will be able to see them at permitted times, if all concerned are of good behaviour,' she replied coldly, walking to the door and holding it open.

Kitty buried her head in her hands. Her shoulders shook.

'Don't let 'em see yer crying,' said a soft voice, out of Miss Feather's hearing.

Kitty leapt back when she felt her arm been stroked gently.

'Oh, I'm sorry, I didn't mean to make yer jump. Follow me, and I'll show yer to the dorm.'

Kitty fought back her tears as she rose and passed Miss Feathers, who went back into her office and closed the door loudly behind her.

She followed Milly, comforted by her reassuring tone. She was of slim build with light brown hair and Kitty estimated she was in her mid-twenties.

'I need to know what's 'appened to my children,' pressed Kitty. 'When can I see them?'

'Try not to fret. There are ways, and, as Miss Feathers says, it is allowed, usually on Sunday afternoons. There are other mothers in 'ere and we watch each other's backs. Put it out of yer mind now. You need to change quickly for tea. If we're late we'll miss out and have go to bed on an empty stomach.'

Kitty's heart thudded as she followed Milly along a long corridor into the women's dormitory. The walls were lined with narrow iron beds covered with thin grey blankets. Milly paused at the end of the room. 'That's your bed. At least the mattress is clean. Now yer must hurry.'

Kitty crumbled inside. Milly spoke softly. 'Yer'll get used to it. I came 'ere when I was ten years old, fifteen years ago, not that I'm counting, but with luck on me side, I'll be leaving soon to take up an appointment as a maid in one of the big 'ouses by the quay. If you do well, the same good fortune will befall you.'

Kitty's face brightened. 'It will?'

'As long as yer don't mind giving Mr Mumbles a favour now and again.'

Kitty's face showed alarm. 'Favours? What do yer mean?'

'You're a married women, so I think yer get me drift. If yer get asked to clean his office, you need to be prepared to provide a few extras.'

Kitty quickly removed her clothing and pulled the grey dress over her head, then topped her head with the white frilly headwear.

'Just leave yer old clothing on the bed for now. Yer can put 'em in the chest under yer bed later. We are all given one of these. We have to go.'

Kitty noticed the panic in Milly's voice and she walked quickly after her, following her into a long room with high windows. There were two long rows of benches and tables, the same as in the day room. Different age groups were seated together, with men and women apart. A high table at the end of the room was raised on a platform with a dozen or so people sitting there, including Miss Feathers.

Kitty wedged herself onto the bench between Milly and another girl with an ashen face and sad eyes who sipped her bowl of watery vegetable soup and chewed slowly on a lump of hard bread.

Kitty rose from her seat, craning her neck to catch sight of her children. A familiar cry reached her ear. 'It's Rosie,' she yelped, lifting her leg over the bench. She was about to hurry towards her daughter when Milly grabbed her arm.

'Don't be daft. Yer don't wanna draw attention to yerself.'

'But I must, I know that's Rosie's voice. She's only four and she needs me.'

'The young girls 'ere are looked after more kindly than the boys. Mrs Fairbairn isn't like Miss Feathers. She won't let harm befall 'em.'

Kitty returned to her seat, her head swivelling in all directions searching for her daughter. After a few moments

28

Rosie's sobs subsided and Kitty fervently hoped that what Milly told her about Mrs Fairbairn was true.

The chatter from the high table became louder and reverberated about the room. She glanced towards it and saw Miss Feathers was seated next to a portly looking man of middle age with thinning hair and greying whiskers down the sides of his cheeks. She was pointing in Kitty's direction and whispering in his ear. Were they discussing her?

From the corner of her eye, Kitty watched him replying animatedly while eating with his mouth full of food. He was hunched over his food, piling it in his mouth before he had swallowed, and was agreeing with whatever Miss Feathers was telling him. She was becoming increasingly animated, throwing back her head and laughing whenever he spoke.

Kitty nudged Milly. 'Is that the man you were telling me about? Is that Mr Mumbles?'

'Yes, that's him. 'Orrible, ain't he? We call 'im The Fumbler. Mumbles the Fumbler, 'cause that's what 'e does to the pretty girls.'

Kitty recoiled, her throat dry. She stared avidly as Miss Feathers had now laid her hand on the guardian's arm and was pressing her face close to his, her lips moving rapidly. He was smiling too and showing increased enthusiasm to what she was saying.

A moment later, the inmates rose and began to quietly file out of the dining room, their eyes gazing down at their feet, the way they were instructed to walk. Feeling curious, and gripped by fear, Kitty made a sideways glance at Mr Mumbles. Her head spun around in the direction that Miss

29

Feathers was pointing out to him. Mr Mumbles nodded vigorously, speaking in her ear.

Kitty's eyes followed the object of their attention. She froze, barely able to breathe. 'Victoria!'

Chapter Four

The following day a pile of crisp golden leaves swirled in the wind in Harry's direction as he stepped along the station platform. He spotted one of the porters nearby and raised a hand to call him over, instructing him to sweep the leaves up.

Harry prided himself on having the tidiest station in the region and it was at its prettiest in the spring and summer when Jessie carefully planted a riot of colourful blooms into hanging baskets and tubs, geraniums and petunias that lasted long throughout the season. The station had to look its best for its royal visitors, and Harry ensured they were always impressed.

Harry observed his new porter, Sebastian Cripps, as he set about his task with the broom with alacrity. Aged fifteen, he was the son of Augustus Cripps, who had been a woodman from the estate. Augustus was one of the Sandringham Company killed in action in Gallipoli on the 12 August 1915 and had been a good friend of Frank Willow. Some said his family was lucky because they knew he was dead and could grieve him, though his body remained in a war grave overseas.

Harry sighed contemplatively. He raised his head just as Ada approached with him his grandson, Leslie, in tow.

'A penny for your thoughts, Father,' asked his youngest daughter. 'It looked like you were miles away.'

Before he could reply, Sebastian's vigorous brush strokes caught Harry on his ankles with a fierce whack. Leslie giggled as Harry leapt up and tried to grab the brush from the porter, who apologised for his clumsiness, his cheeks turning scarlet.

Ada smiled. 'Do you recall when Prince John would sweep the leaves off the platform?'

The station master chuckled. 'I certainly do. And very good he was at it too. Once he started it was nigh impossible to stop him. In fact, I do believe he used the very same broom that almost knocked me sideways a moment ago.'

Ada giggled. 'I could see the pleasure it gave him. He so enjoyed coming here dressed in his sailor's suit because we treated him like a normal little boy, that meant a lot to him. Prince John bore his affliction so bravely. Even so, his death took us all by surprise for someone of such tender years.'

'It did indeed. I can still see his face light up when I gave him a shiny silver threepenny piece when he finished. His nanny would tell me it wasn't necessary, but it was worth it to me just to see the smile on his face.'

Leslie jumped from foot to foot. He tugged on his grandfather's sleeve. 'Can I sweep up the leaves, Grandpa?'

The porter stepped forward. 'Pardon me, Mr Saward, but I couldn't help overhearing that Master Leslie wants to sweep up the leaves. That's all right with me, if you and Miss Ada agree. After all, it's true what they say, "Many hands make light work".'

Leslie begged, 'Please, say yes, Mama? Grandpa? I've done it before, with Prince John, remember?'

32

Harry smiled indulgently. 'Very well, young man, as long as you don't get in Cripps' way. If you see Eddie, by the way, will you tell him to come and see me?'

The station master's daughter watched Leslie traipse off happily after Sebastian, his jug-like ears sticking out like handles on a beer tankard.

Ada asked her father, 'Do you recall how Leslie used to play with Prince John? It seems like it was only yesterday that he passed away, but it must be eight months or so now. It goes to show that it doesn't matter who your family are, money can't fix everything, even if you are the King and Queen of England.'

Prince John's death at the turn of the year when he was only thirteen years old, following a massive epileptic seizure, shocked the tight-knit community on the royal estate. His loss was felt deeply by everyone in the community who had taken him to their hearts. He was a sickly child and had moved into Wood Farm close to the station, where he lived with his devoted Nanny, Lala Bill, away from his parents and siblings at the Big House, playing instead with local children when he was well enough.

Harry nodded solemnly. 'I hear he suffered terribly, poor boy. If only there had been a cure for his fits. The doctors did all they could, but were unable to save him. Still, he had some good times here and enjoyed watching the trains coming and going. I'm glad we were able to give him some small pleasure.'

Ada reflected wistfully, 'Funnily enough, Leslie was asking about Prince John the other day. Even though the prince was older, he had a lovely way with Leslie and enjoyed showing him his toys. Leslie obeyed Lala when she instructed him not

33

to overexcite the prince, or to take any notice if his manner became difficult.'

'I remember the last time he came here before he was taken bad, I kept a close watch while he played. He commented that he was hungry and asked if he could join Leslie and come to my house for tea. Lala protested, but gave in, much to his delight.

'Betty's face lit up when she saw him and he quickly scoffed the scone and egg sandwich, wiping his plate clean,' Harry chuckled, referring to his loyal housekeeper.

Ada stifled a giggle. 'It was a great surprise for Betty when Prince John walked through the kitchen door. She curtseyed, her cheeks flushed, and was all flustered, but she was pleased as punch when he gobbled down his tea. Leslie then showed him the wooden engine you made him and he wanted to take it home; there was a bit of a do over it.'

Harry nodded. 'Yes, there was. I offered to make one for him too, but time flew by and I forgot all about it.'

'None of us could foresee what was going to happen. If I'd known the prince was going to be taken from us so soon, I would have given him Leslie's engine, but he was so attached to it. We only saw the prince once after that.'

'I heard that on his passing, the boy's face bore an angelic smile. Do you recall his funeral at Sandringham church? Every person on the estate went and stood around the gates to pay their respects, and his grave was absolutely covered with flowers.'

Leslie bounded up to the station master then, alongside Sebastian, his cheeks flushed and eyes shining. 'Have I done a good job, Grandpa?'

Harry arched his back and surveyed the platform and grinned. 'You have indeed. It's never looked better.'

'Even better than when Prince John did it? He was always a bit slow.'

'Leslie! Please don't speak about him like that. You know he couldn't help it,' his mother scolded.

Harry produced a silver threepenny coin from his pocket and teased his grandson. 'Guess which hand it's in, and it's yours.'

Leslie shuffled from one foot to the other, reaching out to Harry's left arm behind his back, and then the other.

'This one, no it's this one,' before finally thumping Harry's right arm.

'How did you guess?' his grandfather asked good-naturedly.

Harry then glanced at the station clock. 'I must be on my way now. Queen Maud is arriving soon and I need to check everything is in order.'

Ada's eyes showed interest. 'I do hope I will have the chance to meet her again. I haven't seen her since the war. I heard that she established a fund in her name to assist women living in extremely difficult circumstances during the war and I should love to hear about it, in the hope that her ideas might help families here.'

'Why not write and ask to meet her?' Harry suggested.

'Why that's a wonderful idea, Father! I think I will.'

'Just one more thing, Ada, while we are alone. I hope you don't mind me broaching a sensitive topic.'

As they stepped along the platform an engine steamed in, its shiny sleek sluglike engine coming to a sharp halt, the

35

smoke and hissing sound making Leslie jump and cover his ears with his hands. When it had quietened and they left the platform, they saw the figure of a man crouched at the side of the station, his arms wrapped around his head, facing away from the platform.

Leslie pointed him out. 'What's that man doing there, Mama?'

Ada stared and she froze as she recognised Eddie Herring cowering, in a state of distress. Like her Alfie, although not physically wounded, Eddie was a casualty of war.

She returned straightaway to inform her father, who was unable to coax him out. He scratched his head and was considering asking Dr Fletcher for his assistance when Maria appeared, breathless, her eyes filled with anxiety.

'You can leave us, Harry. I'll see to Eddie,' she announced, her eyes filled with concern.

Harry mopped the back of his neck. 'I'm pleased to see you, Maria. How did you know?'

'The butcher's wife mentioned it and stopped me a moment ago on me way 'ome. Thank goodness she did.'

She knelt down beside Eddie, not caring whether her long skirt became dirty. Harry was called away, promising to return after a few minutes, as the sound of an approaching train sent Eddie into a state of wild panic, its engine sounding louder and louder as it pulled in, covering them with clouds of choking smoke and exhaust gas blowing in their direction.

Eddie choked, gasping for breath, his wide eyes terrified and begging for help. Maria undid his top shirt buttons and his hands gripped his neck. The veins on his neck stood out and his breathing was quick and shallow. He squeezed his eyes shut and repeated over and over, 'No, no. I won't do it. I won't do it.'

Maria clutched his shaky hands and begged, 'Eddie, it's me, Maria. Now listen to me. I want you to breathe slowly. Nobody is going to make yer do anything. You're back in Wolferton with your friends. The war is over.'

His face was sweaty and flushed and he gasped as he fought to control his breathing.

Maria soothed, 'That's better, Eddie. I'm going to take yer 'ome now. You frighten me when you 'ave these turns, Eddie. I want to 'elp yer, if you let me.'

Eddie sniffled. 'Who can 'elp me, Maria? I feel useless. I ain't any good to anyone.'

'Listen to me, Eddie Herring. You're my fiancé and I won't 'ave that kind of talk,' Maria asserted. 'Shall I ask Beatrice if someone at the hospital can 'elp?'

Eddie rose unsteadily, aided by Maria. 'Aye, if you think she can do anything.'

Maria's eyes misted over. 'I love yer, Eddie Herring, and it breaks me 'eart to see yer suffering. Can I ask yer something?'

He stared at her, his eyes blank and after a pause he nodded.

'What did you mean when you cried out, "No, no. I won't do it. I won't do it."'

Eddie's face paled and he clenched his fists. 'I said that?'

'Yes, what did yer mean?'

Eddie's eyes glazed over and he shook. 'I can't ever talk about that. Don't make me, Maria. Do you promise?'

Maria retreated, 'Of course, Eddie, I promise.'

37

As she walked alongside Eddie, supporting him until he reached his home – Elm Cottage, a cosy two-down with lattice windows that he shared with his mother, Mabel – her mind questioned what had happened to make Eddie so fearful, and what was it that he was unable to talk about. Was it the cause of his disturbed mind?

He was only twenty years old, having lied about his age to sign up for war four years ago. She felt a pang inside her as she questioned if she would ever have her old Eddie back with his cheery smile and happy-go-lucky ways. *Yes,* she vowed, she would, whatever it took.

Chapter Five

Eddie's situation preyed heavily on Maria's mind the following day when she set about her duties at the Big House. Mrs Pennywick approached Maria as she was about to enter Queen Alexandra's private chambers, duster in hand.

The housekeeper raised a hand. 'Ah, I was hoping to catch you, Maria. When you have finished cleaning Her Majesty's drawing room, I would like you to come and see me in my office.'

Maria frowned. Mrs Pennywick's tone was brusque, but that was nothing unusual.

'I ain't done nothing wrong, 'ave I?' Maria asked anxiously, her mouth dry. She smoothed down the folds of her crisp white apron which she wore over her black dress, a white frilly mop cap topping her head.

Mrs Pennywick shook her head. 'It's nothing of the sort, I can assure you of that. In fact, quite the contrary.'

Maria's jaw dropped as she watched the housekeeper saunter off with a mysterious smile on her face, leaving Maria feeling puzzled.

What could she want with me? Maria fretted, despite the assurances she had been given that she was not being summoned for a scalding. Although Mrs Pennywick exuded a strict no-nonsense exterior, Maria found she had always been fair to her and respected how she ran the staff and household at the Big House with a rod of iron.

Now in her sixties, Mrs Pennywick showed no signs of retiring. Queen Alexandra had a great fondness for her and liked to be surrounded by familiar faces she could trust, even more so following the death of her husband nine years before.

Maria undertook her tasks diligently, taking great care not to drop any of the delicate Meissen porcelain treasures she dusted, handling cautiously the silver-framed family photographs that occupied every surface. She paused only to glance into the ornate birdcage in the corner of the room where its famous occupant, a parrot called Emerald, shuffled along its perch and came to a halt, tilting her head with its glorious green plumage.

'I hope I ain't done anything wrong,' mimicked the gloriously multi-coloured exotic creature, repeating Maria's earlier words.

Maria chuckled. 'Pardon me, I should have said, "I *haven't* done nothing wrong." I'm trying me best, I mean, *my* best.'

The bird repeated Maria's words again, flapping its wings and chirping merrily. She threw back her head and laughed. 'You'll get me the sack. I have to get on with *my* chores now. I can't let yer distract me as I have to see Mrs Pennywick as soon as I'm done 'ere.'

Maria swept up the scattered bird feed from under the cage, muttering under her breath, 'Who would 'ave thought I'd be spending me day chatting to a bird.'

Emerald was no ordinary bird, but an adored pet of Queen Alexandra. Maria had become used to the feathered creature after their first encounter two years ago. Queen Alexandra enjoyed observing the parrot's high-pitched chatter and startled expressions on the faces of her guests when it regaled them with its cheeky impersonations.

'Who would 'ave thought I'd be spending me day chatting to a bird,' squawked Emerald, making Maria spin around. She chided herself for being caught unawares. Maybe she never would get used to her. She stifled a giggle as she recalled Mrs Pennywick telling her how the Dowager Queen warned visitors not to say anything in front of the bird that they didn't want repeated. Despite the cautionary warning, the visitors would forget and jump in surprise, and sometimes with embarrassment, when their words were repeated, much to her great amusement. It provided Her Majesty with great entertainment, mused Maria.

The large room was bright and airy and a delight to work in. Maria's jaw dropped when she first stepped inside, and she marvelled at its painted trompe l'oeil ceiling panels and panels with doves and pheasants immortalised there, as well as musical instruments. The Dowager Queen's exquisite collection of figures and animals crafted by Carl Fabergé in jade and amber was displayed in glass-fronted cabinets and the room contained many precious gifts given to her by her dear sister, Dagmar, who married Tsar Alexander III.

The gifts were all the more poignant and of sentimental value as the summer before the Empress Dowager's son, Tsar Nicholas, his wife, Empress Alexandra, their five children and loyal servants had been murdered by Bolsheviks. She had survived by fleeing to Crimea and travelling on to London in a battleship with a party of seven Romanovs, and taking refuge with her sister, Alexandra, spending time together with her in Sandringham before returning to her native Denmark.

Maria had been shocked by the Romanov family's downfall and the question most feared in the royal household was, *Could it happen here too?* She shuddered at the thought, being a staunch royalist. But empty bellies and poverty drove revolutions and the country was struggling to get back on its feet after the war. War pensions were paltry, men's jobs had been taken over by women and many found themselves without work, or suffered a disability that made it difficult for them to have their old job back. Widows struggled to bring up their families with little money to live on, with many going to bed on empty stomachs.

She completed her chores speedily, tidied some loose stays of hair and returned downstairs to the servants' quarters, checking in the mirror that she was presentable before making her way down the corridor off the kitchen where the housekeeper's office was situated.

She paused outside and inhaled a deep breath before knocking on the door.

'Come in.'

Maria opened the door tentatively. The housekeeper glanced up from the pile of paperwork and motioned for Maria to take a seat in front of her desk.

Maria shifted uncomfortably on the seat as the housekeeper remained occupied with some paperwork, but eased when she saw her finish writing and look up and smile at her.

'Please relax, Maria. As I said, you are not in any sort of trouble.'

'I'm pleased to 'ear that, 'cause I always strive to do me best 'ere.'

'I can see that, which is why I have put your name forward.'

'Pardon me, Mrs Pennywick. What do yer mean?'

'I have been most impressed with how you undertake all that is asked of you and accomplish it to the highest standard. You have been here four years now, I believe, and so I thought this is the right moment for you to consider a change of position. You can regard it as a promotion.'

'Promotion? Me? But I don't understand,' she retorted, incredulous.

'The thing is, Maria, we have something of a dilemma on our hands. Queen Maud is arriving at Appleton House tomorrow for her autumn break and the recent departure of her regular maid has caused a problem. I have recommended you should take up the position as you are used to working discreetly with royalty. I've discussed this with Miss Knollys, the Queen Mother's lady-in-waiting, and I'm informed she understands entirely. In fact, Her Majesty commented on how you have fitted in very well here, and she was confident you would fit in well at Appleton House too. That is indeed very worthy praise from the highest level.'

Maria's head was in a spin as Mrs Pennywick continued. 'I'm not sure if you are familiar with Appleton House, but it is much smaller than here. You will take instructions from Mrs Watson, who I also trained here at Sandringham. There is the kitchen staff too, and we may take on another maid there.'

Maria could barely take in what she was hearing. 'I don't know what to say, Mrs Pennywick. This is, well, just so unexpected.'

Maria had seen Queen Maud in passing on her last visit to her mother. A portrait of her hung in the Dowager Queen's private chambers and she observed that she had similar facial features to her mother. She'd been told how, as a princess, Maud had married her first cousin, Prince Carl of Denmark, the second son of Queen Alexandra's eldest brother. For Queen Alexandra it was a match made in heaven as she had been born in Denmark and at the age of sixteen was chosen as a bride for Prince Edward, the Prince of Wales. Prince Carl was later crowned King of Norway after Norway's historic union with Sweden was dissolved and the throne was offered to Prince Carl.

Maria had passed Appleton House a number of times, but never set foot inside. It was just one mile from Sandringham and had been gifted to Princess Maud and Prince Carl as a wedding gift by her father, King Edward VII. She visited every year, with a skeleton staff staying on to maintain it in her absence, and it was here that her son, Prince Olav, was born.

Maria was mulling over the unexpected offer, twisting her hands in front of her. 'Do yer really think I'd be up to it, Mrs Pennywick?'

'Yes, I do, otherwise I wouldn't have suggested it. I think you would be perfectly suited for the position. Queen Maud is very much like her mother and takes a keen interest in the welfare of her staff and people around her. I believe she undertook some work during the war to help unmarried women, which raised many eyebrows. She uses her influence and position to help women in need, if they find themselves in your kind of situation, whenever she can.'

Maria's cheeks flushed at the reference to unmarried mothers, a reminder of her own similar situation, and was wondering if the offer to her would be withdrawn if it offended Queen Maud. Mrs Pennywick sensed Maria's embarrassment, reaching over her desk and taking Maria's hand in hers.

'I do apologise, I didn't mean to upset you. My comment was not meant to be a personal affront to your situation. But what I say about Queen Maud is true and I thought you might take some reassurance from knowing a little about her as you are going to be working there.'

'It's all right. I know you didn't mean to be unkind. Queen Maud sounds a lovely lady. I'm still taking it all in. I can barely believe what you are saying.'

Mrs Pennywick's eyes narrowed. 'Well, what do you think, Maria? Shall I send word to Mrs Watson that you will start there next week?'

Maria's radiant glow disappeared in a flash as she remembered Kitty. She lowered her gaze and mumbled. 'Of course, and thank yer for mentioning me, though I feel awkward about it as I'll be taking on Kitty's job after she had to leave the way she did. I saw 'er departing from Wolferton Station yesterday and it broke me 'eart.'

The housekeeper leaned back in her chair. 'Yes, I do believe that is the case. It's all very sad. The estate's agent let them stay as long as he could, but Mrs Willow could not remain indefinitely as the rules are quite clear about only male tenants having tenancy of tied cottages, and with Mrs Willow's husband unlikely to return, I am most sorry to say, it was time for her to leave. The cottage is needed for another estate worker who has returned to his former position in the stables at Appleton.'

'It just don't seem fair that she 'ad to leave, it ain't her fault that her husband is unaccounted for in Gallipoli.'

The housekeeper rubbed the back of her neck. She looked uncomfortable at Maria's challenge.

Maria faced the housekeeper squarely and affirmed. She raised her head and spoke clearly. 'I were just thinking out loud. Of course I'll take the job, Mrs Pennywick. It's a great honour and I won't let yer down. You can rely on me.'

'That's settled then. I shall inform Mrs Watson that you will start there next Monday at seven o' clock sharp.'

'Thank yer, Mrs Pennywick. I promise I won't let yer down.'

Maria's heart raced for the rest of the day and her mind wandered to what her new position would be like, and if Mrs Watson would take to her. She had an extra spring in her step as she made her way lightly along corridors, flicking her duster around precious porcelain objects and over golden gilt picture frames.

When she had finished she set off for the station to see if Eddie had made it to work that day. She was bursting to share her good news with her fiancé. The railway company felt obliged to take on Eddie again as porter when he returned home after he was demobbed. With his mop of black hair and cheeky grin, he had been a favourite with passengers before the war, whistling a tune as he loaded luggage on his trolley and chatting to them in a friendly way.

She was bursting to share her good news when she dismounted from her bicycle at the station. Harry shook his head and confirmed her worst fears, that Eddie hadn't turned up that day.

The news was a shock for Maria, who felt suddenly overwhelmed by Eddie's troubled state and wondered whether anyone could help him.

As she set off for home, she saw Beatrice outside the station master's house. Unable to hold back her emotions, she burst into tears. 'What's happened, Maria? Come in and tell me the cause of your distress.'

Maria followed Beatrice into the front parlour, Beatrice assuring her they would not be disturbed. Through scalding tears, she blurted out her concerns about Eddie and the events of the day before at the station. Beatrice listened thoughtfully. 'Leave it with me, Maria. I'll mention it to Dr Butterscotch when I see him next.'

Chapter Six

Leslie tugged his father's arm impatiently, his cheeks burning. Ada frowned at Alfie's lack of response, the little interest he showed in what was going on around him. His skin was pale and pinched and he had grey rings under his yes. His hair had thinned out on the top, but he had kept his moustache. He sat slumped in an armchair reading the newspaper in the front parlour, sadness painted across his face.

'Please, Papa, will you play with me?' Leslie pleaded with increased determination to attract his father's attention.

Alfie glanced over the page that he had read several times, without taking note of the words. His voice had an irritated tone. 'Later, Leslie. Now be a good boy and run off.'

Alfie caught Ada's eye beseeching her to take the boy out of the room. She could see he was scanning the 'Situations Vacant' column, just like he had done yesterday, and the day before. What chance was there of a position being advertised for a musician of Alfie's calibre? The downturn in the post-war economy was such that even officers who had once held highly skilled positions returned from the war with no work and had taken to advertising for jobs that would suit their skills or accepted work below their skills and education if desperate.

'I'm luckier than many other men,' he had told her the previous evening, his tone subdued. 'Thankfully I still have all my limbs, my hearing and my sight. I read a notice in the paper today from this poor blind soldier who had made it back from Gallipoli saying he requires a cottage with three to five acres of land suitable for poultry and fruit farming to rent for a moderate sum. Replies to be sent to a Captain Woodfield. I wish the poor blighter the very best of luck.'

Sensing Alfie's sombre mood, Ada forced a smile for the benefit of her son. It was on her mind to say, *Stop your self-pitying and please make an effort.* But she bit her tongue and extended her arms out towards her lively son, recalling how two years ago she believed her husband had been killed on a French battlefield, but was found barely alive, lying in a ditch suffering from amnesia. It was thanks to her letters in his pocket that Alfie could be identified and was able to return home. Although his memory had returned, Alfie's pride had been badly hurt when he discovered that his former position as organist and choirmaster in Cromer, a North Norfolk coastal town, had been given to someone else who didn't match his musical talent. He felt hurt and betrayed, believing the position would remain open for him at the end of the war.

'Shall we go and see Aggie? I'm sure she'll let you feed her cats, and I want to hear all about her recent trip to London,' she suggested, extending her hand.

Leslie's face brightened at mention of the moggies and within a quarter of an hour they were walking down Aggie's cobbled path and knocking on the door of Kitty Cottage. As Aggie lifted the latch, two cats skirted around her legs and darted outside in a flash.

Leslie's head swivelled after them, his eyes widening, but they had scarpered into the back garden and crawled under a hedge and out of sight in an instant.

Aggie raised an arm in the air with an exaggerated flourish, the lace edging on the sleeve of her violet dress fluttering in the soft breeze. 'Do come in, and don't worry about Oscar and Helena, they will be back when they're hungry. I'm so pleased to see you, Ada. I have some exciting news to share with you.'

Ada followed Aggie inside. She thought it was strange that Aggie was happy to shrug off the whereabouts of her disappearing cats; she would normally have scrambled around on her hands and knees trying to coax them out of their hiding place. She appeared uncustomarily agitated, but not in an anxious state, more one of excitement, her lips quivering and her eyes sparkling.

Aggie patted her hair with her hand and beamed. She was energised, as if she had been awakened from a long sleep, and appeared younger than her forty-four years. The long face and large teeth she shared as common features with her older sister Magnolia, did not seem as noticeable with her newfound youthful vigour. Neither did Maria notice the birthmark on the side of Ada's cheek that the older woman had once been very self-conscious about and would cover with her hand.

Leslie bent down to stroke a beautiful white long-haired moggy with deep green eyes as she nuzzled her head against his leg. He followed her into the kitchen where the cat snuggled against him again. He giggled and bent down tentatively to stroke her. The cat purred and seemed content, rolling on its back and letting Leslie rub its tummy.

50

Aggie shook her head. 'I've let it be known that I want no more cats. I can't take in any more strays now Magnolia has left.' She paused. 'Especially . . . well, especially as my time will be required elsewhere.'

Ada opened her mouth to speak, but Aggie interrupted. 'Of course, I am delighted that my sister found love and happiness after all these years. Who would have thought it possible, that she would be swept off her feet by the man she had secretly pined for all those years ago, only for him to return, widowed and available.'

Yes, that took us all by surprise. Ada pressed, 'Are you sure you don't get lonely sometimes, Aggie, without Magnolia? I know you have your family of cats and enjoy spending time with Maria and her family, but there must be times when you wish you had company here with you, maybe a gentleman you could walk out with?'

Aggie let the question pass unanswered, though a slight upward turn at the corner of her lips did not slip Ada's attention. Aggie extended her arm, inviting Ada to take a seat around the kitchen table. The dresser was cluttered with plates and china ornaments bearing images of cats, some wearing hats and clothing. Ada picked up a cup showing a ginger cat adorned in a ruby necklace. 'Is this new?' she enquired, smiling.

'It is. I couldn't resist it when I saw it at the Mart.'

'What is it, Aggie? What did you mean when you said your time might be needed elsewhere? Your cheeks are rather flushed too.'

Aggie smiled. 'Well, I do have something to tell you.'

'Is it something to do with your recent trip to London? I almost forgot to ask.'

51

Aggie beamed, her tombstone teeth on full show. 'Yes, it is. I had the most wonderful time.' She paused, vigorously fanning her face with her hand. 'If I appear flushed, it is because I cannot contain my excitement. You see, I have an excellent idea, and I want to ask your opinion and whether you think your Alfie might help.'

Ada's eyebrows arched. 'Alfie? How can he help?'

'Mr Saward informs me that Alfie still isn't himself since the war, and I'm truly sorry to hear that. I know how he excelled at his job at Cromer and that it is no longer available to him, and what a huge disappointment that must have been. It is their loss, without a doubt.'

Ada flinched. 'Indeed it was a blow to him. I'm afraid Alfie still has relapses with his memory and his mood is low, but he is getting better. The doctor says we must be patient, that it takes time. With respect, Aggie, what concern is this to you?'

Aggie's face brightened. 'Well, I may have the answer to Alfie's problem. I have a proposal for him.'

Ada's cup almost slipped through her fingers. She stuttered, 'A proposal? What are you referring to?'

Ada listened in astonishment as Aggie's excitement bubbled over and she described her trip to London to visit her cousin, Violet, who lived in Hammersmith and had started a dance school to bring some gaiety back to people's lives after the horrors of the war.

'Oh, Ada, it is so marvellous. There is so much demand for it. Violet told me dancing is quite the thing these days, and women are now raising hemlines on their dresses so they don't trip up. I hesitated to try it at first, but she insisted and

I must confess I found it quite exhilarating. To my amazement, I found I had quite a flare for the foxtrot and tango.'

Ada stared incredulously. 'I would never have thought it of you, Aggie. Your demeanour has always been so reserved. It's like you've had fire breathed into your veins. But, tell me, what does this have to do with my Alfie?'

'Well, as you can see, I'm in such a fluster. I've been unable to think of anything else since I returned home. My head is full of it and it made me think, if these dances are so popular in Hammersmith, they could surely be a success anywhere. Even here, in Wolferton.'

'You really mean it, *you* want to start a dance school, here, in Wolferton? But where? And would Violet come all the way from London to teach these new dances?'

Aggie's excitement bubbled.

'No, not Violet. I would teach the dance steps. Violet will train me up, though she says my standard is sufficiently high already. She says I'm a natural. I had no idea I possessed this gift. I was thinking that Alfie could play the music for us on the piano, if he didn't consider it beneath him. I appreciate he is used to playing music from our accomplished composers. Do you think this is something he would consider? It might help lift his spirits, and it would be such fun.'

'I'm lost for words, Aggie. I really am. I can see that you are exhilarated about this, and I am pleased to see you so happy.'

'Of course, there will be fewer men, but women can dance together. They don't seem to mind at all. It's a very social occasion with tea and cakes served when we take a break from dancing. There is nothing to compare. I found it so uplifting, which is just what we need at this moment. I am

53

planning to make enquiries about using the meeting room, where they have a piano.'

Aggie rose suddenly from her chair and held an upright pose, folding her right arm across her chest and raising her left arm above her head in an arc shape. She tilted her head to one side and raised it slightly and tiptoed around on the spot, gaily humming a tune and moving to the beat.

The noise made Jasper, Aggie's tortoiseshell moggy, waken from his sleep in the corner of the room. He raised his hind legs and haunch and Leslie went over and stroked his fur gently.

Aggie's enthusiasm was infectious. 'It all sounds most interesting. Can you tell me more, Aggie? I'm intrigued and will certainly mention it to Alfie. Do you think there will be sufficient interest for tea dances here?'

'I certainly do. Come, stand up and be my partner. I feel like I'm floating on air.'

Before Ada could resist, Aggie had swept her off her feet and raised her arm up in the dance hold.

'I'll be the man. Just follow my lead,' Aggie laughed, swirling Ada around the table. They danced around the furniture and bumped into Leslie, who toppled onto Jasper who snarled and lashed out with his paws, scratching Leslie's arm. Blood trickled from a cut and Leslie bawled.

Aggie released Ada from her grip as she attended to her tearful son who was nursing his wound. 'Oh dear, I'm so sorry, Leslie. It's my fault for getting carried away.'

Ada murmured, 'I think we both did. We had better leave now. Maybe you are right, Aggie. Maybe we do need something to lift our spirits and to help us put the grim war

54

years behind us. I believe it could lift Alfie's mood. Yes, it could be just the tonic for him.'

'I can think of no better or pleasurable way of improving dark moods. I was thinking of calling it "Aggie and Marcel's Dance Time". What do you think? I shall be circulating leaflets about it very soon.'

Ada queried. 'Marcel? Why Aggie and Marcel?'

Aggie's face broke into the biggest smile. 'I haven't had a chance to tell you about him. Marcel will teach the steps with me. I met him at Violet's where he taught alongside her. He is keen to leave London and make a fresh start in the country. Wait till you meet him, Ada. He is very debonair and charming. Although he is from France, he speaks excellent English. There is no one else like him in Wolferton and he has awakened feelings inside me. Womanly feelings.'

Ada was speechless and slightly embarrassed at Aggie's outburst. There was no doubt that the Aggie who stood before her was a different woman to one she had known all her life, radiating a new inner glow.

As Aggie led Ada to the front door, she placed her hand on Ada's arm, her smile stretching from ear to ear. 'I see I have surprised you, my dear. I am sure you will approve of Marcel once you meet him. He makes me feel alive, truly alive and gay. I haven't felt so happy for such a long time. Not since Percy.'

Aggie's reference to Percy was a sad reminder of a man she met in the park in King's Lynn and a secret romance developed. Sadly their love never had a chance to flourish as he died suddenly, leaving her bereft.

Ada chuckled, 'You really are going to set tongues wagging, Aggie. I can't wait for your dance classes to start!'

Chapter Seven

Maria's first day at Appleton House was upon her. Queen Maud's arrival was eagerly anticipated by staff and they lined up outside as the chauffeur swept up the drive in a sparkling Daimler. The smiling Queen of Norway stepped out of the limousine and straightened, pausing to look around her, taking in a deep inhalation of breath. The pleasure on her face was clear to see.

She was dressed exquisitely, and her dark green skirt showed off her trim waist. Her jacket was nipped in at the waist and the collar and cuffs were edged with velvet in a deeper green. A pale lemon blouse was worn underneath. Matching velvet buttons finished the garment beautifully.

An attractive slim woman in her thirties with pale skin and finely chiselled features, also elegantly dressed and with white blonde hair tied at the back of her hair in a loose knot, stepped out of the car and stood alongside her.

The housekeeper beamed at her royal mistress. 'I trust you had a pleasant journey, Your Majesty.'

'It was pleasant enough, thank you, Mrs Watson.'

The housekeeper enjoyed visits from Queen Maud, bringing life back into her country home. She smiled and curtseyed as the queen stepped towards her. She raised her eyes when she reached her and they lingered on the tallest woman she had ever seen, towering a head above the queen, standing alongside her.

Queen Maud indicated for her to rise. 'It is so good to be back, Mrs Watson. There is no other place in England that warms my heart like Appleton.'

The housekeeper replied, 'We are very pleased to see you here again, your Majesty. I hope you will find everything to your liking.'

Her eyes strayed to the stranger. Queen Maud extended an arm in her direction. 'May I introduce Hanne Jensen, my new lady-in-waiting. This is her first visit to Norfolk and I'm sure I can count on you to make her welcome and attend to all her needs. She speaks excellent English and has been looking forward to her first visit here.'

Mrs Watson slightly bowed her head. 'Of course, your Majesty. It is my pleasure to welcome Mrs . . .'

'It's Miss Jensen,' said the blonde companion, speaking with only a slight accent.

The Queen turned to her. 'I am sure you will soon enjoy the pleasures of Norfolk as much as I do. For me it is such a joy to be back on the Sandringham Estate where I spent many happy hours riding my darling horse, Trifle, and playing in the countryside.'

The royal mistress and her lady-in-waiting entered the house and Mrs Watson followed them into one of the four sitting rooms situated on the ground floor. The pale lemon wallpapered walls and high ceiling gave the room a light and airy feeling. It was Queen Maud's favourite room. The ornate polished sideboard was adorned with family photos and there were portraits on the walls. Lush green pot plants added a vibrancy.

She swirled around the room, her face brightening. 'Everything looks wonderful, as always, Mrs Watson. I'm so grateful that you and Kitty take such great care of my things here in my absence.'

'Thank you, Your Majesty. Only . . .' Mrs Watson's shoulders dropped.

'You may call me ma'am, Mrs Watson. We have no need for formalities when we are alone. What is it you intended to say?'

The housekeeper stuttered. 'I don't wish to trouble you about our domestic matters, only . . .'

'What is it you wish to say?'

'It's Kitty, she's no longer here. She's left.'

Queen Maud's eyebrows arched. 'Oh? I thought she was happy here. May I enquire as to the reason of her departure?'

'She was, she was very happy. The cottage she lived in with the children was needed by a new estate worker. Seeing as her Frank isn't going to be coming home, not that we know of, and with her not able to stay on as an official tenant, 'cause only men are allowed to, she was asked to leave.'

I'm very sorry to hear this. 'I wish I had known, there might have been something I could have done.'

'We were all very saddened, and her poor little 'uns,' commented Mrs Watson.

Queen Maud pressed her finger to her lip, deep in thought. 'I shall speak to my mother about this. On my last visit here I saw her youngest daughter having a tea party on the lawn for her birthday, she was the sweetest thing. I

58

was in town later that day and bought a topsy-turvy doll for her. I can still see the delight on her face when she pressed it against her chest, she was so enthralled with it. Oh, I hope they will be all right.'

Mrs Watson remained silent, her eyes fixed on the floor. The queen asked, 'In the meantime, are there plans for Kitty to be replaced?'

'Mrs Pennywick has made the arrangements. She came over yesterday after Kitty left and assured me that I have nothing to worry about. The new girl's name is Maria Saward. She should have been here by now, I was expecting her an hour ago.'

Queen Maud replied, 'I expect she will have a reasonable explanation. As this is her first day here, we should give her the benefit of the doubt, in case there was a misunderstanding.'

'Yes, ma'am,' Mrs Watson replied. 'It's not a good start though, is it?'

The queen quipped, 'I'm sure we can rely on Mrs Pennywick's judgement. I should like some lunch now served in the conservatory, for myself and Miss Jensen, and I will then take a short rest before I join my mother for dinner.'

'Very well, ma'am.' Mrs Watson bobbed. 'The table is already laid and cook has prepared watercress soup and some fresh cod caught just this morning which she will serve with a parsley sauce and vegetables from the garden.'

'That sounds just perfect. I should like to freshen up now. I have told Miss Jensen how wonderful Cook is and she is looking forward to sampling our local fare.'

'That's very kind of you to say, ma'am. I will pass on your compliments to Cook.'

Mrs Watson bobbed a curtsey and left the room. She joined Cook in the kitchen who was preparing the lunch. Maggie Hope was in her mid-forties and could work magic in the kitchen and produce a delicious spread from whatever was in the pantry. She, like Mrs Watson, had trained at Sandringham House.

At fifty-one years of age, Hettie Watson prided herself on her climb up the servants' hierarchy and had never put a foot wrong. She considered herself fortunate to have her position at Appleton House as Queen Maud was only in residence a short time of the year, so her duties were not arduous.

The housekeeper moved briskly and cleared away Queen Maud's lunch when she had finished and plumped up the cushions in the sitting room when Her Majesty retired to her bedroom for an afternoon nap.

She returned to the kitchen and yawned. 'I was here till late last night getting everything in order for the Queen's arrival. Where has that new maid got to?'

Cook peered out of the kitchen window. 'You'll find out soon enough. There's someone walking down the path. It looks like she has just arrived.'

Mrs Watson huffed. 'About time too. I was expecting her first thing this morning. I wonder what she has to say for herself.'

Mrs Watson observed the girl rush along the path. She appeared flustered, pausing to straighten her skirt and fasten a button on her jacket. Then she reached for a handkerchief in her pocket and dabbed her eyes with it.

Cook commented, 'Perhaps she's feeling poorly?'

'We'll find out soon enough.' Mrs Watson paused for a moment, checking her hair in the mirror in the landing by the back door, and smoothing down her apron over her dress.

'It's only the new maid, not one of the young princes,' Cook chortled.

'First impressions count, and one must lead by example. Let's hear what she's got to say for herself,' Mrs Watson replied primly.

After hearing three knocks on the back door she opened it. A voice said shakily, 'Good afternoon, Mrs Watson?'

'It is indeed,' the housekeeper retorted. 'And you are Maria?'

'Yes, I'm Maria. Maria Saward. I'm the new maid. I want to apologise for me lateness, only—'

Before she could finish her sentence Mrs Watson interrupted. 'I've half a mind to report you to Mrs Pennywick. I hope you have a good explanation. And I shall know if you are telling fibs, I can smell them a mile off.'

Pale and trembling, Maria muttered, her eyes filled with sadness, 'Please give me another chance. I'll tell yer the truth, cross me 'eart.'

Maria trembled as she followed the housekeeper into the kitchen. Cook pulled out a chair and offered it to Maria. Mrs Watson's lips were pursed. 'Well, what's your excuse?'

'I didn't intend to be late. Please don't tell Mrs Pennywick. I need this job and I swear it won't 'appen again.'

'It depends on what you have to say for yourself. I'm all ears, young lady.' Mrs Watson spoke in an authoritative tone and a nod from Cook who was listening in confirmed she was acting correctly.

61

Maria bit her lip and stared at Cook's face, and then Mrs Watson's. Maria's knuckles were white in her lap as she anxiously twisted her hands around.

'I'm promise yer I'm usually punctual, and I'm a good worker. I pinched meself after Mrs Pennywick gave me the job 'ere 'cause it shows she has faith in me. I worked 'ard to earn that trust and I have no intention of letting 'er down.'

She paused for a moment, as Mrs Watson edged her chair closer towards Maria. 'Well, go on then. We don't have all day.'

Maria sniffled and spoke directly to the housekeeper, her voice faltering. 'I would 'ave been 'ere on time too, but my Eddie 'ad another turn. I couldn't just leave 'im in the state 'e was.'

'Eddie? Who is Eddie? Some relative?' asked the housekeeper.

'Oh, no. Eddie is my fiancé. I don't know what the matter is with 'im, but he ain't been his self since 'e came back from the war.'

'I see. Or, rather I don't see. What exactly do you mean?' probed Mrs Watson, exchanging a look with Cook who shrugged her shoulders.

Maria clutched her throat with her hand. 'I was on me way 'ere this morning and passed by Eddie's house when his ma stopped me. She said Eddie had run off from the station just half an hour before and nobody knew where he was.'

Cook asked, 'Why did he do that?'

'Because his mind is troubled since he came back from the war. He shakes and has a terrible 'ead if he hears loud noises at the station. It brings back terrible memories of what 'appened during the war.'

'Poor fella. I'm sorry to hear that,' Mrs Watson murmured. 'Did you find him?'

Maria paused to sip her tea. Her eyes moistened. 'I searched everywhere and was worried in case . . . Then I saw him, sitting in the churchyard. I'm telling yer the truth, I swear it.'

Mrs Watson placed a consoling hand on her arm. 'I believe you, Maria. Where is Eddie now?'

'He was agitated, but I managed to calm him after a while and accompanied him to his mother's house. Poor Mabel, she is beside herself with worry.'

Cook's hand rested on her chin. She listened attentively and said, 'I've heard of men coming back from war and they are not always right in the head. It isn't their fault, it's something that can happen if they've had a particularly bad shock.'

Maria's eyes were filled with sadness. 'If only someone could 'elp Eddie. Dr Butterscotch is the best doctor I know. He did a wonderful job saving his leg two years ago when he thought he was going to lose it. If only he could heal troubled minds as well as our mens' broken bodies.'

She beseeched, turning to Mrs Watson. 'You won't sack me, will you? I'll make up for me lateness. I won't take any breaks and I will stay longer. Please don't tell Mrs Pennywick.'

'There's no need to fret about that, Maria. Mrs Pennywick has mentioned what a hard worker you are. I know how you care for your ma too. Let's put it behind us. You can make a start by giving Cook a hand, I'll let Queen Maud know you have arrived.'

Maria clutched her hands in front of her chest, her eyes welling. 'Thank yer, Mrs Watson. You won't regret it, I promise.'

Chapter Eight

Hillington Hall, a large medieval country house set in parkland just four miles from Wolferton and owned by Lord and Lady Appleby, was modest compared to grand homes in its neighbourhood, such as Holkham Hall, the magnificent abode of the third Earl of Leicester, and Houghton Hall, the grand Palladian mansion, that had been built for Britain's first prime minister, St Robert Walpole, where the royal family were guests.

Lady Appleby had willingly agreed that its vast rooms in a spacious wing at the back could be converted into temporary hospital wards during the war. Precious furniture, portraits and porcelain were carefully wrapped and stored away while-iron framed beds were installed on either side of the rooms and smaller rooms used as office accommodation or for rehabilitation, which was its primary use now the war had ended.

Larger, better-equipped hospitals were used to deal with serious wounds and amputations while Hillington Hall was making a name for itself by trialling innovative therapies in the treatment of shell shock.

It was here Beatrice began nursing and discovered it was her true vocation. It was a job she would never have considered if it hadn't been for the war. Before this, she assisted her mother at Wolferton post office where she delivered mail and telegrams informing families of their losses on the battlefield. Now, after almost four years on the wards, her dedication and skill were unquestionable. Her professional manner had greatly impressed Matron, Frances Butterscotch, who ran the hospital with a rod of iron, and her father, Doctor Butterscotch, a distinguished surgeon from a leading London hospital.

As Beatrice stepped through the ward, a man's pained voice cried out, 'Nurse. Nurse. Where is that sound coming from?'

A patient was sitting in a chair next to his bed, pointing towards the end of the ward, his face contorted with anxiety.

Beatrice's eyes followed the direction of his finger. His voice wobbled. 'Listen, over there. Can't you hear it? It sounds like a child's voice. What's going on?'

Beatrice spun around and was surprised to see that the patient was right. There was a boy playing outside in the hallway with his toys on the floor, lost in his own world, with his sounds carrying through into the ward.

'I'm so sorry for the disturbance,' she apologised. 'I will see to it straightaway.'

'No, please don't. I don't want you to stop it. Will you bring the lad in here?' the patient pleaded.

Private John Docherty's eyes were fixed in front of him in a glassy stare and he cupped his left hand behind his ear, straining to pick up every sound from outside the door.

Beatrice hesitated. 'Are you sure? I don't want him to upset you.'

'I want to see the child. I want to hear his voice closer. Surely you can't deny me that?'

'I'm not sure Matron would approve seeing as it isn't visiting time until tomorrow.'

'You and your bloody rules. I just want to stroke his face. Hearing him lark about reminds me of my own boy, Tommie. Where's the harm in that?'

Beatrice gulped as she considered the soldier's poignant words. 'If that's what you want, maybe just a few minutes won't do any harm.'

'Thank you, nurse,' the patient replied, his voice croaked with emotion.

As Beatrice stepped away and the boy's voice became louder, she recognised it as coming from her nephew Leslie. She recalled that Ada mentioned she was meeting with Lady Appleby that day to discuss the mother and baby clinic in Wolferton, and she had taken Leslie in with her.

She found Ada in the hallway trying to quieten Leslie. Leslie was pushing his wooden engine across the tiled floor, squealing and making engine noises, then rushing over to pick it up and send it back the other way.

Ada apologised. 'I'm so sorry about the noise, Beatrice. I would have left him with Betty, but she had to go out this afternoon.'

Beatrice assured her that Leslie wasn't causing a nuisance and explained the soldier's request. Lady Appleby responded instantly. 'The poor man is right. If Matron wants to make a fuss about something like this, then let it be on my shoulders. What do you say, Ada?'

Ada knelt down and spoke softly to her son, explaining that the man had been injured in war and had lost his sight, and wanted to meet Leslie as this would give him some comfort and remind him of his own little boy at home. Leslie nodded and clutched his mother's hand tightly as they entered the ward and followed Beatrice to Private Docherty's chair.

Beatrice introduced them and Ada nudged her son, encouraging him towards the patient. Leslie held out his engine to the soldier. 'Do you want to see my special engine that Grandpa made for me? It's my favourite toy.'

The private held out his hands to reach for it, but they were too high. Leslie placed it in his lap. 'Can't you see it?'

'Shush, Leslie. You mustn't ask questions like that,' his mother scolded.

'It's all right. Please don't give the boy a ticking off. He's just curious, and I have to get used to it.'

The private beckoned to Leslie to come closer. 'My Timmy likes engines too. I would like to have a feel of yours.'

He ran his fingers along it and nodded approvingly. 'I can tell it's a good sturdy engine. Your grandpa's a very clever man.'

'Oh yes, he is. He's the station master. I want to be a station master when I grow up,' Leslie babbled.

Private Docherty reached out with his hands and placed them on Leslie's face. His eyes were blank as his fingers gently felt the boy's eyes, nose and mouth. Leslie recoiled.

'Don't be scared, lad. You don't know what a comfort it is for me to speak to you and feel your closeness. I'm

67

leaving 'ere soon to face the outside world as a poultry farmer. I like being outdoors and I've advertised for a small-holding around here. Who knows, maybe we will be neighbours and you can play with my lad Timmy and show him your engine.'

Leslie's tone was earnest. 'I'd like that. My pa is always too busy to play with me.'

Ada's cheeks flushed. 'Your father dotes on you, Leslie. He is just preoccupied at the moment trying to find work, like the gentleman here.'

Private Docherty's voice wobbled. 'I wish him well, ma'am. I'm learning how to live with blindness and, God willing, I will still be able to put food on our table, and not be forced to sell matches on the street corners or beg for a coin, like some poor blind blighters are doing. I have much to be thankful for.'

Beatrice noticed the patient turn his head away, his eyes moist. 'I think we should leave Private Docherty to rest now.'

'Of course,' Ada agreed. She extended her hand towards Private Docherty, but withdrew it when he didn't respond and she realised he couldn't see it.

As they walked towards the door, he called out, 'Come again, if you can, little lad. Your company has been a tonic for me. Don't let a few tears from a silly old soldier put you off.'

'I'll see what I can do. I will need to ask Matron's approval,' Beatrice replied, feeling moved by the heartfelt moment she had witnessed.

She thanked Ada, telling her sister, 'Kindness and compassion can do so much to lift the spirits of our wounded men.'

'I found it quite moving,' Ada replied. 'I'm glad I've seen you, Beatrice. I heard that Eddie had another bad turn this morning. Maria and Mabel are besides themselves with worry.'

'Poor Eddie. I have heard about it too and have mentioned his case to Matron as a matter of urgency and we are hopeful a bed will become available very soon.'

As Leslie and Ada left, her son yanked at his mother's hand. 'When can I see that nice man again, Mama?'

∽

Beatrice arranged to call in at Eddie's on her way home to break the news.

Mabel answered the door, her face etched with lines and deep hollow pockets under her eyes. She dabbed her moist eyes with her apron and she invited Beatrice in, turning her face away.

'What's happened, Mrs Herring? Is it Eddie?'

Mabel spoke falteringly, clearly distressed. 'I'm so glad to see yer, Beatrice. He won't come out of his room. He's been there all day and I don't know what to do with 'im.'

Beatrice placed a consoling arm around Mrs Herring's trembling shoulder. 'That's why I'm here. I may be able to help, or rather, Doctor Butterscotch can, if Eddie agrees to try a new therapy for shell shock. That's what it is called by the medical profession.'

Mabel poured water into the kettle and placed it on the range. 'So it has a name then, other than cowardice, which is what I've 'eard folks call it.'

'No, that is not what it is. Believe me, Eddie can't help the way he is. The doctor thinks he can help. We suddenly have a bed available and can offer it to Eddie if he wants it.'

Mabel tilted her head upstairs. 'I pray you can get him to agree.'

Beatrice picked up the tea that Mabel had poured. 'Let me try. I'll take this up to his room and see how he is.'

She paused as she reached the top of the stairs and knocked softly on Eddie's door, not wanting to bang loudly and upset his senses. She pressed her ear against the door, but there was no response. She tentatively pushed it open, faintly calling his name. The room was darkened with the curtains drawn. In the corner of the room she spied what appeared to be the shape of a body underneath the covers making shaky movements.

'Hello, Eddie. It's me, Beatrice.'

She knew better than to pull back the bedclothes, having been trained that unexpected jerky movements could be unsettling for patients suffering shell shock.

She spoke softly. 'How are you, Eddie?'

She chided herself for her foolish question. 'I'm sorry, I know that's a silly question.'

Eddie remained silent.

'I know you are struggling, Eddie. I came to tell you that I understand why you feel the way you do. You've been through so much . . .'

Her voice trailed off as she hesitated to search for the right words. 'There is a new therapy Doctor Butterscotch is trialling on patients like you. I took the liberty of mentioning you to him and Eddie, he thinks he can help you.'

70

There was a snuffle from under the bedding. 'Nobody can help me,' came the reply, his voice thick with emotion.

Beatrice spoke gently. 'Why don't you let the doctor be the judge of that? He helped you before, didn't he, when you thought you would lose your leg?'

After a few moments, Eddie's face appeared from under the covers. He was pale and his eyes sunken in. He avoided eye contact, holding the bedcover up to his chin, his hands trembling.

'Oh Eddie, it breaks my heart to see you this way. We're all worried for you.'

'I can't bear being like this. I'm not a coward, but the things you see, the horrors all around you, they can break you.'

'I believe you, Eddie. If you give this a chance, you will feel so much better, in time. Doctor Butterscotch swears by it.'

'Really?' he asked, turning to face her. 'I'll try anything, and I trust Dr Butterscotch. I trust 'im with me life, but I don't want that electric shock I 'eard about for fellas like me.'

'I promise you that won't happen at Hillington Hall.'

'What will I 'ave to do?'

Beatrice sat on the chair next to Eddie's bed. 'Doctor Butterscotch has been to talks given on new gentle methods to help men like you who suffered this way. He encourages patients to talk about their experiences and feelings.'

Eddie raised his knees under the covers and huddled over them, his shoulders shaking. 'I can't ever . . . talk . . . about the things I saw, the things I did,' he stuttered.

'He says it will take time, but that is not all. He believes patients benefit by labouring on the land. We are well placed for that here.'

71

'But I know what the other men will say. They'll still point their fingers at me and say I'm a coward,' he retorted.

'No they won't, not those who fought too, they know what it was like. The men who didn't fight don't understand what you went through, the hell you had to endure. You are a young man, Eddie Herring, and have your whole life ahead of you. You can do this, you should do it for Maria and little Joey. They care for you and want you to be well again. We all do.'

Eddie paused before responding. 'Very well, I will try it for Maria's sake, and for Ma. When do I start?'

'I'll confirm the day as soon as I hear, Eddie. I promise you won't regret it.'

∽

As Beatrice arrived at the station master's house, feeling relieved Eddie had agreed to trial the new therapy, her mother called out, 'There's a phone call for you. It's George. He would like to speak to you.'

Beatrice felt a fluttering sensation as she rushed to take the call. George Perryman was the most decent man she knew and through his work as a solicitor he took on cases for the underdog, charging little, or nothing, to fight their corner. It was during a court case when George acted for a boy who stole food packages intended for local soldiers serving overseas, at the behest of his father, that she first met him.

He was calling to apologise for not seeing her recently, having been detained with work. 'I'm busier than ever since the war ended, but I am calling in to Hillington Hall hospital

72

tomorrow to see Lady Appleby and wondered if I could see you then.'

Beatrice's eyebrows furrowed. 'Well, yes, if my work permits, though I will only be able to spare a few minutes.'

She paused, picking up a leaflet that lay nearby, reading it with interest while George chatted on the line. It was Aggie's leaflet advertising the first of her dance classes.

'I've joined the workhouse committee and there is much to see to there,' he told her.

'Really? That's a coincidence. The Willow family from Appleton have just moved there. We are all most anxious about them.'

George promised to ask about Kitty and her children. Their call was coming to an end when Beatrice suggested, 'It's a long time since we've been to a dance. Would you like to join me at Aggie's new dance class here next week, with the mysterious Marcel?'

'In Wolferton? The place is livening up, but you know dancing is not my strongpoint, darling. Not with my gammy leg.'

George was referring to his limp, the result of suffering polio as a child, which still troubled him at the age of thirty-two. She pleaded, 'Maybe we could have a slow dance out of view of everyone?'

She persisted until George finally agreed, adding that she had to clear the night off with Matron. She entered the kitchen where the family were seated, waving the leaflet. Alfie was again scouring the 'Situations Vacant' pages while Ada was upstairs settling Leslie in bed.

73

'George is coming, if I can get the night off. Who else is going?'

Jessie replied, 'I am willing to give it a try. If only I could go with Jack. Who shall I dance with?'

Sarah commented, 'Aggie mentioned that young ladies can dance together. There's a shortage of men at dances these days, on account of the war.'

'I see,' muttered Jessie. 'I'm not sure I'm keen on that, but I would like to support Aggie.'

Jessie added, 'Me too. We could do with some jollity in our lives and I am excited to learn the latest steps so I can surprise Jack when I see him again.'

Sarah frowned. 'Do you know when that might be, Jessie? It will do you good to go out and have a bit of fun in the evenings. If you ask me, I think your Jack could make more of an effort to stay in touch.'

'Mother! That's not fair,' protested Jessie. 'You know he does his best, and I'm accustomed to hearing from him at short notice, due to his secret work as a royal messenger. I worry constantly about him as I know he sometimes has to travel to hostile countries, even to Russia, and sometimes he has been away for months when he journeys through the continent. It's forbidden for him to communicate with me or tell me where he's been for reasons of security.'

'I only mentioned it because, well, you're not getting any younger. Has he said anything about wanting to settle down with you one day?' Sarah asked pointedly. 'After all, you've been courting now for the last four years. It's not decent to keep you hanging on.'

Jessie's cheeks flushed and she opened her mouth to speak, but before she could say anything Beatrice piped up, 'What does it matter, Ma, as long as Jessie is happy? Anyone can see that Jack adores her. I've no doubt his intentions are honourable.'

'Let's hope so, and that he doesn't keep her dangling too much longer,' she retorted, tight lipped.

Jessie shot Beatrice an appreciative glance and mouthed, *Thank you.* Her sister shrugged her shoulders and raised her arms in the air in despair.

However, her mother's words did strike a chord and a sense of unease swept over Jessie. Deep in her heart she had no doubt Jack's feelings for her were genuine, he had declared his deep affections for her and asked her to be patient. She had allowed him time to grieve the loss of his wife, who died after giving birth to their stillborn baby.

Although he was the trusted King's Messenger, she reasoned that the war had ended now, but he was still constantly on call, meaning they could only snatch short spells together. Surely the pressure on his time should be less now, but that didn't appear to be the case.

A warm sensation rippled through her when she recalled how alive she felt when they were together, however brief, and his recent unexpected visit on official duty at Sandringham was no exception. When they were able to spend longer together, she treasured the memories, reliving it all in her mind. Her pulse quickened when she recalled three months before when he had invited her to London, at a day's notice, and they had spent a joyous evening at the theatre. His eyes had barely left her face and her heartbeat quickened as she recalled his tender embrace as they bade farewell.

Pulling her towards him and pressing his lips on hers, she wanted that sweet moment of ecstasy to last forever. His parting words were, 'I'll write, my darling. As soon as I can. We have our whole lives ahead of us.'

He had assured her they would have a lifetime together when the war ended, but how much longer would she have to wait? She narrowed her eyes, her mouth drying, as her imagination began to run riot. She dare not speak the thoughts running wild in her head – *had Jack's head been turned by someone else?*

She stared into her lap, her rambling thoughts making her blood run cold. A moment later, she dismissed any doubt she had about Jack's feelings. Beatrice was right, there was no better or truer man than Jack, and she was suddenly enveloped with guilt.

Beatrice was still chatting about the dance classes. 'Are you going to try it, Mother? Dancing is for all ages. You can bring Father along.'

Her mother pulled a face. 'Stop your jesting now. My dancing days are long past.'

She went on, 'I can't speak for your father though. There was a time he did whisk me off my feet.' The corner of her lip curled and her eyes softened as she dwelled on a tender recollection of Harry's surprising sure-footedness on the dance floor when he swept the farmer's daughter off her feet. They had met at a country dance in Whittlesey, a Fenland market town in Cambridgeshire, where Harry worked at the time. He knew her family from church and she agreed to have the last dance with him. She had encouraged him to apply for the royal station master's post when it came up. At the age of just twenty-five years, he beat off stiff competition from one hundred and twenty other applicants to secure the much coveted appointment.

Jessie turned to her mother. 'Where is Father this evening?'

Sarah retorted, a serious expression on her face, 'He was called suddenly to the Big House for a meeting.'

'Really? What meeting? What's going on there?' asked Beatrice, her ears pricking up.

Sarah pondered, before replying. 'I was going to let your father tell you the news when he returned home, but I may as well tell you.'

'Tell us what?' asked Beatrice and Jessie in unison.

'It's to do with the whereabouts of the missing men from the Sandringham Company and the land agent, Captain Frank Beck.'

Alfie placed his paper in his lap and looked up. 'What about them? Is there any news?'

Sarah answered, 'I believe so, and it's thanks to the determination of our royal family to find out what happened. It's believed there has been an important discovery of . . .'

Sarah couldn't finish the sentence.

'You mean, the bodies of the men have been found? After more than four years?' asked Alfie, incredulous.

Beatrice choked. 'Oh no! Do the families know? So many families still hold out hope they will return one day.'

Sarah bit her lip. 'I can't say any more. You must wait to hear it from the man himself, the chaplain, Reverend Pierrepont Edwards, who was out in Gallipoli at the same time as the Sandringham Company. Queen Alexandra personally asked him to go to Gallipoli and return with answers, which he has done.'

The mood in the room was sombre as the news sunk in. The station master's wife continued, 'All I know is that the chaplain is here now, your father greeted him at the station and they are at the Big House together. A public meeting is to be held as soon as possible. The chaplain intends to make a statement about his discovery, and he wants Harry to help.'

Chapter Nine

Their happy memories in Wolferton now seemed like a dream for the Willow family as they settled into their new life of harsh routine.

Kitty followed Milly into the washroom for her morning wash, her shoulders slumped. She took her place along the line of steel sinks and shivered as she splashed the cold water over her face. Just over a week had passed since she had first set foot in the workhouse. Her hands were now red raw from scrubbing the laundry that the workhouse took in from outside, her brow wrinkled and prominent circles had appeared under her eyes due to fretting over her children.

Her mood lifted in the day when she caught the odd glimpse of them at meal times, and her eyes searched particularly for Victoria. She had spotted her yesterday from a window. She was walking in line across the courtyard, her head down. Kitty had felt a sharp pang. There was no spring in her daughter's step, and her shoulders drooped as if she were an old lady. The girls wore loose grey dresses with long white pinafore aprons over them, while the boys wore scratchy grey shorts that fell below the knee, teamed with white shirts and grey pullovers. Kitty wondered if the children were eating enough, her heart aching at the thought of them going to bed hungry each night, as she did, refusing the meagre food placed in front of them – tasteless grey gruel and scraggy cuts of meat fit only for animals, with rock-hard bread. Her worse fears were if the guardian had singled out Victoria for his attention, and she prayed this had not happened.

The only day their meal resembled anything edible was on a Sunday. This was the day they were joined by the workhouse committee of do-gooders who came in to check that all was well. She wondered if they were astute enough to see how ravenous the inmates were, if they could judge this by their eyes popping out as a tasty meat pie, vegetables and thick gravy were served, and how quickly they shoved the food into their mouths.

After Sunday dinner, served at noon, the women were expected to sit quietly and embroider in their common room. Milly warned Kitty how they had to not only be on their best behaviour during visits by the committee, but were expected to sing the praises of the guardian and Miss Feathers as the workhouse was endeavouring to improve and modernise and treat its inmates more humanely.

Kitty could barely believe what Milly said. 'I shudder to think what this place was like before then.'

A strong emphasis was being placed on finding jobs for the inmates by providing training and skills to equip them for life in the outside world. Management was expected to rule with compassion, not cruelty, but Kitty wondered how much had really changed. She sat alongside Milly working on their sewing, picking different coloured threads for the tablecloth she was embroidering from a pattern she had been given. The design of partridges with glorious golden brown plumes appealed to Kitty and she learned this was a special commissioned piece. Kitty and Milly were both accomplished with the needle and Miss Feathers informed them that their work was to be of the highest standard as the commission had come from a very important person.

'I wonder who it could be for?' queried Kitty.

Milly shrugged her shoulders. She was using a similar design for matching napkins. 'Well, Miss Feathers says the order came from the top.'

'It's probably someone from the committee then. Look, here they come now, with Miss Feathers. What should we do?'

Milly whispered, 'Keep yer head down, keep stitching, and only speak if they speak to yer.'

Kitty observed Miss Feathers from the corner of her eye stopping to speak to one of their fellow inmates at the end of her table, a girl of eighteen or nineteen called Emily. She was accompanied by three well-dressed gentlemen and an austere-looking woman. They appeared to admire her embroidered sampler with the solemn words 'When my Father and my Mother forsake me, the Lord taketh me up', stitched in a square surrounded by beautiful flowers and trees.

The woman nodded approvingly, telling Miss Feathers, 'Quite so. I hope these . . .' She pointed her finger at the seamstress, her lips juddering as she struggled to find the word she was searching for.

'Ladies? Is that the word you are searching for?' enquired one of her distinguished-looking gentlemen companions.

Miss Feathers steered the group towards Kitty. Her ears had pricked up when she heard the gentleman speak. It was the first time she had heard a kind tone since she entered the workhouse.

81

The man with the kind voice stopped behind her. 'May I ask, what are you stitching? Your work is exquisite.'

Kitty glanced up and saw a pair of kindly eyes staring down at her. She opened her mouth to speak, but Miss Feathers stepped forward. 'This is a special commission cushion cover for Her Majesty, Queen Alexandra, who has a fondness for pheasants. She is our patron and takes a great interest in our work here.'

The kind gentleman leaned forward and enquired again about her work, but his words went unheard as Kitty panicked about her predicament.

'Are you all right? You appear to have come over unwell?' he asked, showing genuine concern.

'Of course she's all right,' Miss Feathers replied, stepping forward and raising her chin, holding herself in an authoritative stance.

Miss Feathers' face showed displeasure, while the gentleman stared at Kitty, tilting his head, waiting for her to answer.

Kitty stuttered. 'Yes . . . yes, sir. I was just taken aback to 'ear I am making this for Queen Alexandra.'

'And why would that be? What concern is it to us?' asked the haughty woman, dressed from top to toe in an expensive royal blue skirt and jacket, a jewelled brooch clasped to her collar. She had an icy stare that made Kitty freeze. She estimated they were both in their late forties, with the woman, judging by the lines criss-crossing her face, maybe a couple of years older.

The kindly gentleman smiled. 'I can see you are very accomplished with your task. Her Majesty will be most impressed.'

As Miss Feathers ushered her guests towards the end of the room, Kitty's ears pricked up when she heard the gentleman enquire about her circumstances. Miss Feathers described how Kitty had been forced to leave the Sandringham Estate, and the reasons why, exclaiming that the charity was doing its utmost to help Kitty and her family.

The kind man muttered, 'That explains it then, poor woman.'

Kitty watched him walk away. She wondered how influential he was at the workhouse. She could tell he was a professional gent from his fine attire; dressed in a dark grey suit and white shirt, with a pale blue and green striped tie, a matching handkerchief in his top jacket pocket. His thick greying hair had a bouncy wave on the top of his head. He nodded in Kitty's direction, his mouth curling in the corners, and their eyes met. Kitty's cheeks flushed.

Milly nudged her, making her snap out of her day dreams. 'Are you all right, Kitty? You did come over all funny.'

'I'm fine, I really am. Hearing Queen Alexandra's name was a shock, and I dread the thought that she might visit if she's a patron. I'd be so ashamed for 'er to see me like this.'

'You mustn't think like that. She'll understand,' Milly sympathised.

'I don't want any pity. I must get this done now, else I'll 'ave Miss Feathers after me.'

'Yer not the only one who's 'ad it 'ard. I've just been told the lady's maid job I wanted 'as been given to someone else. I thought I 'ad a chance to leave this place, and now I ain't,' Milly flared.

'I'm sorry to 'ear that, Milly, I really am. It's no wonder you are feeling low.'

Milly shrugged her shoulders. Her auburn hair was tied back showing a clear freckled face and bright green eyes that were filled with mystery. Kitty had immediately sensed a sadness about Milly and gradually coaxed out the reason behind this.

'Tell me, Milly, how did you end up here? You've never said.'

'It's all in the past now, I don't like to talk about it' Milly replied, casting her eyes downwards.

'Please, I'd like to know. We're friends, aren't we? You can tell me anything.'

Milly whispered, 'Very well. I'll try.'

Milly's words were slow to spill from her lips at first. Kitty didn't rush her. She listened agog to every word that Milly spoke in a matter-of-fact way, without a shred of pity for herself. Her father, Wilfred, had been a chimney sweep, like his father before him. When she was ten years old he became very ill and struggled to breathe, coughing up tar like thick phlegm. He died shortly afterwards from a painful respiratory condition which doctors said was caused by breathing the soot.

After his death her ma, Sylvie, went to pieces and left Milly in charge of her brother, Toby, who was one year younger than her. She could remember the day she arrived at the workhouse as clear as if it were yesterday.

'Ma brought Toby and me here, telling us we were on 'oliday, and would be back for us after a week. That was the last I saw of 'er,' Milly said, the words beginning to choke her.

'I can't believe a mother could be so cruel. I'm so sorry, Milly.'

'I believed Ma when she said she would be back, I kept asking Miss Feathers if she had heard from her. Then one day Miss Feathers told me I should forget her, saying she had gone off with a docker and was never coming back for us.'

'You can't be sure of that,' Kitty bleated, knowing she didn't sound convincing.

'We 'ad nowhere else to go, but when he turned fifteen, Toby ran away, 'e joined the crew of a ship leaving from 'ere and is in Australia now, I get one letter a year from 'im at Christmas, 'e says 'e aint coming back. I'm all on me own. I'm scared to leave though, does that sound silly? I don't know how I'd cope outside.'

'I do understand, I really do. I just wish there was a way out for you, for us all. One day, it will happen.'

Milly sniffled. 'I ain't ever spoken of this before. I'm used to it 'ere now. Maybe I'll never leave'

'But you can't want to stay 'ere forever? Maybe that kind gentleman would help, if we could let him know about your situation.'

Milly shrugged her shoulders. 'I dunno.'

'But that's the real world out there. You said yerself they want us to move on. There is goodness out there too. I only wish Victoria had a chance to leave as I 'aven't been able to put out of my mind how Mr Mumbles' eyes were fixed on her. If that man lays a finger on her, I swear he will live to regret it.'

'Your Victoria is a pretty girl. I can see why she caught 'is eye. He ain't a good man. There was a time he used to . . .'

Kitty grabbed Milly's arm before she could finish the sentence. 'You mean, he . . . ?'

Kitty was uncertain how to finish her sentence. Milly elaborated, 'I were fourteen and 'e took a shine to me. Miss

Feathers said he 'ad requested me to take his nightcap to him in his office. At first, that's all it were, and then he moaned about aches and pains on his body and asked me to rub them better. One night I could see he became very excited when I were rubbing his knee and then the top of his leg. He took my 'and in his and placed it, you know where. I was scared and pulled away, but he grabbed me 'and made me rub his manhood until it exploded with juice.'

Kitty was enraged. 'That is despicable. Did you report him?'

'I didn't know who to tell. Miss Feathers knew, she stayed outside his room while I were there.'

Fuming, Kitty cried, 'My Victoria is an innocent. What if he tries this with 'er?'

Milly contended, 'Try not to fret about 'er. If she's as bright as I think she is, she'll be able to look after 'erself.'

Kitty persisted, her frown deepening. 'Yes, my girl is bright, and she has courage too, which should stand her in good stead if he tries anything untoward. I'll never forgive myself if he lays a finger on her.'

Kitty couldn't put out of her mind what Milly told her. That evening, when Victoria sat on the bench in the dining hall, her mother watched her expression. It seemed to be evasive and unwilling to look up, while Mr Mumbles wiped his mouth after finishing his food and stared intently in Victoria's direction.

Kitty barely slept a wink that night and struggled to keep her mind on her work the next day in the wash house. Working in the laundry was back breaking, and she got the impression that all new women started there as a rite of passage. The morning routine began by filling the copper wash boiler with cold water and lighting the fire underneath with wood, coal and any scraps to heat the water. The coloured items were separated from the white ones and garments with the worst stains were soaked overnight and then scrubbed on a washboard with Sunlight soap.

Although Kitty was used to laundry work as a mother of six and had done these duties in the royal household, she had never had to deal with huge piles of dirty washing in such great quantities. Spending all day in a room filled with steam made her face constantly drip with sweat and her back ached from stooping and carrying. As soon as one pile was finished, another basket overflowing with dirty washing was dropped at her feet and she pressed on, refusing to show signs of fatigue.

∽

The following Sunday afternoon Kitty and Milly were seated in the common room. Kitty had almost completed her tablecloth and was holding up her handiwork and admiring it when she heard Miss Feathers' raised voice in the background.

'I am very sure we can accommodate you, Mr Bell. I shall ask the young lady concerned to join us in my office straightaway.'

She came over to their table and spoke to Milly, while the kind man's attention was diverted, in deep conversation with the same haughty companion, who appeared to be shaking her head.

'I have some good news for you, Milly. Our chairman, Mr Bell, is looking for a kitchen maid who possesses all the necessary skills and I put your name forward. He wants to meet you. Now don't let me down, will you?'

Milly's heart pounded. She gripped Kitty's arm. 'Me? Why me?'

Miss Feathers snorted. 'It was Mr Mumbles' suggestion. He said it is time for you to leave as we have taught you everything you need to know for the outside world.'

'Leave? But I don't want to. Haven't I always pleased Mr Mumbles?'

Kitty gasped, but Miss Feathers ignored Milly's comment. 'That's enough of your silliness. You can't stay here forever. Now, please follow me, you ungrateful girl.'

Kitty rose too, and hugged Milly, who scraped a hand through her hair. 'You must go, Milly. This is your chance of a new life and you should take it. Remember what I said, there are good people out there, and Mr Bell seems kindly, so do not be afraid.'

Kitty watched Milly walking off nervously with Miss Feathers. They were joined by Mr Bell and his haughty female companion. He paused at the door and turned. Kitty dropped her chin slightly and glanced into her lap feeling awkward that he had caught her staring. When she looked up a few seconds later they had left the room.

Milly returned to the common room fifteen minutes later, panting. 'Oh Kitty, I'm to start tomorrow morning. The gentleman says 'e wants people like me who 'ave been 'ere years to 'ave the chance to start their lives on the outside. 'E seems ever so nice.'

'I'm so happy for you.' Kitty beamed. 'You deserve this chance. Is it a sudden vacancy?'

'Their kitchen maid is in the family way and her baby is due next week. She kept it secret from them, but their housekeeper found out about it when she fainted from tiredness. She wanted to stay on right up until the birth on account of her man losing a leg in the war and them only 'aving his pension to live on. But Mr Bell insists she leaves now, for 'er own good, and will send her a weekly food parcel till they get settled. Oh Kitty, do yer think it will work out all right? I'm scared of not being good enough and being sent back 'ere.'

'Now put those notions out of yer 'ead, Milly. You will be absolutely fine. Do you know who the woman is with him? She seems to have a sour face. Is that 'is wife?'

Milly shrivelled her nose. 'Oh no, that's his sister, though you'd never know it, they're like chalk and cheese. She is very 'oity-toity and looked down 'er nose at me. I 'ope she won't go on at me. Her name is Lucinda and she were telling 'im off for being so soft to 'is kitchen maid, but 'e took no notice.'

'Oh dear, Milly. Try not to fret. Once you settle in, I'm sure everything will work out. You are lucky to have this chance of a fresh start.'

Milly leaned closer to Kitty. 'This might be of interest to you. I 'eard the gentleman say they needed a companion for his ma who is ailing. I straightaway mentioned your name, it just came out of me mouth. Miss Feathers gave me one of 'er looks, but Mr Bell seemed interested.'

'A lady's companion? Me?' Kitty exclaimed. 'I ain't ever done that. I've always been a maid.'

Milly's eyes flashed. 'So what did yer say to me, *this is your chance and you should grab it.* Well, I say the same to you, Kitty Willow.'

'It's out of the question. There is no way I would leave Victoria 'ere at risk of that foul man. He might try to take advantage of 'er.'

Half an hour later Kitty was surprised to be summoned to Miss Feathers' office. The kind gentleman was standing in front of the window, his hands behind his back, staring outside, watching the trees shed their leaves under the dull grey sky.

She caught the haughty woman's unfriendly gaze and smiled weakly, bobbing her knee slightly. Lucinda Bell was seated in a corner of the room, her back upright, and Miss Feathers invited Kitty to take the seat in front of her desk.

'I won't beat about the bush, Mrs Willow. Mr Bell is a very generous benefactor to our institution, and it is his express wish to help those who are, how should I put it, in a less fortunate position, those such as yourself, so they can be given a chance to improve their situation. We are most fortunate to benefit from his unstinting and selfless support.' Miss Feathers clasped her hands in front of her chest and smiled appreciatively.

Mr Bell raised a hand in protest. 'Please, Miss Feathers, I seek no acknowledgement for what I do. My reward is to see the people here flourish under my scheme. I thought it would make sense for Mrs Willow to start together on the same day as the new maid, Milly, seeing as they get on well. From what you have told me of Mrs Willow's background working in the royal household and her exemplary reference from them, I am sure she will advance admirably with us, isn't that so, Lucinda?'

The question was directed to his stony-faced sister who replied, 'Indeed, brother, though I believe your faith in human nature is misguided at times.'

Kitty took a step forward. 'Please, sir, may I ask, what is it you are proposing I should do? I'm not sure I would be best suited. Perhaps there is someone else 'ere who could benefit from your kindness?'

Miss Bell's nostrils flared. 'The insolence of the woman, asking questions of us and telling us whether she is suited or not to a golden opportunity like this.'

Kitty's eyes faced the floor and her fingers twisted in front of her. 'I do apologise, sir, ma'am, for I didn't intend it to come out that way, and what you are doing for Milly is wonderful.'

Miss Feathers intervened, staring icily at Kitty. 'I think you've said enough, Mrs Willow. Please leave now.'

Turning to Mr Bell, she fawned obsequiously. 'I apologise most sincerely. I'm sure Mrs Willow means no offence.'

Mr Bell asserted, 'I agree. I'm sure the good lady didn't. Do you mind, Miss Feathers, if I question her for a moment?'

Miss Feathers appeared flustered, but he insisted. The kind man's eyes softened as he spoke. 'I apologise too, Mrs Willow, we have been talking over your head without informing you of the details of our offer, and you may require some time to consider it, rather than it being forced on you. I'm conscious too that we haven't been properly introduced. My name is Josiah Bell, I am a solicitor in the town and chairman of the workhouse committee. I am accompanied by my sister, Lucinda, who is also on the committee. It is our desire to make changes here for the benefit of the residents.'

Kitty gasped. 'A solicitor? Oh, I've never met a solicitor before. I'm pleased to meet yer both.'

Mr Bell cleared his throat. 'It is my preference to offer employment opportunities when I can to residents here, to try and give them a chance in life to improve their fortunes. Milly has agreed to be our kitchen maid and I am also in need of a lady's companion for my elderly mother. Your name was mentioned.'

Kitty's heart raced at his words and the realisation of his tempting offer sunk in.

She clenched her fists, her knuckles turning white. 'I very much appreciate yer kind offer, sir, but I'm afraid I can't accept. You see, there is one matter troubling me.'

'Tell me, what is it?' he asked, raising his hand and sending a glance in the direction of Miss Feathers and his sister to silence them.

Kitty paused, aware that she couldn't blurt out her concerns about Victoria in the presence of Miss Feathers. She bit her lip as she contemplated what to say without refer-ring to Mr Mumbles directly and came up with a plausible excuse. 'I 'ave me children 'ere and I couldn't leave them, if I 'ad to sleep in, sir. I need to know they are all right and I live for the moments I catch sight of 'em at meal times.'

'How ungrateful. I told you it would be a waste of time.' Lucinda scowled, tilting her nose up.

'I warned you she would say that,' retorted Miss Feathers, glowering. 'There may be another person I could suggest who would be more suitable.'

Mr Bell rubbed his chin. 'I like your thoughtfulness, Mrs Willow. I believe you are exactly the person whose company my mother would like, and the position will help you improve your station and remove you from this dreary place.'

'Mr Bell, I do protest!' retorted Miss Feathers lamely.

'I don't want to see Mrs Willow waste her life here. If you agree, Miss Feathers, I see no reason why she can't return here at night to sleep, and for arrangements to be made for her to see her children as she wishes. I wouldn't want them to suffer further because of their mother taking up this position.'

Kitty was overcome by Mr Bell's kindness and felt instinctively she had to accept the post, but needed to be sure Miss Feathers would agree to his suggestion. She nodded. 'If Miss Feathers gives me her solemn word and sticks to it, that would make a difference.'

Miss Feathers' lips were twitching. She seethed, 'I do not see how I can refuse your request, Mr Bell, as one of our most important benefactors. I am sure we can accommodate it, though Mrs Willows will be expected to pay for her overnight stay from her salary.'

Mr Bell nodded. 'I will pay any costs incurred by her here while she is in our employment. How does that suit you, Mrs Willow?'

'Thank you kindly, sir. In that case, I would like to accept your offer. I'm anxious to see my children as soon as possible. I am only able to catch a scant glimpse of them at meal times, and as soon as I catch sight of them, they are moved on.'

Miss Bell crossed her arms in front of her chest and tut-tutted. Her brother caught Miss Feathers' eyes. Her lips were pursed.

'I see no reason why this cannot be arranged. It's perfectly understandable. I'm sure Miss Feathers will make the necessary arrangements,' Mr Bell replied.

'As you wish, I shall arrange for you to see the children later,' Miss Feathers muttered between her teeth.

'Thank you, Miss Feathers. I fret about 'em constantly,' Kitty said. 'Tell me, are they well?'

'We do our best for them, but I'm afraid to inform you that your boy, Philip, was punished by his teacher for fighting with one of the other boys and placed in solitary confinement. I'm sure that's taught him a lesson and he won't be doing that again. And Victoria, well, she is doing very well. In fact, I have suggested she be one of the chosen few who are given extra tuition from Mr Mumbles himself in return for helping him catalogue his library.'

Kitty's legs gave way at these revelations. Pip, fighting? That was so unlike him. She also recalled what Milly had told her about the way the guardian abused his position with young girls and was scared for her daughter.

She forced herself to keep her concerns to herself for now.

Miss Feathers asserted, 'I will arrange for you to see them in the common room after tea this evening at six thirty. I ask that you don't overexcite their emotions and cause them anxiety. You will start your new position tomorrow.'

Mr Bell smiled. 'That's settled then. We will expect you at seven o'clock tomorrow morning. Miss Feathers will give you the address.'

Chapter Ten

Milly was elated to hear that Kitty would be working in the Bell household too. As they sat together at the trestle table for their evening meal, they did their best to contain their delight, so as not to arouse jealousy from the other women.

Kitty anxiously chewed on a lump of bread and cheese, washing it down with lukewarm watery tea. She fidgeted constantly, arching her neck to raise her head and look in all directions to catch sight of her children.

She spotted Pip and Laurie enter the dining room and stood up, raising her arm to catch their attention. Laurie's face broke into a wide smile and he mouthed *Ma*. Pip nudged his brother to look away, not wanting them to get into trouble.

'I can't 'elp meself, Milly. I can't wait to see them in the common room and hug them.'

'I don't 'ave anything to me name that's worth taking. Ma and Pa never left me anything. I only 'ave these ol' rags I'm wearing. Miss Feathers said she would sort me out something that belonged to a dead 'un if I wanted anything else.'

As Kitty made her way to the common room her thoughts turned to her beloved Frank. He was the best husband and father she could have wished for, always putting family first. Was he still alive? Part of her felt he was dead, though she couldn't help clinging to the hope he had somehow survived. Maybe he was a prisoner of war? Or languishing in a hospital with memory loss? A thought flashed through her mind: as she was going to work for a solicitor, she could ask him if he had contacts, or might know who to approach, to help her discover the truth, one way or another, unaware that news about their fate was reaching Wolferton at that moment.

∽

After their meal, Kitty made her way to the common room. Miss Feathers was already there and informed Kitty that the children were on their way.

At that moment the door opened and a child's voice cried, 'Mama!'

'Rosie, my sweet angel. How've yer been? Oh how I've missed yer all.'

All her children were there, their eyes filled with tears of joy. They gulped back sobs and made quiet whimpering sounds, wiping their runny noses on the backs of their sleeves.

Kitty asked, 'Please, Miss Feathers, would you leave us alone for a few minutes.'

'You have ten minutes.'

When she had shut the door behind her, the children clambered around Kitty, releasing the tears they had held back. She embraced them tightly, fighting back her own sobs. Victoria's arms were around her neck while Pip stood back a few paces, giving space to Laurie and Billy, who clung to her apron around her waist, while Iris and Rosie were enveloped in her arms too, and gasping for air.

'We only have a short time, but I wanted to see you before I begin my new job tomorrow.'

'Are you leaving us 'ere?' the chorus of voices cried.

Kitty bit her lip. 'I'll be back at night. I'm going to be a lady's companion. My employer is a kindly solicitor and once I've settled in, I'm gonna ask 'im to 'elp me get yer out of 'ere.'

Rosie snivelled. 'Mama, please don't go. I don't like it 'ere. I can't 'elp it if I wet the bed.'

She'd seen the soiled linen herself from the children's beds that piled up in the laundry. Had some of those been Rosie's? And was it true what the other women said, that a child would have to sleep in the wet bedding to teach them a lesson? Had that happened to her?

Before she could ask Rosie about it, Laurie blurted, 'Pip's been fighting again, Ma. He's going to be in more trouble if he don't behave.'

'It weren't my fault,' the older brother replied indignantly. 'I stood up for meself when one of the boys kept saying we didn't 'ave a father. He said we were all bastards. I ain't, and I told him that, and he kept saying it so I punched him in the face.'

'He knocked 'is two front teeth out, Ma, and he were twice the size of Pip,' Laurie divulged.

'Serves 'im right!' declared Pip. 'He deserved all 'e got. He kept saying it, so I did it again.'

'Oh Pip. You need to have cloth ears. As long as we know what the truth is, that's all that matters. Did yer get a thrashing for it?'

Pip remained tight lipped, but Laurie revealed, 'He had a caning from Mr Mumbles, his bottom is red. I want to hit that man, he's 'orrible.'

Her face reddened with rage when she finally persuaded Pip to show her the red wheals clearly visible from his beating. 'That man will answer for this. I'm sure Mr Bell will be appalled when I tell him what's going on 'ere. I am going to work in his house and he is a good man. Please give me your words that yer won't get into any more scrapes. I will come for yer all, as soon as I can, and take you away. I promise you, with me life.'

They clung to each other, and as they were pulled off one by one by the superintendent who had entered the room, Kitty kissed them softly, leaving Victoria till last.

She stroked her pretty face, which shone with innocence. Kitty wrapped her arms around her and whispered a warning. 'I want you to listen carefully. You must not be alone with the guardian, not just because of what he did to Pip, but because I'm told he has a liking for pretty young girls like yerself and sometimes behaves improperly. If he tries anything on, tell 'im sharpish you will report him to Mr Bell. I believe Mr Bell is a man of influence and I will be sure to inform him. Will you promise me that?'

Victoria lowered her eyes and nodded. Kitty feared the worst. 'He hasn't touched you yet, has he?'

'Oh no,' Victoria responded sharply. 'He tried once to fondle me when I bent over to pick up some papers he dropped in his office, but Miss Fairbairn came in and he stepped back very quickly. He ordered me to return to the classroom, and I haven't been alone with him since. But he does scare me, Ma. He stares at me a lot.'

Miss Feathers returned to the common room carrying Kitty's bags. 'Come along now, Victoria. I can't stand here waiting all evening.'

Victoria pulled away from her mother. 'I love yer Ma. I promise to do as you say.'

∞

Kitty retrieved her suitcase from Miss Feathers and flung it on her bed when she got back to the dormitory. She opened the lid, and rummaged among its contents. 'Oh no. My money, it's gone!' she cried.

'What money?' Milly enquired.

'It was a collection from me friends in Wolferton to be used during emergencies. Now I don't 'ave a brass farthing to me name.'

'You can kiss goodbye to that. It's bad luck for you, but there's nought you can do about it without proof you 'ad money in yer bag,' Milly stated.

'But there was more than ten pounds. Miss Feathers would know who had access to it,' Kitty protested.

'Well, unless you 'ave proof it ever existed, you don't stand a chance of getting it back. If you'd been given a receipt specifying it then that would have been proof.'

Kitty slipped under her bedcovers and was unable to settle. She listened to Milly's heavy breathing and the gentle snores from other women in the dormitory filled her ears. Eventually, Kitty's eyelids became heavy and clasped shut, but she slept fitfully and was surprised to be shaken awake by Milly at sunrise.

'Wake up, Kitty. It's time to get up. I've already washed.'

Kitty rubbed her eyes and propped herself up on the bed. Milly was pulling a dark blue blouse over her head. She had been given a drab grey skirt to wear with it by Miss Feathers.

Kitty eased herself out of bed. After a quick splash she hastily dressed in the same dark blue dress she wore when she arrived. She wrapped a shawl around her shoulders.

'Ready?' asked Milly. 'I'm too excited to eat anything.'

Kitty gulped, her stomach flipping as she followed Milly. The other occupants were rising too, and as she passed them, she felt their eyes bore into her and heard their mutterings, 'Why is she favoured to leave so soon? She's only been 'ere five minutes.'

'Ignore them,' whispered Milly.

Kitty placed her bag under her bed for now, painfully aware that she would be returning to lay her head there that evening.

The two women stepped out of the back door that led into a courtyard. They held each other's hands and walked out of the iron gates, excitement rising within them about the new opportunities opening up for them.

∽

Kitty and Milly arrived at the Bell household at 23 Quayside after a fifteen-minute walk through alleys and up cobbled streets. In front of them was a fine looking double-fronted property with two Roman pillars at the side of the black-painted front door.

Kitty read the brass plaque outside: *Josiah Bell & Son, Family, Defence and Commercial Solicitors at your service.*

Kitty's eyes widened. 'He sounds a very important man.'

Milly shrugged. 'Shall we find the back door? They won't be pleased if we ring the front bell.'

A passage at the side of the Georgian property led to the side gate, which they opened, stepping into a small yard. A large outer building was attached to the rear of the property and a washing line stretched across the yard.

The back door was flung open by a woman in her fifties before they had a chance to knock. 'I saw you both gawping at the front of the house when I went in the front parlour to draw the curtains. You must be Kitty and Milly. Follow me. I've been expecting you.'

Kitty and Milly introduced themselves nervously and exchanged worried glances. 'We didn't mean to stare in,' Kitty apologised.

Once inside the warm kitchen, the woman introduced herself. 'I'm Henrietta Finchley, Miss Finchley to you. I've been the housekeeper here more years than I care to remember. We can familiarise ourselves later, as you see, I am up to my neck in it.'

The smell of bacon wafted under their noses. Milly blurted, 'Oh, that smells just wonderful. I can't recall the last time I had crispy fried bacon.'

She immediately covered her mouth, her cheeks turning scarlet.

'You'll be able to sit down and tuck into some later. I'm sure the master won't mind. He likes his staff to be properly fed . Would you like an egg and toast to go with it?'

Kitty could scarcely believe her ears. 'Do you really mean it?'

'Of course. Meals are included with your terms of employment, and that includes breakfast. The servants usually eat after the ladies and gentlemen of the house have finished theirs. I'm getting the breakfast ready now. Let me show you quickly where to put your things, then I need you to come straight down and give me a hand.'

Kitty explained she would not be staying the night, but followed Milly up to the attic room. It had several partitions and a brass bed covered with a neat patchwork bedspread was positioned in the corner in front of the window, a bentwood chair positioned next to it. A small wardrobe and marble-topped washstand filled most of the remaining space. Milly beamed, spinning around on the spot.

'I ain't got much to put in that wardrobe, but I'm gonna save up for some new clothing. I have to pinch meself, we 'ave struck gold coming 'ere.'

'We have, Milly, we have. I can scarcely believe it meself.'

Miss Finchley was frying more rashers of thick bacon over the range when they returned to the kitchen and the aroma of the sizzling fry-up made her mouth water. She pointed to some slices of cut bread on the table and asked Milly to toast them on the toast plate, warning her not to burn them.

'The ladies like the crusts cut off, and the bread soft and slightly golden,' she instructed.

Kitty was instructed to make some pots of tea, including one for Mr Bell's mother. A tray had already been laid with a pretty lace-edged cloth and napkin, and a dainty porcelain cup and saucer were placed on it.

Kitty was so preoccupied seeing to her task that she didn't hear the door open. Mr Bell stood there holding a folded newspaper under his arm. 'I thought I heard you arrive. I wanted to welcome you both. Miss Finchley is like one of the family after being with us for many years. She will explain your duties to you.'

Turning to the housekeeper, he added, 'I need to leave for a meeting in London within the hour, Miss Finchley, but my sister will be here.'

Kitty and Milly lowered their heads and bobbed a knee. 'There is no need for those formalities here.' He smiled.

'Breakfast will be ready in five minutes, Mr Bell. Shall we bring it through with the tea?' Miss Finchley asked.

'That will be splendid,' replied Mr Bell, retreating out of the kitchen.

Kitty observed that the housekeeper was well spoken. Her pale features retained a fine bone structure and her blue eyes were clear. Her countenance shone and it was clear for Kitty to see that she was a good person. Her medium height and frame displayed a slender figure, her tawny-coloured hair showing a few grey streaks.

Miss Finchley asked Kitty to wheel the breakfast trolley into the dining room. A bowl of fried mushrooms and some kidneys were placed on one of the shelves ready to be served on the warmed plates the housekeeper had just removed from the oven.

A mahogany oval table with carved legs was positioned in the centre of the elegantly furnished dining room. The walls were covered in a rich embossed mint-green paper decorated with elaborate white lilies, complementing the velvet drapes made from a darker shade of green with gold braid edging that hung from the large front window.

Three places were set around the table. Mr Bell was seated at the head. He was talking animatedly to a younger gentleman in his early thirties who was seated to his left. He was also very well dressed and wore a dark grey suit with a burgundy paisley waistcoat which was set off with a burgundy tie and matching handkerchief in his jacket. Like the older man, he had a kindly expression.

Mr Bell was showing him an article from the local newspaper. 'It says here the chaplain of the Norfolk Regiment has returned to England from Gallipoli with news about the missing men from the Sandringham Company.'

'I fear what that news might be,' the younger man replied.

'No!' cried Kitty, the plates she had been holding slipping through her fingers. Her face paled.

A moment later she dropped to her knees, picking up the shattered pieces. Her hands shook. 'I'm sorry for the breakage, sir. You can take the money out of me wages.'

Mr Bell knelt down alongside her. 'We will do no such thing. It was insensitive of us to mention this in front of you. Your husband's situation slipped my mind.'

Kitty gulped. 'Can you tell me what the paper says?'

The younger man took hold of the paper and read from the page. 'It appears that a meeting is to be held in Wolferton called for by a chaplain who has recently returned from Gallipoli and invites anyone with an interest to attend.'

Kitty clutched her throat. 'I would like to go, if possible.'

Mr Bell nodded. 'Indeed you must, and so must you, George. You may be able to offer your services to families.'

'That's an excellent idea, I shall certainly do so and perhaps I could escort Mrs Willow there. By coincidence my work is taking me to Hillington Hall today to attend to some legal correspondence for Lady Appleby and I shall attempt to speak to Beatrice about this at the hospital. If she has no further information about it, then I shall call in on Mr Saward at the station on my way home he is bound to know about it.'

Kitty blurted, 'You mean, Mr Harry Saward, the royal station master? And Miss Beatrice Saward? Do you know them?'

Before he could reply, Mr Bell intervened. 'Mrs Willow, I don't believe I have introduced you to my very affable nephew, George Perryman. George, may I introduce Mrs Willow who joined our household today. She is to be a companion to my mother and comes to us with the highest recommendation from the royal household.

'Mrs Willow, my nephew George works with me, though due to his soft nature we frequently lose more money than we make as he is dedicated to helping the underdog for little or no fee, relying on me to make up our fortunes from our affluent business clients.'

Kitty's cheeks flushed. She wasn't sure how to respond. It was not customary to be introduced to her employer's family in such an informal way, let alone them discuss details of their business with her. She bobbed a curtsey and lowered her gaze, hoping she didn't appear foolish.

'Sir, it's a pleasure to make yer acquaintance.'

George put her at her ease. 'Welcome to our home, Mrs Willow. I am impressed to hear of your high recommendation. I know of you from Beatrice, she speaks most highly of you.'

Kitty noticed George's eyes brighten when he mentioned Beatrice's name. 'That's very kind of you to say. Mr Saward and his family were very kind when I was forced to leave our home on the royal estate. Jessie is like a second mother to my daughter, Victoria, and Ada's son Leslie is one of Rosie's playmates.'

'Well, it is a small world. I should like to know more about your circumstances and your husband's disappearance. If I can be of any assistance, I will be happy to help.'

Kitty's face brightened and she took his hands in hers and kissed them. 'Oh thank you, sir, thank you.'

Turning to his uncle, she asked, 'You mentioned the royal household and me being *highly recommended*? Did someone there vouch for me?'

Mr Bell smiled. 'Indeed they did. Your unfortunate situation was brought to my attention by a senior member of the royal household.'

Kitty gulped. 'I 'ave no idea who that might be, but I have wondered why you bestowed so much kindness on me when there must be other deserving cases at the workhouse.'

'I am aware of that, Mrs Willow, which is why Milly is here, else the chances are she would have remained at the workhouse for the rest of her life. You have a guardian angel, my dear, and your dire situation has not gone unnoticed by those in the highest quarters.' Miss Finchley entered the

106

room. Her eyes fixed on the broken crockery. 'I thought I heard a crashing sound. I shall send Milly in to sweep up. I'm afraid the damage will have to come out of your wages, Mrs Willow.'

Mr Bell intervened. 'There's no need to concern yourself about that, Miss Finchley. It was an accident caused by Mrs Willow having a shock as a result of something I said.'

The housekeeper remarked, 'It must have been a big shock. Come along, Mrs Willow, I'll show you around the house.'

Chapter Eleven

The head gardener at the Sandringham Estate, Mr Usher, had mentioned to Harry in passing that a delicate pair of hands were required to work with the queen's fragile and exotic collection of orchids in the hot house. Ideally, he needed someone with a flair for flower arranging too.

Jessie immediately came to mind as being ideal; she shared her father's love of gardening, keeping the blooms in good order at the royal station, and she had also impressed as a land army girl during the war. Harry's suggestion was immediately accepted and he got in touch with Mr Usher to arrange a meeting. Two days later, Jessie cycled over to meet him, full of eager anticipation. Mr Usher, a small man with a wizened face, was waiting for her by the glasshouses.

She extended her hand nervously and introduced herself. He rubbed the soil from his hand and shook hers. 'I've seen your work in Queen Alexandra's garden at the station and it's top-notch. I know too how hard you worked as a land army girl. I am very impressed.'

'That's so very kind of you to say.'

'We need a steady pair of hands in the glasshouses. You may not have done this kind of work before, but you'll soon learn.'

'Oh yes, I would like that very much, if you will give me a chance.'

Mr Usher was in his sixties with thinning hair on top. He rubbed his chin with his stubby fingers, the skin dry and reptile looking.

'We've not taken on female gardeners before; you'll be our first. Leave it with me, I had best get approval from the land agent. If he is fine with it, then the job is yours.'

The following day, Mr Usher informed her she could have the job, but on a one-month trial. 'I'm in no doubt you will be excellent,' he praised.

Jessie's work was exemplary and with her boundless enthusiasm, and coaching from Mr Usher, she felt she had found her perfect vocation. However, it soon became clear that her presence was not welcomed by some of the other gardeners. She sensed their resentment towards her and over-heard their mutterings that the job should have been given to a man instead, a veteran who had returned from the war and fought for his country. Her father advised her to ignore the comments, but she still felt their hardened stares boring through her back. She decided on a plan to win their favour.

One evening, when most of the gardeners had finished, Mr Usher approached Jessie when she was potting up. 'Shouldn't you have finished an hour ago?'

Jessie shook her head. 'I need to finish this first. Jacob brought these plants in for me to see to and they can't be left, they are so delicate.'

'He did, did he? I've heard what the men have been saying about you, and it's not right. It looks like you've put their noses out of joint as you are doing such a good job.'

'Oh no, please don't say anything to Jacob, Mr Usher. That will make matters worse,' Jessie pleaded. 'He needed to get home early today as his ma has been taken poorly and he's been fretting about her all day.'

'Very well. But remember, you only take instructions from me from now on. Or maybe we should play him at his own game and let him see what a good worker you really are, that will put a colour on his cheeks.'

Two days later, Jessie spotted Jacob, a sturdy man in his fifties, planting hundreds of spring bulbs. He was complaining how back breaking the job was, standing up and rubbing his back.

'Need a hand?' asked Jessie cheerily, getting a nod from Mr Usher who was a few feet away.

Jacob stared in astonishment, and before he could reply she returned armed with a spade and dug into the soil alongside him, neatly spacing out the daffodil and crocus bulbs.

When it was finished, Jacob's face was reddened and he groaned from the aches he felt, stretching out his back. Jessie produced a flask of ginger beer and offered it to him.

'Can we be friends now, Jacob?'

'Aye, I know when I'm beaten,' he replied. 'I take my hat off to yer, you're as good a worker as any of the men here.'

Mr Usher approached. 'She's put you in your place now, Jacob. What will the other lads think of you, letting a girl do your job?'

Before Jacob could reply he winked at Jessie and turned, whistling a tune and chuckling.

∽

The following day, when Jessie entered the domed orchid hothouse, her eyes fixed on a dozen or so branches of autumnal foliage and she gawped in admiration. The magnificent exotic blooms with their dainty petals in varying shades of pink, yellow and white were a favourite with the royal family and had been much admired when the gardens were opened to the public for the first time before the war.

Jessie was instructed to ensure the orchids faced east to get the morning light, and to water them sparingly, looking out for spent blooms to cut. She was not allowed to pot them, the head gardener alone could see to that to ensure they were planted in the correct bark mixture, with a layer of moss on top.

Another hothouse, situated alongside the orchids, contained a glorious row of cultivated potted chrysanthemums with blooms the size of tea plates and had won prizes in horticultural shows.

Jessie stored all her new experiences in her head and vowed to write them on paper at the end of the day when she wrote to her beau, Jack. His secret duties with the King were keeping him in London, though she was thankful he had less frequent travels overseas on his confidential missions. She missed him desperately and longed for the day he would propose to her, her heart telling her he was the man she wanted to spend the rest of her life with and bear his children, and she was sure he felt the same towards her.

A special task had been set for her that day by Mr Usher; this was her chance to prove herself again. Her nerves were beginning to pinch inside her as she concentrated hard on Mr Usher's instructions.

'Queen Alexandra is hosting a family dinner this evening in honour of Queen Maud. His Majesty, King George, and Queen Mary, will be in attendance and she asks that the dining room is adorned with an abundance of autumnal decorations. Can I leave this with you, Jessie? Will you scour the gardens for cuttings and use your artistry to create a glorious display fit for a king and three queens?'

Jessie's voice wobbled. 'I would be delighted, if you think I am up to it. It would be an honour.'

'I'm sure of it. I've been impressed with your floral displays in the Big House.'

There was no shortage of greenery to choose from. The garden had an abundance of Virginia creeper crawling along the wall, its trails of red, russet and gold leaves snipped off and placed in her basket, alongside cuttings with red and yellow leaves.

Feeling satisfied with her selection, she retreated to the potting shed and made four balls of soft clay. She placed each one in a clay potting saucer which had been covered with silver foil.

Mr Usher popped his head through the door as Jessie was wiring the leaves and berries and sticking them into the clay. His smile stretched across his face. The beam on his face showed his pleasure. 'This is wonderful, just what I hoped you would do. Our queen will be delighted.'

'I do hope so. I was thinking that these long trails of Virginia creeper could trail along the length of the table, with these decorations interspersed in-between. We may need some more, I wanted to ask your opinion,' Jessie told him.

'That would be just perfect,' he admired, his pale blue eyes bright glinting appreciatively. 'It will look spectacular and be very well liked by the royal family. You have quite an artistic talent, Jessie.'

Jessie's cheeks flushed at the compliment. She set about collecting some more ivy and grabbed some steps from a nearby shed. She climbed on top of them, armed with her secateurs, and snipped the desired length and quantity of trailing ivy with its warm hues.

Mr Usher complimented Jessie when she returned with the ivy. 'Mrs Pennywick is waiting for it. Can you take it to the Big House?' he asked.

The housekeeper nodded approvingly when she saw Jessie arrive at the back door of Sandringham House with a laden wheelbarrow of golden ivy.

'Your arrangements are very beautiful. If you like, I will show you how we have laid the table, and you can add these final pieces.'

'I'd love to.' Jessie beamed and followed Mrs Pennywick, both of them laden with ivy, along the maze of corridors and up the stairs from the basement until they reached the dining room.

She stared open mouthed at the sumptuous surroundings, her eyes soaking up the exquisite embroidered Spanish tapestries by Goya, a gift from King Alfonso XII of Spain to the Prince of Wales in 1876, which hung from the wall. A turquoise, gold and white Minton dinner service was laid out on a sideboard.

Sparkling crystal glasses and silver cutlery were laid out on the mahogany table, her decorations carefully placed there, and arranged tastefully around the room too. Jessie and Mrs Pennywick arranged the remaining ivy on the table, making adjustments here and there.

Jessie's eyes narrowed as she took in the final table decorations set in place. 'You don't think it's, well, a bit too much?'

'Queen Alexandra isn't averse to having lots of decorative objects around her, so I don't think we are in danger of overdoing it.' The housekeeper smiled. 'It's just beautiful.'

∞

The following morning, Queen Alexandra strolled around the garden, linking arms with her daughter while leaning on a carved walking stick with her free hand. The sun was thin, but bright enough to light up a pale-blue sky. They approached the greenhouse where Jessie was carefully watering the orchids with tepid water.

Jessie had her back to them as they entered and she overheard Queen Maud say wistfully, 'If only we could grow magnificent flowers like this in Norway. I fear the climate would be too cold and not suit them.'

Jessie spun around and curtseyed to them both. 'Your Majesties. This is an unexpected surprise.'

Both queens were beautifully dressed in matching skirts and jackets, the older queen wearing dark blue with a high-necked white blouse underneath and a cameo brooch clasped at the throat, with strings of pearls draped down her front, while her daughter wore a moss-green outfit and white bouse with matching green buttons down the front and an open neckline where a necklace fell on her pale skin.

114

Queen Maud praised, 'I always say that no visit to Sandringham is complete without admiring your orchid house.'

The older queen addressed Jessie. 'I wanted to thank you personally for the beautiful floral arrangement you created for our table last night. I didn't realise you were working here, Miss Saward. Are you still assisting your mother in the royal retiring rooms?'

Jessie confirmed she was. Queen Maud asked, 'Do you happen to know the Willow family who left Wolferton recently?'

'Why yes, I do,' Jessie confirmed.

Queen Maud imparted this information to her mother in a loud voice. The younger queen said, 'Mrs Willow and her husband Frank served our family well over the years and we would like to help them if we can. We understand they have gone to a workhouse.'

Jessie tilted her head. 'I believe that is the case. My relative, Maria Saward, was telling me she intends to visit Kitty on her next day off.'

The Norwegian queen replied, 'Ah, yes. I do recall Mrs Watson mentioning Miss Saward to me, informing me she is our new maid in place of Kitty Willow.'

Jessie raised her chin. 'Excuse me, ma'am, if I may say something. I am also concerned about the Willow family since they left Wolferton. I used to help keep an eye on the older children when Kitty and Frank were working, they're like family to us.'

Queen Maud replied, 'I quite understand your concern. You can be assured that this matter is also on our minds.'

Queen Alexandra interjected, cocking her ear, 'Is there any news from them?'

'Not yet, not that I am aware of, ma'am,' replied Jessie, in a raised voice.

The older queen looked thoughtful. 'I shall be looking into this personally. As patron of the workhouse, perhaps I should pay a visit. Before we leave I would like to compliment you, Miss Saward, on your wonderful work here. The orchid house has never looked so lovely.'

'It really is a delightful,' her daughter agreed, gently ushering the Dowager Queen towards the door.

Chapter Twelve

Maria's mind drifted to Eddie who was due to start his treatment the next day. Beatrice had left a message at her home saying a bed had suddenly become available. Her thoughts were on how Eddie would respond to the therapy as she rubbed a cloth over the silver cutlery until she could see her reflection in it. She inspected the shiny fish knives with great satisfaction, her mood lifting as she dreamt of their future together, with Eddie back to his old cheery self. She dreamt that, one day, her Eddie could be considered for a position on the Sandringham Estate and have his name on the tenancy of a tied cottage, a home for them to share with Joey.

His future lay in the hands of Doctor Butterscotch and Beatrice assured her he had given his word that Eddie would not be strapped to a chair, the method still practised by some medics, with an electric current applied to the pharynx of a soldier suffering from mutism or to the spine of a man who had problems walking when they returned from war.

'So, what exactly will the doctor do?' Maria had asked her anxiously when Beatrice explained the new treatment to her.

'It's called psychotherapy, and is proving very successful,' Beatrice had replied.

'I don't understand any of it, this psycho . . . whatsit.'

'It's new and very few hospitals are using this method. Eddie will be encouraged to talk every day about his experiences in the war and spend the rest of his time doing gentle pursuits, something like gardening, at Hillington Hall, under Matron's watchful eye when her father is not here. Even listening to pleasant and calming music could help him. Please be assured we all want what is best for Eddie.'

Maria was brought back to the present when a voice spoke sharply, catching her off guard, her elbow knocking the silver cleaning solution all over the table at Appleton House.

'Maria, you've not heard a word I've said. Now look at this mess. Please clean it before it leaves a stain.'

The words choked in Maria's throat and her eyes moistened. 'I'm sorry, Mrs Watson. I'll see to it straightaway.'

Maria's hand shook and she then knocked into a chair which fell onto the floor. Mrs Watson's eyebrows rose. 'What's got into you today? Your mind is all over the place. Is it something to do with Eddie?'

Maria's chest heaved and she nodded, her eyes welling up. 'I'm worried about Eddie, in case the new treatment don't work, or if it makes him feel worse. He's going into hospital tomorrow, it's come so sudden.'

Mrs Watson consoled her. 'If Beatrice thinks this new treatment will work, then I would heed her words. I've heard about the wonderful work at Hillington Hall under Matron and Doctor Butterscotch and how highly regarded he is in the medical profession.'

Maria sniffled. 'I know that's what Beatrice says, but I can't stop worrying about 'im.'

'Now dry those tears. I have a suggestion that will put a smile on your face.'

The housekeeper handed a leaflet to Maria. She managed a half smile. '"Aggie and Marcel's Dance Time"? Ada did mention this, but no, it's not for me. I have two left feet. And I couldn't possibly go. I see it's on Friday evening, the day after tomorrow. I couldn't go without Eddie, it don't seem right.'

'You need a bit of fun, and I'm sure Eddie won't mind. You can get there for the last hour or so after work. Why not put your head through the door, even if you just sit and observe. Your Joey will be with your ma, so you have no worries there.'

Maria pondered. 'I must admit I'm curious to see who this mystery Marcel is.'

'You and the rest of Wolferton. Now tuck that paper away in your apron, and finish putting a shine on those fish knives.'

Maria felt uplifted after the housekeeper's words and she began giving some thought to the dance class. She was unsure about asking her mother to keep an eye on Joey. Earlier that morning Ruth was wheezing and short of breath. Her mother had shooed her away and assured Maria she would pick up after a rest. She had seen her mother's spirits revive after forty winks before and was hopeful her condition hadn't taken a turn for the worse during the day.

When Mrs Watson stepped out of the kitchen, Maria retrieved the leaflet from her pocket and read it again. 'Aggie and Marcel's Dance Time. We bring you instruction in the latest dances – the Jazz, Hesitation Waltz, Foxtrot and

Tango. £1 1 shilling for four lessons. Wolferton Meeting Room, 7 p.m. – 9.30 p.m., every Friday.'

The idea suddenly appealed to her.

∽∞∽

When Maria returned home that evening Joey was playing on the kitchen floor with a rainbow-coloured spinning top Ada had given him for his last birthday. He ran to greet his mother and she scooped him in her arms.

'You will soon be too heavy for me to lift.' She smiled, ruffling his hair affectionately.

She placed him on the floor and he held up a wooden elephant. She asked, 'Where's Grandma?'

He pointed upstairs. Maria ascended the narrow staircase to her mother's bedroom. Ruth was propped up in bed, her face pale and her greying hair hanging over the front of her nightshirt. Ruth reached for a bowl on a chair at the side of her bed and coughed into it. Maria stared into it and her hand flew to her mouth after spotting traces of blood in the green phlegm.

'Oh Ma,' she cried. 'You look dreadful. I shall call for the doctor.'

Ruth whispered, 'No, don't do that. I don't want a fuss. Just leave me be, and it will pass. It always does.'

Ruth covered her mouth with a handkerchief and coughed some more, showing more spots of blood. Her arm was stick thin and Maria felt an inner sense of dread. Her mother's eyes were sunken in and her shoulders appeared frail and bony as she hunched forward trying to catch her breath.

'Where are Freddie and Archie? Are they 'ome yet?'

120

'Archie is staying late helping Lizzie on the farm and Freddie should be back any minute.'

Maria was concerned about some fellas her brother Freddie was spending time with. They were renowned militant railway workers, but she hid this from her mother. It would be frowned upon by Harry if he believed Freddie was involved with their activities. The workers were demanding an increase in pay and threatened strike action if they didn't have their way and were encouraging railway workers up and down the line to protest with them. Freddie was headstrong and likely to show an interest.

Ruth raised her arm and beckoned Maria closer. She spoke softly. 'I'll be all right. You go down and see to Joey. You know I've had these turns before and pulled through.'

'Well, if you insist. At least let me fetch you a hot drink and some broth. And if you are not showing signs of improving in the morning, I shall send one of the boys out for the doctor then.'

Ruth managed a weak smile. 'There won't be any need for that. I didn't get the Spanish flu, after all. I'm a tough old bird.'

'I only wish that were true. How did yer manage with Joey after school in this state? He must 'ave been a handful for yer'.

Ruth shook her head. She spoke slowly. 'Mabel stopped by to see me. She insisted I came to bed and she looked after Joey.'

'That was kind of her,' said Maria. 'I expect she will be relieved that Eddie can start his new treatment. I'll call in tomorrow morning on my way to work, to see if I can catch him before he leaves.'

'Mabel told me he's nervous about it, and they are placing all their faith on this Doctor Butterscotch.' Ruth reached for Maria's hand. 'I 'ope it works out for him, for yer both.'

She pressed her mother's hand to her lips, noticing how thin her skin was, the veins and bones protruding through.

Maria popped downstairs to check on Joey, who had curled up in a ball in a high-backed chair and fallen asleep. She carried him upstairs and lay him on his bed, leaving him with his clothes on and covering him with a blanket. She returned downstairs and made her mother a hot drink and felt slightly cheered seeing her mother sip her tea and broth. She settled her down, deciding not to mention the dance the following evening. Shortly afterwards, she heard the back door open and Freddie stepped in, throwing his cap on the table.

Maria scalded. 'It's past nine o'clock. Where have you been all this time? I've been worried sick about yer, and so has Ma. She's been taken poorly again and . . .'

She saw a leaflet hanging out of his jacket pocket and lurched forwards and removed it before he could stop her. 'What's this?' Her face reddened as she read the words. 'Don't tell me yer going on a march? Not after everything Harry has done for yer?'

'For you, maybe. Not me, sister. I'm entitled to fair pay for a day's work. The lads 'ave asked me to join in a demon-stration and I've said yes.'

'Oh no yer not. Over my dead body!' Maria spluttered. 'What will Harry say? It ain't right.'

Freddie fumed. 'I don't care. You can't stop me. I'm a member of the National Union of Railwaymen. We stand together, shoulder to shoulder, and demand a fair wage. The government thinks it can reduce our pay and not keep its word to give us what was promised. We ain't 'aving it and we're going to show them.'

∽

The day arrived for Eddie to be admitted to Hillington Hall. Beatrice arranged to meet him at the hospital first thing. Mabel told her he wanted to go alone, and promised to do everything the doctor advised.

Beatrice was peering out of one of the side windows when she saw him pedal up to the building and park his bicycle along a rack. She watched as he took some steps back and glanced upwards at the building. A nurse walked by pushing a patient in a wheelchair, deeply engrossed in conversation. Eddie rubbed his hands behind his neck and paced on the spot, walking round in circles. He paused and then scratched his head and removed his cap, squeezing it tightly in his hand. He took a few steps towards the door, then hesitated and retreated, walking back towards his bicycle.

Beatrice rushed outside and reached the cycle rack just as he mounted it and was about to ride off. She pretended she hadn't seen and welcomed him with a warm smile. 'Hello, Eddie, I'm so pleased you are here. You won't regret it. Shall we go in?'

'Er, I'm not so sure now, Beatrice. I'm scared.'

'It's natural to be afraid of the unknown. Doctor Butter-scotch will explain everything. I promise you, Eddie, the therapy he uses could change your life.'

He shuffled from foot to foot. 'Ma and Maria tell me I should trust yer, so all right. I'll try it.'

As he dismounted from his bicycle, a shotgun was fired in the distance and he cowered, covering his head with his arms.

'It's just a gamekeeper shooting rabbits,' Beatrice told him gently, with a frown, as he jumped and looked around him.

He turned his head sideways and pointed up to the sky. 'Can you 'ear them? It's the enemy. They're nearly on us. Quick, duck low else your 'ead will be blown orf.'

'No, Eddie. No. That was someone shooting a rabbit, you know what it's like round here. Please, give me your hand, I'll take you to see the doctor. I promise you, you won't regret it.'

Eddie's rapid breathing began to ease. 'I don't want to be like this for the rest of me life. I want to be like I was before.'

'I know. We can help you. Come, let's find Doctor Butterscotch. His room isn't far away.'

Doctor Butterscotch had complained previously to the landowner about shots being fired, explaining that it could be detrimental to his patients while undergoing therapy. Eddie looked up and Beatrice touched his arm gently, encouraging him to follow.

He shuffled behind Beatrice and entered the hospital, passing along the corridor and pausing every now and again when he was gently coaxed by Beatrice to take another step. Doctor Butterscotch was talking to a patient at the end of the corridor. The patient leant on a stick, his head tilted towards the doctor as he spoke. A moment later the patient wobbled off, swaying past them, pointing his stick out in front and at the sides, his arms spread out in all directions.

'The poor bugger. He must have been gassed,' Eddie commented. 'I'm thankful I still have me sight, it's inside me 'ead I'm messed up.'

Doctor Butterscotch came over and introduced himself to Eddie. 'I heard about you from Nurse Saward and I commend you for taking this first step by coming here. Shall we step into my room and I will explain our therapy to you?'

Eddie nodded and followed behind Beatrice. As they reached the door, he grabbed her arm. 'Will I 'ave to stay here?'

She answered, 'We think that's for the best, for a while.'

The doctor soothed. 'Please do not worry yourself about this, Eddie. If you don't wish to stay, nobody will force you to. You won't have to do anything you don't wish to do, that's not how we work here.'

Eddie instantly relaxed and sat in the seat offered by the doctor while Beatrice hovered behind him, brimming with admiration at the doctor's empathic approach.

'You may leave now, Nurse Saward,' the doctor instructed. 'Eddie and I will be just fine, won't we?'

'Oh yes,' Eddie agreed instantly.

As Beatrice stepped out of the room, she heard Doctor Butterscotch say, 'Now tell me, Eddie, old chap, what happened? Don't hold anything back.'

She went to the nurses' station where matron told her, 'I'm afraid I can't let you have Friday night off. Two of our nurses are off sick with dysentery and I need all the hands I have. I am sorry.'

Beatrice accepted the disappointing news, thinking wryly that George would be relieved to hear it. She recalled she was due to meet him at the hospital and asked Matron if she had seen him. 'Why yes, there he is,' she confirmed, pointing to the rehabilitation room. 'He is with Nurse Riley, and from what I've heard, it's been a heated discussion.'

She inched the door open where Nurse Riley, a pretty nurse in her early twenties with blonde curls and sapphire blue eyes, was resting her head on George's shoulder. He had his arm around her and she appeared to be upset.

Although Beatrice had no cause to mistrust George, she was taken by surprise at their closeness. 'Fleur! George!' she cried, in a high-pitched voice.

Fleur rose, her voice shaky. 'I'm just leaving, Beatrice. Thank you for listening, George. I feel better for telling you.'

Beatrice raised an eyebrow. 'What did she mean? I didn't know you knew Fleur?'

'She is quite an exceptional woman,' he said, his eyes bright. Seeing Beatrice's questioning expression, he added, 'In the purely professional sense, of course.'

'What do you mean, "purely professional"? What business does Fleur have with you?'

'Please don't press me on this, my darling Beatrice. You'll find out soon enough.'

She let the matter drop, but a nagging feeling in her gut churned away.

'I came to tell you I'm afraid our waltz at Aggie's dance is going to have to wait a while. I have to work Friday night,' she informed him.

He rose and stepped towards her, and in mocking tone he said, 'I am truly devastated to hear that. Is Matron looking? Good! I want everyone to see you are my girl.'

Before Beatrice could protest she was wrapped in George's arms and melting as his lips pressed firmly on hers.

Chapter Thirteen

Kitty had been alarmed by her mistress's forthrightness at their first meeting. 'I believe you are tasked with keeping me amused. I hope you have plenty to say for yourself and won't just sit back like a mouse. I like a woman with a bit of spirit.'

Mrs Bell's voice had a mischievous tone which put Kitty at ease. 'I shall do my best, ma'am. I ain't ever been a lady's companion before. I'm not sure what is required of me, but I shall do me best. I'm an 'ard worker and honest too.'

'That's the spirt. As we will be spending time together, I hope you won't object if I offer a suggestion or two to improve your speech. Let's start with, "I ain't". Can you repeat after me, "I have never been a lady's companion before."'

Kitty's cheeks flushed, feeling embarrassed at her poor pronunciation. She repeated her words more carefully. 'I have never been a lady's companion before.'

'That's much better. Something tells me you're a fast learner. I like that.'

Kitty eyed the walls and drapes of the room, which were tastefully adorned in pale blue and a swirling ivory pattern. A plump eiderdown filled with soft goose feathers covered the bed.

Mrs Bell urged Kitty to tell her story. This seemed most unusual to Kitty; surely she was there to work and not natter. Mrs Bell assured her it was important for her to understand as much as she could about her companion if they were going to be spending time together.

After a faltering start, the words tumbled out of Kitty's mouth and she described the events that led to her present situation. Mrs Bell listened to every word with keen interest, never interrupting. When Kitty finished, her mistress pressed her delicate hand firmly on Kitty's and said, 'My dear, thank you for sharing this. I believe you were sent here for a purpose and fate works in mysterious ways.'

❦

Kitty's tasks involved washing and dressing Mrs Bell in the mornings, and seating her comfortably in her armchair by the window so she could watch the passing pedestrians. When asked, she sat on a stool by Mrs Bell's seat and read to her, with the occasional interruption from Mrs Bell commenting on her pronunciation.

She saw little of Mr Bell and his nephew, who were both fully immersed in their work, but exchanged pleasantries when their paths crossed. She took her instructions from the housekeeper and gladly helped out with sewing and polishing when Mrs Bell had her afternoon nap, while Milly lit the fires and did the main household chores, cheerfully cleaning the house from top to bottom.

One evening, Kitty overheard Mr Bell ask Miss Finchley how she and Milly had settled in, and her lips curled at the glowing praise that came from the housekeeper's mouth.

Pleased as punch, she quickly settled into a pleasant routine and found she was enjoying the books she read to Mrs Bell, with P. G. Wodehouse and W. Somerset Maugham among her favourite authors.

One day, Mrs Bell noticed Kitty was distracted and asked what was on her mind. Kitty brushed off the question, but her mistress persisted, asking how her were children were, and if the sleeping arrangement was working to her satisfaction.

Kitty turned her head away, unsure how to answer. She was still returning to the workhouse at night to sleep, and every morning when she left for work she glanced up at the window where she knew her children slept, hoping to catch a glimpse of them.

She had twice been allowed to see the children all together on a Sunday afternoon, but as Miss Feathers remained with them in the common room she was unable to question Victoria freely. She seemed to be retreating into herself, holding back when asked how she was, instead of being the happy and sunny child she'd been at Appleton.

The children appeared cautious about what they could say, glancing at Miss Feathers for approval and Kitty thought she noticed from the corner of her eye that she cast Victoria a warning glance when she asked her about her work with Mr Mumbles.

Victoria answered her mother falteringly. 'I feel privileged to help our esteemed guardian if he requires assistance in his office, sorting out his books. He has so many of them and they need putting in the right order on his shelves.'

Kitty saw Victoria glance at Miss Feathers nervously. 'Couldn't one of the boys help Mr Mumbles instead?'

Kitty's skin prickled when the wardress stroked Victoria's hair as it shone in a sheet down her back.

'Oh it's regarded as an honour, I assure you, Mrs Willow. Victoria is doing just splendidly. You have nothing to concern yourself about.'

Kitty had departed with a heavy heart and a sinking feeling, arranging to see them again the following Sunday. She counted the days until the weekend arrived. Although the children appeared well physically, they now had a sadness in their eyes. Little Rosie still clutched her topsy-turvy doll and Iris, her little tomboy, appeared much quieter than before.

When the following Sunday had come the heaven's opened and the pouring rain scotched her plans for them to go for a walk in the park, away from the prying eyes of Miss Feathers, so they sat in a corner of the common room under her watchful eye once more. Rosie plonked herself on Kitty's lap and pressed her head against her mother's chest. The boys became restless after a while and asked if they could be excused to play with some lads they had befriended. Iris followed after them, saying it wasn't fair she was a girl.

Kitty pressed Victoria about how things were, but her replies were evasive, and she avoided eye contact. When she mentioned Mr Mumbles' name, Miss Feathers appeared from the corner of the room and hovered over them, listening for Victoria's response to confirm that all was well. Kitty saw Victoria's face redden and her body stiffen at mention of the guardian's name. She was unsure what to do, who to raise her concerns with, in case it got back to Mr Mumbles.

Now Mrs Bell had asked about the children, she found she couldn't hold back and blurted out her fears.

Mrs Bell listened attentively to Kitty as she poured out her heart.

'I see, this all sounds very concerning. No wonder you appear so anxious. Is there anything I or my son can do to help?'

'Please, ma'am. I beg of yer not to say anything, in case word gets back to Mr Mumbles.'

'Very well, if you insist, I shall say nothing for now. Your fears may be well founded as I have heard my son question the guardian's behaviour. He has seen for himself what a slippery character Mr Mumbles is, behaving in the most despicable way when he is in a position of trust and is determined to do something about it. I believe George is as well.'

'That's reassuring to hear. Thank yer for listening, ma'am.' Kitty gushed gratefully. 'I hope Victoria will be able to stand her ground until Mr Mumbles is somehow made to stop.'

In the afternoon, Kitty assisted Milly with dusting down two smaller bedrooms at the back of the house and a room in the attic.

Miss Finchley told her, with an air of mystery. 'They haven't been used for a number of years, but I believe that may change . . .'

To Ada's surprise, a queue formed outside the meeting room for Aggie and Marcel's Dance Time class. An air of eager anticipation and nervous expressions on the faces of those in attendance were signs it was going to be a night to remember. Alfie was inside tuning the piano and placing his music sheets at hand. Alfie had hesitated at first, questioning if this was the right time for frivolity, while the mystery of missing estate workers at Gallipoli was still unexplained. Ada had assured him he must do what he felt morally comfortable with. He discussed his dilemma with the vicar who helped him make his mind up. 'The Bible says, Let them praise his name with dancing. Praise him with tambourine and dance.'

Small tables covered with white lace tablecloths, floral teacups and saucers were positioned around the side of the room. A posy of flowers was placed at the centre of the table adding the finishing touch. Gazing down from the wall were large portraits of their beloved King and Queen. Arrivals continued to pile in and find seats, huddling in small groups, with women outnumbering men by two to one.

Ada and Jessie, along with a number of fashion-conscious ladies, wore shorter skirts on Aggie's recommendation so they did not trip up.

Jessie gave a twirl, her expression anxious. 'I hope Jack won't disapprove of me showing my ankles. Do you think it's too short? It is certainly more comfortable for spinning around.'

Ada assured her. 'I'm sure he wouldn't mind at all. Don't forget, you were one of the first women to wear breeches as a land army girl, you broke the mould then and he didn't object, so I don't see how he can object to this. After all your new dance skirt covers far more of your leg than those ugly breeches did.'

Ada's eyes scanned the room for Aggie. She spotted her at the end of the room talking to a tall dapper-looking man with a confident poise wearing a smart black suit. His dark hair was thinning on top, and his striking dark handlebar moustache stretching across the front of his face and curling at the ends forced you to stare. He was younger than she had expected, possibly ten years younger than Aggie, with an ebullient manner, his arms making exaggerated gestures in the air as he spoke.

Ada approached Aggie in astonishment, with Jessie following. Her cat-loving friend was almost unrecognisable. Her friend's new style of dress was elegant and simple, a far cry from the elaborate layers of frills and adornments she usually wore, and Ada wondered if Marcel had influenced her choice of outfit – a well-cut skirt in black satin, which fell above the knee and showed a shapely calf and fashionable black strappy sandals, teamed with a white silk fitted blouse with matching buttons. A string of double pearls draped down her chest and a wide belt nipped tightly around her surprisingly trim waist, which Ada hadn't noticed before, hidden by her fussy outfits.

Aggie's makeup had always been discreet. She had barely used any before, but she stood before Ada with her cheeks covered with thick white powder and her lips heavily rouged.

Her hair was piled on top of her head in curls with the loose strands dangling down the side of her cheeks, a change from how it was usually worn conservatively in a neat bun tied back at the nape of her neck.

Aggie's dance companion toyed with a loose strand of hair dangling down her cheek. He tucked it gently behind her ear, whispering something to her, making her cheeks flush even more. It was a tender and intimate moment that made Ada look away embarrassed.

'*Ma chérie*, you should not hide your beauty behind your hair. Your lovely face should be seen and appreciated by everyone.'

Aggie's eyes sparkled and she lowered her gaze and stifled a girlish giggle behind her hand.

Marcel addressed the sisters, making an elaborate bow. 'Allow me to introduce myself. I am Monsieur Marcel Fovargue and it is my honour to partner with Mademoiselle Agatha on the dance floor. I am deeply grateful to her for this, more than words can express.'

'Mademoiselle Agatha?' queried Jessie, the corner of her lip curling.

'It's the French way of saying my name,' Aggie explained, returning her companion's admiring gaze. 'Marcel prefers it, he says it has a more refined air. It is my real name, after all. Aggie was a pet name from when I was a child and seems to have stuck.'

'That is true. For me you are Mademoiselle Agatha. It is a popular name in my country and means *good*. I know no other woman with as much goodness as you.'

Aggie beamed at Marcel as Ada and Jessie introduced themselves. Marcel took their hands in his in turn and brushed his lips against them. 'I am charmed. Mademoiselle Agatha has told me about you and I am delighted to make your acquaintance. Please, allow me to escort you to a table.'

They were shown to an unoccupied table at the front of the room. Aggie's sister, Magnolia, and her husband, David, were already seated and greeted the sisters enthusiastically. Their table was close to the piano; there were now few seats left, and a quick count showed there were around forty

135

people present. Alfie's fingers ran expertly along the keys playing a piece by Rachmaninov, Ada's favourite composer. She applauded when he finished and their eyes locked. 'That was so beautiful,' she mouthed.

Marcel whispered something in his ear and Alfie fumbled with the music sheets. The French dance instructor beckoned Aggie to his side and she raised her hand, to silence the room.

'I speak for us both when I say Monsieur Fovargue and I are delighted to welcome you here. We have learnt these new dances at a dance school in London where they are flourishing and cannot keep up with demand.

'We shall demonstrate the dance first of all, then repeat it slowly. If you can stand and take your partners at the side of the room. Firstly, we ask that you observe closely how our feet move to the music, and once you have tried this and mastered it, watch our upper bodies, our poise, the angle of our heads, shoulders and arms.'

Marcel added, 'Please, ladies and gentlemen, do rise and take your partners. It is acceptable for women to partner each other, with one leading, and then changing over. We shall show you two dances this evening, the slow hesitation waltz and the foxtrot. You shall leave here walking on air, with the lightest steps.'

An excited buzz filled the air. One woman whispered to her friend, 'Wait till I get home and show my Rupert. I'm not sure what he'll think of a Frenchman showing me how to dance, but I don't care. Aggie looks ten years younger too, good on her. Her friend replied, 'I can't wait to learn the tango. My Horace was too shy to come, he says he has two left feet and would make a fool of himself. I'm hoping he'll change his mind. He might come along next time.'

Alfie's fingers confidently glided along the keys to Strauss's 'The Blue Danube', perfect for the waltz. The tempo increased when he caught Marcel's eye who nodded in his direction. Marcel held an erect pose and extended his arm out for Aggie. She placed one arm on his left shoulder and the other around his waist, their heads held high as they counted in the beats of the music, then moving on cue at the start of the dance and sashaying around the floor.

Their movements around the floor were graceful, smooth and self-assured. At the end they made a small bow and the room filled with applause.

Jessie shook her head. 'Who would have thought Aggie had it in her. She is a dark horse.'

Magnolia beamed. 'I'm told our dear mother was in great demand at parties as a dancing partner. It is to be anticipated that my sister and I will have inherited her talents.'

'Indeed, I would expect nothing less,' retorted Jessie, stifling a laugh. Turning to her sister, she said, 'I assume we will have to partner with each other as we are without our men. I only hope I don't stumble and tread on your toes too much due to my poor hearing.'

Ada encouraged her. 'I will help you. Try to read my lips when I repeat any instructions and watch what everyone is doing. You can be the lady and follow my lead.'

Before they could start, Ada felt a tap on her shoulder. It was Maria. She was panting, having just hot-footed it to the dance lesson after finishing her duties at Appleton House, hurriedly changing from her maid's clothing into her own blue skirt and cream blouse before she left.

'I came as quickly as I could,' she gushed. She shook her head, her face showing disbelief. 'I can't believe how many people are here. Is that really Aggie, all made up to the nines like a theatrical lady of the night? And who is the man with the big moustache she is with?'

Ada laughed. 'That is *the* Monsieur Marcel Fovargue, her dancing partner. We're just about to start our first dance, it's the slow waltz. Why don't you watch first time round, and see if there is someone you can team up with as a partner.'

Ada and Jessie fumbled with putting their arms in the correct position, glancing at Aggie and Marcel as they walked around the room checking that partners were in the correct hold.

From the corner of her eye, Ada saw Maria speak to Annie Gilbert, one of the kitchen maids at Sandringham House. It was no secret that her husband had a foul temper and beat her. The last she heard he had run off with a barmaid from Hunstanton, it was definitely a case of good riddance to bad rubbish.

Jessie's eyes narrowed. 'Ada! You're treading on my feet. Will you concentrate? Or should I take over as the lead?'

Ada averted her gaze. 'Oops, I'm so sorry, Jessie. I was distracted for a moment. Now where was I. One, two, three, one, two three . . . that's it, you move forwards and I go backwards.'

After a few clumsy steps, knocking elbows with their fellow dancers who were also grappling to find their pace and tempo, they found their rhythm had improved and they swayed around the room with a light step.

When the music finished their faces beamed. 'I don't believe it. I can dance.' Jessie glowed. 'It wasn't as difficult as I thought it would be. It's hard to explain, but I can almost feel the music through vibrations, and staying close to Alfie certainly helped.'

Magnolia and David rushed over to share their thrill. 'If I hadn't been a singer I'm sure I would have been a dancer. It comes so naturally to me.'

David smiled good-naturedly. 'My dear, I sometimes feel that with your excitement you take the man's lead and I follow you, when it should be the other way around. Could I suggest a little less fervency? Then we will have perfection.'

'Oh, but I find it difficult to contain myself when I feel the music pulsating through my body. I deliver the same passion with my singing. But I will try, dear husband, I will do my best to deliver the perfection you deserve from your wife.'

Ada noticed that while the dance was rapturously received by many, a number of women at the back of the hall were talking behind their hands and staring towards Aggie and Marcel, shaking their heads in disapproval.

Ada pointed this out to Magnolia. 'What do you think they are saying?'

Magnolia snorted. 'Why it's obvious that they are jealous because Aggie has started the dance school and has made a success of it, and with a Frenchman.'

Ada spun around as Aggie and Marcel approached them, their joyful expression showing they were oblivious to the talk going on behind their backs.

Aggie suggested, 'We shall demonstrate the dance one more time, only now, let's change partners. Marcel, why don't you dance with Ada and give her the thrill of dancing with a professional? I will partner Jessie and show the ladies how they can dance together.'

Before they could object they were scooped into their new partners' arms and stood erect in their start positions. Marcel whispered to Ada, 'I know how highly dear Mademoiselle Agatha regards you in her affections. I do hope we can become friends. It's true I am younger than her, but to me age is just a number. She is a divine woman of unequalled goodness. I would like you to know my intentions are entirely honourable.'

Taken aback by his candour, Ada gulped. 'I know I shouldn't ask this, but . . .'

'But what, Madame Heath? You think I will take advantage of a good woman I am blessed to have met?'

Ada's throat tightened. 'I can see how happy Aggie is in your company and my concern is that I do not wish to see her feelings hurt or for her to make a fool of herself. Can you swear your intentions are honourable?'

The Frenchman made an exaggerated gesture with his hand, sweeping it over his eyes and swaying sideways. 'I swear it on my life. From the moment my eyes first saw Mademoiselle Agatha I saw a deep inner beauty within her that needed to be awakened. As you can see, she is a different woman now because of the love she feels for me. You know, she is a very passionate woman, and music and dance has helped bring that out.'

Ada felt herself redden from top to toe at Marcel's causal talk of passion. As he led her expertly around the dance floor,

140

they paused at the group of gossiping women whispering to each other behind their cupped hands. Marcel caught their astonished expressions and, tilting his head in their direction, smiled politely before whisking Ada across the floor.

'I see that my arrival here has caused some talk. Please, believe me, Madame Heath, there is nothing in my past that brings shame to my name and I will care for Agatha like the precious jewel she is. And now, I must return to her. It is time to show you the foxtrot.'

Chapter Fourteen

Maria busied herself dusting Queen Maud's bedroom, pausing to glance out of the window at the splendid views that extended across the grounds. The gardener was raking leaves that had fallen onto the paths from the horse chestnut trees so her mistress would not slip on them. She recalled how two years before conkers from the entire Sandringham Estate were gathered in great quantities. They were dispatched to a manufacturer in King's Lynn and the cordite from them was used to make explosives for the military following a shortage of shells.

Signs were posted in local schools urging children to help.

THIS COLLECTION IS INVALUABLE WAR WORK
AND IS VERY URGENT. PLEASE ENCOURAGE IT.

They willingly responded to the appeal. Joey thought it was a great lark scrambling around the grounds gathering the shiny fruit. Some of the older children threw sticks up at the prickly green casings on the higher branches to make them fall. The War Office paid a bounty of 7s 6d for every hundred weight that was handed in.

Maria recalled that the children's efforts were so successful that they collected more conkers than there were trains to transport them. Operation Conker had succeeded and helped win the war.

∞

Later that afternoon, Mrs Watson and Maria were sharing a cuppa in the kitchen while Queen Maud, accompanied by her lady-in-waiting, was visiting her mother at the Big House for the day. The chores had been finished in good time and Maria was permitted to have half a day off in order to visit King's Lynn in the hope of seeing Kitty.

'That's very good of you, Maria, on top of all your other worries. May I ask, is there any news of how Eddie is getting on at the hospital?'

'It's early days, but Beatrice says he's been able to talk about what 'appened, and that is important for the treatment to succeed. She is going to tell me when I can visit.'

'I hope that won't be too long now. I'm sure seeing you will be just the tonic he needs. Be sure to give Kitty our very best wishes.'

'I will do. Joey wanted to come when 'e 'eard me say I was going to visit Kitty, but I 'ad to explain I wasn't sure if I could see them. I've written another letter to Kitty and want to deliver it meself seeing as I didn't get a reply to two that I wrote before.'

Mrs Watson shook her head. 'That's not like her. Ah, the poor lass. I wonder if she's heard about the meeting Mr Saward and the chaplain are holding regarding Gallipoli?'

'I will be sure to mention it to Kitty if I see her. It crossed me mind that she might not have written back 'cause she was upset with me on account of me 'aving her job, but what was I to do?'

Mrs Watson scratched her head. 'I'm sure there's a good explanation. Our Kitty has a soft heart and isn't the sort to hold a grudge.'

'I shall be glad to have Jessie's company,' said Maria as she finished her drink and rose to leave. Mrs Watson disappeared into the pantry and returned with some dainty cakes. She wrapped them in brown paper, tied them with string and handed them to Maria.

'Here, give these to Kitty.'

Maria clutched the cakes and made her way to the back door. 'She'll be pleased to have these. I have some sweets and chocolate for the children too.'

'You are a good friend, Maria. I'll see you tomorrow then.'

Maria cycled to the station where Jessie was already waiting. She also had some cakes in her basket, as well as lemon slices that Betty had baked that morning and a bunch of red, russet and gold chrysanthemums that Mr Usher said she could take with her, once he knew who they were intended for.

'I couldn't turn up to see the Willow family empty handed now, could I?' Jessie asserted, as they seated themselves on the train.

Jessie produced a letter from her bag and reclined in her seat, deeply engrossed, while she read its contents. Maria noticed her eyes brightening and her finger touch her lips, her face breaking into a smile.

144

She placed the letter in her lap. 'It's from Jack. He's joining the King on a visit to Sandringham. I think it's soon, but he couldn't say exactly when or the nature of his business here for security reasons. I was just beginning to think his feelings had cooled, and then he writes to me out of the blue.'

Maria reached forward and gripped Jessie's hands. 'I'm sure that's not true. What makes you think such a thing?'

'It was something Ma said that got me thinking. I will hopefully see Jack soon enough, and I'll know inside here,' said Jessie, pointing to her heart, 'how I feel for him.'

'Funny you should say that, 'cause that's how I still feel when I see Eddie, even now, the way 'e is. I can't wait to see him either.'

The train rocked gently from side to side and in just over half an hour they arrived at King's Lynn and made their way towards the docks. Within ten minutes they were standing outside the gloomy, imposing building of the workhouse.

Maria stared at it and shook her head. 'So this is where I could 'ave ended up if it 'adn't been for you and yer family, Jessie.'

'That's all in the past. Just looking at the place gives me the shivers. Come on, let's knock on the door.'

Jessie lifted the latch on the iron gates and it creaked open. They stepped onto the courtyard as a group of boys were being marched across the front.

'Look' said Maria, excitedly, pointing to the group. 'Look, there's Pip and Laurie. I'm going over to them.'

The two brothers, aged twelve and ten respectively, stopped in their tracks, faces lighting up as they recognised her.

'Pip, Laurie," she called, 'it's me, Maria.'

Suddenly, a man stepped forward and clipped the boys round the ear. He forced them back into line again.

Maria took some steps towards them, but Jessie stopped her, placing her hand on her arm. 'Leave them be, for now,' she advised. 'We don't want to get them in trouble.'

'Did you see the way that man glared at me?' Maria cried, feeling helpless watching the boys disappear around the corner of the building.

Jessie's eyes narrowed. 'I'm very concerned at what I've seen. They looked so unhappy and appear to have lost weight. I suspect the other children are the same. Come on, let's go and find out. I do not intend to leave until I see the whole family. I shall demand to know how they are.'

Maria's eyes widened as she stared in admiration at Jessie, usually the quietest of the three Saward sisters due to her hearing impairment. With her eyes blazing and cheeks flushed, she was fired up in a way Maria had never seen before.

Maria followed Jessie, who marched up the steps to the front door and rang the bell. They stood back and waited.

The door was answered by a pasty-looking woman in her mid-twenties wearing a drab gown, her shoulders hunched and with a scared look on her face.

'I would like to see the guardian,' Jessie demanded sharply.

The girl stuttered in a soft voice, her eyes looking down. 'Mr Mumbles ain't in.'

'I can't hear you. What did you say?' Jessie repeated, her eyes peering over the woman's shoulders, who she presumed to be an inmate.

146

The woman raised her eyes. 'He ain't in. The guardian ain't available. Can anyone else 'elp?'

Jessie ignored her, stepping around her, with Maria on her heels. The inmate scuttled off saying she would find someone else. Jessie pointed to a room off the hallway where the door was ajar. Maria stepped towards it and signalled to Jessie to come over. She mouthed, 'I can 'ear voices inside? What should we do? I don't want us to get into trouble 'cause legally we're trespassing.'

Jessie pointed at her basket. 'I was thinking I could tell a white lie if I have to and say I am from the royal estate and people there want to know how the Willow family are. Yes, that's what I'll say, and that way I can ask to see Victoria. If they are in a classroom here that shouldn't be a problem.'

'That's a good plan, I didn't know you could be so devious, Jessie. I'll knock first, and then we can enter the room together.'

Jessie nodded, having read Maria's lips, and knocked three times on the door, then they entered the room together.

A girl stood on the top of a stepladder placing books on shelves, her back to them. A stout man had his hand on her ankle and was running it along her bare leg, while lifting her skirt, saying, 'Careful, my dear, you pretty young thing. Mr Mumbles will steady you so you don't fall. You know you are my special girl here.'

The girl's voice sounded fearful. 'Yes, Mr Mumbles. Thank yer, Mr Mumbles'

'Victoria!' they cried, rushing over to her, pushing the man away.

147

The book she was holding in her hand fell to the ground and Victoria wobbled. 'Maria! Jessie! What are you doing 'ere?'

Jessie blurted. 'We were worried about you, my darling girl, and with good reason, I see. Who is this man? And why is he behaving in this outrageous way towards you?'

The guardian wiped saliva from around his thick lips. 'How dare you make such outrageous accusations. I demand you get out of my office immediately, and then I shall be prepared to put this misunderstanding behind us.'

Jessie fumed. 'How dare you lay a finger on that girl. I shall report you for improper conduct.'

Victoria climbed down the steps, staring sideways at the flustered guardian. Jessie embraced her, her heart pounding. Victoria appeared shocked and relieved. 'I'm so 'appy to see you both.'

The guardian stepped forwards to defend his ground. Jessie shielded Victoria from his advances. He extended his arm towards her, whining, 'Victoria will tell you herself that my behaviour has been nothing more than how a guardian's should be towards a young lady in his care. Isn't that so, my dear?'

Victoria remained silent, her hand tightly gripped in Jessie's firm hold.

'It's clear to me that this girl is terrified of you. You are vile and I shall lodge a strong complaint based on what I have witnessed to the workhouse committee stating you are unfit to remain in this position.'

Maria glared at him. 'If you lay another finger on 'er, or any other young girls in your care, you'll be for it. We have connections with the royal family and we will let them know of our concerns.'

Mr Mumbles rubbed his head, his face becoming anxious. 'There's no need for that, I assure you, it's just a misunderstanding, and Victoria will say as much when she finds her tongue.'

The next moment a distinguished gentleman entered the room followed by an anxious-looking woman. 'I could hear loud voices as I entered the hallway, what has been happening?'

Mr Mumbles had positioned himself behind his desk when the two people entered, attempting to look occupied with his work.

Jessie interjected, 'May I ask your name, sir, as I have a complaint of the strongest nature I would like to make against the guardian.'

'My name is Josiah Bell and I am a solicitor and chairman of the workhouse committee, and this is Miss Feathers, who is in charge of the women in our care here. Would you care to explain the nature of your complaint.'

Jessie and Maria introduced themselves and blurted out what they had seen, insisting they were not exaggerating. Mr Mumbles' face puffed out and turned crimson while Miss Feathers rushed to his side, agreeing with the guardian that Jessie and Maria had overreacted and misinterpreted what they saw.

Mr Bell's eyes strayed to the book that lay by his feet and reached down to pick it up. It was the book that fell from Victoria's hands and its pages were filled with scantily dressed women.

'Mr Mumbles. I assume this salacious book belongs to you?'

The guardian squirmed, covering his eyes with his hands. 'Oh no, Mr Bell. It has no place in this establishment. I have no idea how it got there.'

'That is not the only thing that has no place here – neither do you. This is an exceptional case that needs prompt action to protect the young girls in our care here. The poor girl is clearly distraught and I shall take her to my home this evening to join her mother—'

Before he could finish his sentence Maria blurted, 'You mean Kitty Willow? She's living with you?'

Mr Bell confirmed she was working for his family as companion to his invalided mother. 'I live in a large house and have room for all of her children. I will make the necessary arrangements for them to move in immediately.'

Victoria's face brightened for the first time. 'Thank yer, sir. Thank yer so much. I can't wait for us all to be together with Ma.'

Mr Bell smiled. 'We need to make the rooms ready, but, yes, you can all come.'

Maria beamed. 'This is just wonderful. I 'ave a letter for Kitty, if you would be so kind to give it to her. And cakes too for the children.'

'I'll make sure they get them,' Mr Bell said.

'You can be assured I shall see to Mr Mumbles' immediate departure from the premises and will decide on a course of action regarding Miss Feathers. As a philanthropist, it is my intention to raise the standards here to the highest level.'

Maria's head was in a spin taking in everything. She pictured the joy on Kitty's face at being reunited with her children, and marvelled at the kindness of gentlemen like Mr Bell. *Philanthropist?* That was a new word for her, and she was bursting to tell her mother and Eddie about it.

∽

Kitty could scarcely believe her eyes when Victoria stepped into the house with Mr Bell at the end of the afternoon. She stared at them with utter disbelief. Victoria ran straight into her mother's arms, tears streaming down her cheeks. Kitty cried too, tears of joy.

'I don't understand. Why are you 'ere?'

Mr Bell broke the news to her about what had happened, and that he had made an offer allowing all of Kitty's children to move into his house.

'I stand by that offer,' he declared. 'As chairman of the workhouse committee, I feel partially responsible for the actions of that man and wish to make amends.'

Kitty warbled, 'How can I ever thank you, Mr Bell. It's not your fault. Of course I accept your generous offer.'

Mr Bell tactfully left the room for mother and daughter to have time alone.

'Rosie misses yer so much, Ma. I did me best to care for her. There's a teacher, Mrs Fairbairn, who has a soft spot for her, but this makes the other children jealous. They are spiteful and pull her 'air and call us horrid names.'

Kitty stroked Victoria's hair, long soothing strokes with her hand. She held her chin up. 'Rosie will be with us soon. How fortunate it was that Jessie and Maria were there to see

151

that man's wickedness. Tell me, truthfully, did Mr Mumbles ever do anything . . . intimate?'

Victoria shook her head. 'No, Ma. I swear, but 'e did say I was his special girl, and if I behaved 'e would give me a treat. A couple of other times Miss Feathers asked me to see Mr Mumbles in his office, but Mrs Fairbairn told 'er I had schoolwork to finish. She's nice, she looked out for me.'

Later that day, on hearing the news, Milly expressed delight at the guardian's demise and hastily set about making up beds in the spare room for her and Victoria, but Kitty insisted on returning to the workhouse to sleep until there was room for all of her children to move into their new lodgings.

∽

The next day, Victoria insisted she was well enough to start at her new school in the town and Kitty was relieved to hear from Mr Bell that Mrs Fairbairn passed on her best wishes to the girl.

He told her, 'Mrs Fairbairn is a credit to the school and I can see she has a soft spot for Victoria. She says you were a natural as a classroom assistant. I didn't know about that. She asks if you would consider staying on as a helper?'

'Oh, I'd like that,' blurted Victoria. I enjoy 'elping the younger ones who struggled with their writing and arithmetic. Please say I can.'

'Very well,' replied Kitty. 'Let's see how it goes.'

It was decided that Kitty and Victoria would share a large double bed and a small bed would be purchased for Rosie that could be positioned by the window. Pip, Laurie, Billy and Iris would sleep in the attic where two single beds were pushed against the eaves, no longer required by staff who had once slept there. It would be two to a bed, but they were used to that. Miss Finchley would arrange for new bedding to be delivered and she had instructions from Mr Bell to provide whatever else was required for the Willow family.

∞

Maria's elation came to an abrupt halt when she returned home and was confronted by Archie yelling at Freddie. 'How could you think about marching with the union, after everything Harry has done for you?'

'Because it's right and men are struggling to provide for their families on the pittance we are paid.'

Maria cried out, 'What are you two rowing about? Stop it this minute. You know Ma's head can't take all this shouting. Where is she, and where's Joey?'

Archie looked sheepish. 'I'm sorry. Ma's in bed. She was feeling feverish and said her chest was playing up again. I put Joey down a few minutes ago, he should be settled.'

Maria flew up the stairs, two at a time, and went to her mother's bedside. Ruth's eyes were closed. Maria felt her warm brow and frowned. Her breathing was strained too, and Maria decided to keep an eye on her overnight in case her condition worsened. It felt as if she had barely slept when Maria awoke exhausted to the sound of the dawn's chorus. She stretched her arms above her head, rubbing her eyes and moved out of her chair.

Ruth's eyes opened slightly. Maria knelt by her bedside. 'Oh Ma, I've been so worried. How are you feeling?'

153

Ruth coughed and gripped her chest. She attempted to sit up and Maria assisted her to a comfortable position, her back resting against an extra pillow. She went to the marble-topped washstand and poured a glass of water.

Ruth sipped a few drops and thanked her, her voice soft. 'It's nothing, just a cough. I'll get up and take Joey to school.'

'You'll do no such thing. One of the boys can do it, you must rest.'

Ruth slumped back in her bed and nodded, her eye lids closing. 'Oh Ma, I'm worried about you. I think I should call for the doctor.'

Ruth's breathing was laboured. 'Give it another day or so. I'm sure I'll pull through. You know how it comes and goes. I'll be as right as rain later.'

Maria's brow furrowed. 'You're so stubborn, always refusing help. I'm going to make you some tea, Ma, a nice hot brew might help you feel better. Will you have some eggs as well?'

It didn't seem the right moment to share her news about the Willow family and Maria let it pass from her mind so she could focus all her attention on her mother. She heard Freddie's and Archie's footsteps climb the stairs and turned to see them standing by Ruth's doorway, looking in on their mother, their expressions showing concern.

'Shush, don't disturb her. And no more rowing!' Maria told them sternly.

'She's gonna be all right, isn't she?' Archie croaked.

'You know Ma. She has these turns, and then picks up after a rest. She thinks she will be up and about tomorrow

154

dropping Joey off at school, but I don't see her being well enough for that.'

Archie offered, 'I'll help, if yer like. You've only got to say, Maria.'

Maria pondered. 'That would be a big help, thank you, Archie.'

Ruth had dozed off when Maria went back in to see her. Her heavy breathing seemed to have eased slightly. Maria leant down and kissed her mother on the forehead. Ruth opened her eyes slightly and closed them again.

Assured that her mother's condition did not appear to have worsened, Maria left the house as Joey was just waking, giving strict instructions to Freddie and Archie to keep an eye on Ruth, saying she had planned to stop off to see Mrs Herring and ask if there was news of Eddie, and would ask her to look in on her later in the day.

She reached the Herrings' cottage within five minutes, just after the church clock struck seven times, and walked briskly along the side of the house. She found Mabel in the back garden gathering eggs. It didn't escape her notice that weeds had grown and the front garden was untended. The garden had once been Mabel Herring's pride and joy, fully stocked with carnations, roses and marigolds and a vegetable garden in the back scented by sweet trees that trailed up a trellis. It was clear that Mrs Herring was struggling now. Maybe this was something Eddie could help with, once he was back on his feet.

'Good morning, Maria. I was hoping to see you today. Is everything all right?'

155

'I'm sorry to come so early and unexpected, only . . .' Maria's faltering words stuck in her throat and she was unable to finish her sentence.

Mrs Herring placed her basket of eggs down and placed her hand on Maria's arm.

'Maria? You look upset? Is it Joey?'

'No, isn't Joey. It's Ma. She has taken poorly again and I wanted to ask if you would be able to look after Joey after school today. Ma thinks she'll sleep it off and doesn't like to make a fuss, you know what she's like.'

'Don't worry your pretty head about a thing. I'll look after Joey, he's no trouble at all and it will take me mind off things. I'll look in on Ruth later this morning as well.'

Mrs Herring's kindness made Maria well up. 'She looks so frail these days, I'm really worried about her.'

'I know you are. It's a lot for yer to take on, on top of Eddie. I have some news that will put a smile on your face.'

Maria sniffled, her face brightening. 'Really? What news? Is it about Eddie.'

'It is indeed. Beatrice stopped by last night to tell me he has responded very well.'

Tears welled in Maria's eyes. 'That is wonderful news. Do you know when I can visit him?'

'The doctor says very soon, if he continues to make good progress.'

Maria clutched her hands to her chest. 'That's such good news, I'm so happy to 'ear it, and can't wait to see him.'

She embraced Eddie's mother and set off for work. She was passing the royal station when the figure of a young woman, three or four years older than her, clutching a brown suitcase, caught her eye. She had a young boy with her who was a year or so younger than Joey. The woman had an oval face with pretty features and thick blonde curls that fell down her back. She wore a plain dark grey skirt and matching jacket with a blue blouse and she appeared to be unsure which way to go. The woman gripped the boy's hand tightly and he was wrestling with her to loosen her grip. She saw the woman stare in both directions, confusion etched across her face, and retrieve a sheet of paper from her pocket. She read its contents and looked around again, clearly unsure where to go.

Maria braked alongside her. 'Excuse me, I don't mean to intrude, but are you looking for somewhere. Can I 'elp?'

'I am, as a matter of fact,' she replied crisply. 'Can yer tell me where I might find the Reverend Frederick Rumbelow at The Vicarage in Wolferton.'

'You want to see the vicar?' asked Maria surprised. 'At this time of day?'

'That's what I said,' retorted the woman, with an indignant air.

Maria pointed out the path she needed to take past the turreted royal station master's house from where the church steeple was visible in the distance. The woman whistled softly. 'That's a grand-looking house for a station master.'

'It is indeed. In fact, I am related to the station master, Mr Saward. My name is Maria Saward.'

'Pleased to meet yer, I'm sure, Maria. Me name is Ruby Gatesby. We'll be on our way now. Thank yer for yer assistance.'

She watched Ruby walk off clutching her suitcase in one hand and pulling along her protesting son with the other.

'Come along, Piers. We're nearly there,' she urged, loosening her grip.

Maria's ears pricked up, thinking it strange that the boy should have the same uncommon name as the vicar's son. Piers Rumbelow was a medic who had died heroically while serving in the war. He was an only child, a much beloved son, whose loss had broken his parents' hearts, his mother leaving his bedroom untouched since the last time he was there.

How peculiar. What a coincidence, Maria mulled, as she continued on her way to Appleton House.

Chapter Fifteen

Florence Peter's head swivelled at the sound of the latch on the front gate being lifted at the vicarage. She stopped sweeping the leaves on the side path and wondered who would be calling at eight twenty in the morning. Perhaps a parishioner with an urgent need to see the Reverend Rumbelow, who had just finished his breakfast and was already in the study.

Her ears pricked up as the footsteps crunching over the gravel footpath approached, voices reaching her.

'Ouch. You're 'urting me arm, Ma,' wailed a boy.

'Well stop dragging yer feet then,' a woman replied, in an exasperated tone.

Florence placed her broom against the wall. She was young for a housekeeper, not quite twenty years old, but had a wise head on young shoulders. She had cared for her mother's house when she was ill and didn't shirk from hard work. Beatrice knew her well and gave her a glowing reference. She had been engaged to Florence's brother, Sam, who died in the war, and had been impressed with Florence's neat and efficient house management when her mother's nerves gave way.

That was four years ago. The vicar and his wife had initially hesitated to take on someone so young when their housekeeper announced her retirement, but Beatrice convinced them to give Florence a trial. She tactfully suggested that her gentle approach towards her mother had helped her to restore her health, and that this experience would stand her in good stead with Jane who still suffered the painful loss of their son. The vicar's wife's hair had turned white overnight from the grief of losing Piers. After a few weeks training under Gladys's wing, Florence had proved herself more than capable.

Florence suddenly came face to face with their visitors in the garden. The boy had just snapped off a head of a large chrysanthemum and stamped on it. Florence was aghast, knowing how much Mrs Rumbelow loved all her flowers.

'Stop it. This minute!' ordered the woman who was with him, grabbing the boy's hand and shaking him.

Florence stepped forward. 'Please, don't hurt the child. I'm sure he didn't mean any harm,' she said diplomatically.

'I'm afraid we are making a bad impression, and we ain't even met the vicar and 'is wife yet.'

Florence eyed the woman from head to toe. 'Are they expecting you? I don't believe I know you. Are you from these parts?'

'I'm from Cambridge and I've come on a delicate personal matter. I apologise for me early arrival, as I said, it's urgent. Besides, I didn't think yer needed an appointment to see a vicar, I thought yer could just turn up.'

'Reverend Rumbelow has just finished his breakfast. I will see if he is free as I believe he is preparing notes for a meeting. Mrs Rumbelow doesn't rise until later in the morning, not since . . .' Florence paused. 'What name shall I give?'

The woman raised her chin and Florence could see she had a flawless pale complexion and pretty features. The boy with her had quietened, holding his mother's hand, his wide eyes staring up at her. She could see her knuckles whiten as he pressed them tightly.

She replied in a soft voice. 'Ruby. Ruby Gatesby. Tell him I used to be acquainted with their son Piers.'

'Follow me,' instructed Florence, walking past the study where the vicar was sitting at his desk. She stopped when she reached the back door. 'Please wait here until I say otherwise.'

Ruby waited a couple of moments after Florence left and then scooted to the side window and peered inside. She spied the vicar with his head down at his desk. He wore his dog collar and black clergy shirt and she ducked as Florence entered the room, raising her head a moment later to observe Florence speaking to him. She saw his face pale, plastered with a pained expression. He rose quickly and Ruby rushed back to the door as he suddenly appeared. His startled expression flickered from her face, and then to the boy at her side.

'Florence tells me you knew my son, Piers?'

'Yes, that's right, sir. Me name is Ruby Gatesby.'

Ruby stepped forward and extended a hand, which the vicar took in his and shook politely. She held her son close to her side. 'The name isn't familiar. May I enquire, what brings you here?'

'I apologise for not giving notice. What I have to say is of a personal nature. Could I step inside for a moment, please?'

'Very well, if you say you knew our son.'

161

He stepped aside and Ruby swept past him, her eyes resting on a silver-framed photograph of Piers Rumbelow dressed in his army uniform placed on a table in the entrance hall, a posy of fresh flowers next to it. The boy clutched the woman's hand tightly. The vicar bent down and asked, 'What is your name, young man?'

The boy shuffled his feet and stared up at the woman's face. 'That's what I've come to talk to yer about. The thing is . . .'

A woman's voice called out from the top of the stairs, its tone incredulous, with Florence standing behind, having rushed upstairs to inform the vicar's wife of their visitor. 'Jonathan, is it true? Florence tells me a woman has turned up here with a child and says she used to be acquainted with Piers. Is she still here?'

Ruby walked to the bottom of the stairs. She glanced up and saw the vicar's wife.

'Yes, I'm still here. I was just going to explain the nature of my visit to the vicar.'

'Well, do wait for me, I should like to hear it too.'

Jane Rumbelow descended the stairs cautiously, holding on to the banister for support, with Florence following behind her. Jane's hair hung loose down her back and she wore a robe adorned with flowers over her nightgown.

When she reached the bottom of the stairs, Jane paused for breath. 'I look forward to hearing what you have to say. Could you bring some tea to the breakfast room, Florence. Some of your delicious cupcakes too. I imagine this little man would like that, wouldn't you?'

'Oooh, yes, I would,' Piers replied instantly, his face breaking into a big grin.

The woman scolded, 'What did I tell yer, Piers, about saying "please" and "thank you".'

Jane gasped and swayed to one side, her arms reaching out to a chair for support. Her husband stepped over and took her arm. She croaked, 'His name is Piers? That's just extraordinary.'

'I'm sorry, I didn't mean to shock yer. I was unsure whether to write or just turn up. I thought this was the best way, as it were going to be a surprise whatever way I told yer.'

The vicar asked, his eyes fixed on the boy. 'Tell us what? I would like to hear it from your own lips. But as a man of the world, I think I have an inkling what you are about to say.'

Jane grabbed her husband's arm. She quaked. 'It is such a coincidence that the child is called Piers. Do you think it could possibly be . . .' Her words trailed off as her watery eyes fixed on Ruby's face.

'Yes, he's Piers's son,' she confirmed.

The vicar and his wife's faces paled and they exchanged glances of disbelief.

The vicar asked, 'You must see this is a big shock for us both, especially as Piers never mentioned being in a relationship.'

Jane took shaky breaths, her voice cracking with emotion. 'My Piers would never have a relationship with an uneducated woman like you. How can you prove this is his child.'

Ruby glared. 'If you are throwing accusations like that at me, I shall be orf. Come along, Piers, let's go.'

The vicar stood between the two women and turned to Jane. 'Do you not think you are being hasty, my dear? We

163

should hear Ruby's story in full. After all, this could be our grandson. Whatever the circumstances.'

Jane acquiesced. 'You're right, of course. You always are, my darling. I'm sorry, Miss Gatesby. I apologise for my outburst. Can we start again?'

Ruby stared at the fixtures around her. They were standing in the light and airy breakfast room which had a tall bay window that looked across the beautifully maintained garden that was Jane's pride and joy. A round table was placed in the front of the window with four chairs around it. A chiffonier sideboard was covered with photographs of Piers from when he was a baby and with his proud parents.

A wooden cross was fixed to the wall, as well as a framed picture of Jesus Christ. A copy of the Bible lay opened on a side table next to an armchair and a standard lamp with a large tasselled floral shade was positioned behind it.

'It's a lovely room. I can picture Piers sitting here in front of the window while you are sat in yer chair reading the Bible,' Ruby said in a soft voice.

'Why yes, that's what we used to do. And Jane would sit there and write to him. It's the loveliest room in the house,' the vicar told her.

Ruby pointed to a footstool for Piers to perch on. He hugged his knees and glanced anxiously at his mother. Jane pulled her robe around her and smiled. 'I'm sure Florence can find a nice glass of milk for you.' Turning to her husband she exclaimed, 'Do you know, I do believe I can see something of Piers in his face. Or am I imagining it?'

'Yes, I can see it too,' agreed Ruby, pulling a chair from the table to sit on. The vicar and his wife sat on either side of her and exchanged questioning glances as she unclipped her brown case and produced a bundle of letters tied together with blue ribbon.

'These were all written by Piers to me. Proof that I am speaking the truth. I would never lie to a religious man 'cause I know I would be struck down.'

Florence entered the room then with the refreshments, including a glass of milk for Piers, and looked with interest at the opened letters on the table. She suggested, 'If it helps, I can take the lad off your hands. I'm used to little boys, seeing as I have two younger brothers meself, though they are strapping lads now.'

Piers shook his head at first, but was persuaded by Florence after she suggested they went in search of conkers, which lay in abundance down the lane.

'Is an hour sufficient time?' she enquired.

'I believe so. I shall need to finish preparations for my sermon tomorrow and have some calls to make,' the vicar replied.

After Florence and Piers had left, Ruby blurted out her story. 'My mother used to clean some of the student rooms at Cambridge, including Piers's. He weren't as stuck up as some of the others and always found time to ask how she was.

'One day, Ma was unwell and I offered to do her rooms as she couldn't afford to lose her wages. That's how I met Piers. I was seventeen at the time and working as a cleaner in The University Arms Hotel. I could fit it in around me hours.

'Ma said how kind he was, that he was the son of a vicar, and wouldn't you know it, as goodness poured through his veins. He was concerned about Ma's failing 'ealth and said

165

he had warned her not to overdo it the last time he saw her. Ma is a big lady and struggled to walk up the narrow stone spiral staircase to the students' rooms at the top.'

Jane dabbed her moist eyes with a dainty handkerchief. She sniffled. 'That sounds like my Piers. He was always a thoughtful boy. Do you know his name means "rock"? He was always kind and thoughtful, a steady *rock* you could count on in your hour of need.'

'I admit I quickly developed an affection for him. Piers would compliment me whatever I did, he had the most cheerful disposition. He asked me about my education, encouraging me to improve the words I could read and write. He even helped me himself sometimes, insisting it was no trouble. He said I was a good learner.'

The vicar choked, 'My dear boy. Do you recall, Jane, how Piers would help at the Sunday school? I thought his path lay as a teacher or an academic, if not the ministry, but he was determined to be a doctor. He saw the way families struggled if they weren't given proper medical care and wanted to help them.'

Ruby's eyes brightened. 'He told me this too. He was unlike any other man I knew. I spent more and more time with him over the next six months, and even though Ma was well enough to do his room again, I did it instead, so I could be close to him, and gave her the money. I saw his eyes light up when I entered his room. I wasn't just Ruby, the cleaning girl. He made me feel more than that, that there was another life at my fingertips if I wanted it.'

Ruby paused and bit her lip. Jane commented in a soft voice. 'Are you saying Piers had feelings for you?'

'I believe he did. We became close and couldn't stop ourselves when it happened. Piers was conceived from love.'

The vicar's and his wife's faces reddened.

Jane gripped her husband's arm. Her voice shook. 'When exactly did this happen?'

Ruby bit her lip. 'As you know Piers decided at the beginning of the war to sign up with the Medical Corps. On our last evening together before he left for training camp, Piers promised me he wouldn't be away for long. Then, he kissed me, and I kissed him back. It was our first kiss. We couldn't stop ourselves. I really thought he would be back, and everything would be all right. Afterwards, he told me loved me.'

Jane twisted her fingers, her bottom lip juddering. 'I find it hard to believe that Piers would behave in such a way out of wedlock. He knows it's a sin.'

The vicar rose and walked to his wife, taking her hand in his. 'Yes, Piers knew that, but he was not a sinful person. He loved this girl, and we must love her too.'

He reached for the Bible and flicked through the pages, his finger running along the lines of Luke, chapter six, and quoting from verse thirty-seven. '"Do not judge, and you will not be judged; do not condemn, and you will not be condemned. Forgive, and you will be forgiven."'

He took Jane into his arms. She shook, gulping large breaths, her heart pounding. Her husband comforted her as she rested her head against his shoulder.

'I was just coming to terms with his death, and now I am reliving his memory and suffering all over again. It's so painful, Miss Gatesby,' she confessed.

Ruby was holding out his letters. 'You can call me Ruby. Would you like to read these? There are only half a dozen, before he was taken from us.'

The vicar read one of the letters and became visibly upset. He placed it back in its envelope. 'I don't think I can manage any more today. It's been such a shock for us. Tell me, what did Piers say when you told him you were with child?'

The words stuck in Ruby's throat. 'He never knew. I didn't want to write it in a letter, and then he died.'

Jane's eyes moistened and she took a couple of steps back. She exchanged a shocked expression with her husband. She reached out and took Ruby's hand in hers. 'That is so dreadful. One can only pray that Piers is looking down on us now. Your poor son has never known a father's love or guidance, but I hope that from now on we can help and be a part of his life.'

'Jane is right. Can we, as his grandparents, who are missing our son dreadfully, get to know little Piers? This boy could have been sent to heal us, like a gift from God. You are right, Jane, I can see the likeness between them and it will help us with our grief.'

Ruby took a breath and spoke softly. 'I believe that is what Piers would want, and it is why I came to see you today. Ma died last week and the slum lodgings we lived in are being pulled down. I thought this would be the right time for a fresh start. Before Piers left he made me promise that if ever I were in trouble, I would come to you.'

Jane reached forward to hug Ruby. Her throat clenched. 'This is all so extraordinary. I can't believe it; we have our Piers back. Of course, you can both stay here. We have a spare room for you, Ruby, and our dear grandson can have his father's room. It's not been touched since we lost him.'

Ruby beamed and lurched forward to kiss Jane's cheek. 'I was 'oping you would say that. I accept your kind invitation.'

The vicar quipped, 'It's true, the Lord certainly moves in mysterious ways. I would never have expected our son's own flesh and blood to walk through our doors. We are so blessed.'

Chapter Sixteen

Maria was bursting to tell Mrs Watson how Victoria had left the workhouse and the family were now staying with Kitty's employer, the solicitor, Mr Bell.

'The poor things. They've had one ordeal after another,' she muttered.

They were interrupted when Miss Jensen entered the kitchen with a brisk manner. She began reciting precise instructions to Mrs Watson about how Queen Maud liked her breakfast to be served. Maria could tell the housekeeper was only half listening and was seething.

'We have our own ways here, Miss Jensen, and I can assure you I have never served an overcooked soft boiled egg to Her Majesty. I know how she likes them. Her crusts will be cut off the freshly baked bread and our butter was fresh from the dairy yesterday. We have the freshest kippers too, which I know Her Majesty is partial to.'

Miss Jensen appeared taken aback by the housekeeper's abruptness. 'I was just making sure. Thank you, Mrs Watson.'

'The cheek of it!' exclaimed Mrs Watson, throwing her head back, her hands on her hips, when the Danish lady-in-waiting was out of earshot. 'I hope I made it clear who the boss is in my kitchen.'

Maria retorted, 'You certainly stood yer ground, and I don't blame yer.'

∞

Later that morning, after the breakfast dishes had been cleaned away, Queen Maud entered the kitchen dressed in a satin robe over her white nightgown. Maria and Mrs Watson leapt up and curtseyed.

She addressed the housekeeper. 'I gather from Miss Jensen that you spoke rather curtly to her this morning. I expected better from you, Mrs Watson. Can you give me your word that from now on you will make every effort to be amenable to her?'

Mrs Watson's jaw dropped to the floor and her face turned scarlet. She started to stutter, but stopped herself as she caught sight of Miss Jensen. She was smiling at her, and not in an unkind way.

'Of course, ma'am, I do beg yer pardon. I apologise, Miss Jensen. It was just a silly misunderstanding on my part.'

Miss Jensen said in a conciliary tone, 'Your apology is accepted. The breakfast was delicious.'

Mrs Watson beamed at the compliment, her cheeks flushed as Queen Maud and Miss Jensen left the room. She heaved a sigh of relief and muttered to Maria, 'I made a fool of meself then, didn't I? Me and my big mouth.'

'I'm sure it's forgotten about,' Maria consoled.

Maria went in search of some beeswax polish to give the dining room furniture a good shine and returned with a duster and the polish. 'There's something else you might like to know. It's very odd, come to think of it.'

'Oh yes? What do you mean?'

'I saw a woman outside the station on my way in this morning. She wanted directions to the vicarage. She 'ad a young boy with her about the same age as my Joey, by the name of Piers! I 'eard 'er call him by that name. Don't that seem strange to you, seeing that's the name of the vicar's dead son?'

'Well, it is a bloomin' coincidence,' retorted the house-keeper.

'That's what I thought. Did yer know Piers?'

'I did. He was well liked. His death hit his parents hard.'

'I remember the day Beatrice took the telegram to the vicarage. She was working with her mother then at the post office. They say Piers died a hero.'

Mrs Waton nodded. 'He did, he was that kind of person. He went to the aid of an injured soldier who was being carried over to him on a stretcher under fire. Piers spotted a sniper behind the stretcher bearer and stood up to warn him to keep his head down. He ducked just in time, but Piers took the shot straight through his heart. He didn't stand a chance.'

Mrs Watson glanced at the clock as it struck nine times. 'That's enough chatting for today. Her Majesty has asked for an early lunch. She has a guest coming over this afternoon, Lady Appleby, from Hillington Hall. Maria, when you have finished your polishing, can you lay the table and make sure everything sparkles. We need fresh cut flowers around the house too.'

∞

Maria was relieved when the end of the day came, her mind on her mother and Eddie. She stopped off at Mrs Herring's home on her way home and was relieved to be given some good news.

'I called in at the hospital, you can go and see Eddie in a couple of days. He's been asking after you.'

Maria flung her arms around Mabel's neck. 'That's the best news. I'll go on me next day off, the day after next.'

When she pulled away her eyebrows furrowed. 'Did you 'ave a chance to see Ma today?'

'I did, and I can put yer mind at rest there. I took her some broth and she tucked it away with relish. I then 'elped her wash and change into fresh clothing. Before I left she felt well enough to walk down the stairs, and I left her sitting in her chair in front of the stove with a blanket over her legs. Joey is taken care of – he went to play with Leslie after school, and Ada offered to give him tea and bring him home.'

'It feels like a weight 'as been lifted off me mind. Thank you, Mrs Herring . . . Mabel.'

'You can call me Ma Mabel, seeing as yer already like a daughter to me.'

'I swear I'll be a good daughter and the best wife to Eddie. I can't wait for that day.'

Just as Mabel had said, Ruth was sitting comfortably by the fire when she returned home and Archie was cleaning up the dishes. Ada brought Joey home, yawning and rubbing his eyes, after his energetic game of chase with Leslie in the station master's garden, and he went to bed without complaint. Freddie arrived later, after everyone else had gone to bed. A tightening of her stomach and the way he averted his eyes from her face when he brushed past her made her

173

feel uneasy, and she vowed to speak to him when they were alone.

∽

Two days later, Maria mounted her bicycle and ducked under the overgrown branches as she cycled down the country lanes, rising high in places, giving her a bird's eye view across the marshes. She placed a packet of custard creams in her front basket, Eddie's favourites. The two small squares of sugary biscuit with a layer of smooth vanilla fondant sandwiched between them were a melt-in-the-mouth favourite.

As she approached the hospital, she followed the track to the back of the premises, almost colliding with someone pushing a wheelbarrow. It was filled with weeds and cuttings that had been pruned back from shrubs and wobbled from side to side.

'Eddie!'

'Maria!'

She flung her bicycle down and threw herself into his arms, almost knocking him over. Her heart was pounding and she felt his body tense. He stepped backwards, confusion etched across his face. A moment later, his face lit up.

'Maria! I wasn't expecting to see you 'ere today.'

There was an awkward pause as Eddie's brows furrowed. Maria made her voice sound cheery. 'I 'ope your happy to see me, Eddie. Beatrice said I could come and told me how well you are doing. I'm seeing Doctor Butterscotch with yer.'

'I saw him for a short while, he gave me this job to do. Look, I've pruned all these branches from the bushes.'

174

'And nearly got yourself run over too! Well done, Eddie, you've done a grand job.'

The doctor stepped out of the back door and walked towards them. He smiled and extended a hand. 'Ah, there you are, Eddie. I'm pleased to see you have found Maria. Eddie has done himself proud here, after everything he has endured.'

Maria's forehead furrowed as she caught Eddie give the doctor a sideways glance as if to silence him. The doctor placed his arm on Eddie's shoulder. 'Shall we all go inside? There is something we need to tell your future wife.'

Maria followed the doctor and Eddie along the corridor, her eyes peering into the wards out of curiosity. Many of the patients sat in chairs by their beds reading a paper, or pretending to, while some played card games, or chatted with visitors or nurses. Some lay in bed, the covers pulled up to their necks.

The doctor stopped at his door and invited them both in. Instead of sitting behind his desk, the doctor pulled his chair out and sat next to the two chairs occupied by Eddie and Maria.

The words gushed from Maria's mouth. 'Is Eddie ready to come 'ome, Doctor? Is 'e well enough to return to the station?'

The doctor raised his hand. 'One question at a time, Miss Saward. I think you are getting ahead of yourself. Firstly, I'd like to thank you for coming here today. Eddie has spoken very fondly of you and Joey.'

Maria's hand reached out to hold Eddie's. Eddie flinched, and pulled it away, his jaw tense. She caught the doctor's eye, and his expression told her to let it be.

Doctor Butterscotch cleared his throat. 'As you are to be married, Eddie has given me his consent to speak to you about what happened to him so you understand why he feels the way he does. Isn't that so, Eddie?'

Maria reached out again and took Eddie's hand in hers. He glanced down to his lap and then turned his face away.

The doctor leant forward. His eyes were kind and his voice soft. 'I would like to start by commending Eddie for his fulsome support of this new programme. It takes courage to place your trust in a stranger and to bare your soul, even if I am his doctor.'

Maria beamed proudly at Eddie as the doctor continued. 'Our therapy is specially designed for brave men like Eddie who are haunted from the war, day and night, by the atrocities they experienced and witnessed.'

Eddie lowered his head and sniffled. The doctor continued. 'Unless you have lived on a battlefield, it is impossible to understand the senseless brutality of it and the fear our good men faced constantly. Loud explosions are to be expected; this is war, after all. But for some poor souls, when they return home, the trauma and shock suffered by them remains. They cannot free themselves of it. These are not physical wounds that the naked eye can see, but invisible wounds inside the mind; that's what makes our trial here so significant.'

Maria asked, 'What do yer mean, Doctor?' Did something really 'orrible 'appen to Eddie?'

'I'm afraid so, Maria.'

'I see,' she muttered, glancing at Eddie's face, her pulse beginning to soar.

The doctor continued. 'Some of my traditional medical colleagues believe the best way to overcome a fear is to face it. In other words, soldiers who retreat into themselves and suffer considerably from their nerves after the war should be forced to face loud noises constantly, to face what they call their demons. They believe the poor men who cannot face their *demons*, as they put it, are regarded as cowards and made to work doubly hard in noisy environments. I have no doubt that going back to Wolferton Station would make Eddie relive his ordeal, for the time being, at least.'

Maria bleated, 'Eddie's no coward, but what else can 'e do, Doctor? It's the only work he's ever done?'

'I know that, but Eddie's life will need to change when he leaves hospital. Here, Eddie spends his days attending to the gardens. We encourage him to be outdoors and walk around the grounds, and to talk to us too so he can understand that what happened was not his fault.'

'What do yer mean, "not his fault"?' queried Maria.

'There was a traumatic event that has had a deep impact on Eddie. It's not just the shattering sounds of shell explosions that can damage a man's mind.'

Maria's eyes narrowed. 'I don't understand. What do yer mean?'

Eddie rose and began to pace around the room, clenching his fists, his body tensing. The doctor's eyes followed his movements. 'We can take a break if you would like?'

Eddie returned to his seat and inhaled a deep breath. 'No, carry on. I'm all right now. I want Maria to know everything, if she's gonna be wed to me.'

'Very well, but please do let me know if you would like me to stop at any time.'

Maria placed her hand in Eddie's again, pressing it between both her palms and listened attentively as the doctor spoke.

'While out in Gaza, in the Middle East, Eddie became good chums with a lad from Dersingham by the name of Simon Styles. He was a cobbler, the youngest of four boys, who had only just turned twenty. Before he left for war he wed his childhood sweetheart. Like many of the lads, he kept a photo of her tucked inside his jacket, close to his heart.'

Maria cast her mind back, recalling that Eddie had mentioned Simon who he had known since they were children at school together and wrote to her saying how good it was to see him again, but wishing it could be anywhere other than the sweating desert of Gaza.

'What's Simon got to do with my Eddie?'

The doctor stared at Eddie, who nodded, indicating for him to speak, biting his lip, the muscles on his face tightening. 'What I will now recount is very tragic. One of Simon's brothers, Ezra, was a fisherman. He drowned at sea during a storm the month before war broke out. Simon's two older brothers, John and Joseph volunteered and were posted to France. John died from typhus within six months, leaving just Joseph and Simon. Simon signed up too. He had been at Gaza five weeks when he received a letter from his mother informing him Joseph had been killed by mustard gas; the poor man inhaled too much of this poisonous substance in his lungs and throat to survive. That just left Simon.'

The doctor paused as Eddie buried his head in his hands. 'I'm sorry you are having to go through this again, Eddie. Would you like me to stop?'

Maria's face showed confusion. 'That poor mother, to have suffered so much loss. But what happened to Simon? I don't understand.'

Eddie squeezed his eyes shut and stifled a sob. Maria sensed the pain coursing through his body and stroked his arm to soothe him.

Doctor Butterscotch continued. 'Private Styles was distraught, knowing how heartbroken his mother would be if she lost the last of her three sons. He made a plan to return home without anyone knowing and confided this to Private Herring.'

The doctor paused, his eyes fixed on Eddie's face. Eddie clasped his hands over his ears as the doctor continued.

'You mean, he deserted?' asked Maria, incredulous.

'I'm afraid he didn't consider the consequences. He told Eddie he had to return home as soon as possible. It was a foolhardy plan, but his intentions were brave and courageous.'

Maria's voice wobbled. 'What did he do?'

'He decided to steal some woman's clothing and disguise himself. As I said, it was a foolhardy plan. He had a slight build and was able to find a nurse's uniform in the laundry. He then seized his chance to escape by climbing onto the back of a wagon that had delivered provisions to the camp. He hid under a cover and thought he could somehow make his way back to Blighty, across the channel, and on to Norfolk.'

179

Maria's hand flew to her mouth. 'Oh my goodness. He got caught, didn't he?'

'I'm afraid so. He wasn't aware the cart was going to drop off some of the troops at another camp. When they climbed into the back and lifted the tarpaulin, they found him. He was charged with being a deserter.'

'I see,' murmured Maria. 'There's only one sentence for that, isn't there? Death by firing squad.'

The doctor nodded. Eddie's shoulders shook and he clenched his fists, his knuckles turning white. 'It's not right. Simon asked his commanding officer if he could have time off on compassionate grounds, but he dismissed it. It was downright cruel of them. I told the sergeant that special allowances should have been made for Simon, that it weren't right.'

Maria's eyes filled with admiration. 'That was so brave of you, Eddie.'

'I could see that speaking up for Simon the way I did set some of the officers against me. The sergeant told the colonel I needed to be taught a lesson.'

'A lesson? But you did nothing wrong, Eddie.'

Eddie's head jerked. He croaked. ''E said I would have to . . . that I should . . . show others what 'appens to deserters, and those who support them.'

Eddie slumped, burying his head in his hands. His shoulders shook. Maria reached over and enveloped her arms around him. She consoled, 'Shush, my poor Eddie, you don't have to say any more.'

Eddie raised his head and wiped his eyes dry. 'You should 'ear it all now, seeing as I've said this much.'

His distraught face stared straight at Maria. 'There were four of us in the dawn firing squad, including me. I was ordered to shoot 'im or be disciplined for disobeying orders. I 'ad tears in me eyes as I watched Simon shaking as they tied his 'ands behind 'is back and they put a blindfold over 'is eyes. My 'ands were shaking as I 'eld up the rifle. When the order came to shoot, I fired deliberately over his 'ead to miss. But me nerves were so bad and me 'ands were shaking and I think . . .'

Eddie was visibly upset and buried his head in his hands. Beads of sweat dotted his forehead and his breathing was fast and erratic. The doctor shot a warning glance to Maria, pressing his finger against his lips.

Eventually, Eddie's rapid breathing eased and he raised his head, gulping large breaths of air.

The doctor spoke softly. 'I know how hard this is for you, Eddie. Shall we take a break?'

'No, Doctor. I want Maria to 'ear it all from me.'

Maria coaxed gently, 'You should never 'ave been put in this situation. What they made you do was unforgivable. It's the most heartless and appalling thing I've 'eard.'

Eddie rubbed his chin and held Maria's gaze. 'That's the side of war people don't get to 'ear about. I can't get it out of me 'ead. I ask meself, was it my shot that killed him? Can you imagine how that makes me feel?'

Eddie broke down and turned away from Maria, collapsing to his knees. He cried and whispered his friend's name. Maria knelt in front of him and took his hands in hers.

'You mustn't think that. It weren't yer fault, Eddie. None of it were your fault. That poor boy didn't stand a chance once 'e bolted.'

The doctor rose and glanced at the clock. 'I think that's enough for one day. Reliving this will have been very traumatic for Eddie. I shall leave you alone for a few minutes and will arrange for some tea to be sent in.'

'Thank yer, Doctor, for everything you've done. I could never have imagined anything like this 'appening to Eddie. No wonder 'e's so shaken up.'

'I am pleased he can open up about this traumatic experience. All he can do is take one day at a time. I am assured he will be in the best of hands with you, Miss Saward, when it is time for Eddie to leave.'

'I will do me best for him. Should I tell his mother what 'appened?' Turning to Eddie, she added, 'That is, if Eddie agrees.'

Eddie rose and shook the doctor's hand. 'No, I want to tell Ma meself. 'Earing all this again, having to relive it, as hard as it is for me to bear, has made me come to a decision.'

Maria and Doctor Butterscotch stared at Eddie and said in unison, 'What might that be?'

'I've decided I shall write to Private Style's family and tell his ma and missus he wasn't a coward, that he died out of love for them.'

The doctor patted him on the back. 'That is an admirable suggestion, and progress indeed, Eddie Herring.'

Chapter Seventeen

Two days had passed since Mr Bell's encounter with the disgraced Mr Mumbles. The shamed guardian had packed his bags and departed the workhouse under a cloak of darkness. His sudden departure was the talk of the town. A couple of his cronies on the workhouse committee announced their resignation in protest. Others appeared genuinely shocked at discovering him for the rogue he was.

Mr Bell was praised for his swift response to a delicate situation that could have attracted negative publicity. Miss Feathers fled later when her part in assisting Mr Mumbles' insidious deeds was uncovered, slipping out of the back door with a suitcase, a hood covering her face.

An advertisement was promptly placed in the local newspaper for a new guardian and women's wardress. In the meantime, John Hopper, who was in charge of the men's section, was asked to stand in as interim guardian until a new appointment was made. Mrs Fairbairn, who was popular with both the women inmates and hard-working staff, agreed to fill Miss Feathers' shoes on a temporary basis. Mr Bell considered them both suitable for the posts, but due processes for senior appointments had to be adhered to and all staff were invited to apply for the positions.

Interest was expressed by Theobald Barber to become the next guardian. He was a senior teacher at the school and felt aggrieved to work under Mr Hopper's supervision, saying he was better qualified. Mr Bell had heard whisperings that Mr Barber had a fierce temper and was known as Thunder Theobald by the boys who had suffered at his hands. Mr Bell invited him to meet him and his fellow committee members to share his vision for the workhouse. His worst fears were confirmed when Mr Barber, his double chin juddering, produced a cane and flicked it through the air making a whooshing sound.

'I believe in the tried and tested method of caning pupils as the best way to instil respect into them and that hard work should not be shirked,' he declared with a flourish, and air of macabre satisfaction.

Mr Bell rose from behind his desk and spoke indignantly. 'You are mistaken, sir. Not only are you unsuited as guardian to meet our future aspirations and vision for the workhouse, but you are no longer required to work here under Mr Hopper.'

Later that evening, back in his house, Mr Bell was in his office when he heard Kitty and her children's voices coming from another room. He had taken it for granted that his mother, sister and nephew would agree to him offering the Willow family a refuge and had acted instinctively.

Mr Bell believed his actions were setting an excellent example to the wider community on the importance of being non-judgemental and showing compassion to those less fortunate. He wanted to demonstrate how the lives of families, thrown into turmoil and poverty through no fault of their own, could be transformed if given the right encouragement and kindness. To his surprise, his mother's eyes lit up and she readily welcomed the idea. His nephew, George, shared his values and was a man after his own heart, and had heartily patted him on the back as a gesture of approval. His sister was scathing, which he expected, but she was planning an extended visit to a cousin who resided in London within a few days, so would not be involved in the same way. Before leaving, she offered her resignation on the workhouse committee, which was a relief to Mr Bell, who had been concerned that she aligned herself too much towards Mr Mumbles and Miss Feathers.

Mr Bell had been impressed to see how Kitty, Victoria, Milly and Mrs Watson had worked miracles to transform the attic into liveable accommodation. They scrubbed the walls clean of cobwebs and dust, washed the flooring and hung fresh gingham curtains. Some of the sheets and bedding retrieved from a chest of drawers were usable, but new bedding was also purchased, along with new eiderdowns. Mr Bell kindly allowed the children to purchase two sets of nightwear and a new outfit each *for best*. Kitty had insisted Mr Bell take payment for this from her salary, but Mr Bell wouldn't hear of it.

Mr Bell noticed how his mother seemed to perk up with their new residents now settled in. She enjoyed spending time with Victoria, who read to her when her mother was busy around the house, stumbling over some words that Mrs Bell was only too happy to correct. Rosie cheered her with her charming childish ways, telling her stories about her topsy-turvy doll, and she was very impressed to hear it had been given to her by Queen Maud.

185

She found the boys too noisy, though Iris amused her with her tomboy ways after she recounted her mischievous antics with her brothers and the pranks they got up to. Her favourite was hiding with a sheet over her head when it was dark and then leaping out to scare Rosie.

∽

One Saturday evening Kitty was brushing Victoria's long fair hair and preparing to go to bed when her daughter asked, 'Is it true, Ma, that there is a meeting in Wolferton tomorrow about the estate workers who went to Gallipoli? I read your letter from Maria where she mentions this.'

'Yes, it's true, but I didn't want to say anything, in case there is no news about yer pa. Mr Perryman is attending and has offered me a lift in his car. I 'ear it is being held after the church service. It will be strange to be back in Wolferton. I wonder how I will be received there.'

Victoria flung her arms around her mother's neck. 'We've done nothing wrong, Ma. You and Pa worked for the royal family all yer life and he went to war to do his duty for his King, for us all. We're not to blame for how things worked out.'

Kitty kissed her daughter's forehead. 'That's what Mr Perryman says but I still feel a sense of shame. Even though Maria has my old job, I bear 'er no ill and will most likely see her there tomorrow. I shall need you to look after yer brothers and sisters. Mrs Finchley will prepare yer meal, and if it's dry tomorrow, you can take them to the park.'

Victoria's eyes moistened. 'I'm scared, Ma. Pip says Pa is dead. He says they're all dead.'

Kitty turned her face away, not wanting her daughter to see the tears trickle down her cheeks. How could she tell her that she was haunted by the same fears, that she may never see her father again.

∽

The following day, Kitty felt overcome by nerves about attending the meeting and the information that would be disclosed. Her nerves were heightened too by the fact that this would be her first return visit to Wolferton since she'd left for the workhouse. She was thankful to be accompanied by Mr Perryman, who was held in high regard in the village.

A church service was to be held ahead of the meeting and Jessie arrived in good time to put the finishing touches to her autumnal flower arrangement at the front of St Peter's Church in Wolferton. She shuffled some of the more colourful flowers around to make them more prominent. The golden chrysanthemums were grown by Harry in his garden and their enormous eye-catching blooms were proof that they were worthy winners of the gold prizes they garnered at the horticultural show.

She stood back to check her arrangements were displayed to their best advantage, viewing the blooms from all angles, making a few small tweaks to the positioning of the orange Chinese lantern stems so they could be admired by all, and felt satisfied. There was plenty of greenery on the estate with rose hip berries and trailing ivy for Jessie to help herself to, but it was the golden globed chrysanthemums that made the arrangement stand out.

Due to her poor hearing she was unaware of the footsteps behind her that approached. As they stopped, a man's voice make a coughing sound, which Jessie ignored. He coughed again, before speaking in a loud clear voice, 'Jessie.'

Jessie spun around, dropping the foliage in her hand, and yelped with joy.

'Jack! It's you!'

'Yes. It is. I'm sorry I couldn't let you know I was coming, I didn't know myself for sure until last night, and my plans can change at a moment's notice. I called at your house and your mother told me you were here. I came straight over.'

Jessie glanced around to check they were alone, and then, within seconds, she was in her sweetheart's arms. He raised her chin towards his face and kissed her softly on the lips.

She returned his kiss coyly, her cheeks flushed. He led her to a pew, holding her hand firmly in his. He said, 'Let's sit here and talk for a couple of minutes before we are disturbed. I'm only here for the day on an official matter and want to make the most of every minute we can spend together.'

'I've missed you so much, Jack. It's the best surprise I could have wished for, but it's a sad day for us here. If your visit is official, am I allowed to ask you the reason for it?'

Jack stroked her cheek and murmured, 'His Majesty is keen for me to report back to him from the meeting this afternoon about the King's missing men in Gallipoli. I assume you are going?'

'We all are. The vicar is expecting a larger congregation because of it. He feels it's important to provide spiritual support to the bereaved, but at times like this, words of comfort are hard to find.'

'Reverend Rumbelow knows only too well how these poor families feel. After all, he lost his only son and grieves his loss as they do.'

A moment later, they were joined by a group of men and women, estate workers or relatives of those who had connections with the royal estate, as they made their way in, dressed in their Sunday best. Harry strolled in and took his position as church warden at the back, handing out hymn and prayer books to the congregation as they entered. Jessie and Jack moved closer to the front to a pew reserved for her family.

Once seated, Jack pressed Jessie about her new position in the hothouses that she had written to him about, and she gushed, beaming as told him it was the best job she had ever had.

'I'm very proud of you, my darling. You have a special talent, you know.'

An elderly woman shuffled along in the pew behind her and chatted animatedly to her companion. Jessie spun her head around to see if she knew them as she thought she heard them mention visiting a medium. Because of her hearing impediment, she couldn't grasp the full exchange, and she asked Jack what they were saying. The elderly woman described how she and her daughter had been to see a spiritualist the week before in King's Lynn and had been in touch with her dead son, Daniel, who was killed in battle in the Middle East. He told the medium to pass on a message to his ma, to tell her that his suffering had been brief and he had been laid to rest in the corner of a field under a tree, and that she should get on with her life.

Jessie gasped and turned to face the women. 'Are you interested to know what happened, dear?'

Jessie nodded, while Jack pressed his hand to her arm, throwing her a warning glance.

The woman ignored him and continued, with Jessie listening agog. 'Now where was I? Oh, yes. Then the medium said something I couldn't believe, that I was not to forget that Bertie missed him too, and to remember that he likes to be tickled on his tummy. I mean, how would she know that about Bertie?'

Jessie blurted, 'Who's Bertie? Oh dear, I'm sorry to interrupt.'

'Bertie was Daniel's mongrel. He's been mourning his passing too. Animals are clever creatures. I never gave Bertie a thought since my son died, but I did as she said and he howled and howled. When he stopped, he lay by my feet as I sat in the chair and rested his head on my lap. The medium said Bertie is my connection to Daniel. Now, whenever I stroke his stomach, I see an outline of Daniel's face on the dog's. Just for a split second, but it's clear as water, it's like he's with me. I reach out to touch him, and then the apparition of Daniel's face is gone, there's nothing there, just dear old Bertie.'

Jessie's jaw dropped. 'Doesn't it scare you? I did read that the writer Arthur Conan Doyle communicates with the other world – he started doing so before the death of his son – and bereaved women are turning to these mystics for comfort. If we believe in heaven and Jesus, there surely must be an afterlife. I can see it would be a comfort for you to have a message from your Daniel.'

The companion leaned in towards Jessie. 'That was how her Daniel liked to be touched as a babe, to have his tummy rubbed, just like she said. Now how would the spiritualist know that?'

Jessie had no answer. Distraught bereaved families, rational men and women, were turning to spiritualists for solace. It lifted their grief to have *words* from their dead sons told to them.

The vicar and Jane were at the back of the church talking to a young woman she did not recognise with a young boy. Jane Rumbelow appeared more cheered than her usual downcast demeanour. She walked along the aisle and took her place at the front pew. Jessie leant towards Jack. 'This is a surprise. Mrs Rumbelow rarely attends church since her Piers died. I wonder what brings her here today.'

She jerked her head back as the vicar's wife moved along the pew and the woman and boy sat alongside her. The pews were soon filled. Magnolia and David Fellowes were joined by Aggie. Since Magnolia wed David, her flamboyant taste in dresses had become less showy, while Aggie retained her extravagant flair; this was toned down for the church service, with only the white feather in her black hat, matching the white buttons on her jacket, a sign of her individual eye-catching style, while Magnolia opted for a smart matching tweed jacket and skirt with a cream blouse and dainty pearl buttons.

Sarah, Ada and Alfie took their places in the second row from the front, followed by Maria, while Leslie remained at the station master's house with the housekeeper, Betty, who had offered to keep an eye on Joey too, saying the boys could play together while she prepared lunch. Beatrice was on duty at the hospital, but Lady Appleby, dressed elegantly in a dark suit with a fox fur collar, arrived and took her place in front of the Sawards.

Harry took his seat with his family just before the vicar stepped to the front. He raised his hands and waited for the chattering congregation to quieten. He welcomed them on this momentous day, urging them not to feel forsaken by God, saying the Almighty gives life and knows the pain of personal sacrifice as he gave up Jesus Christ.

The worshippers were invited to stand as Alfie, as organ-ist, belted out, 'Abide With Me'. Just as it finished and the congregation was seated again, the church door creaked open and in walked a woman and a gentleman.

All eyes were fixed on Kitty who held herself bravely, her head high and her eyes fixed forward. She had trem-bled outside the church for half an hour feeling too anxious to hear the vicar's address, but George had gently coaxed her to go inside. She was dressed in a smart new outfit, a dark green dress under a black jacket. She stood alongside George Perryman, who took her elbow and gave her a look of encouragement, guiding her along the aisle, swaying from the ball of one foot to the other with his rolling gait. Her eyes stared directly ahead as they made their way to the front of the church, avoiding the curious glances as she passed. When she reached the front, Lady Appleby stepped out of her pew and invited Kitty and George to join her. Kitty appeared unsure, but George nodded for her to take her seat. She smiled meekly and took her place between the solicitor and Lady Appleby, nodding to Jessie as she did so.

Jessie nudged Jack and whispered in his ear, 'Poor Kitty, her family has been through a tough time. I hope she isn't given bad news.'

The service continued without further incident. After two more hymns and prayers, the vicar stepped into the pulpit and waited for a hushed silence. His eyes fixed on his wife and the young woman and child in front of him and he smiled.

He told the congregation. 'I see before me a church filled with heartache and loss, a sacrifice my dear wife, Jane, and I share with you. A day never passes when we wish we could turn back the clock to before the war and have our husbands, fathers, sons and brothers back with us. Some may question if the price paid was too high for the freedom we have today, but there can be no doubt it was worth it as freedom is price-less, and one hopes that our future generations will be told of the sacrifices made, the scars and terrible disabilities and amputations some are left with. For some here, the anguish of not knowing if their man is dead or alive continues. I offer heartfelt prayers for the families in our midst who suffer every day of their lives.'

Kitty shuffled uncomfortably at this and dabbed her eyes with a handkerchief. The vicar paused and muffled sobs could be heard from the congregation.

He continued, 'I'm so sorry that my words bring dis-tress. This afternoon we will hear from the chaplain who has returned from Gallipoli with news about the fate of the missing King's men with the Sandringham Company. I shall be there to offer spiritual comfort. This has always been a strong and united community and our King and Queen have done their utmost to care for families who serve them on the estate.'

Kitty shook her head and bit her lip. Jessie could hardly blame her anger at hearing this as she had been forced out of her tied cottage by the estate's agent – just for being a woman.

Jessie observed fretful expressions on the faces of some parishioners, some placing a comforting arm around the person next to them.

The vicar raised his voice. 'Our Lord works in mysterious ways. He takes from us, but he also gives to us. I would like to share with you a blessing that recently came our way.'

He glanced in his wife's direction again and met her gaze. She tilted her head slightly and the vicar continued, his voice becoming emotional. 'You will have noticed that my wife is accompanied by a young lady and a child today. They are newly discovered members of our family who have moved into the vicarage. It was a surprise to us to learn that our son Piers had a son with the woman over there, Ruby. The boy next to her is our grandson. We are overjoyed and give thanks to the Lord for giving us this unexpected gift. He is called Piers too, after his father.'

The air filled with gasps. 'Your reaction is to be expected. It was a great surprise to us. Although Piers was not married, he had a loving union with Ruby. Their friendship may seem unusual to some, it developed while he was at Cambridge and she cleaned his room. He saw something special in Ruby, and now we have got to know her, we see it too. Ruby and her son, our dear grandson, are now part of our lives. We welcome them with open arms and I ask that you welcome them here too, as we have done.'

Jessie's chin dropped to the floor and the church filled with astonished exclamations. The woman behind her muttered, 'I can't believe what I just heard. The child is well, a . . .'

The vicar raised his arm. 'Yes, I know what you are thinking. The boy was born out of wedlock. I ask you to question your consciences before you make hasty judgements. The Lord tells us to love our neighbour as ourselves, he tells us that if we forgive others, then he will forgive us our sins. How many people here can truly say they have never committed a sin?

'I ask you to show kindness and compassion to Ruby, who is recently bereaved of her mother and came to us hoping we would understand and not show her the door. Piers was conceived through love and I hope you will not judge her harshly, for in doing so you also judge my son. You only have to look at young Piers's face to see how alike it is to our son's. I ask you to open your hearts and minds and welcome them here in Wolferton. Ask yourselves this, would you not do the same if you were in our shoes?'

When he finished speaking there was an uncomfortable silence. Jessie said, 'I was not expecting to hear that. It must have taken some courage for the vicar to speak so forthrightly. I never realised what kind of man John Rumbelow is until today, a man of courage.'

Jack agreed. 'What a shock for everyone to hear this. He is right to say how easy it is to judge.'

'We felt that way with Maria at first, but now she and her family are part of our family, and she has fitted in well with the community. Given time, I'm sure the same will happen for Ruby.'

Chapter Eighteen

The mood in the meeting room was sombre. It was filling up with estate workers and their families, their faces tired but showing determined expressions, as the Sawards arrived. Reverend Rumbelow was already at the front of the room talking to another vicar, a slender man with a gentlemanly air about him and twinkling eyes. He wore a monocle on one eye and had a benevolent expression. Lady Appleby was seated on the front row with George and Kitty. They were joined by Harry and Maria on the two spare seats at the front, while Jack and Jessie sat themselves on the row behind.

As a sergeant of the Sandringham Company, Harry had thoroughly enjoyed attending training camps in lieu of his holidays, such was his dedication to King and country. His age went against him when it came to volunteering; at the age of fifty-six he was too old. A day never passed when he didn't think of his dear friend, Captain Frank Beck, the Sandringham land agent who was two years younger than him. He had bravely insisted on leading his men despite his age and being asked to by the King not to go. He too was missing with the rest of the Sandringham Company.

There was a heavy sombre atmosphere in the hall and soon every seat was taken, with those arriving last having to stand at the back. The group comprised of many of the people who had been at the church that morning. Some had already received the dreaded telegram announcing the death of their husband, son or male relative and were there to support a relative or friend whose loved one's fate had still not been officially declared. Some already had tears in their eyes.

On their way to the meeting room Harry had recounted the bravery of Reverend Pierrepont Edwards. Jessie was astounded to hear that he known as the Fighting Parson, and queried how this came about.

'He used to be a curate in an East End mission before the war, and it was rumoured he was not afraid to use his fists to settle a political disagreement. He was a staunch supporter of the Conservative Party and was ready to defend his political beliefs with both actions and words during meetings and marches.'

Jessie narrowed her eyes and leant forward to scrutinise the chaplain with her father's words at the forefront of her mind. She could only see a gentle and modest countenance, which belied the courage and spirit of God's man beneath his black cloth.

He had sailed to Gallipoli with his battalion from the East Anglian Division with the 5th Norfolks and Sandringham Company and was present when the terrible battles claimed the lives of hundreds of young, fit men.

Jack acknowledged Harry's account. 'Yes, this is a man of great character who speaks his own mind. You do know he doesn't approve of women wearing trousers in public and ignores them.'

Jessie covered her mouth to conceal a chuckle. 'My land army days may be at an end, but that is a rather antiquated view, considering how women did men's work during the war.'

Families were distraught that the fate of many unaccounted for remained a mystery more than four years after the last battle they were known to have fought in. This was intensified when General Ian Hamilton, who led the Mediterranean Expeditionary Force, recounted by way of explanation, 'In the course of the flight . . . there happened a very mysterious thing. Amongst these ardent souls was part of a fine company enlisted from the King's Sandringham Estate. Nothing more was ever seen or heard of any of them. They charged into the forest and were lost to sight or sound. Not one of them ever came back.'

Jessie knew that good news could not be expected, but answers were needed and would come soon.

Lady Charlotte Knollys suddenly entered the meeting room and the Reverend Pierrepont Edwards walked forward to greet her, offering his arm for her to take. Everyone knew she was there as Queen Alexandra's eyes and ears as her trusted private secretary, the first woman to ever hold this position, despite her own advancing years, being in her eighties. Harry rose and led her to reserved seating at the front, alongside Lady Appleby.

The station master positioned himself at the front of the hall and faced the audience. He was taller and stouter than their guest, and his voice carried well as he spoke across the hushed room as he introduced Reverend Pierrepont Edwards.

'This is no ordinary parson. He is the bravest man of God I know, he was awarded the Military Cross for his bravery, going out to no-man's land under heavy enemy fire to rescue wounded soldiers.'

Harry read from his citation, which described how the fearless chaplain had volunteered to collect the wounded who had been out all night.

The Reverend Pierrepont Edwards raised his arm. 'That's enough about me, Mr Saward. I am here to tell these people of my discovery in Gallipoli.'

Choked sobs could be heard from the assembled audience. He cleared his throat and informed them of his return to the Turkish peninsula as officer in charge of the War Graves Commission Registration Unit in Gallipoli; this was permitted under the terms of armistice with Turkey, which enabled the British Army to revisit the battlefield in search of the missing men, or any identifiable items.

He spoke softly, looking directly at the anxious faces that stared intently at him. 'It is only now I can speak of this, having submitted my official report on my findings to King George and Queen Alexandra, who I assure you have been persistent in their demand for answers about the missing estate families.'

An angry woman from the back called out, 'Tell us what yer know. We've been waiting long enough.'

The chaplain ignored the heckling and continued. 'It's with great sadness I have to tell you . . . the search after the war led to the discovery of a Norfolk's regimental cap badge from under the sand. While searching for similar identifiable objects – a shoulder title, military equipment with names stamped or scratched into them – I'm afraid the remains of a number of soldiers were discovered.'

Kitty leapt up. She cried, 'What do yer mean, *remains*? Was one of them my Frank's?'

Another woman stood up. 'And my Ezra? Can you tell me if his remains were among 'em. I want to know where his body is. I can't take any more of this.'

Three more distraught women rose. Before they could speak, the chaplain raised his arm. 'Please. Let me finish. It grieves me to say that we cannot say for sure whose remains have been found. What we did find was scattered over an area of a square mile around the ruins of a small farm. The search continues.'

Lady Appleby caught his eye. 'May I ask a question? Can you tell us how many bodies you have found?'

'I believe to date there are one hundred and eighty bodies.'

The cries and wails from broken-hearted families filled the room. It was a desperate heartbreaking scene. After a while the Reverend Pierrepont Edwards was asked to continue.

The vicar lowered his eyes. 'I am sorry I am the bearer of this terrible news. We hope to identify some of the bodies, but it won't be possible to identify them all. We believe one hundred and twenty-two have been identified by shoulder titles as belonging to the 5th Battalion, The Norfolk Regiment, who our Sandringham Company was with. The bodies of three officers were found, but it was impossible to identify them. We found only two identity discs with the bodies of the 5th Norfolk's, neither of them was from the Sandringham Company.

'It's a small comfort, I know, but all the remains that we recovered have been given decent burials in fenced cemeteries and their graves are marked with wooden crosses.'

'And what about those yer couldn't find? Or you can't identify?' asked an angry woman from the back of the room.

The chaplain's tone was calm. 'We believe some were taken prisoner and make up our unaccounted numbers. We shall continue with our search and enquiries until every one of them is accounted for.

Miss Knollys rose, rather unsteadily, and asked, 'What about Captain Beck? Is there any hope?'

The chaplain shook his head. 'I'm afraid not.'

∽

Kitty clung to George and sobbed. 'So that's it. I'm none the wiser. What will I tell the children? Am I to assume my Frank is dead?'

'I'm sorry, Kitty. It seems there is no hope of anything more official than this report. It was personally requested by Queen Alexandra, who is anxious to get to the truth. At the very least this means I can help you apply for a pension, if you wish. Reverend Rumbelow has offered his time with this too. I can speak to him now about it, if you would excuse me a for a moment.'

Kitty buried her face in her hands when George left her side. Women all around her were red faced, sobbing and comforting each other. She was deep in her own thoughts when she felt a tap on her shoulder and ignored it. She was in no mood to speak to anyone.

Maria's voice trembled. 'Kitty, I'm so sorry. I wish there was something I could say, or do . . .'

Kitty glanced at her. 'There's nothing anyone can do. I 'ave to carry on, Maria. That's all I can do, seeing as I have six children to fend for.'

'That must be hard. How are they all? Have they settled in their new home?'

'We are blessed in that respect, but they miss their pa, and they didn't have an easy time at the workhouse, especially my Victoria. We want our own place again.'

'That will come in good time, Kitty. You've 'ad a terrible shock. It makes sense for you stay put for now,' Maria consoled.

Kitt's eyes moistened. 'You're right, Maria. I don't know how I'll find the strength to carry on. But I will.'

'Just tell yerself these dark days won't last for ever.'

Kitty sniffled. 'I'd like to thank yer for what you and Jessie did at the workhouse, and for yer letters. I only got them the other day. I didn't mean to sound ungrateful a moment ago as we are very fortunate to be placed under the care of Mr Bell. And Mr Perryman, who brought me 'ere, is so kind to us too.'

Maria shuffled her feet. 'I'm pleased how things 'ave turned out for now. There is something else I want to say, Kitty. I want yer to know I didn't ask for yer job at Appleton House, it were offered me by Mrs Pennywick and I didn't feel I could refuse. I feel guilty about it and I'd give it back to yer tomorrow if I could.'

Kitty scoffed. 'There's no way I would go back there, after the way we was turfed out.'

Maria let the comment pass as she observed George Perryman walking towards them. 'Hello, Maria. I have a message for you from Beatrice. She asks if you can call in and see Eddie and the doctor again at your earliest convenience. Beatrice tells me Eddie has made excellent progress and can be discharged. Seeing as his mother isn't able to be there, she wondered if you could go instead.'

Maria's face broke into a huge smile. 'Discharged? Now? So soon? Why that's wonderful news.'

George agreed. 'It is excellent news. I am very happy for you both.'

Maria gushed, 'Seeing how he's taken to gardening so well, I hear there may be an opportunity coming up at Appleton House that would suit him.'

'That would be wonderful for you, Maria . . .' Kitty replied softly, turning her head away.

Maria's face crumpled, realising she had invertedly referred to Eddie filling Frank Willow's old job.

She stuttered, 'I'm so sorry, Kitty, please forgive me. Me and my big mouth. I shouldn't have said that.'

Kitty shrugged her shoulders. 'What will be will be. At least you are lucky enough to have your Eddie back in one piece.'

Maria twisted her hands in front of her. It was true she had Eddie back in one piece, but his mind needed time to heal from the atrocities he'd experienced and the terrible act that had been forced on him, the guilt hanging heavily from his shoulders. Nobody could say how long that would take, yet, she reasoned, he still had a life to live, and she vowed to make it the best.

Chapter Nineteen

Three weeks had passed since Maria learnt of Eddie's dark secret. Sharing it had helped his tortured mind come to terms with what had happened, and his recovery had progressed at such a pace that the doctor said he was well enough to return home.

Beatrice welcomed Maria as she arrived at the hospital and led her to Doctor Butterscotch's office. On their way there, Beatrice commented, 'Eddie is looking forward to seeing you, Maria. He can't wait to start afresh and talks about wanting to be the best husband to you and the best father to Joey.'

Eddie's face shone as Maria entered the room and he rose from his seat and took hold of her hand.

'Can yer believe it, Maria. I can leave today.'

Maria's eyes moistened and she embraced him. 'I'm very proud of yer, Eddie Herring. Your ma is waiting and has yer room ready. And little Joey is excited to see yer too. We've all missed you.'

The doctor made a coughing sound from behind his hand. 'Would you both like to take a seat. There are some matters we need to discuss before Eddie leaves.'

They sat where indicated and held hands tightly. Eddie fixed an adoring gaze on Maria's face while the doctor spoke. He leant back in his chair. 'I can't state strongly enough how much progress Eddie has made in the quickest time I have known. I believe this is because he could unburden himself and speak truthfully about what happened, as well as wanting desperately to return home and begin a new life with you, Maria.'

Maria felt overcome with emotion. She turned to him and spoke with tenderness. 'You've been through so much. I promise on Joey's life that I will never leave yer side. Look at me, shedding tears 'ere in front of the doctor.'

She reached for a handkerchief in her pocket. The doctor spoke gently. 'This is a safe place where anyone can feel free to unburden their emotions. I wanted to explain that the agreement for Eddie's early discharge is on condition that he continues his gardening work, which has proved so therapeutic for him, and I am told he can do this at his mother's house to start with and, in due course, on the royal estate. I have been in touch with the land agent to discuss this, and they are in agreement he can start there two days a week, on a trial basis, to see how he gets on.'

Maria clasped her hands in front of her, an expression of sheer delight on her face, while Eddie beamed. 'I'm a lucky man, thanks to you, Doctor Butterscotch.'

'All I ask in return is that you don't rush things. You will feel tired after you exert yourself and should rest then. Remember, we are here for you whenever you need us. In fact, we will be arranging a follow-up appointment. Beatrice will be in touch with you about this.'

They rose and Eddie shook the doctor's hand and thanked him profusely. Maria's lips quivered as she thanked him for giving her her old Eddie back.

Eddie and Maria linked arms and marched out of the hospital feeling on top of the world. He stopped and asked her, 'Did you mean everything you said in there? Are you sure you want to be with me, Maria?

She looked up into his face, her heart fluttering. 'Eddie Herring, what a thing to say. Of course I do. I love you more than ever. Right now you're making me go all weak at the knees again.'

He bent his face down and they kissed softly. The sound of someone whistling made them stop and look around.

'Are you too lovebirds ready for a ride 'ome then?' Old Abel was seated on his cart.

They grinned at each other and walked hand in hand over to him. Old Abel was chewing on a piece of straw. He had long white bushy sideburns and his hands were gnarled, but he had a soft heart and a fondness for the couple.

''Ello, boy,' said Abel, with a kindly smile, his eyes crinkling.

'Ello Abel,' replied Eddie. 'Thank yer for coming 'ere.'

'That's all right, me boy. Your ma is looking forward to seeing yer.'

Eddie and Maria hopped on the front of the cart and sat alongside Old Abel, their hands clenched together. Maria rested her head on Eddie's shoulder as the cart rumbled on. The ride home was slow and Old Abel reminded them his nag had been due for the slaughterhouse, and he'd bought her for a song. The nag trotted slowly back to Wolferton and they chatted amiably along the country lanes.

As Abel pulled up outside Eddie's cottage, his mother was on her knees in front of the gate, a trowel in her hand. She leapt up from her weeding and ran towards her son, her arms outstretched. Her voice was filled with emotion. 'I'm so 'appy to see yer 'ome, Eddie Herring. Oh, how I've prayed for this day.'

She flung her arms around his shoulder, her shoulders shuddering as she embraced him, her emotions welling up inside her. 'Silly me, crying like a girl.'

Eddie's shoulders shook too. His mother stepped back. 'How are you faring now, Eddie? You look a different boy from the one who left here. I'm glad to see you have that spark back in yer eyes.'

'I'm much improved, Ma. I'm sorry for the worry I put yer through, and Maria.'

'Don't be so daft,' scolded Mabel Herring. 'Come on, let's go inside. I have a nice brew waiting and some tongue sandwiches.'

Maria and Old Abel declined, allowing mother and son some time on their own, with Maria promising to look in on Eddie the following day. He took Maria aside for a moment and whispered, 'I 'aven't forgotten what I said. I'll tell Ma tonight. I'll tell 'er everything.'

'What's that you've got to tell me?' asked his mother, suddenly appearing.

'It's a long story, Ma. I'll tell you later,' he replied, walking towards the garden his mother had been tending. 'You don't 'ave to worry about the weeding. I'll see to it tomorrow.'

As Maria left the house, she smiled, as Eddie put his arm around his mother's shoulders and stepped into the house with her.

It was a short walk back to Honeysuckle Cottage and Maria's mind was full of the day's events, but as she turned a corner, she stopped in her tracks on seeing a woman on the path sobbing.

'Ruby! What's the matter? Why are you crying?'

Maria spotted a group of women walking ahead at a fast pace, their heads close together. They were laughing and turned round, giving Ruby a haughty glare before all disappearing into one of the houses.

Maria fumed. 'Did they say something to yer?'

Ruby nodded, pressing her finger against her mouth.

'I can imagine what they said, the spiteful . . .'

'You're the only one that's been kind to me. People think I'm an imposter. But I ain't. I swear to God I didn't mean to fall with child, but I don't regret it. How could I regret having a beautiful son?'

Maria's stomach tightened. She had been in the same shoes as Ruby when she arrived in Wolferton. She empathised with her anguish, but knew it would take time for her to fit in, and Ruby would have to prove her good character.

She consoled her. 'Take no notice of them, Ruby. I believe you. And as long as Mr and Mrs Rumbelow believe yer, that's all that matters. Where is Piers, by the way?'

Ruby sniffled. 'He's playing soldiers at the vicarage with some old toys they found in the attic. They used to belong to Piers. It's so good to see how settled he is already. He enjoys playing in the garden and being made a fuss of by his grandparents. They've been wonderful and can't do enough for us.'

Maria linked arms with Ruby. 'Do yer want me to walk with yer back to the vicarage?'

'Yes, I'd like that. Do you know of any jobs going? I need to do something to occupy myself. I've only done domestic

208

work, but I'm good at it. That's how I met Piers, when I was cleaning his room for Ma at the college.'

'I'll ask around for yer,' replied Maria, mulling it over. 'Did yer bring yer references with you?'

'Well, no. Do you think that will be a problem?'

'If you want to work in the royal household, if that's what yer thinking, you will need references.'

'Oh, I see. Only, I weren't officially employed by the college, it was me ma they took on, and I did her work for her when she were too unwell. Did you have references?'

'The station master vouched for me, and seeing as we are related, and the high esteem with which he is regarded in the community and with the King, that was good enough for them. I've worked 'ard to prove meself, rolling up me sleeves and knuckling down. I've kept me nose clean and given no one cause for complaint.'

'You're lucky then, not to 'ave any worries on yer shoulders.'

'I didn't say that exactly. I fret about Ma's poor health, I worry about Eddie with his troubled mind and I worry about me brother Freddie. I have a feeling he is mixed up with some troublemakers from the railway union.'

'You do have a lot on yer mind then. Please, don't you worry about me. I know how to look after meself. The vicarage is in sight, I'll be all right from here,' Ruby brightened.

'I like you, Ruby. Your worries will sort themselves out, you wait and see.'

Maria embraced the other woman and they parted company. She recalled how before she set off for work that morning, she'd found a leaflet in Freddie's pocket about

209

a railway workers' meeting that evening. She'd pleaded with him not to go, rallying support for a march, but he'd remained tight lipped and avoided her gaze.

Honeysuckle Cottage was quiet when Maria lifted the door latch and let herself in. Her mother had retired and Archie had put Joey to bed. Maria cut herself a slice of meat pie and buttered a chunk of bread before sitting down in front of the fire. Freddie had not yet returned from work, he was late again and her stomach flipped as she sensed trouble. She wrapped a shawl around her shoulders, deciding to wait up for him, worry gnawing at her.

∞

Freddie had had enough of being told what to do by his sister. Tonight, he decided, he would show them he had his own mind. He might only be seventeen, but he was big for his age and looked older and had been the man of the house for these last four years since his father died.

He fished out the leaflet from his pocket and read the words calling for railway workers to meet at the Railway Arms that evening to discuss a march they planned to hold in King's Lynn in a couple of days. He was fired up and excited at the thought of taking part. He found life in Wolferton quiet and uneventful and he yearned for adventure. His passions were stirred up at the thought of marching shoulder to shoulder with men who were taking on the railways. The thought of it made him feel strong and empowered and ready for action.

When his shift finished at the royal station he leapt on the train to King's Lynn and within forty minutes he stood outside the public house, his stomach beginning to churn. He plucked up some courage and entered the smoke-filled room and, looking around, he spotted Rufus Fagan who came over to greet him. 'So if it ain't Freddie Saward. You snuck off under Harry Saward's eyes then. Get yerself a drink and grab a seat.'

An older woman at the bar, revealing an ample cleavage, and the worst for drink, asked, 'You look like a good lad, what are you doing with them ruffians?'

Freddie's cheeks coloured. Wanting to appear important, he replied, 'It's railway work.'

She threw her head back and roared. 'Oh yeah, and my name's Queen Victoria. Just watch yerself, laddie, hanging around with the likes of Rufus Fagan. He can be nasty when he's had a few drinks. Where he goes trouble usually follows, though his ma never sees what's under her nose.'

She pointed to the landlady who was bringing over Freddie's ale. Freddie grabbed his drink and returned to Rufus and his gang. The ringleader, his mop of greasy hair like thick black tar covering his slug-like eyebrows, turned to him and said, 'I 'ope you've got a good voice on yer because we want to 'ear it loud and clear tomorrow when you shout out what we think of them railway bosses.'

Freddie's eyes showed concern. 'Oh yes, I do, but, there won't be any trouble, will there? It will be a peaceful march, won't it?'

Rufus pushed his face close up against Freddie's. He hissed, 'Are you daft, or something? What's more, you can be at the front. That will make a good picture for the paper.'

Freddie quaked. 'What do you mean, "the paper"? I can't have me picture in the paper. Harry will sack me if he sees it. I'll be at the back though, we need marchers at the back too, don't we?'

Rufus snarled, his face turning red. 'Are you trying to outsmart me?'

'No, no . . .'

Rufus staggered to the bar where his mother refilled his tankard. As Rufus turned, his arm knocked into the man behind him and his drink went flying. Suddenly Rufus's gang circled the man, who was wearing khaki, a soldier who had re-enlisted after the war and was celebrating being home on leave.

He held his hands up in the air in an attempt to calm the situation and caught Freddie's eye, pleading for help. Unable to stand by and do nothing, Freddie yelled, 'Stop it. Please. Stop it. It were an accident. You can see he's a soldier on leave. Just let 'im go.'

Rufus sniggered. 'So yer 'ave got a voice on yer then. That were no accident, was it boys?'

'That weren't,' chorused Fagan's mob and laid into the soldier, who vanished as the other men piled on him.

Freddie's heart pounded as he stared incredulously around the bar at the handful of customers who turned their backs on the unprovoked assault. The woman at the bar tilted her head towards the door, indicating Freddie should make a hasty exit. He saw blood on the floor and fled, feeling a wave of nausea rise within him, vowing never to get involved with the union again. He ran a few yards down the road and his stomach heaved, bringing up vomit. Tears streamed down his cheeks as he chided himself for being so stupid. He tidied his appearance up as much as possible so as not to arouse suspicion when he stepped off the train at Wolferton.

Freddie was still shaking when he arrived home. Maria had dozed off, but her eyes flickered open as soon as she heard the door open. He called out *good night* before she could question him and ran straight up the stairs and flung himself onto his bed, thumping his fists into the pillow, crying, 'I 'ope they didn't kill the man. Please let 'im be all right.'

Chapter Twenty

The following day Mrs Watson and Cook's heads were locked together, poring over menus, when Maria arrived for work. Freddie had left earlier than usual. Over breakfast, Archie asked Maria, 'Do yer know if Freddie were all right last night when he came in?'

'I didn't really see. He came in and disappeared straight to his bed. I thought it was because he were tired. Why do yer ask?'

'I thought I 'eard him crying and it woke me up. When I asked what the matter was, he said, "Nothing" and told me to get back to sleep.'

Archie's comments made Maria uneasy and she couldn't get them out of her head, on top of her worries about her mother and Eddie.

She was relieved Mrs Watson didn't notice how pre-occupied she was when she announced, 'Her Majesty has arranged a small gathering here this afternoon to help widows with their pension forms. She would like us to prepare afternoon tea for a party of eight in the yellow drawing room, so we need to get started sharpish.'

'Shall I go through and give it a good dusting again?' offered Maria. 'It's such a pretty room. I can clean the table and arrange the napkins and cutlery. We need to have space for the china too. Which china do you suggest we use?'

Miss Jensen entered the kitchen at that moment. 'I can answer that question. Her Majesty would like the white Meissen tea set with gold gild frilly edging and hand-painted flowers.'

'Yes, Miss Jensen,' Cook replied coolly. 'You needn't bother yourself with domestic matters here, everything is in hand. You might see we do things differently here, but Her Majesty will find it is all to her liking.'

Maria and Mrs Watson stared open mouthed at Cook's stern gaze, which was fixed on Miss Jensen's face, the earlier admonishment from Queen Maud to the housekeeper ringing in her ears. The two women stared each other for a moment, both glaring and challenging the other to speak.

Miss Jensen straightened her back. 'That is very good to know. That bread in the oven smells very good. May I take the menu for Her Majesty to approve?'

Mrs Watson handed the menu to her. It included dainty sandwiches with fillings, including fresh chopped egg with cress, cucumber from the greenhouse, fresh-baked gammon and tongue, grated cheese mixed with cream, celery and nuts, and some sweet treats from Mrs Beeton's book, including a blancmange which had by luck been made the night before so it would set in time, fluffy jam puffs, fruit scones and a walnut sponge. Miss Jensen glanced over it quickly, nodded approvingly and swept out of the kitchen.

'I bet her ears are burning now. Honestly, doesn't she see how much extra work has been landed on us without notice? I ain't scared to say me piece,' Cook proclaimed.

'We can see that, you have a nerve, but you need to watch it so you don't land us all in trouble. We have to make a show of getting on. You have a point though. Our hands are more than full, with lunch to see to as well,' Mrs Watson retorted.

She turned to Maria. 'Can you help Cook today? I'll see to laying out the room and will call you when I need a hand moving furniture around. It's going to be all hands on deck today.'

Maria grimaced. Baking was her least favourite task. However hard she tried her scones and pastries never melted in the mouth as they did when her mother or Betty made them. Cook dismissed her concerns with a friendly smile, telling her she simply needed more practice.

Maria rolled up her sleeves. 'Do we know who is expected?'

'The good and the worthy and let's hope some good comes from it to 'elp them widows,' Cook muttered.

Mrs Watson butted in. 'From what I've been told, as well as Her Majesty and Miss Jensen, we can expect Lady Appleby and Mr Perryman, the vicar and his wife, Ada and Magnolia. Aggie was invited too, but is preparing for her next dance class.'

Maria raised her chin. 'If anyone can do some good, these folk can. And God knows those poor women need all the 'elp they can get.'

'That's very true. Maria, if you can get the flour out of the pantry, Cook will give you the scone recipe.'

Elbows flapped and flour flew in the air as Maria set to work under Cook's careful instructions. The kitchen was filled with the aroma of sweet smelling bakes that were brought out of the oven, golden topped and soft to the touch.

216

The bread was sliced thinly, the crusts removed, and filled. With the cakes laid out alongside them on the table, and a hasty, early luncheon finished, Maria glanced at the kitchen clock. The front doorbell rang as it struck two o'clock.

Miss Jensen stepped into the hall and invited their guests into the yellow drawing room. A thin autumnal glow flickered through the large window that looked across the lawn, which was covered with confetti-like russet and gold fallen leaves.

The room filled with guests and echoed with polite chatter. Maria paced the hall outside, curious to know what was being said, and making an excuse to Mrs Watson that the flower arrangement in the hall needed some adjustments.

She pressed her ear against the door and heard Reverend Rumbelow speaking in a slightly raised voice. His tone had a hint of suppressed anger.

'I've officiated at three weddings recently of widows with young children they couldn't afford to feed and clothe, and not a smile on their faces.'

Queen Maud queried, 'Really? And why would that be?'

The vicar replied, 'These women didn't marry for love. They married men they were not suited to for convenience. If they were fortunate, they could make the best of their situation, but others were badly treated by husbands who made it clear to them they should count themselves lucky for being given a roof over their heads.'

Maria leapt back when the housekeeper snapped. 'What do you think you are doing? How dare you eavesdrop on private conversations in the royal household? I have a good mind to report you.'

Maria's chest tightened. 'Please, Mrs Watson. Please don't do that.'

She returned to the kitchen sharpish. A moment later, the bell from the drawing room was rung, their cue for the tea to be prepared.

Mrs Watson warned Maria sternly. 'If you ever do anything like that again, I won't be reporting you; I will be giving you your cards. Do you understand?'

'Thank yer, Mrs Watson. I swear it won't 'appen again. Shall I go in and ask what they want?'

'Very well. But come back here straightaway, and keep your nose out of other people's business.'

Queen Maud was pacing the room, her arms behind her back, when Maria knocked on the door and entered.

'We are ready for our refreshments. We have a real thirst following our discussions, so please make sure there is plenty of tea. Perhaps some ginger beer and lemonade too?'

Maria curtseyed and left the room, then together with Mrs Watson, they returned with the refreshments on a trolley.

Maria saw the housekeeper's ears prick up as they poured tea, catching the tail end of a conversation between Lady Appleby and Mr Perryman. She was saying, 'I was appalled to hear what the Reverend Rumbelow just said. I did wonder why a pretty young girl in her twenties would want to marry old farmer Piggott; he is well into his seventies.'

The solicitor retorted, 'I hear he works her hard on the land and is not kind to her young ones. Sadly, there is nothing we can do. In the eyes of the law they are man and wife. Yes, it's troubling that these poor women are so desperate for security that they will succumb to this.'

'Poor sods,' mumbled Mrs Watson, when they were back in the kitchen. 'You know, a war widow with three kiddies, is given a pension of twenty-six shillings and three pence, less than the weekly wage of a working man. I read it in the papers, and to think they've lost a husband and father and have to manage on their own. With pensions held up, it's no wonder they go orf and marry any Tom, Dick or Harry who offers them a home.'

Maria shuddered as Cook preached, 'There are them that try and take advantage. I 'eard the other day of one greedy woman who forged her widow's pension papers from four to fourteen, then 'ad the cheek to say she knew nothing about it. Serves her right for getting caught and going up before the beak.'

Mrs Watson shook her head. 'I don't know how they have the nerve. There are those too who fraudulently took a widow's pension without declaring they remarried, while others have to carry on without a farthing to their name. It ain't right.'

Maria commented, 'Ma was telling me the other day about the widow of Corporal Boxford who was on a pension of twenty-six shillings a week for herself and her little 'un, while she were married to another man at the same time, while 'onest women who need it are going without.'

An hour later, the bell rang in the kitchen again. Mrs Watson instructed Maria to answer it. 'I expect they want more tea.'

Maria knocked on the door tentatively and stepped in. Miss Jensen asked her to remove the dirty crockery and bring in more tea. Her ears pricked at mention of Ruby's name. A smiling Mrs Rumbelow was seated next to Queen Maud, telling her about her newly acquainted grandson. 'It was quite a surprise, I can tell you.'

The queen dabbed the corner of her mouth with her napkin. 'The child and mother are indeed fortunate to have you and your husband take them under your roof. What I have seen in Denmark, and is common here, is that women have frequently been taken advantage of. The man then shows no regard for the girl or the child that he helped bring into the world. I congratulate you both for your compassion.'

'When it's your own flesh and blood, and your son has been taken from you, it's the only choice there is,' said Mrs Rumbelow.

'Exactly. But for those whose lives are destroyed by the selfish gratification of men, and no guardian angel such as yourself and your husband, what chance do they stand? I am hoping that the women we encounter in that situation on the royal estate will take up training at the needlework school my dear mother founded, and that this will enable them to be sufficiently skilled to seek employment.'

The vicar's wife beamed. 'That is just splendid. Your visit is most timely, Your Majesty. During the war, women and girls at the needlework school knitted socks and produced anything that was needed. Their embroidery is just divine. It was used on the backs of chairs made by our craftsmen trained at the technical school, though this was disbanded during the war.'

The queen listened with interest. 'There is so much talent around us. So many lives have been broken and we owe it to them to pick up the pieces again. I know it won't be easy, but

I feel the pain of our families and the men they lost. What can be done to help their widows and orphaned children?'

Maria's interest was sparked as she hovered by the queen carrying a handful of dirty plates. The words tumbled out of her mouth before she could stop them. 'Please 'elp Kitty if yer can, Yer Majesty. Excuse me for speaking out, but you know Kitty Willow and her little 'uns, she used to work 'ere. They've had a terrible time at the workhouse, and though she 'as been taken in by Mr Perryman's kind uncle, she is very anxious as she still has no news about her Frank.'

Miss Jensen stepped forward and glared at Maria. 'Miss Saward, you should be aware by now that the correct proto-col demands that you wait for the Queen to speak to you . . .'

Queen Maud raised her hand. 'That is quite all right. This is an informal gathering and how can I help people unless they approach me directly?'

Maria gushed, 'I'm sorry if I spoke out of turn, Yer Majesty.'

'Just "ma'am" is sufficient,' replied Queen Maud, with a slight smile.

Maria tensed and fumbled with her fingers, kicking herself for her faux pas in front of the Queen's gatekeeper.

Queen Maud put her at her ease. 'We are aware of Mrs Willow's circumstances. Mr Perryman has kept me abreast of her situation. I wish I could offer an answer or words of comfort, it really is a distressing matter.'

Maria bent a knee and dipped slightly. 'Thank you, ma'am. I am 'eartened to 'ear how much you care. Mr Perryman and his uncle are good men and the Willows are most fortunate in that respect.'

'Thank you for your comment, Miss Saward. It would appear the Willow family have a good friend in you. Our meeting has drawn to a close now.'

The Queen rose and thanked her guests for attending. 'It has been a most informative meeting and I am encouraged and grateful to have your support. Let's go forth now and do all we can for our women.'

∞

Maria cycled over to Eddie's house after work thankful her eavesdropping hadn't landed her with a caution for misconduct. As she braked by the gate to the cottage, she paused to admire the garden. There wasn't a weed in sight.

Mabel greeted Maria with a smile. 'You're welcome to come in, but Eddie is sleeping. He tires easily and was exhausted when he finished digging over the vegetable plot at the back.'

'I better get back home, but do give Eddie my love and tell him I stopped by. He's done so much work today, no wonder he's worn out. The doctor said he would be. He said we 'ave to take one day at a time, Mabel, and today it looks like Eddie has taken several huge strides.'

∞

As Maria reached home she felt a sense of dread in the pit of her stomach. A man's black bicycle was propped against the hedge and she recognised it instantly as belonging to Police

Constable Rickett. Had something happened to Ma? To Joey? To either of her brothers?

She burst through the back door and ran into the kitchen. Ruth sat in an armchair, a shawl wrapped around her shoulders and a worried look on her face. The constable had a small notebook and pencil in his hands and was making notes. Freddie stood next to the constable, his head hanging low. He shuffled from foot to foot, avoiding his mother's gaze and biting his lip.

Ruth asked him with her soft weary voice. 'Tell me, Freddie, is it true what the constable says?'

He remained silent, staring down at the floor.

Maria's chest was pounding as she looked at them all. 'What 'ave yer done, Freddie? What's all this about?'

Ruth answered. 'He's been fighting. That's what he's been up to with them railway union fellas. The officer says Freddie took a glass to a soldier for no good reason and he's in 'ospital and could lose an eye.'

Maria cried, 'But that's terrible. Freddie. I can't believe it. When did this 'appen?'

'Last night,' Ruth replied. 'I'm so ashamed, Freddie. You've brought shame on the Saward name.'

Freddie clenched his fists, speaking at the top of his voice. 'I didn't do it. I swear on me life. I swear on Joey's life. I didn't do it. I'm innocent.'

The constable referred to his notebook. 'There's no need to raise your voice. Were you not at the Railway Arms last night with Rufus Fagan and his associates?'

Freddie replied lamely, 'I was, it's true to say I were there. But that's all I'm guilty of.'

Maria fumed. 'I can't believe me ears. What were you doing there with that lot? I warned yer to stay away from them.'

223

'I wish I had,' mumbled Freddie. 'But I swear I never laid a finger on the soldier. It were Rufus. I told him to stop, but he ignored me.'

The constable grunted. 'Do you have a witness that can verify your account?'

Freddie scratched his head, his eyes fearful. 'There were a lady at the bar who saw it all, but I don't know 'er name. There's the landlady too, and there were other customers. Maybe one of them will speak up.'

'Oh yes, and pigs will fly before the landlady says anything against her son and the regulars at the Railway Arms will speak out against him and his thugs. They're too scared of them, but we intend to crack down on their law-breaking activities.'

'Can I ask, how bad is the soldier? I wanted to 'elp, I really did.'

'It's not good. When he is well enough we will question him and hope he can recall who attacked him.'

Relieved, Freddie blurted, 'So he's gonna live then? I'm so glad to 'ear that.'

'He is,' the officer confirmed. 'But no thanks to you from what I have heard.'

Freddie's expression changed from desperation to one of defeat. 'You must believe me, I ain't part of Rufus Fagan's crowd. I got sucked into seeing them through me own stupidity. I wish I'd never gone to the meeting, but they goaded me. Said I was chicken if I didn't go 'cause I was scared of Harry.'

Maria whimpered, 'Oh Freddie. You've let us all down, but, most of all, yerself.'

Freddie hung his head in shame. 'I know it. I wanted to prove I was a man, and that I don't hide behind the Saward name with its royal connections.'

'Freddie Saward. How can you say that after everything Harry's done for us? He is yer step-brother after all, and deserves your loyalty.' his mother scolded.

Maria's eyebrows drew together. 'You're only seventeen, Freddie. You're not a man yet, and you ain't like them ruffians. And Ma's right. You should remember it's thanks to Harry you have a good job with prospects. It's 'im you owe your loyalty to, not them bad 'uns.'

The constable chipped in, 'I'd like to ask Freddie how he got himself in this mess in the first place.'

Freddie spoke falteringly, rubbing the back of his neck. 'Rufus Fagan came 'ere to Wolferton Station. He put his arm around me, all friendly like, and asked me if were satisfied with my lot. A lot of the railway lads look up to him and I felt important, him talking to me.'

The constable interjected, 'We know Mr Fagan. Carry on.'

'He said he had some railway fellas 'e wanted me to meet, that they 'ad 'ad enough of living on fresh air and were planning on holding a demonstration. To be honest, I thought he 'ad a point. I didn't think it would do any 'arm to demonstrate for a fairer wage. I agree with that.

'Once I arrived at the Railway Arms I could see they were a tough lot and I felt uncomfortable. They seemed more interested in drinking than talking about the demonstration. Rufus picked on the soldier for no good reason and laid into 'im, and then 'is cronies joined in.'

Maria asked, 'So how come police are questioning you about your part in this?'

Freddie shrugged his shoulders. 'I dunno. I swear I didn't lay a finger on anyone. I'd never 'urt anyone.'

Maria nodded. 'I believe yer, Freddie. You were in the wrong place at the wrong time with the wrong crowd. What happens now, Constable Rickett? You've heard what Freddie said, do you think he's innocent, knowing what Rufus Fagan and his cronies are like?'

The constable snapped his notebook shut. 'That might be the case, but seeing as his name has been put forward as the perpetrator, he remains under police investigation. We also have a witness.'

Freddie shook. 'That can't be true. I swear on Ma's life.'

The constable raised his chin and spoke sternly. 'I advise you, Freddie Saward, to stay away from the Railway Arms for now. A decision on further action will be made later by my superiors.'

Freddie grabbed Maria's arm, pleading, 'None of it's true. I swear! You gotta believe me.'

Maria thought for a moment, then asked the constable. 'Do we need to inform Harry about this right now? I mean, you won't say anything yet, will yer, not until you've gathered all yer evidence, just in case no charges are pressed against Freddie?'

The policeman pondered. 'Mr Saward is a highly esteemed member of this community and I couldn't tell him a lie or not disclose information I felt was of importance. However, I anticipate it will take a week for police to speak to everyone. We will have a clearer idea then about who is being charged. If Freddie is among them I'll have no choice but to inform Harry, if word doesn't reach him before then.'

Freddie said nervously, 'Thank you, Constable Rickett. I give yer me word I won't have any more to do with that crowd. All they've done is get me into trouble.'

'I'm glad to hear it. I'll be on my way,' the policeman said.

Constable Rickett took a few steps towards the door. Maria followed. 'Thank yer for not saying anything to Harry for now. Only, I worry Freddie might lose his job. He wouldn't want to upset Harry.'

The policeman replied sternly, 'He should have thought of that before. There are plenty of men back from war who would take his job willingly, given the chance.'

After the constable had gone, Maria glanced with concern at her mother. She seemed even frailer and the upset appeared to have worsened her condition. Her eyes were sunken and she struggled to cough, pressing her clasped hand across her chest.

Maria whimpered under her breath, 'Oh Freddie, you stupid boy. What have you gone and done? If word of this gets out, we're finished.'

At that moment, Ruth gasped and bent over, clutching her chest, her breathing rapid.

Freddie whimpered, 'I'm sorry, Ma. I'd do anything to undo it.'

Chapter Twenty-One

The following morning Kitty appeared withdrawn as she plumped the pillow behind Mrs Bell's head and smoothed down the bedcovers. She avoided Mrs Bell's direct gaze, and her reserved manner did not go unnoticed.

'I was sorry to hear about the meeting in Wolferton. I can't imagine how unsettling it is for you to not know what happened to your husband.'

'Maybe one day someone will find out the truth. I 'ave to carry on, I 'ave the children to think about.'

Mrs Bell picked up a letter from the side of her bed. 'It appears Lucinda is enjoying city life and plans to stay on a while. I apologise for her sharpness, it can't be pleasant for you, but I'm sure she doesn't mean to be unkind.'

Kitty said nothing. Mrs Bell continued, 'I hope her absence will help you feel more at ease here. You can be assured we are very happy to have you and your family under our roof. I enjoy hearing the children's voices. Pip is handy around the house, I'm told, and it is a real pleasure to have Victoria read to me. She tells me she wants to be a teacher.'

'Yes, ma'am. That's right. Some afternoons Victoria returns to the workhouse when she has finished school and helps the young 'uns with their reading. She impressed Mrs Fairbairn with her quick learning. She said Victoria has the patience and good understanding of children's ways, being an older sister to her brothers and sisters, and would be of great assistance.'

Mrs Bell enthused. 'Victoria will make a wonderful teacher one day and it is a credit to her nature that she can face returning to the workhouse after what happened to her. I hear Pip is obliging too and helps with chopping up wood and bringing in coal. As for the younger ones? Well, I may see less of them, but I enjoy hearing their laughter. They're bringing some life to this big house.'

Kitty's face brightened. 'That's very kind of you to say, ma'am.'

'On another matter, I fear my hair is somewhat tangled under this mob cap. You have such a gentle touch and I would like you to brush it for me. My hair used to be my crowning glory. It reached down to my waist and was thick and wavy and I would dress it with the prettiest ribbons.'

'Of course, ma'am, but you still have lovely hair. I wonder if you would like to try stretching your legs a little, take a few steps towards the dressing table and sit there for a change, instead of having your hair brushed in bed.'

Mrs Bell thought for a moment. 'Do you know, I think I would like that. The doctor has encouraged me to try to move about a bit, but I feel such a feeble fool. I'm worried I will fall again and break my leg. If I can lean on you and have my walking stick for support, I should be able to manage it. I'm told my bones are brittle and I don't have strong muscles in my legs. There was a time I could walk for miles through the country lanes, but those days are long gone.'

Kitty pushed the bedding away and her mistress shuffled her legs across the side of the bed. Kitty placed her feet in her slippers and helped her into a white satin dressing gown decorated with embroidered flowers. Kitty stroked her fingers across the fabric and marvelled at its softness.

'My husband brought this for me from China. He used to be a merchant and would recount many exciting stories about his travels. It's rather beautiful, isn't it? I think of him every time I wear it.'

'Yes, it's very beautiful. May I ask, what happened to him?'

'He died in the South China Sea, during a terrible storm, twenty years ago. His ship, *The Verity*, hit a rock and, it saddens me greatly to say, his body was never found. Some fragments of the ship were discovered the following week by a passing vessel that identified it. So you see, Kitty, we have suffered the same in that respect.'

Mrs Bell carefully got up from the bed and steadied herself. Kitty gripped her left arm tightly while her sturdy walking stick gave her the support she needed on her right side. She hobbled tentatively, shuffling a few inches, her confidence growing. The dressing table was a few feet away, and when she reached it, Mrs Bell heaved a sigh of relief. She smiled back at her reflection in the mirror and passed the hairbrush to Kitty. It was made from engraved silver and was placed neatly next to a matching comb and hand mirror.

Kitty removed the white mob cap that kept her mistress's hair neatly tucked away. It was very fine silvery grey and flowed down the full length of her back like a sheet. She gently stroked the brush through the soft strands, imagining how lush it would have been in her younger days. 'I'm sorry to hear of your loss, ma'am. I didn't know you had suffered the same way. I find it so hard not knowing, not even after our meeting in Wolferton, and not having a body to lay in a grave that I can visit with flowers.'

Mrs Bell turned to face Kitty and pressed a hand to hers where it rested on her shoulder. 'That's exactly how I feel. I felt my husband's loss deeply. If only he had listened. I pleaded with him not to go on that last trip. He enjoyed the thrill of life on the sea and promised me it would be his last. Alas, those words proved to be true, but for reasons we did not anticipate.'

Kitty's attention was distracted by raised voices from outside. Mrs Bell heard the noise too. 'I wonder who is causing such a disturbance? It's usually as quiet as a monk's abbey here. Would you be a dear and go and look?'

Kitty peeped through the net curtains, her hand flying to her mouth at what she saw. Standing on the pavement opposite were two men having a heated exchange.

'Who is it? What is all the fuss about.'

Kitty stepped back from the window. A cold shiver ran down her spine. 'It's him. Mr Mumbles. 'E's with another man and looking up at the 'ouse.'

'How dare he! That man has no business here. I shall be sure to inform Josiah of this,' declared Mrs Bell.

After a moment the men walked off, leaving Kitty in a state of panic, asking herself *Is he after Victoria?*

∽

Miss Jensen pointed to a corner of Queen Maud's drawing room. 'Are you able to clear the newspapers away, Maria?

And afterwards, the flowers need replenishing. But it appears you are in a world of your own today.'

Maria didn't hear a word of Miss Jensen's instructions, despite her speaking louder than usual to gain her attention. Maria was rooted to the spot, holding the latest edition of *Lynn Advertiser*. A headline screeched at her, 'Royal Station Master's Relative Questioned by Police over Attack on Soldier'.

A burning sensation rippled through her as she realised the headline must be referring to Freddie. She shoved the paper in with some other rubbish she was cleaning away, and apologised to Miss Jensen for her absent-mindedness.

Maria's mind was in turmoil. There was no doubt that Harry would now hear what was going on. It would break her mother's heart and she cursed Freddie for the shame he was bringing to the Saward name.

Mrs Watson entered the room looking bothered. 'I thought I heard raised voices and came in to see everything was in order.'

To Maria's relief Miss Jensen made no reference to her absent-mindedness, but her ears pricked up at her unexpected announcement. 'Her Majesty will not require luncheon here tomorrow. She has an early appointment at the workhouse where she will be officiating at the opening of a new hospital wing and refreshments will be provided there.'

'Why that's where Kitty and her young 'uns went after leaving 'ere,' Maria said.

Miss Jensen interrupted. 'Yes, Her Majesty is aware and will enquire after their well-being. She is stepping in in place of her mother who is feeling under the weather.'

Maria was left to complete her tasks when a voice from behind caught her by surprise. 'It's a lovely morning, isn't it?'

Queen Maud smiled at her warmly. She was wearing a lilac dress with a straight skirt, the high neck and sleeves edged with a cream lace collar and cuffs. Like her mother, strings of pearls adorned her chest, and large pearl earrings dangled from her lobes.

Maria bobbed a knee. 'Pardon me, ma'am. I am almost finished, but can come back later if you wish.'

'I would like to ask how you are settling in, Miss Saward, and your own circumstances? I know you came highly commended by the Big House and are related to the royal station master. Are you married with a family?'

Maria shifted from one foot to the other uncomfortably, her eyes downcast. 'In truth, the answer is no, and yes, in that order.'

Queen Maud raised an eyebrow. 'I'm afraid I do not understand what you are saying. You mean, you have a child, but not within marriage?'

Maria remained tight-lipped, avoiding her direct gaze. The Queen spoke softly. 'Please do not think I will judge you for a moment. I helped many women in Denmark during the war who found themselves in your situation, if my assumption is correct.'

Maria bit her lip and nodded. With some gentle prompting from the queen, she told her everything – how Walter Jugg forced himself on her, how she turned to the royal station master for help when she was desperate, the kindness extended towards her by Harry and his family. She told the Queen about her love for Eddie, who she was going to marry, and finally described his struggles to overcome his tormented mind, his fear of loud crashing sounds that made him want to hide, and the flashbacks to the horrors he witnessed on the battlefield.

'My dear girl, that is quite a story. I feel it is important we look after the welfare of our staff. If there is anything we can do to help you, please let me or Mrs Watson know.'

Maria shuffled her feet. 'Well, ma'am, there is something I would like to ask, but I hesitate to mention it in case you think I am speaking out of turn.'

The Queen, surprised by Maria's chutzpa, stared at her servant's face with interest. 'Let me hear what you have to say, and I shall be the judge of that.'

Queen Maud listened attentively as Maria recounted how gardening and being out in nature played a key part in Eddie's rehabilitation. She responded, 'I will write a note to our land agent about it today mentioning Eddie's situation and suggest that perhaps he could come here and work in the garden with Mr Gilbert on an informal basis, seeing as the good Doctor Butterscotch may have already broached the subject with the estate.'

Maria's face shone. 'I'm so grateful, ma'am. You're so kind. I can't wait to tell Eddie.'

Miss Jensen entered the room then and Maria bobbed a curtsey to the Queen. Her ears pricked as she walked towards the door and overheard the Queen instruct her lady-in-waiting, 'There is an urgent letter I need to write to the land agent today. Could you please ensure it reaches him.'

Kitty listened to the clock ticking away, her fists clenched. She jumped as it chimed eight times and stared at the kitchen door, waiting to see the latch lift and Victoria walk in.

She had taken a hot chocolate to Mrs Bell and made her comfortable in bed before hastily returning downstairs where she sat at the kitchen table with Miss Finchley, who was flicking through a magazine. Her voice conveyed her concern. 'I don't understand it. She should have been back by six o'clock. What could have delayed her?'

Miss Finchley soothed. 'Try not to fret, Kitty. She may have stayed behind to help with some other task. You know how soft Victoria is, she would never say *no* to anything Mrs Fairbairn asked of her.'

'No, that's true enough. But if she isn't back soon, I shall send Pip to see what's happened.'

Rosie tugged at Kitty's skirt, gripping her upside-down doll in her free hand. She stared up at her mother's face. 'Where's Victoria, Ma? I want her to read me a story.'

Kitty concealed her concern. 'I'll tuck you in this evening. When you wake up, Victoria will be back and will walk you to school tomorrow.'

Rosie clung to her mother's neck as she settled her in bed, pulling the bedcovers up to her chin. Bending down, she stroked her hair and kissed her cheek gently. Her doll lay on the pillow next to her and Rosie closed her eyes, taking the doll and pressing it close to her chest. When she returned downstairs, Kitty found Pip cleaning Mr Bell's boots in the kitchen. Her voice was strained. 'Can you leave that for now, Pip? It's almost nine o'clock and Victoria still hasn't come home. Can you go to the workhouse and ask if they know anything?'

Pip's face showed concern. 'She'll be all right. She's sensible.' He looked at his mother's anxious expression. 'Yer don't think anything untoward has happened to her, do yer, Ma?'

'I saw Mr Mumbles outside the front of the 'ouse today with a man, it can't be a coincidence.'

Without saying a word, Pip grabbed his jacket and flew out of the back door. The bell from the mistress's bedroom rang down into the kitchen. Kitty went up to answer the call.

Mrs Bell asked, 'Where is Victoria? I would like it very much if she could read to me. I find her voice so soothing.'

'I'm sorry, ma'am, she hasn't returned home from the workhouse school. I've sent Pip there to find out what's happened, and to bring her home.'

'Oh no, that is concerning. I believe Josiah and George are at a meeting there this evening. If she can't be found, we must ask them to help.'

Downstairs, Milly tried to distract Kitty from her anxious thoughts. Milly mentioned how much happier the house seemed without Lucinda's bad temper to contend with.

Miss Finchley overheard and commented, 'Yes, it's true that Miss Lucinda is remaining in London for a while; she finds a house full of children too much for her nerves.'

Milly asked, 'Have you been with the Bell family very long, Miss Finchley?'

'Indeed, I have. My acquaintance with the Bell family goes back many years, though I'm sure it's of no interest to you.'

Kitty's interest was roused. 'On the contrary, I should very much like to hear. Mrs Bell told me how her husband died on a ship in the South China Seas. Like me, she has no grave to lay flowers on and weep the loss of our husbands.'

'I never knew that,' gasped Milly.

Miss Finchley elaborated, 'That's very true, unfortunately, and many good men died with him. He was a fearless man, highly regarded by both his seamen and the community here.' She paused, recollecting memories from the back of her mind. 'It should have been my father leading that ship as its captain, instead of Mr Bell. They were the best of friends and business partners, but the day before the ship was due to sail my father went down with a vomiting fever and didn't have the strength to walk. Mr Bell insisted he stay behind, rather than pass his sickness on to his seamen. If he hadn't made that selfless gesture, he may still have been alive today.'

Kitty reached over and placed a hand on Miss Finchley's arm. 'I'm so sorry, I 'ad no idea. I didn't mean to open painful wounds.'

'That was a long time ago, Kitty dear. Mrs Bell was beside herself with grief and Lucinda was due to get married on her father's return, but she was abandoned when her fiancé found out the family had no money any more as they used what they had left to pay some recompense to families of the crewmen who were lost at sea. Her life took a downward turn and changed her to the unhappy person she is today.'

Miss Finchley paused. 'It affected my family too. You see, the insurance company wriggled out of paying compensation for the ship due to some technicality that was false and the business went bust, leaving my mother and me penniless. It was during this time that Mr Bell was being trained by his father to work in the shipping business. Because he was so furious with the injustice of the insurance company in refusing to pay up, or compensate the widows of the shipmen, he decided to train as a lawyer and be a voice for those who are unable to speak up for themselves. George has followed in his footsteps, with his uncle, who now takes on some well-to-do business clients to keep the wolf from the door.'

Before Kitty could question her further, Pip burst into the kitchen. He was breathless and his lips trembled.

Kitty rose and walked to the door, grabbing him by the shoulder. 'Where is she, Pip? Where's Victoria? Why isn't she with you?'

He opened his mouth to speak, but the words stuck in his throat. Miss Finchley took his hand and asked gently, 'Tell us what you know, Pip. Has something happened to your sister?'

His voice shook. 'Mrs Fairbairn says she left before six o'clock. She suggested she might have been detained doing something else at the workhouse, maybe helping one of the younger girls. She told me to hurry back home and said she was sure Victoria would be back here now. But she isn't, is she?'

His mother pressed, 'She isn't here, Pip. Why are you crying?'

Pip's bottom lip wobbled. 'There's something else, something Old Dobbins said on the gate.'

His mother shook his shoulders. 'What did Old Dobbins say?'

'He saw Victoria leave; she was wearing her favourite blue shawl. His attention was drawn by a couple of men who appeared from nowhere and pointed towards her, muttering, "That's the girl."'

Kitty's hand flew to her chest. 'What men? Did he see their faces?'

There was a tremor in Pip's voice. 'He didn't say, Ma. I don't know any more. Why would they want to follow 'er?'

Kitty's mind flashed back to the two men she had seen outside the house the night before. She froze, her veins beating a visible pulse beneath the skin.

Her eyes fearful, she instructed, 'Pip, listen carefully. We 'ave to act quickly. I want you to return to the workhouse straightaway and inform Mr Bell and Mr Perryman what's 'appened. Ask them to get the police out looking for 'er.'

Chapter Twenty-Two

Victoria had willingly followed the unknown men when they told her Pip was in trouble. They led her down some alleys lined with warehouses, some with pulleys on the first floor to haul up cargo for storage. As they turned the corner and headed towards the docks, a sense of unease gripped her. Pip surely had no business in this part of town. She paused. 'Where is he? Where's Pip?'

'It's not far now. Come on with yer,' one of the men replied gruffly.

'Pip! Pip!' she cried. The men pushed her forward and she stumbled. She attempted to flee, but her arm was grabbed roughly and a large hand placed over her mouth. 'Stop making a fuss. You'll see him soon enough.'

She had no choice but to do as she was told, sensing strongly something was amiss. After five minutes they stopped outside a row of run-down warehouses by the quay where the murky water from the wash was lapping against the side. She glanced up at the corner building at the end of a row of terraced houses that had a derelict look about them; it was where sailors and drunks found lodgings. The sun had set and the glow from the moon showed they were close to a wide river with cargo ships bobbing on them. A few dockers were idly loitering around smoking cigarettes and took no interest in her presence.

'Where's Pip?' she asked again, screwing up her eyes. It made no sense to her that Pip would venture to this area.

A man's voice from behind sneered. 'Why don't you come inside and find out, my sweet little thing?'

Victoria spun around, her voice quaking. 'Mr Mumbles! What are you doing 'ere? Have you seen Pip?'

She watched helplessly as he inched towards her, his eyes bulging, holding a damp cloth. She attempted to push past him, but was no match for his weight as he pushed her against a wall and pressed the cloth against her face. Just as she registered the foul smell coming from the cloth her mind went blank and she passed out.

When she opened her eyes, she was lying in a heap on the floor of a cellar. She felt drowsy and realised she had been drugged. Her chest tightened with fear. Why had she been left in this cellar and why was Mr Mumbles here?

She wrapped her shawl around her and began to cry, scared and alone. Her first thought was that her mother would worry about her and have no idea how to find her.

After a while, her eyes became accustomed to the darkness and she could see some barrels, fishing nets and grubby sacks scattered around. Water trickled down the brick wall close to a trapdoor at ceiling height where a sliver of light filtered through and, staring up, she saw some steps on one side of the basement leading to a door.

She summoned up the courage to climb up the slippery steps. When she reached the top she turned the door handle. It was locked. She pressed her ear against the door and could hear faint voices. She made out the muffled sound of Mr Mumbles saying, 'That is your lot. You're not getting a farthing more!'

Her blood froze and she pulled away. What did he mean? Why were these men in the pay of Mr Mumbles?'

An angry man's voice challenged the guardian. 'You said you'd give us double. It's worth more than that to yer if yer want us to keep our mouths shut. Kidnapping is a serious offence. She's a pretty thing too, what do yer plan to do with her?'

The hair on the nape of her neck rose and she shivered. She heard Mr Mumbles throw more money at the men and order them to get out.

She heard a door slam shut and the voices of the men leave the house, laughing and boasting loudly how well they had done, their voices fading as they walked into the distance.

She steadied herself and rose slowly, summoning up the courage to bang on the door. 'Mr Mumbles. Please, let me out.'

She almost fell backwards when he flung the door open. He stood in front of her, his clothes dishevelled and face brimming with expectation. 'I was just coming for you . . .'

Summoning all her might, she tried to push past him, but he grabbed her by the throat. He threw her into the room where the men had been and she fell to the floor.

She saw she was in an empty room apart from a couple of rickety chairs and a wooden table with a scratched surface. A few empty hessian sacks and wooden crates

242

were dotted around. It smelt musty and a lattice window offered no light – it was covered in so much grime and cobwebs that it was impossible for daylight to glimmer through.

She huddled on the floor and her heart pounded. She raised her head and rubbed her neck where he had grabbed her. 'What do you want with me? Where is Pip?'

Mr Mumbles stared down at her and snarled, 'Pip? Ha, ha. Look around. Do you see any sight of him? I just told the men to say that to get you here.'

Victoria shook, her lips and chin trembling. 'But why? I don't understand. It must be a mistake. Please let me go, and I swear I won't say a word about this.'

'It's no mistake. I didn't expect it to be so easy to capture you, my little bird. You flew straight into my cage.'

'I'm not your bird,' Victoria wailed. 'I want to go home.'

Victoria felt the wall with her clammy hands and clung to it while she pulled herself up from the floor. Her eyes scanned the darkened room for the door. She looked from the corner of her eyes for an outside door and spotted one. Mr Mumbles' bulky frame blocked her full view of it, but it was there, and she guessed this was the exit his accomplices had left by. There was also a door that was closed, which led into the main rooms of the house.

She shoved him with all the force she could muster and made a dash past him for the outside door, but he grabbed her by the arm. She sunk her teeth into the sleeve of his jacket, and he tossed her aside, smirking at her distressed state as she curled into a ball in the corner.

'You can blame the interference of the so-called do-good lawyer you are staying with for me losing my job. And Miss Feathers too, who was always very kind to you, was forced out of her job.'

Victoria exclaimed, 'I didn't say a word. I swear on my life! On Pip's life! On Rosie's life!'

'Well now you can make it up to me.'

The guardian lurched towards her and Victoria, shuffling along on the floor, kicked out so he tripped. His response was quick enough to haul himself up, spin around and pin her against the wall.

Victoria shook uncontrollably, panting for breath. 'Help. Help!' she screamed, at the top of her voice, but her cries were weak.

'Ha, you think anyone can hear you? Scream all you like, you stupid girl. The door is locked, so there's no point in you trying that. I'm not daft.'

He produced a key from his pocket and sneered. She flinched away, the colour rising in her cheeks.

'What are you going to do with me? Please, please let me go. I won't tell anyone what happened. I promise.'

His podgy face leered and he licked his lips. 'I like a girl with fire in her.'

'Please, no, not that. Please don't touch me.'

'Well that depends.'

'Depends on what?'

'On how cooperative your Mr Bell is. Seeing as I am ruined and need to start afresh, I need a helping hand to move on.'

'What do you want from him?'

244

'I want you to write your nice Mr Bell a note saying I never laid a finger on yer, and asking him for a reference.'

Victoria's voice warbled. 'A reference? I don't understand.'

'Miss Feathers and I have been offered new appointments in America, but we both need to post out an excellent reference from the Board of Guardians before we set sail on the ship in two days' time. I would like Mr Bell to provide these as its chairman, with a small remuneration for, how shall I put it, the inconvenience we have suffered. If Bell is a reasonable man and wants your return, I am sure he will understand.'

Victoria pleaded. 'All right. I'll do it. Will you let me go tonight if I promise to do as you ask?'

'I will, and my two friends will be watching you and waiting for you to get that letter – and the money, too. We know where you live, so if you try anything on, we will come after you.'

'I won't. I promise. Ma will be worried about me. Can I go now?'

'You must be patient a moment longer, my pretty little thing. I shall go to my lodgings and collect some paper for you to write on.'

With one swift movement, Mr Mumbles lifted Victoria, clutching her against his chest, opened the cellar door and thrust her inside, slamming it shut and turning the key.

'I'll be back in half an hour with the paper.'

Victoria banged on the door. 'Open the door. Let me out. Please!'

Her cries were in vain. She sunk to the cellar floor and cuddled her knees up to her chest, tears cascading down her cheeks. *I'm scared. I want to go 'ome. I want my ma.*

Mr Mumbles stormed out of the building and locked the door behind him, kicking out at an elderly woman who was crouched on the ground nearby, dressed shabbily, pulling a shawl wrapped tightly around her.

She held out a bony hand and stared up at his face, which was sweating profusely.

She slurred her words. 'Can yer spare a farthing, Mr Mumbles? Only I ain't 'ad a bite to eat for these last two days.'

He seemed taken aback to be recognised by a woman, who was a well-known drunk in these parts.

He hissed, 'What, so you can drink yourself into a stupor on my money? Get out of my way, Bess Roper. And stay away from here, or else . . .'

She taunted, 'Or else what? Oh, somefinks got under yer skin today. What's all that banging about for in there, anyway? You don't scare me.'

'Oh no? We'll see to that,' he threatened, his face turning purple as he raised his hand to strike her.

Suddenly, he gripped his chest with both hands and swayed, gasping for breath, and then he fell, hitting the ground with a thud. His legs twitched and his hands clutched his throat as he fought for breath, before making a final gargling sound and then silence, his eyelids closing and his head falling to one side.

Bess rose up unsteadily and stared around. There wasn't a soul in sight. She stepped over his body and grimaced. 'Huh, and 'e thinks I've 'ad one too many.'

Crouching down, she delved into his jacket pocket, her face brightening when she found a wad of notes, which she stuffed into her bag.

'Blimey, it's me lucky day. Thank yer, Mr Mumbles. I'll be 'aving one or two on you,' she cackled, stumbling off to the nearest tavern.

∽

Mr Bell burst into his house with George and Pip following. He asked, 'Is she back now?'

Kitty shook her head, her voice quavering. 'No. I thought that was her now. I hoped it was.'

Mr Bell asserted, 'We'll bring her home, Kitty, I promise. I put in a call to the police from the workhouse and they are on their way to Mr Mumbles' lodgings, in case he is behind this. Police are also searching the area near the workhouse. For now, all we can do is wait.'

Kitty was overwrought and pressed her clenched fists against her chest. 'But I can't do nothing. Please, please, find my daughter.'

Mr Bell declared, 'We will find her, I give you my word. If that man Mumbles is involved, he will face the law and answer for his actions, I swear it.'

Miss Finchley entered the room and raised an enquiring eyebrow at her employer. He shook his head. 'I've put the children to bed and Mrs Bell is settled too. Let's hope we have some news soon. Victoria is a bright girl, she'll keep her head straight.'

Mr Bell's tone was urgent. 'I think it's best if I go to the police station. I want to be there when their officers return with any news.'

Pip piped up, 'Can I come with you? Just in case you need a messenger.'

Kitty reached out and held his arm. 'No, my darling. We don't know who's out there. I don't want to lose two children in one day.'

'I'd fight them, I would, Ma.'

George persuaded him to stay. 'I'll go with my uncle. Tell you what, Pip. How about you be the man of the house in our absence?'

'Very well,' he retorted, his expression serious. 'I'll be in charge.'

'Please, hurry,' Kitty beseeched Mr Bell. 'Please bring my Victoria home with yer.'

An hour later they returned, their expressions desolate. Mr Bell said, 'I'm sorry, Kitty. There's no sign of Mumbles at his lodgings. He hasn't been seen since this morning, and Miss Feathers swears she has no information. She was shocked to hear that Victoria is unaccounted for.'

Kitty beat her fists on Mr Bell's chest. 'Where's my daughter? You said you would find her. If you hadn't sacked Mumbles my Victoria would still be 'ere.'

Chapter Twenty-Three

It was with a heavy heart that George left King's Lynn the following morning with no news of Victoria's whereabouts. He was expected in Wolferton for a meeting at the vicarage with the war pensions group for disabled servicemen and widows. Some bereaved families had poor literary skills and were unable to complete application forms for war pensions, and payments were delayed. Villagers turned to their vicar, and educated people in their community, to assist with this. George knew of their suffering, their struggles with poverty, and was determined to help them. He promised Kitty he would return as soon as possible.

On police advice, George and his uncle agreed to their request to keep Victoria's disappearance secret for a few more hours while they continued their search.

It was felt that Jane Rumbelow would be able to deal with the latest batch of applications alone with George as Ada woke up that morning with a throbbing head and gave her apologies and Jessie was working at the royal gardens and also unable to attend.

Mrs Rumbelow outlined one of the cases. 'I have one here from a blind man whose livelihood relies on selling matches outside King's Lynn railway station. He was blinded by gas in the trenches, and lost both his feet to gangrene. He has been forced to succumb to this terrible way of life. It's beyond belief.'

George scanned the form and nodded. 'He appears genuine to me. I will check all the details have been correctly filled in ready for him to sign.'

George was asked for his views on another application where it was felt the woman was not truthful about her present marital status. Mrs Rumbelow handed one of the forms to him and he studied it closely.

He glanced up. 'This woman's details do indeed seem familiar. She has changed her last name on the form, but her address remains the same. I believe she has tried this once before, claiming the man she was married to was her uncle who was killed fighting in France. It seems she is trying it on again. If you leave this with me I will discuss it with my uncle and delve deeper with the appropriate authorities.'

Jane Rumbelow interrupted. 'What you say may be true, but I believe she has ten children and is in desperate straits, and this is why she is duplicitous. She is not seeking financial benefit for herself, but to feed and clothe her children.'

George picked up a handful of forms. 'Every one of these is a tragic story due to the war. I will certainly do what I can to help and sift through those that appear not to be truthful for speedy processing. Her Majesty is keen to know what progress we are making and has asked to be kept informed.'

When all the forms had been scrutinised, the vicar's wife commented, 'We don't appear to have a war widows' application from Kitty yet. Would you like to take one for her?'

George had raised the matter with Kitty who had been undecided when the time was right for her to do so. He thanked Mrs Rumbelow for the form and promised to mention it to Kitty again.

He left two hours later and stood waiting on the platform at Wolferton Station for his return train when he was almost sent flying by someone rushing past.

'Hey, hey, Freddie. Steady on. What's the rush?' the solicitor asked, grabbing him by the arm.

Freddie stood trembling and shook himself free from George's grip. He mumbled a few words under his breath by way of explanation, his chest pounding and his eyes moist. His words were drowned out by the hissing of steam from the black engine as it pulled into the station. It was George's train, but he couldn't leave Freddie when he was so upset.

He took Freddie by the arm and led him to a quiet spot at the back of the coal shed. 'What's happened, Freddie? I've never seen you in this state before.'

Freddie stared down at his feet, his face red.

The solicitor moved closer to him. 'Nobody can hear you. Tell me what has upset you. I might be able to help.'

Freddie's voice was unsteady. 'I'm in a terrible mess. I've only got meself to blame. I was stupid. How I regret going to King's Lynn that night.'

'What are you talking about?'

Freddie blurted out the events that landed him in hot water pending the outcome of the police investigation, and how it had made headline news in the local paper. He told him everything, including the false accusations against him, and his concern for the injured soldier. He asked meekly, 'Is there any way you can find out how 'e is? I'm really worried.'

George listened to Freddie's confession without interrupting him. He responded after a moment's pause. 'You have got yourself in a terrible mess, mixing with the likes of Rufus Fagan. I'll see what I can find out about the soldier, and when he is well enough, I will see him to ask if he can verify your account.'

George placed a reassuring hand on Freddie's shoulder. 'Try not to worry, the truth will come out, one way or another. As it is, I have to go to the police station on another matter and will make a few enquiries about their investigation on your behalf.'

Freddie gratefully accepted the offer. 'Please don't tell anyone. I'm scared. I don't want Harry to see the newspaper. I don't want to blacken the Saward name. That would be the end of me 'ere, for sure.'

'Come, come. I'm sure it won't come to that. You are innocent until proven guilty, you will have to deafen your ears to gossip, especially as it's been in the papers, and Harry is bound to get wind of it. I suggest you return to your duties and keep your head down until this matter is resolved. I'll be in touch as soon as I hear anything.'

A few minutes later, he spotted another train pulling in that would take him to King's Lynn. He saw Fleur arrive on the platform and walked over to greet her. Although she worked with Beatrice, her relationship with George was on a professional standing. He held the carriage door open as she boarded the train, her eyes meeting his. 'How wonderful. Are we taking the same train? Perhaps we can share each other's company on the journey?'

'It would be my greatest pleasure, Miss Riley.'

'Oh Fleur, please,' she laughed, inching closer towards him in the carriage. 'There is no need for formalities between us, George. May I ask if the matter you are investigating is going as well as you hoped?'

George reached forward so his face was close to Fleur's and other passengers could not hear their conversation. 'I am very grateful to your brave input, but I'm afraid progress is slower than I would like, with my work on the war pensions and seeing to other clients. Please be assured, it's all in hand.'

George's back faced the window and he was oblivious to the tapping on the glass of someone trying to catch their attention. Fleur was resting her arm on his shoulder and leaning into him, catching his every word.

She straightened. 'Look, there's Beatrice.' Fleur pointed out of the window.

George immediately rose and rushed to the door, flinging it open as the guard blew his whistle and raised his flag.

'Beatrice!' he cried.

She turned for a brief moment and he saw a puzzled expression on her face, before she turned her back and walked off briskly.

'Damn,' muttered George under his breath, promising he would call on her later that evening and invite her out for supper.

❧

George returned home at the same time as two police officers were knocking on the door. One had three stripes on the sleeve of his jacket and was in his fifties, while his colleague was younger, in his twenties.

George blurted. 'Is there any news of Victoria?'

The sergeant spoke. 'I believe you know Mr Mumbles?'

'Well yes, I do, through my work on the Workhouse Committee. My uncle is the chairman, he is better acquainted with him. Why do you ask?'

'May we come inside for a moment. Mr Perryman, is it? I recognise you from your visits to the station. There is some news I need to inform you about.'

The officers removed their police hats and were shown into Mr Bell's study. Mr Bell and Kitty were there with another officer who was taking notes about Victoria's disappearance. Kitty was dabbing her eyes, her face anxious and distraught.

'What is it? Do you have news?' asked Mr Bell, his voice tinged with urgency when the two officers entered the room. Kitty gripped his arm tightly.

The sergeant cleared his voice. 'There has been a significant development. A body was found by a warehouse in the vicinity of the docks today . . .'

Kitty didn't wait for the officer to finish his sentence and burst into tears. 'Oh no. Please, don't say it's my Kitty?"

'No, Mrs Willow,' the officer continued. 'If you let me finish. A body was found earlier today – the body of a man – and we believe it to be Mr Mumbles. His body is being identified as I speak by Miss Feathers, seeing as he has no close relatives here.'

Kitty shrieked. 'I don't understand. How did he die? Did you find Victoria?'

Miss Finchley had been sitting in a corner. She stepped over and held Kitty while the tears poured from her eyes.

Mr Bell asked, 'Do we know how Mr Mumbles died? He was a scoundrel, but I wouldn't have wished this on him.'

'We can't say yet. The coroner has been informed and no doubt a post-mortem will be required to determine the cause of death,' the sergeant said.

He cocked his head, indicating he would like a private word with Mr Bell. Mr Bell led the two officers into the hallway and listened in stunned disbelief. 'These latest developments mean we have to keep all our options open. First, we had a report last night of a missing girl and were led to believe it could be connected to Mr Mumbles.'

'Yes, that's correct,' murmured Mr Bell.

'And then the body of Mr Mumbles is discovered, minus a large amount of cash, his life savings, we are informed, and there is no sight of this girl. It's quite a coincidence, don't you agree? So, you must understand this is a line of enquiry we have to follow.'

'Now look here,' thundered Mr Bell. 'I cannot believe what I am hearing. How dare you insinuate that Victoria had anything to do with the death of that vile man.'

Kitty stood in the open doorway, listening to every word. She levelled up to them and raised her chin, her face burning. 'How dare you. Get out of this house and find my daughter so and bring her back to me.'

∽

Mr Bell was in two minds whether or not to postpone the royal visit. With no guardian or wardress for the female inmates, and rumours swirling about Mr Mumbles' death and Victoria's disappearance, it couldn't have come at a worse time.

But the workhouse committee felt they should continue as special preparations had been made and there was a frisson of excitement too, especially on learning Queen Maud was to visit, instead of Queen Alexandra. Although the older queen was well liked, it was rare for them to see her daughter who was renowned for her compassionate nature. It was decided that her lady-in-waiting would be briefed on the situation, without going into the full details.

As soon as Queen Maud stepped into the workhouse, murmurings rippled through the building of how exquisitely dressed she was in a beautiful dark green velvet skirt and matching jacket that nipped in at the waist. Her cream blouse had a frill down the front and showing below her jacket sleeves too. Her hair was piled high on her head with pearl pins to keep it in place. Miss Jensen accompanied her royal mistress, carrying the bouquet of flowers that had been presented to the Queen.

Mr Bell was joined by his bristling committee members, all stalwart members of the local community. Queen Maud praised them on their new hospital wing, with ten beds on one side of the corridor for male patients and ten for the women on the opposite side.

When the visit was coming to an end the royal party stepped into the common room, the table decorated with freshly picked flowers, for refreshments. Sandwiches and cakes were brought in by the inmates who acted coyly, their cheeks turning pink when they were spoken to.

After the refreshments had been eaten, the Queen asked the committee to leave the room, with only Miss Jensen and Mr Bell remaining. She told him, 'I commend you on the changes you are putting in place here and your desire to advance the prospects of your inmates.'

'Thank you, ma'am. I am pleased you approve. Your visit here has raised the spirits of staff and residents alike.'

'I would like you to tell me exactly what is going on though. Why did your guardian and wardress leave under what is clearly a very dark cloud, and I have been asked to enquire with you about the well-being of Mrs Willow and her family, who are residing with you. I cannot leave until you tell me the truth.'

'It would be a great relief to tell you everything, ma'am. There has been a lot happening. The ex-guardian, Mr Mumbles, was let go due to improper conduct and has since been found dead. We are all frantic with worry about Victoria Willow, who has been missing for two days.'

He blurted out the full story and Queen Maud listened with great interest.

When he finished speaking she cleared her throat. 'Mr Bell. Perhaps there is some way I could help. I would like to offer a reward of £500 for information leading to the safe return of Victoria. Can you please see to this immediately, and make sure posters are put about town with a picture of her face, and add the words, "By Royal Command".'

Mr Bell was exalted. 'I shall see to it immediately. Thank you, ma'am, it's a most generous gesture and is bound to bring in information. After all, money talks.'

Chapter Twenty-Four

Maria was stretching her feet out in front of the fire after a busy day at work when there came a knock on the door. She shot a querying glance at her mother and brothers, feeling a sense of unease. 'Who can that be this time of night?'

'Well is someone going to answer it?' asked Ruth.

Freddie was closest to the door and dispatched to do so. A man's voice could be heard faintly. 'Hello, Freddie, can I come inside?'

Freddie led the way into the sitting room. Constable Rickett addressed him solemnly. 'I'm sorry, Freddie. I've been asked to take you in for further questioning.'

Maria stepped forward. 'What do you mean, "further questioning"? He's told you everything he knows. I thought you believed our Freddie?'

'It's not a matter of whether I believe him or not. As I explained when I last saw you, further investigations were continuing, and a witness has stepped forward to say Freddie was involved in the bust-up in the pub. The courts want to set an example to others that they will not tolerate unruly behaviour of this kind.'

Freddie protested, his eyes flashing. 'But it's not true! Who is this witness? They're making it up.'

'The landlady of the pub says she saw you. The sergeant has asked that you come to the station first thing tomorrow morning for an identity parade. If she identifies you, and other witnesses back her story, you will be charged with causing an affray and criminal damage, as well as the assault.'

An anguished cry, followed by a fit of coughing, silenced them. Ruth stood and confronted the police officer. 'Anyone with an ounce of sense would know that woman is lying to protect her son. Surely you don't believe her?'

'As things stand it's her word against Freddie's. We have to thoroughly investigate all complaints.'

Ruth swayed, crumpling into a coughing fit. Maria rushed over to steady her mother and eased her into a chair. She passed her a handkerchief.

Constable Rickett advised. 'I'm very sorry, Mrs Saward. My advice is for Freddie to get himself a good lawyer. In the meantime, Freddie Saward, will you give me your word that you will appear at King's Lynn police station tomorrow morning at nine o'clock and confirm you agree to participate in an identity parade? Otherwise I shall have to take you in now.'

Freddie appealed to Maria. 'It's a stitch-up, I know it, 'cause I didn't go along with the railway union men. I'm worried if I go that the landlady will point her finger at me and I'll be used as a scapegoat. I'm innocent, you have to believe me.'

Ruth became increasingly distressed and clung to Maria. She dug her fingers into Maria's arm and pleaded, 'Freddie's right, Maria. We must get word to George Perryman and beg him to speak up for Freddie.'

The constable warned. 'Do I have your agreement, Freddie. Otherwise I shall have to ask you to accompany me now to the station where you will be detained overnight.'

Freddie's voice wobbled. 'Very well. I give you my word I will be there tomorrow.'

Maria pledged. 'I'll come with you tomorrow, Freddie. It's me day off. We'll sort this out.'

'Good lad,' said Constable Rickett. 'I don't like any of this either. I've known your family since you first came here and you've never caused any trouble, but it's out of my hands, I'm afraid.'

When the constable had left, Ruth beckoned Freddie over to her. She grabbed his shirt collar and pulled him towards her. 'Promise me you will clear yer name, the Saward name.' She took his face in her small shaking hands and stared into it. 'Do you promise me?'

Gulping back tears, he sobbed, 'Yes, Ma, I will. I just want to see you well again.'

Turning to Maria, she asked, 'Promise me you'll do all yer can for Freddie, and see if Mr Perryman can help. I can't fathom why people would make up such wicked lies. What 'ave we ever done to wrong them?'

She readily agreed. 'Nothing I know of, Ma. Of course, I promise, and maybe Archie can leave Joey with Mabel for me while I'm with Freddie.'

'I feel better knowing you'll be there, Maria. Will you help me to me bed now?' she whispered.

Ruth rose unsteadily, with Freddie and Maria supporting her arms on either side. She struggled to climb the stairs, stopping every couple of minutes as her legs gave way. Her cough worsened and she wheezed and spluttered her way until she reached the top of the stairs. Maria threw open the bedroom door and helped her mother inside, where she slumped on the bed.

Within seconds, Ruth's eyes were closed and her handkerchief fell from her pocket to the floor. Maria picked it up and let out a small cry. It was filled with a thick yellow-grey mucus.

She had noticed this before in smaller quantities and her mother had fobbed off her concerns. Maria made Ruth as comfortable as possible, propping up her back and placing an extra pillow beneath to help clear her airways. Her mother's skin was hot to the touch and her cheeks were flushed. Maria chided herself for failing to notice her mother's condition had worsened.

Ruth's rapid breathing eased slightly and Maria pressed her ear against her chest. She heard a rattling sound that intensified, and then lessened as her chest rose and fell. Her mother spluttered and brought up more thick phlegm, and then settled back in her bed. Maria settled herself in a chair in her mother's room for the night, barely sleeping.

∞

The following morning, before the sun had risen, Maria checked on her mother. Her condition was no better. 'We have to go for the doctor now, Ma. I'm worried about yer breathing.'

Ruth shook her head and struggled to speak. 'No, I want you to leave me and see to Freddie.'

'But, Ma . . .'

Ruth whispered, 'You must go, Maria. 'Elp him clear his name. The boy needs you.'

261

Then Ruth slumped back into her bed and closed her eyes, the rattling sound on her chest audible. Maria felt her cheeks and they were burning.

'All right, Ma. Of course I shall 'elp him, and I'll get word to George Perryman and ask if he can 'elp. But please, let me send Archie for the doctor.'

Her mother's eyelids closed and she didn't answer. Maria called out for Archie, instructing him to bring Dr Fletcher over straightaway, to press on him the severity of their mother's illness, and to call in and see Mabel on his way home to ask about having Joey.

Archie glanced at his mother's frail condition, hearing the sound her chest was making. A tear trickled down his cheek.

'She'll be all right, won't she?' The words stuck in his throat.

'I 'ope so, Archie, but I've never seen 'er this bad. Ma's always pulled through, but I don't like the sound of her chest this time.'

Overcome with emotion, Archie leant over the bed. 'Ma, I love you. I know I don't tell yer enough, but I do.'

Maria sniffled. 'I love yer too, Ma. We all do.'

Archie wiped his eyes with his sleeve. 'I'm going for the doctor, Ma.'

'I've scribbled an urgent note for Beatrice too,' said Maria, handing it to her brother. 'It's important you drop if off at the station master's house and ask them to urgently telephone Mr Perryman and beg him to meet Freddie and me at the police station. Now go, and come back as quickly as you can. Here's the note for Mabel.'

262

Archie asked, 'But what will Mr Saward say if 'e knows Freddie 'as to be at the police station? Isn't 'e supposed to be at work?'

'I've explained it all in my letter. I've learnt that it doesn't pay to hide the truth and you should ask for 'elp if it's needed. I've written a note for Aggie as well, if you could drop that off at Kitty Cottage, asking if she could come over and look in on Ma later in the day.'

Freddie hovered in the doorway listening. He had black crescents under his eyes. 'Is there anything I can do?'

Maria answered, 'I can see you didn't get much sleep last night. You could make up the fire in Ma's room, while I go downstairs and put the kettle on.'

Joey came into the room and asked why everyone looked sad.

Maria took his hand and led him to the room they shared then lifted him onto her bed. He nestled his head against her chest and threw his arms around her waist. 'I love yer, Ma.'

'I love yer too, you funny boy. What's brought this on?'

'I heard you say it to Grandma Ruth. Is she going to die?'

Maria squeezed Joey. 'No, oh no. She is very unwell, but the doctor will be 'ere soon and will make her better. You must be quiet for 'er while I wash and change quickly before he comes.'

Joey kissed his mother's cheek. 'I'll be a good boy, Ma. I want Grandma to get better.'

Maria placed a kiss on Joey's forehead. 'You are a darling boy. How about you go downstairs and play with yer soldiers. I'll be down in a minute and will make some breakfast, and later you can visit Mabel.'

263

Joey leapt off her lap and crept down the stairs as quietly as he could. When Maria was assured her mother was as comfortable as could be, she went downstairs and heated up some porridge. She also took a cup of tea upstairs to her mother and left it by her bedside so it was at hand if she woke up and was thirsty.

Downstairs, Freddie restlessly paced around the room, rubbing the back of his neck. Maria told him, 'There's some porridge on the range for yer. Try and eat something before we leave. We don't know how long you will be detained.'

Maria immediately chided herself for her careless words as Freddie's eyes filled with panic. She vowed to put on a positive face for Freddie, but felt uneasy as she recalled Constable Rickett's warning that the courts wanted to make an example of troublemakers.

She gulped down a cup of tea and forced herself to eat a few spoonfuls of breakfast. Freddie sat glum faced doing the same, just as the doctor arrived with Archie. Dr Fletcher knew the house well and rushed up the stairs two at a time to Ruth's room, clutching his medical bag. Maria followed hastily. 'Thank yer for coming so quickly, Doctor. I ain't ever seen Ma this bad before. Her chest is making a strange noise and her skin is hot to the touch.'

Dr Fletcher's face was sombre as he eyed his motionless patient, listening to her rasping breathing. He removed his stethoscope from his bag and gently undid the buttons down the front of Ruth's nightdress.

He then sat by her bed and took her pulse. He turned to Maria and indicated that he wanted to examine Ruth in private and Maria retreated to the kitchen where Archie joined her.

She asked, 'Did you leave the notes with Beatrice, Mabel and Aggie?'

'I did. Mabel saw me coming and said she will be here within the hour. Beatrice was just about to leave for the hospital. Harry had already told her that Freddie was in some sort of trouble, so it didn't come as a surprise. She said she would call George straight away, though she said she knew he had some other pressing business to deal with involving Kitty. Aggie was very concerned about ma and will call in later and stay with her until you return.'

Maria's eyes clouded over. 'That gives me some peace of mind, but I wonder what is troubling Kitty to be in need of Mr Perryman's assistance?'

Maria glanced out of the kitchen window and her face brightened as she rushed to the door.

'Eddie!' she exclaimed. 'What are you doing here?'

'Ma told me about Freddie being in trouble and needing to go to the police station today. I had to come straightaway. I'll come with yer, I want to 'elp, just as you 'ave done for me.'

The gratitude showed clearly in Maria's eyes. Eddie cupped her chin in his hands and kissed her lips lightly.

'I would be glad of yer company, especially if Mr Perryman is delayed. I ain't been to a police station before.'

Freddie stepped forward. 'I'm scared, Eddie. I feel like a criminal and I ain't done anything wrong.'

At that moment the doctor walked downstairs. Maria asked anxiously, 'How is she, doctor?'

'She needs plenty of rest to see this through. I'm hoping her chest will clear, as it has done before, but each time it has left her weaker. Like you say, it's the worst it's been.'

'So ... so ... she isn't going to die?' Freddie asked, his voice unsteady.

The doctor shook his head. 'I don't see why she should, but I doubt she will regain her former strength. She seemed to be worried about something and mumbled Freddie's name under her breath. I strongly advise that she is kept calm and trouble free while she is in this frail and unstable condition. Give her plenty of fluids, try honey in warm water, and also mop her brow with a cold flannel to keep her temperature down.'

Freddie turned his head away from the doctor's inquisitive gaze. Dr Fletcher produced an odd-looking contraption from his medical bag that Maria had never seen before. It was an earthenware vessel with a spout and glass funnel. He handed it to her and she read the words engraved on the front, 'Improved Earthenware Inhaler Manufactured by S. Mawson & Thompson, Aldersgate Street, London'.

She queried, 'An inhaler? What's this for? Is it for Ma?'

The doctor nodded. 'It is. This is the Nelson-type inhaler and could prove very effective for Ruth. I used this on my father when he had breathing difficulties, as well as other patients who vouch for its effectiveness. It belongs to me personally and I hope it will bring some comfort to your mother.'

Maria tilted her head. 'That's a funny-looking thing. Do yer really think it will 'elp? What do you do with it?'

'It's very simple to use,' he told her. 'You just pour boiling water into the vessel and she inhales the steam directly from the funnel. An infusion can be used, some herbs, such as rosemary, sage or thyme. This should be added to the infuser first, and the boiling water poured on top. Inhaling this should help clear her chest and lungs of mucus. I recommend placing a towel over her head while she inhales the steaming infusion so she gets the full benefit of it.'

Maria clutched the inhaler as if holding a precious jewel. 'I shall see Ma uses this as soon as I return from an urgent matter in King's Lynn; I wouldn't want to trouble Aggie with it.'

Dr Fletcher told her, 'I am passing Aggie's on my way home. I can mention this to her and ask if she can cut some herbs from her garden to bring along. The sooner Ruth begins using it the better.'

Maria's eyes watered. 'You're so kind, Doctor. How much do we owe you?'

Dr Fletcher raised his hand. 'We can settle that another time. I need to catch Aggie without delay. So, you say you have an urgent matter to attend to? It must be very important if you are having to leave straightaway.'

Maria noticed his eyebrows lifting and his gaze fix enquiringly on her face. Freddie was shuffling his feet and averting the doctor's gaze. She replied, 'It's a misunderstanding that needs clearing up. It's Ma's wishes that I attend to it.'

'Very well. I won't detain you any further,' the doctor told her, walking briskly towards the door. 'However, If your mother's breathing worsens or she complains of chest pains or a sore throat, come for me straightaway.'

After he had left, Maria placed a jug of fresh water by her mother's bedside. She stroked Ruth's brow and her mother murmured slightly, her eyes remaining firmly shut. Her breathing was still heavy, but the rasping, rattling sound appeared to have eased a little. The tea Maria had brought her earlier remained untouched.

Freddie and Eddie were ready by the back door and within a flash Maria had buttoned up her coat and joined them, leaving Archie to care for Joey until Mabel arrived.

'We need to rush if we are to get to King's Lynn police station for nine o'clock,' Eddie pressed.

They made it to Wolferton Station and speedily purchased their tickets. The sky had storm clouds gathering and was as black as charcoal.

As the train steamed in they boarded in a flash and found seats on the hard benches in the third-class carriage. The presence of other passengers meant it was impossible to discuss the appointment they were going to keep. Maria's pulse quickened as the train rumbled on. She gripped Freddie's hand tightly, but he released it, rubbing the back of his neck and fidgeting.

A thin bespectacled parson with greying hair sat opposite, staring at him over the rim of his glasses.

'Are you quite all right?' he asked, his expression concerned. 'Only I can't help noticing you seem restless.'

'I'm sorry if I'm disturbing yer,' Freddie replied, avoiding the question.

He remained rigid for the remainder the journey, gripping his cap in his hand and staring down at the floor.

Maria had to remind herself that Freddie was only seventeen. He had had a rough time following the death of their father when both brothers were sent to London to live with their Uncle Gus after their mother became too unwell to care for them, and he squandered the money she gave him intended for their keep.

When they arrived at King's Lynn and alighted from the train the heavens suddenly opened. Thick raindrops lashed down and within minutes they were soaked.

Maria pulled her jacket tightly around her. Eddie offered her his jacket to cover over her head, but she refused. 'It's already dripping wet. It's almost nine o'clock, we'd better rush.'

She lifted the hem of her skirt and sploshed across the road as the rain lashed down relentlessly on them. Maria dashed into a shop doorway for cover a short distance from the police station. It was Batterbee's Bakery and the enticing smell of freshly baked bread made Maria's stomach groan.

A vexed-looking man wearing a long white apron came to the doorway and stared at them. For a moment she thought he was going to tell them to clear off. He said nothing, but returned a moment later with a young woman around Maria's age.

Maria was drenched, shaking from the cold. She was taken aback to recognise the woman's voice. 'We just had a boy in who made off with a loaf without paying and Pa was going after him. Then he saw you standing here and thought your face looked familiar.'

Conscious of the time, Maria didn't want to stand chatting, but her curiosity had been roused. She racked her brain and tried to recall if they had met before.

The girl pressed. 'Don't you remember us? We have a royal warrant to make patisseries for the King and Queen at Sandringham. You were always kind and gave us a cuppa when we delivered them to the Big House. Look how drenched you are. Do you want to come inside?'

Maria now recognised the kindly young woman as Alice Batterbee and her father, Bernard. She had been in such a rush that she failed to notice the coveted royal warrant hanging above their front door. She could have cried with relief and wanted to hug Alice, but time was against them.

'Oh Alice, what a blessing to run into you, though I wish I didn't look like a drowned rat. We have urgent business in town now and I cannot delay and take you up on your invitation, but if you should have an umbrella I could borrow, that would be much appreciated. I promise to return it on my way back to the station.'

'Of course I do,' she replied. 'I'll be back very soon.'

Freddie nudged Maria. 'Why did yer 'ave to come in 'ere?'

'Shush, we will only be a minute. I'm soaked through.'

Alice returned with the umbrella and a dry coat which Maria gratefully accepted. Alice pressed, 'Now promise me you will call in and take some of my bakes back with you afterwards. I'll pop some in a box and leave them under the counter for you when you return. I have some nice apple turnovers and iced buns. How does that sound?'

'That sounds wonderful, and they smell so delicious. I can't thank you enough, Alice. I'll return these on my way home,' Maria said, throwing her arms around her neck.

'It's almost nine o'clock, Maria. Quick, we must rush,' Eddie urged her.

Alice glanced at Maria's companions with interest, but it wasn't the appropriate time to introduce her to her brother, who was increasingly edgy, and her fiancé. She bade her farewell and Maria felt Alice's eyes following them as they stepped out into the street, until they turned a corner and were out of sight. The police station was a five-minute walk away and they arrived at the marketplace where it was situated just as the clock opposite on St Margaret's Church struck nine times.

Maria glanced up at the distinctive building, large black-and-white-check stones on its frontage. The fact that it was also used as a magistrates' court and gaol could be seen clearly. Above the arched doorway was a Georgian facade with a recess panel containing iron shackles and chains and a barred window, all symbols of imprisonment and a warning of the fate that awaited felons, from drunkards and thieves to rapists to murderers alike. Maria shuddered as she pondered on how the most violent of men and the worst of mankind had walked through this doorway. Freddie was not like them.

They shook the rain off their clothing and Maria clasped Freddie's cold shaking hand in hers. 'Let's get this over with. Remember, you're a Saward and you are innocent. Just tell 'em the truth, and then we'll be on our way.' Eddie gave him an encouraging nod.

As they entered the reception area, a young officer was pinning a notice on the wall. Maria's shaky finger pointed to it. She gripped Eddie's arm. 'Look, that's Victoria's face. It says she's missing and a £500 reward is offered for information leading to her recovery. What could have happened?'

'Do you know her?' the officer asked, resting his elbow on the wooden counter and staring at them with interest.

'We do indeed. What's 'appened to 'er? Poor Victoria. Her poor ma must be in pieces. I had no idea,' said Maria, visibly shaken.

The sergeant eyed them with suspicion, his eyes running up the length of their shivery bodies, starting with their feet, which shuffled uncomfortably, and finishing with their faces.

'We're searching for her as I speak. Unless you have information about her, I would ask you not to waste our time as your lad has his own problems to worry about.'

Maria read the name on the counter, 'Sergeant Catcheside'. He had a forceful manner that made Freddie quake, his lips trembling. The sergeant tapped his pen on the paper in front of him and shoved it in front of Freddie. 'Sign this.'

Maria stepped forward, trying to hide her discomfort. 'What is it?'

'I weren't addressing you, miss, if you don't mind.'

Maria leapt back, inhaling a sharp intake of breath. Eddie stepped forward, but she put her arm out to stop him.

Freddie took the pen from the policeman's stubby fingers.

'What is it you want me to sign?' Freddie asked, his lips trembling.

'This is your agreement to participate in an identity parade. They're waiting for you, outside in the yard. When you've signed that, follow the constable down to the cells, and he will take you out into the yard. Inspector Jericho is there waiting.'

Freddie shot a fearful look at Maria and Eddie. Eddie blurted, 'Can I go with him? You can see how frightened he is.'

'What's he got to be frightened of, if he is innocent?' The sergeant smirked.

Summoning her inner courage, Maria approached the counter once more. 'He is innocent. Nobody can say otherwise.'

'Well, that remains to be seen. I would like you and the fella with you to step back and stay seated on the bench. I don't want to hear another word from you. Have I made myself clear?'

Eddie took Maria's arm and they watched as Freddie followed a police constable who had been seated behind the counter.

He was a young man in his twenties and he threw a reassuring glance towards Maria as if to say, *Don't worry, he will be back soon.*

When Freddie had disappeared into the room, Maria approached the sergeant. 'May I use your telephone please? I would like to call our friend, Jessie Saward. She is very close to Kitty and her family and will want to know Victoria is missing.'

The sergeant's tone became friendlier. 'Seeing as she is the station master's daughter, a man of the highest regard, I can permit it. But keep it short in case anyone wants to call in with vital information about the girl.'

Chapter Twenty-Five

After the call was made, Maria paced backwards and forwards, rubbing her neck and then sitting and twisting her fingers in front of her. She turned to Eddie, her eyebrows furrowed. 'Why is it taking so long? I can't stand the waiting, and I need to find out if there's any news about Victoria.'

She rose again and paced the floor, walking restlessly past the sergeant's desk. It had seemed an eternity since Freddie had gone behind the door and Eddie's words of reassurance fell on deaf ears.

Suddenly a woman burst through the door that Freddie had disappeared through and stormed into reception. Her face was puffy and she had loose leathery skin and her small eyes were cold and dark like currants.

She cast a sideways glance at Maria, making her shift uncomfortably on the bench.

With her lips pursed, a defiant expression fixed on her round face, the woman barked, 'My duty is done, Sergeant. Will I be paid for me lost time at work?'

He cleared his throat and leant forward. 'That will be all for today, thank you, Mrs Fagan. The Norfolk Constabulary does not pay members of the public for doing their duty.'

With a flounce of her skirt, she snorted and stormed out into the rain, pausing at the doorway to fix her hat in place. Maria whispered to Eddie, 'I wonder if she's had anything to do with the identity parade. She seems horrible. Where is Freddie? I'm worried he isn't back.'

Before Eddie could answer a friendly voice took her by surprise. 'Maria. Eddie. I was hoping to see you. I hope I'm not too late.'

Maria rose to her feet, clutching her hands. 'Mr Perryman. I'm so pleased to see you. Did you get our message? Can you help Freddie? He's down in the cells, and we don't know what's 'appening.'

George's eyes fell on the poster showing Victoria's face. 'I did, and I will help in any way I can. But first I must see if there's any news about Victoria. We are all terribly worried about her, as you can imagine. Poor Kitty hasn't slept a wink since she vanished.'

Maria said, 'Of course, I understand. I am shocked and very upset to 'ear about this. I know everyone in Wolferton will be too. I was able to telephone Jessie a moment ago from 'ere, she is coming straight over to be with Kitty.'

He shook his head. 'She will appreciate that. The police have officers out everywhere and Queen Maud has asked to be kept informed. With Mumbles now dead, and Miss Feathers unaware of why he should have been by the docks, the police have nothing to go on. Poor Kitty is naturally besides herself with worry.'

George approached the desk. 'Sergeant Catcheside, what do you know about the Freddie Saward case? I am here to represent him while I await news of Victoria Willow.'

275

Maria overheard the sergeant brief George and she let out an anguished cry. 'What did the sergeant mean by saying, "the Saward boy is going to be here for a while"?'

Eddie did his best to soothe Maria. George instructed, 'Follow me, we have the use of a room where we can talk in private.'

Maria and Eddie followed the solicitor out of the lobby door that led to police interview rooms, passing a steep set of stairs that snaked down into oblivion. It was pitch black at the bottom and she couldn't help but wonder what poor souls had walked down them, and what it was like beyond.

She paused, wondering if that's where Freddie was being held, and could just about make out the outline of a door at the bottom. In the next moment, the door was flung open and a number of men filed out. One was in his sixties and toothless, another balding and as round as a barrel and unlikely to see his fortieth birthday again. As they clambered up the stairs she recognised another as Larry, a poacher from the Sandringham Estate who was only fifteen, and then there was another man she didn't recognise who sent a shiver down her spine. The police constable who had accompanied Freddie appeared at the end of the line was setting them free and they walked up the stairs and out of the door leading to reception. Surely they couldn't have been In the identity parade?

George addressed the policeman. 'Constable Thompson, where is Freddie Saward? Is he still being held?'

'He is, Mr Perryman. He was picked out in the identity parade. He's being held in the cells for now until we take his statement.'

'No. No. No. It can't be true,' Maria cried. 'There's no comparison between Freddie and those men who just left. It's a stitch-up.'

George stepped forward. 'Leave him, Maria. I will get to the bottom of this for you. Constable, can you tell me who is in charge of this investigation?'

'Inspector Jericho, sir. He is with Freddie at the moment and should be up very soon.'

Maria pleaded, 'There's been a terrible mistake, Mr Perryman. I swear Freddie is innocent. He must be terrified down there. Can I see him?'

'I'll ask. I don't like the sound of this. Beatrice told me on the telephone about the accusations and his avowed innocence. I believe him.'

'Thank yer, Mr Perryman. I don't like to put on yer as you've enough to see to with Victoria, but I don't know where else to turn. I need to be 'ome as well to see Ma as she needs a special infusion to clear her chest. I must get back for her urgently, but I can't leave without seeing Freddie. I promised Ma I would 'elp him.'

Eddie suggested, 'I'll stay and see to Freddie, if you like. It's important you get back to Wolferton and see to yer ma.'

George agreed. 'There's nothing more you can do here. I give you my word I will go down and do all I can for Freddie.'

Eddie promised, 'I won't leave without him, Maria. You can count on me.'

'Thank you, Eddie. I'll be looking out the window and praying for yer speedy return.'

'Don't forget this,' Eddie said, holding out Alice's umbrella and coat.

Maria took the umbrella and coat and left the room, walking past the sergeant behind the front counter who was deep in conversation with the police constable. As she stepped outside, the rain had eased and she walked in the direction of the bakery, brooding over Freddie.

She toyed with the idea of going to the Railway Arms and having it out with the landlady. She must have been the one who picked Freddie out of the line-up.

But Eddie's words of caution came to mind, warning Maria not to approach her.

She was at the bakery within minutes and the bell on the door jangled as she opened it, catching Alice's eye behind the counter who had just finished serving a customer.

'Are you alone? Where are your companions you were with earlier.'

Maria opened her mouth to speak, but her eyes creased. She had no idea what to say. She stuttered a few words that were barely audible. 'They had to stay on, but I need to return home and see Ma. She's very unwell and needs an infusion to ease her breathing.'

Alice replied softly, 'I'm so sorry to hear that. I'm due a break now, how about a cuppa? Father can take over for a few minutes. You look, well . . . I've never seen you in such a state.'

'Oh no, I couldn't possibly detain you. I stopped off to return the umbrella and coat. I really must get back.'

Alice stepped around the counter and gripped Maria's hands firmly with hers. 'I think you should stay awhile until you have calmed down. Besides, your clothes are still wet and you will catch a chill. Is that what you want? Your Ma

278

wouldn't want you to walk around in these damp garments. Let me dry them off in front of the range.'

'But I . . .'

Maria raised her hand in protest, but Alice was having none of it. The baker's daughter called her father in. Mr Batterbee was a cheerful man in his sixties whose torso was as round as one of his currant buns. 'Take all the time you need, Maria. Our busy period has passed. I hear you have a new position at Appleton House. Congratulations. I delivered an order to Sandringham a short while ago and Cook said you had moved on.'

At that moment, Maria gasped for breath and her heart began pounding. Her head began spinning and her legs gave way. Alice caught her by her arm and, with the aid of her father, they assisted her through to the kitchen at the back.

The warmth of the room made her feel drowsy and she let herself be led to a comfy armchair in front of the warm range. A phial was pressed under her nose.

'Breathe in the smelling salts, my dear girl. And then Alice will give you a strong cup of tea,' urged the baker, his face almost pressing against hers, his eyes as round as saucers, filled with concern.

She sneezed as the smelling salts took effect, shaking her head and holding the end of her nose. Alice passed her a handkerchief and she blew her nose hard, coming back to her senses.

Alice knelt by her side. 'You had us worried then. Here, sip this hot drink.'

'I can't stay, I mustn't,' Maria protested. 'I have to get back for Ma. She needs me.'

Alice insisted. 'Very well, I believe you. But I couldn't bear it if anything should happen to you. Who would look after your Joey and your Ma then?'

Maria croaked, her eyes welling up. 'You're right, Alice. Thank you. Have you 'eard about Victoria Willow? She's gone missing from the workhouse and the old guardian there by the name of Mumbles is dead and could 'ave been murdered.'

Alice's face showed concern. 'Yes, I heard. It's the talk of the town. I know Kitty Willow from my deliveries to Appleton House. We are all devastated for her and hope Victoria will be found soon.'

Before she could stop herself, Maria blurted, 'I'm afraid, Alice. I'm scared for Freddie and Victoria.'

Alice gently stroked Maria's tear-stained cheek. 'Shush, I know you are, but there's nothing more you can do right now. You're as white as a sheet, Maria, and trembling all over. Shall I call the doctor?'

'No,' cried Maria, shivering, wrapping her arms around the front of her chest. 'That won't be necessary.'

'I would rather I did, but if you insist. The least I can do is bring you some food and a nice cup of tea.'

'Thank you, Alice. I would appreciate that.'

Alice returned a few moments later with some tea and pastries.

Maria sipped on her tea and, at Alice's insistence, she accepted a buttery shortbread biscuit. Maria had no appetite, but the biscuit melted in her mouth and the sweetness brought some colour back to her cheeks.

'I don't know how to repay you for your kindness,' said Maria gratefully. 'I've put you and your pa to so much trouble.'

'Put such thoughts out of your head. I'm a good listener,' Alice soothed. 'You know what they say about a problem shared being a problem halved. It's very true.'

Maria was moved by Alice's kindness and the words tumbled out with ease as she told her everything about Freddie's troubles. Alice listened carefully without interrupting her.

When Maria finished, she asked, 'What do you know about this Mrs Fagan from the Railway Arms?'

Alice's eyebrows creased. 'She's not a good person, Maria. Her son, Rufus, is a troublemaker. I heard about the punch-up from a neighbour living near the Railway Arms who complained to a passing policeman about the din just as the fight kicked off. The neighbour came in the next day and told me about it. She said she saw a man leave before the real trouble started. From what you've told me, and her description, this could have been Freddie.'

Maria gripped Alice's arm. 'Is she sure of this? Would she swear to it?'

'I can ask. She heard some men shout out after him and the name Freddie was mentioned, but he ignored them.'

Maria's mouth was dry. 'Her testimony could save Freddie, if she's prepared to give it and isn't afraid to stand up to the Fagans.'

'She's had enough of them and the trouble from the pub. I think this proves your suspicions are right, that Freddie has been framed by them.'

Maria gushed. 'There's not a moment to lose. I will inform Mr Perryman straight away. Oh, thank you, Alice, and please thank this lady too.'

Alice remarked, 'I hope your Mr Perryman is good at his job. From what I hear, the landlady is on good terms with the police, they turn a blind eye to the late drinking and brawling there.'

Maria looked aghast. 'Mr Perryman is the best, we 'ave the utmost trust in him.'

Alice offered, 'If you like, I can call him for you and explain. You need to get back home quickly to see your ma and let her know about this, it will put her mind at rest.'

Maria embraced Alice. Her voice quaked. 'Would you really do that? Oh thank you, Alice. You are an angel. I can never thank you enough.'

Alice pressed a box of bakes into Maria's hand tied with red ribbon. 'I promise I shall do so today. There's something for you to eat when you get home, with our compliments. I hope you will find your ma's condition has improved. I hear the inhaler can be most beneficial for breathing difficulties.'

Maria glanced up at the grey sky as she left the bakery, tightly clutching the box under her arm. It had stopped raining and a thin streak of yellow peaked through the clouds. She spotted a poster at the railway station with Victoria's face on it and felt a pang as she imagined Kitty's agony. What could have happened to her?

Alice kept her word and immediately put a phone call through to George Perryman's office. He was still at the police station, but she left an urgent message with his uncle, and only hung up when she was sure he understood fully that the important information she was passing on needed to be acted on immediately.

When Maria arrived back at Wolferton she collected her bicycle from the station and pedalled home as quickly as she could, placing the delicate cakes carefully in her basket. As she approached Honeysuckle Cottage, her heart skipped a beat when she saw Dr Fletcher's car parked outside.

She flung her bicycle down and rushed to the back door, bursting into the kitchen. Aggie sat at the kitchen table, a solemn expression on her face. She rose instantly and embraced Maria. 'I'm sorry, Maria. The doctor . . .'

'What do yer mean?' asked Maria, puzzled.

'There was nothing he could so, Maria. Your ma . . .'

Before she finished speaking Maria pushed her away, crying, 'No!'

She entered the bedroom as the doctor was pulling the bedcovers over Ruth's pale face. Maria collapsed to her knees. 'Ma. Ma. Oh Ma. I'm sorry I weren't 'ere for you.'

'It was very sudden, Maria. There was nothing you could have done. I'm so sorry,' the doctor consoled.

'But how? Why? Did you know when I saw you earlier?'

Dr Fletcher nodded. 'Your ma didn't want you to worry about her. She confided in me about Freddie and wanted you to be with him. You did as she asked, which pleased your ma, you could have done no more and have nothing to reproach yourself for.'

Maria yanked back the covers and stared at her mother's corpse. Her hands were folded neatly across her chest and her face looked at peace. A bowl at the side of the bed was filled with muslin soaked with sticky green mucus and some blood-streaked phlegm. The Nelson inhaler was nearby.

Maria stuttered. 'The infusion, I thought that would 'ave saved her?'

Dr Fletcher placed a comforting arm on Maria's shoulder. 'I hoped it would, but it seems she was at an advanced stage of bronchitis, caused by her respiratory tract disease. She hung on much longer than I thought after my first examination of her. It was her wish for you not to know the seriousness of her illness after it worsened. She was very proud of you, Maria.'

'But she was only fifty. It was her dream to see me and Eddie walk down the aisle, and now . . .'

The doctor spoke kindly. 'And so you must, all in good time. Eddie is a very good man.' He paused, letting Maria absorb what had just happened. He offered, 'Would you like me to stop off and inform Harry and Sarah? They will help you with the necessary arrangements, I imagine.'

Maria wept. 'I can't believe I'll never see 'er again.'

The doctor left and Maria lay her head against her mother's motionless body, with tears gushing down her cheeks.

She eventually rose and stepped to the window. She gazed up at the sky as a glint of light broke through the grey clouds. Suddenly, a streak of bright yellow flashed in front of her. The breath stuck in Maria's throat and her heart pounded as she pressed her face against the windowpane and stared at the flashing beam until it vanished from sight.

Her spine tingled as a voice in her head told her, *Do not mourn me. Live the life you deserve.*

A moment later, a yellow beam spiralled high into space and infinity. A tiny cry escaped. *I will, Ma. I will.*

Chapter Twenty-Six

Maria sat Joey on her lap and squeezed him tight, her words faltering as she told him his grandma had gone to heaven and was with the angels.

He cried, 'I don't like those angels. Why couldn't they make grandma better and leave her here?'

Harry arrived within the hour. 'I came as quickly as I could, I've just heard the news from the doctor. I'm so sorry, Maria, none of us was expecting this.'

Maria pressed a handkerchief against her wet eyes. 'It was so sudden. I wish I'd been 'ere for her, only Ma insisted I go to the police station with Freddie.'

Harry solaced. 'You did what your ma wanted. Ruth was a sick woman, and Dr Fletcher told me her condition was worse than she wanted to let on.'

Maria fumbled with her fingers. 'I don't know how I'm going to break it to the boys.'

Harry looked out of the window. 'Here's Eddie, but he's on his own. Where could Freddie be?'

She flung open the door. 'Where's Freddie?'

Eddie shook his head. 'I'm sorry, Maria. They're keeping him in.'

∞

Meanwhile, back at the station, George left Freddie in his cell promising to be back the next day.

He begged the solicitor, 'Please tell Ma I love 'er, and I'm staying strong and will clear our name.'

George promised he would. He spoke to Constable Thompson who assured him. 'Don't worry. I'll keep an eye on him.'

He handed George a note from his uncle that had been dropped off while he was detained with Freddie. It read, 'I have news of the coroner's report. Please come home quickly.'

George cursed his leg that dragged as he walked as quickly as possible to reach his home at Quayside. He was close to the river and stopped when he saw a couple of men tearing down the poster from the wall appealing for information about Victoria's disappearance.

He cried out, 'Hey, you two. Stop that. What do you think you're doing?'

He approached them and recognised their faces having seen them in court on offences of theft and assault. One of the men darted off, but the second man lingered.

George screwed up his eyes. 'Tobias Scott? Care to explain?'

'It says 'ere there's a reward for information about this girl? Is that right?'

'Yes. What of it?'

Tobias spat out the remains of a cigarette stub from his lips. 'I think that's the girl me and Bernie Roper took to old Mumbles the other night.'

George thundered, 'What are you saying, man? She's been gone almost three days and she's only thirteen. If you know anything about this, I demand you tell me.'

286

'Mumbles paid us to bring the girl to him, but that was all. We didn't say anything 'cos Bernie kept saying we would be pinned for Mumbles' murder. It were nought to do with us. He were alive when he paid us off, I swear. And I 'ave no idea what 'e did with the girl.'

George shrieked, 'We don't have a moment to lose. If you don't want to be skinned alive, show me where you took her. Now!'

'As long as you promise I won't be done for Mumbles' murder.'

Enraged, George cried out, 'You're in no position to strike a bargain. Now take me there this minute, else I swear I shall strike you.'

George's face was purple and he raised his walking stick.

'Steady on. I stopped, didn't I? I could 'ave run off with Bernie. We're after the reward, seeing as me missus is 'aving another baby next week, that's another mouth to feed.'

George took the man by his shirt collar and pushed him along the path. He raised his voice even louder. 'Now, I said. Take me there this minute.'

Tobias raised his hands in protest and nodded, freeing himself from George's grip.

'We took 'er to an old warehouse, just around the corner. We'll be there in a couple of minutes.'

He glanced at George's leg and added, 'Well, maybe longer, seeing yer leg.'

'Don't worry about me, I'll keep up with you. And on the way, I would like you to tell me how you came to access this property, if other people are involved.'

Tobias paused for a moment. 'Mumbles said a man owed him a favour and agreed to let him 'ave the use of it for a few days, no questions asked. I've no idea who he is.'

George dragged his lame leg behind Tobias, leaning on his stick and, in spite of doing his best to ignore the pain that walking speedily caused him, he needed to pause after every two or three minutes. He followed him down a cobbled ally lined with tall warehouses on either side. Eventually, after fifteen minutes, Tobias stopped and pointed to the dark brick building in front. It had small square windows, three storeys up, and three across, which were all boarded up.

'That's where we took her,' he said.

'Come with me, I want you to show me inside.'

As they approached the building, George kept his eyes fixed on the man. The door was swinging on its hinges. Tobias followed the solicitor inside and rushed over to the door that led to the cellar.

He rushed down the steps and George waited at the top and stared down into the darkness.

Tobias yelled, 'She's not 'ere. She's gone.'

George bellowed, 'If you've deliberately brought me to the wrong address I swear to God you will regret it!'

Tobias returned upstairs. 'She was 'ere, look, I found this. She left it behind.'

He handed George Victoria's blue shawl. 'My God, what has happened to the girl? How in God's name can I tell Kitty this?'

George dragged Tobias by the arm. He spluttered, 'It were Bernie's idea. Bernie Roper. His ma, Bess, stole a pile of money from Mumbles and threw it around like confetti. She told her son how Mumbles collapsed in a 'eap in front of 'er. She were hoping to find a pound or two of change, but struck gold as he 'ad taken out his savings from the bank to travel to America. That's what he said. I wonder if Roper has snatched the girl for the reward and is "olding her in his place.'

'That is the most despicable thing I have heard. You must take us to his address, but first, I must let my uncle and Kitty know that we have a lead.'

∽

When he arrived back at the house, George unlocked the door and his uncle rushed into the hallway. On seeing Tobias he asked, 'Who is this man? What's going on?'

'This is Tobias Scott and he and an accomplice, Bernie Roper, lured Victoria to a cellar by the docks on Mumbles' orders. He took me there, but she is gone. She left this behind,' George told him, handing over the scarf.

George added, 'He can tell us where Roper lives. He thinks he might have the girl with him there. We should go now. It's just as well Jessie is here, she has been a comfort to Kitty.'

Mr Bell told Tobias, 'You had better wait outside. I don't want Kitty to see you, it will only upset her. I have two officers here and they will go to the address straightaway.'

∽

Mr Bell handed Kitty the scarf recovered from the basement. 'We'll find her, Kitty. There is a man outside who says he knows where she might be. Officers, can you please come. We need to go now to the address he has given us.'

Kitty leapt up. 'I want to go too. Please, let me go with them.'

She was restrained by Mr Bell. 'Let them do their business, my dear. They'll bring Victoria straight here.'

Kitty dug her heels in. 'No, I ain't staying here while my daughter's out there. I'm going after them. I ain't standing by and doing nothing. I've had enough of sitting around waiting.'

George spoke up. 'Very well, if you insist, but I'm coming with you.'

Jessie rose too. 'If Kitty is going, I am too. Try and stop me.'

Outside, the police demanded, 'Well, Scott, what is Roper's address?'

'It's 13 Backyard Lane,' he replied. 'Do you want me to come with you?'

Kitty had just appeared and cried, 'Absolutely not. You ain't going anywhere near her ever again.'

Tobias hung his head. 'I'm sorry, miss, honest to God I am.'

Kitty squared up to him, enraged. 'Do you have any idea what you've put me through. If just one 'air on her 'ead has been 'armed, you'll answer for it.'

'I'm sorry. I truly am. That's why I'm 'elping yer now. Roper always takes things too far. He always wants more, the greedy bugger. After Bess showed him what she took he went back to see if there was anything else worth taking from Mumbles, his body stiffening, and stole his gold pocket watch and cufflinks. That's when he saw the keys to the warehouse and went back the next day to see the girl. Mumbles' body 'ad gone by then.'

George urged, 'We don't have time for this now. We must go.'

Mr Bell waved them off, saying he would arrange for police to collect Scott. Kitty and Jessie ran through the back cobbled streets, turning off by the marketplace, with George hobbling along behind, doing his best to keep up with the police officers. He pointed ahead. 'It's at the end of that passage.'

They followed the direction he was pointing in, skirting around patches of manure on the cobbles left by cart-pulling horses. This was an unsavoury part of town that Kitty and Jessie never usually visited, where small back-to-back houses had shared lavatories in enclosed courtyards.

Number 13 Backyard Lane was easy to locate. Police arrived at the same time and she rushed past them in the hallway and into a room, crying out her daughter's name. The front room, with its sparse tatty furniture, was littered with rubbish lying around and a foul smell permeated throughout. There was no sign of her daughter.

She stepped out into the hallway and glanced up the stairs where a constable was a few steps ahead, and shouted, 'Victoria! Victoria! Where are you?'

A faint voice from inside a room replied, 'Ma. Is that you?'

'Yes, it is, my darling Victoria. Thank God you are 'ere. We're going to get you out of there.'

Victoria rattled the door handle. 'I'm locked in, Ma. But I'm scared. Is that man who brought me 'ere downstairs still?'

Suddenly, two more police officers appeared. A man wearing a plain suit took charge. He tapped on the door. 'I want you to listen to me, Victoria. You are safe and the perpetrators

291

are not here. They have escaped, and we are hunting them down. If you stand back, my man will force open the door.'

As he finished speaking, another officer placed a wrench behind the lock and applied tension to it, then heaved it open, splintering the wooden frame.

Victoria rushed straight out into her mother's arms, her throat clenched. 'Oh Ma. I never thought I'd see you again.'

Tears streamed down her cheeks. Kitty cried tears of joy and embraced her daughter tightly. Police exchanged relieved glances, handing over their handkerchiefs.

After a few moments, when their sobs had subsided, Kitty asked, 'Are you all right, my darling girl? Did they hurt you?'

'No, but I was scared. I thought Mr Mumbles might hurt me, though I haven't seen him this past day or so. I've been held by a man and an older women. They talked about a reward, but it didn't make sense. Where are they? Have police got them? I want to go home.'

Kitty glanced at the police officer whose eyes cautioned her response. 'Come, Victoria, let's go home. You are safe now, nobody can hurt you.'

Jessie had waited downstairs, allowing Kitty time alone to be reunited with her daughter. She cried tears of joy and sniffled, 'I'm so happy to see you, Victoria. Your ordeal is over.'

As Jessie hugged Victoria, Kitty turned to the detective and spoke softly. 'Thank yer for all you've done, Officer. Do you know where the Ropers might be?'

'Not right now, but we are speaking to all their known associates.'

The officer turned to George. 'We have you to thank, Mr Perryman. None of this would have been possible without your quick thinking. Please allow us to drive you home and my men can take statements tomorrow.'

Victoria nestled her head on her mother's shoulder on the back seat of the police car and Jessie clutched her hand. When the car drew up at their address, Mr Bell and Miss Finchley were waiting outside, and the children bounded out of the house, throwing themselves at Victoria.

Kitty placed a protective arm around her shoulder. 'Shush, children, Victoria needs time to settle.'

Rosie crept up to her eldest sister and placed her tiny hand in hers. Her innocent face stared up. 'I've missed you, Victoria. Will you read me a bedtime story tonight?'

'Maybe just a little one.' Victoria smiled as they walked into the house together.

Chapter Twenty-Seven

The week following Ruth's death was a blur, a cocktail of high emotions and intense gratitude. A day was set the following week for Ruth's funeral, six days after her death, which Maria still found hard to believe. Ruth's passing caused Joey great anxiety. After the undertakers removed her body, Joey became increasingly clingy, fearing the angels might take Maria too.

Mrs Watson called in to see her the following day, bringing with her a bouquet of white lilies and a basket of fruit and cold meats. 'Queen Alexandra and Queen Maud asked if I would deliver you these, with their deepest condolences. Everyone at the Big House is sorry for your loss. There's something for Joey too.'

Mrs Watson handed her a carved wooden farm, complete with all the animals. She told Maria. 'It came from Wood Farm as it's no longer needed in their nursery, I believe it used to belong to Prince John.'

Maria's eyes welled up as she stared at the generous armful of gifts that Mrs Watson left on the table. 'Queen Mary suggested little Joey might enjoy playing with it. She sends her condolences too.'

Maria stuttered. 'I don't know what to say. Everyone's been so kind.'

'The royal family and staff look after their own here. I baked a sponge for you too, Maria, I know how Joey enjoys it. As the royals are away in London, we've agreed that there is no need for you to return for work until after the funeral.'

Maria warbled, 'I appreciate that, there's so much to see to. Will you please thank everyone for me.'

Maria was overcome by the kindness of folk offering their condolences, even those she barely knew. She would open her door to find food packages left on her doorstep with a card. Magnolia delivered some home-made meat pasties that she said was a favourite of David's; there was a pork pie and some currant buns from Betty; a creamy custard tart from Aggie and a lean cut of ham from the vicar's wife which Ruby dropped off. There was also fresh eggs, milk and cream from Lizzie Piper at Blackbird Farm that she insisted Archie bring home with him. Eddie's mother, Mabel, delivered an abundance of fresh cockles that had been caught in the Wash. She kept a kindly eye over her future daughter-in-law by taking her washing in without a murmur, returning everything freshly laundered and ironed. Eddie, Jessie, Beatrice and Ada had called in every day to be a shoulder to cry on and help in any way they could. She couldn't have felt more loved.

Despite this, Maria had barely slept a wink over the last few nights, her heart pounding as grief and uncertainty over Freddie's situation gnawed at her. He was still detained in a police cell where George had been informed him of his mother's death; he was inconsolable, blaming himself for the stress and worry he brought the family over the trouble he was in. However, there was some good news George passed on that offered relief – the soldier who had been attacked in the pub that night had been released from hospital, his injuries not as bad as expected.

''Phew,' exclaimed Maria, through misty eyes. 'I'm so glad to hear that.'

Maria passed on the latest news to Harry when he called in one evening to see how she was. He stroked his moustache and looked thoughtful. 'There is something I think you should know.'

Maria's eyebrows arched. 'Is it to do with Freddie?'

'Could be. I've been giving his arrest some thought, and I wonder if my refusal to put Rufus Fagan forward for a trainee engineer's position had something to do with it. I made it clear that I couldn't recommend a troublemaker from the union. I let it slip that I had someone else in mind, and he asked if it was Freddie. I didn't reply, I told him it was no concern of his, and he stormed off mumbling I would regret it.'

'You must tell George. The police need to know. This is further proof that Freddie's arrest is a stitch-up.'

'We think so too. George told me Alice had been in touch with some very helpful information too,' replied Harry. 'When this is unpleasant business with Freddie is over, I should like to put his name forward to train as an engineer. Do you think he'd be interested?'

Maria clutched Harry's hands tightly in hers. 'Thank yer, Harry. I'm sure Freddie would be grateful for the new position, and I 'ope you get the chance to ask him yourself soon.'

∞

All too soon it was the day of Ruth's funeral. Maria had barely slept a wink and she shivered as she stepped to the window in just her nightgown. It was a chilly morning and the light was beginning to break. Freddie was still detained in the police cells. Maria grasped her hands in front of her chest and whispered, 'I'm sorry, Ma. I'm doing my best for yer. I'll never give up on Freddie.'

As she spoke she spied a robin fluttering past the window before perching on the garden fence. She gasped. 'Is this a sign from yer, Ma? Is yer spirit 'ere?'

The red-breasted bird remained there for a while, before flying off when a stray dog bounded along the lane. A sob stuck in her throat. She washed and dressed in a black blouse and skirt and descended the stairs with a heavy heart. Archie was already up and dressed in a new pair of black trousers and a jacket Lizzie loaned him that had belonged to her husband. It was too big for him, but would get him by. Harry had lent him a spare black tie.

Archie had taken his brother's arrest badly. He had looked up to his brother and though he was the quieter of the two, wishing he had a sprinkling of Freddie's confidence, he believed Freddie should have taken heed of the warnings he was given earlier about his unsavoury associates. Archie preferred spending his time with animals and creatures of the woodland around Wolferton, believing they would never let him down or cause him trouble.

Like his sister, Archie believed the sight of a robin was a sign of their mother's spirit. After she told him she had seen it that morning, he replied, 'It's been here all week. I've been feeding it scraps each day.'

297

'But why didn't you tell me?' she bleated.

'I thought it might upset you. I first noticed him the day after Ma died and sometimes he follows me to Lizzie's farm.'

∽

Harry arrived and placed a comforting arm around Maria's shoulder and straightened Archie's crooked tie. She accepted his offer to accompany her to the church by horse and cart with Abel behind the reins, accompanied by Eddie and his mother. The vicar had arranged for Joey to stay with Ruby and little Piers while the service took place.

Harry's suggestion of using a motorised hearse for Ruth's last journey was dismissed by Maria, saying her ma wouldn't want a fuss or anything fancy, that a horse-drawn hearse would be good enough. It was arranged this would leave first from Honeysuckle Cottage and they would follow.

Harry kept watch at the front of the house and informed her when it arrived. Maria glanced in all directions for the robin when she stepped outside, but it was nowhere to be seen. 'Ready?' asked Harry, his eyes filled with compassion.

Abel, dressed in a dark jacket and black tie, bowed his head respectfully. He helped her up into the seat next to him, Maria hanging on to the black-veiled hat she wore, lent to her by Aggie. Harry, Archie, Eddie and Mabel took a seat in the cart, as well as Joey, who was being dropped off at the church and met there by Ruby who would look after him.

The church was only a five-minute trot away. As the cart rumbled along the lane, Maria's throat began to tighten.

The vicar greeted them by the lych gate. He was joined by a line of twenty or so villagers dressed in black, among them the blacksmith and butcher, the carpenter and laundress, who had turned out and bowed their heads to pay their last respects. Maria held onto Joey's squirming hand as he began to cry. Her eyes searched the faces in front of her and was relieved to spot Ruby near the vicar.

Ruby stepped forward with Piers and produced a sweet from her pocket to entice Joey away, mouthing that Joey would be fine with them and she wasn't to worry. Maria thanked her, then reached down to hug Joey, but he had taken little Piers's hand and walked towards the vicarage just a few yards away, with Ruby following behind and bending down to speak to them.

Joey had vanished from sight when the coffin was lifted down from the hearse and hoisted onto the shoulders of six pall-bearers. Maria dabbed her moist eyes, poised herself and began walking slowly into the church. She stopped in her tracks and grabbed Archie's arm, pointing to the lych gate, 'Look, there he is, our robin is with us. I only wish Freddie was.'

They walked solemnly side by side along the church path, the black veil concealing Maria's reddened eyes. Archie sniffled, his head slightly bowed. Maria's legs wobbled as she stood at the church entrance as Alfie's fingers glided softly along the keys playing the first piece of funereal music to denote the service was about to begin.

The choir rose from their stalls, their voices soft and harmonious as they sang melodically to Beethoven's 'Für Elise', suggested by Alfie whose judgement she trusted on such matters. The voices reached a high-pitch crescendo, doing justice to this powerful composition capable of generating great emotion. Maria had never heard it before and found it very moving, a lump forming in her throat. The composition roused her heightened emotions and she had tears trickling down her cheeks.

The coffin was placed on a stand at the front of the church, a spray of white lilies on top. She and Archie shuffled into the front pew. Harry and Sarah and Eddie and Mabel sat behind them. She glanced sideways and saw the three Saward sisters and Alfie, as well as Magnolia and David, and Aggie and Marcel. Dr Fletcher was there too.

Swinging her head around further, she spotted some distant relatives from Audley End where Ruth and Maria had lived before Wolferton, their heads respectfully bowed.

The church door creaked and footsteps could be heard on the tiles. It was Mrs Watson, her face flustered, making the sign of the cross across her chest and taking a seat at the back next to Mrs Pennywick.

Maria had no idea that her mother was held in such high esteem within this community. She bowed her head and dabbed her moist eyes as the vicar spoke warmly of Ruth, of her modest and unassuming ways, how she asked for nothing for herself and only wanted the best for her family, to be respected in Wolferton, and how she had achieved this for herself and would be a loss in this tight-knit community.

Maria knelt on the embroidered hassock as prayers followed, also praying for her future. *Please, Ma. Guide me through our troubles. Give me wisdom and courage to live my life the way you wanted.*

She rose unsteadily for the next hymn, 'Abide With Me', aided by Archie who placed a protective arm around her shoulder. She opened her lips to sing, but the words stuck in her throat and she dabbed her eyes with her handkerchief.

More prayers followed and then the vicar invited them to reflect on their memories of Ruth. Archie nudged Maria, pointing upwards. 'Look, what do you see?'

She cried, 'It's the robin! It's Ma's spirit saying farewell.'

The bird flew to the back of the church, catching everyone's attention.

As it did so the church door groaned and opened slowly. Every head in the church swivelled around and stared as it opened wide enough for the bird to swoop down and escape outside. Gasps were expelled when a moment later a figure stepped inside.

'Freddie!'

Maria rose to her feet and swayed, looking to the back of the church. Eddie and Archie grabbed each other's arms, shaking their heads in disbelief. Every person's face was fixed on Freddie as he walked down the aisle. George was a few steps behind and found a seat at the rear of the church.

'You made it,' Maria gulped as Freddie made his way into the pew next to her.

'You didn't think I was going to miss Ma's funeral, did you?'

'I'm so glad you're 'ere,' she choked.

Archie shuffled along to make room for Freddie. After the final hymn, the pall-bearers took their position alongside Ruth's coffin. Without warning Freddie stepped out to join them. Archie followed suit and stood alongside his brother, their arms linking across the coffin as they carried their mother to her final resting place.

She was to be placed in a sheltered corner plot under a yew tree, its drooping branches hanging overhead. This tree symbolises death and resurrection and is said to purify the dead, which Maria acknowledged appreciatively. There was a catch in Maria's throat as the vicar recited his burial words, 'Ashes to ashes, dust to dust . . .'

Maria took a handful of soil from his hand and threw it on the coffin. As she did so, she leant over the grave and whispered, 'Our Freddie is home. You can rest in peace, Ma.'

∞

Everyone made their way to the station master's house afterwards for the wake. Betty worked tirelessly to prepare a spread of sandwiches, cold meats and pickles followed by trifle and fruitcake.

Kitty had wanted to come, but Maria insisted she needed time to spend with her family to recover from their ordeal. Police had kept watch outside Mr Bell's house, day and night, in case Bernie Roper tried to harm them, but there had been no sight of him or his mother since they ran off six days ago.

'Can Freddie and I have a moment together?' Maria asked Harry.

Harry offered them the use of his study, but asked if he could join them as he wanted to hear what Freddie had to say.

Maria and Freddie agreed, and once they were all in the study, joined by Eddie, Maria pressed Freddie, 'It's so good to have you back. Is it all over? Are you in the clear?'

'I am, Maria. I didn't think I would make it in time for Ma's funeral. So much has happened.'

'The worry of it was more than I could bear. Everyone was doing their best for you,' Maria said.

Freddie's eyebrows furrowed. 'I know that, and I shall forever be grateful. I would still be at the station if it wasn't for Mr Perryman and the girl from the bakery.'

Maria looked confused. 'Alice? Alice Batterbee from the bakery?'

'Yes, that's her. I shall forever be indebted to Alice.'

Harry listened attentively, stroking his moustache. 'Why don't you start at the beginning, Freddie. I've not had a chance to speak to George. I'd like to hear your account of what happened.'

Freddie turned to the station master. 'I'm glad you are here, Harry. It's important you believe I am innocent.'

Betty knocked on the door and entered carrying a tray with three cups and saucers and a pot of tea. 'I thought you might like this after today's events. I expect you have some catching up to do.'

After their thirst was quenched, Freddie recounted his story. 'Firstly, I want to apologise for the worry I caused Maria, and you too, Harry, for being stupid and getting involved with these troublemakers. I didn't realise what Rufus Fagan was like. I was taken in by him. I've since learnt he wanted to blacken my name 'cause you turned him down for the trainee engineer's position, Harry. He thought if I ended up in the nick, your good name would suffer too because of it and you'd lose your job.'

Harry's face darkened. 'I wondered if that was his wicked plan! Too right I wanted nothing to do with him. I could see he was trouble, with his swagger and cocky ways.'

'Tell us more, what 'appened to bring about yer release?' pressed Maria.

'Rufus's ma is landlady of the Railway Arms and one day she popped into Batterbee's Bakery. According to Alice, she was heard bragging to another customer that no Saward was going to get the better of her family after turning down her son for the position. She accused the Sawards of being snobs and said she knew how to bring them down a peg or two.'

Maria's jaw dropped. 'That's unbelievable.'

Freddie continued, 'It was also very stupid. Another customer was there at the same time, the wife of Constable Thompson. She told him what she had 'eard. Later that evening, Constable Thompson called in at the Railway Arms, dressed in plain clothes. The landlady was the worse for drink, shouting her mouth off and boasting about how she fooled the police and got away with it. Needless to say, the constable immediately made his identity known and escorted 'er to the station, right in front of everyone! He 'ad been clever enough to confide his plan to a trusted colleague who arrived dressed in uniform, and cuffed Mrs Fagan. She was enraged and spitting, but, surprisingly, none of her cronies tried to intervene, they let the police get on with their job.

'Thankfully, Alice told Mr Perryman who acted on the new information. I'll never be able to thank her enough.'

Harry addressed Freddie. 'I'm sorry you had to suffer as a result of me.'

'I want to be a station master one day. I'll never be as good as you, but I want to make you proud of me.'

'I'm sure you will.' Harry smiled. 'What about her son, Rufus? Where was he during all this?'

Freddie shrugged his shoulders. 'Nobody knows, but Mr Perryman says it won't be long afore he is caught and charged with making false statements and assault on the soldier.'

Maria was still taking in what she had heard. 'How can people be so wicked? It was good of Harry to apologise, but he 'ad no idea this was going to 'appen. I can't understand what could drive someone to behave this way.'

'Envy, I guess,' Harry answered.

Freddie continued, 'It's all thanks to Mr Perryman that I was finally freed.'

'I'm waiting to hear, how did he help?' Harry asked.

'It was quite by chance he was at the station when Constable Thompson escorted Mrs Fagan in. He was there on account of Victoria and saw me being brought up from the cells. He instantly stepped in and sorted out all the paperwork with the desk sergeant to arrange my immediate release. Mrs Fagan made a right scene, saying she 'ad friends in high places and would make an official complaint and 'eads would roll.'

Harry rubbed the back of his neck. 'I expect they will, but not the ones she has in mind. It was very fortunate for you that Mr Perryman was there.'

Freddie straightened. 'You can say that again. As it 'appens, I'm not sure if this is confidential. It turns out there could now be a big scandal high up the police ranks, and it's connected with Mrs Fagan. Constable Thompson already had his suspicions about her, someone had grassed

305

that she asked Sergeant Catcheside and Inspector Jericho to stitch me up at the identity parade and plant evidence against me.'

Harry's eyebrows rose. 'That's a very serious allegation. Are you sure about this?'

'I am. I was told she was plying them with free drinks at the Railway Arms and she was known to provide them with women in her upstairs room. She was blackmailing them. She kept shouting for Inspector Jericho to see her and return the favours he owed her. Sergeant Catcheside was off duty, but he will have questions to answer too.'

'I see,' mulled the station master. 'They will now face the consequences of their actions and, if any heads roll, it will be theirs. I must thank George. Where is he?'

Maria replied, 'He's with Beatrice. I think they 'ad a misunderstanding and wanted a minute. I knew we could count on George. To think police connived to throw an innocent man in the cells is a disgrace. I hope they end up locked up themselves, and someone throws away the keys.'

'They'll be forced out of the force, without a doubt if these allegations are proven,' Harry retorted.

'Good riddance to bad rubbish, that's what I say. Three cheers for Constable Thompson,' cheered Maria.

She embraced her brother. 'It's over now, you can put it behind you.'

'And that engineer's training job, Freddie. It's yours for the asking if you're interested.' Harry grinned.

'Need you ask? I really mean it when I say it, I swear I'll do yer proud.'

306

A moment later, the telephone rang and Harry answered it. He listened intently, commenting, 'I see, That's excellent news. Thank you for letting me know, Mr Bell.'

'Well . . .' everyone asked. 'Who was that?'

At that moment George knocked on the door and entered, followed by Beatrice and Jessie, to say people were asking for them.

Harry pressed his thumbs into the waistband of his trouser and thrust out his chest. 'You've come just at the right time to hear latest news from your uncle, George. Police have found Roper and his ma.'

Gasps of astonishment filled the room. 'Does Kitty know? How and when did this happen?' asked Jessie.

'Did my uncle tell you the circumstances of their capture?' enquired George.

Harry raised a hand and waited for quiet. 'It was quite by chance, as it turns out. Mrs Fagan spilled the beans on them, though it took almost a week. It appears Mrs Fagan had profited handsomely while they were on the run by hiding them in one of her rooms at the Railway Arms. She agreed to take them in, in return for a cut of the reward, and charged a good sum for their bed and board, but after Victoria was freed she blackmailed them in return for her silence of their whereabouts. It's all over now.'

Jessie queried, 'But why weren't the Ropers discovered before, if Mrs Fagan's part in Freddie's arrest was brought to the attention of police earlier after Alice Batterbee informed George about it?'

Harry replied, 'That's a very good question. There was no known connection between the Fagans and Ropers. A few days after Mrs Fagan was released by police and charged for providing false information, the Ropers told her they planned to leave that evening and lie low elsewhere. She demanded more money from them in return for her silence and they laughed in her face.

'She's a conniving woman, that Mrs Fagan, and thought her court case would go in her favour if she informed the police of their whereabouts, which she did, and fabricated a story about having no idea of their involvement with Victoria's disappearance.

'The Ropers were caught as they were about to flee. They are a rotten lot, the Ropers and the Fagans, and are now all locked in police cells.'

George announced, 'This calls for a celebration, that is, if Maria doesn't think we are being disrespectful at her mother's wake.'

'She'd be celebrating too. After all, we 'ave Freddie back.'

Harry asked, 'What about Mumbles? Do we know if the Ropers were involved in his death?'

George answered, 'I haven't had a chance to tell you, an autopsy showed he died of natural causes. He had a heart attack. Police believe that Bess Roper's strong assertion she was not aware of this at the time when she robbed him, that she was too drunk to notice.'

Maria tilted her head. 'Who would 'ave thought that the day we lay my ma to rest is one that brings love and peace to us.'

Eddie placed his arm around Maria's shoulder and squeezed it, pressing his cheek against hers. 'Your ma would be 'appy to know it.'

George turned to Beatrice and whispered, 'Are we friends again? I have the impression you are avoiding me. If it's because of Fleur, I can explain . . .'

Beatrice's cheeks turned pink and she flounced out of the room.

George shrugged his shoulders, 'It's not love and peace for us, I'm afraid. But I won't give up.'

Chapter Twenty-Eight

The day after the funeral Maria returned to Appleton House. It was also the first day of Eddie's trial there as a gardener, thanks to the intervention of both Queen Alexandra and Queen Maud.

The land agent was impressed to read Doctor Butterscotch's glowing testimonial, praising Eddie as an exemplary patient which read, 'With the right support, this opportunity could be the start of a new life for Mr Herring, one that leads back to normality. I shall keenly observe his progress in the hope his success will pave the way for other shell-shocked soldiers whose lives have been blighted by their mental scars.'

Eddie felt instantly at ease with his tranquil surroundings. He had an affinity with and understanding of nature that he hadn't previously realised. He became expert at identifying birdsongs and would *speak* back to them in their language, the long-tailed bearded tit and large-eyed barn owls being his favourite feathered companions. He willingly assisted Mr Gilbert with all the back-breaking bending and any heavy carrying and the two got along famously.

At the end of the week, Eddie told Maria he felt well enough to undertake something he hadn't felt able to do before.

'I want to visit the family of Simon Styles. It's been on me mind a while now. Doctor Butterscotch told me I would know when the time was right to see them and I'm ready now.'

'Would you like me to come with you?' asked Maria gently.

'It's something I want to do alone, and I should go soon. I've heard his mother has taken poorly and might not have long left to live and I want to return the letters she wrote to him. I have Simon's pocket watch to give his missus as well. I have to tell them Simon was not a coward.'

It was arranged that Eddie would visit their cottage in Dersingham, two miles away on the edge of the royal estate, the following Sunday afternoon. He wrote to the family first and was delighted they agreed.

On that day, Maria decided to visit Kitty, accompanied by Jessie who wanted to see the Willow family too, and Ruby readily agreed that Joey could play with Piers, the two having become good friends.

'You've settled in well, Ruby,' Maria remarked when she dropped Joey off at the vicarage.

Mrs Rumbelow beamed as Piers ran around her playing catch with Joey. She noticed how much more cheered Mrs Rumbelow was since Ruby and Piers had moved in, giving her a new spring in her step and a cheerful countenance.

Ruby chased after the boys and the vicar's wife accompanied Maria down the path. 'They've given us a reason to get up in the morning, to smile and be grateful for our lives. It was so empty before.'

Maria, dressed in black mourning, nodded empathetically. 'I know what you mean. We can't change the terrible

311

things that happened in the past, but I've learnt there are good people who can 'elp you through bad times, if you let them, and give you 'ope for the future. Thankfully, for me, those people are here in Wolferton.'

The vicar's wife tilted her head. 'Why, Maria, I didn't realise you were such a soulful person, but you're right. Ruby and I have become very close in a short time, she is like a daughter to me, and I couldn't imagine life without our darling grandson, he is so like his father was . . .'

'I'm glad for yer, Mrs Rumbelow, I really am. I believe Ruby and Piers were sent 'ere for a reason to bring you solace during your loss. Few people are offered that.'

∽

The first stop at King's Lynn was to call in at Batterbee's Bakery. Maria wanted to purchase two boxes of assorted patisseries.

Maria introduced Alice to Jessie and Alice greeted them warmly.

Alice shook her hand. 'I'm so very pleased to meet you. We're all so very happy that Victoria is home again. What a terrible ordeal the poor girl endured.'

Jessie acknowledged her greeting, turning her eyes towards the bakes. 'These look so delicious. I would like to buy some, a mixed selection of your recommendation.'

Maria interjected, 'I'm on me way to see Constable Thompson and wanted to purchase some of your best cakes to give 'im by way of thanks as well. I would like another box too for Kitty and her family. Can you pick out a selection of your best bakes for us.'

'I certainly can, but he's no longer a constable, Maria. Thanks to his quick thinking, Sergeant Catcheside and Inspector Jericho have been slung out of the force, and he was promoted to sergeant.'

'It's very well deserved. Any copper who is in cahoots with criminals deserves to be made an example of,' Maria retorted.

'That's what's going to happen. Mrs Thompson has been keeping me informed. She says they were under investigation anyway after a disgruntled police informer snitched on them. It was only a matter of time before they would be caught, but, thanks to Constable Thompson, I mean, Sergeant Thompson, they now have sufficient evidence.'

Hearing this was music to Maria's ears and she smiled gleefully. Her nostrils sniffed the sweet aroma that filled the shop. She leant towards the glass counter where a delectable array of sugary and creamy desserts was spread before her eyes; they were all so tempting, each and every one of them.

'I can see why you have the royal warrant,' murmured Jessie. 'Mrs Watson and Cook can turn out an excellent sponge, but they would never be able to match what you do with such finesse.'

'It's very kind of you to say, Jessie. Pa went to Paris and learnt everything he knows from the great Monsieur Pierre Clement who ran a patisserie school – that's a fancy name for pastries and cakes – and then he taught me everything he knows.'

Jessie expressed interest. 'What brought you to King's Lynn?'

'My mama came from Paris and met my father at a dance class there, now you mention it. Sadly, she died just after giving birth to me, so there is just Father and me.'

Maria's heart went out to Alice for never knowing her mother. Maria counted herself fortunate to have at least had her mother's love for the past twenty years.

'I'm sorry to 'ear that. Not having a mother must 'ave been so 'ard.'

'It was, and that's the reason we came here because it's where my father's family originate from. They gave him the support he needed to get on his feet and buy this shop.'

Maria and Jessie leaned over the counter, their mouths watering at the range of delicacies in front of them, all made by the hand of Alice or her father. It was impossible to choose between the pink and yellow checked Battenberg cake, the glistening tangy lemon drizzle cake topped with an exquisite lemon icing, a moist ginger sponge covered with icing and daisy decorations, lavender iced cupcakes which Alice said was one of their best-sellers, and, finally, oozing cream horns that looked too good to eat. It was easy to see why the Batterbee bakes were so popular with the royal family.

Maria had considered purchasing some jam tarts, scones or currant buns, which she eyed at the far end of the counter, no doubt for customers who had a more traditional taste, or their purses could not stretch to such extravagances. But she decided to splash out on the best, and blow the extravagance, as it was a small price to pay for Freddie's freedom.

Maria stared open mouthed, afraid to ask the price. As if reading her mind, Alice began packing some cakes into two boxes and told her, 'We do not want your money. Please accept these as a gift from my father and me.'

'I couldn't possibly accept. It don't seem right. Please let me pay,' Maria blurted.

'I insist. I would be in serious trouble from Pa if I took money from you. You see, we make a good living from the royal family.'

Maria stuttered. 'I don't know what to say . . .'

Alice turned to Jessie. 'It would give me the greatest pleasure if I could provide you with a mixed selection for your family. Please accept them with our best wishes.'

Jessie's and Maria's protests fell on deaf ears. Jessie produced her purse, but Alice insisted she put it away, and she accepted the white box wrapped in blue ribbon, while Maria was handed two prettily decorated boxes.

Alice held the door open for them. 'I hope you both come and see us again.'

Jessie smiled. 'I promise I will, Alice. I would like to hear more about your life in France and people's different ways there. Thank you again for your generosity.'

Maria clutched both boxes with great care as she trod along the cobbled path, finding herself outside the police station in a blink as her mind reflected on the last time she had taken these steps with her brother and Eddie.

She strode in, followed by Jessie. 'Good morning, Sergeant Thompson.' Maria smiled. He was sitting at his desk behind the counter attending to some paperwork and rose immediately and greeted Maria as she entered. His face was open and honest and he genuinely seemed pleased to see her.

'Good morning, Miss ... Mrs ... Saward,' he started, awkwardly.

'Miss Saward is fine, until I become Mrs Herring.' Maria grinned. She turned to her companion. 'This is Miss Jessie Saward, the royal station master's daughter.'

'I'm pleased to meet you, Miss Saward,' the young sergeant replied. 'I'm happy to say the Ropers are locked up downstairs. We have also nabbed Rufus Fagan. A neighbour alerted us when he was seen loitering at the back of The Railway Arms.'

Jessie tilted her head. 'May I enquire as to what will happen to them?'

'They will appear in court tomorrow and their charges are so serious they will be sent to Norwich Assizes where stiffer sentences can be given.'

'I'm very glad to hear it, and will let Kitty know. We are on our way to see her now.'

Maria slid a cake box across the counter. 'We called in 'cause I'd like to personally thank yer for what yer did to clear Freddie's name. I never thought 'e would make it back in time for Ma's funeral, and that would have broken 'is 'eart.'

Sergeant Thompson's face exuded gratitude. 'I'm very touched by your kindness, but there's really no need, I was only doing my job.'

Maria insisted, 'Mr Perryman says it was thanks to you, and I would also like you to pass on my thanks to your wife for being alert and setting the wheels in motion for Mrs Fagan's arrest.'

Jessie spoke up. 'And that, thank God, led to the capture of the wicked Ropers. We couldn't have hoped for a better outcome.'

'I'm sorry for Freddie that he got caught up in this mess. I will personally see that we write to Freddie to offer our sincere and humble apologies. It is his right to make a formal complaint for wrongful arrest. I would urge him to do so in order that those responsible will be shamed and made fully accountable.'

Maria listened with astonishment. 'We 'ad lost faith with police. It's thanks to you our faith in them is restored. I'll be sure to pass yer message to Freddie.'

Maria pointed to the cake box. 'Go on, open it.'

Sergeant Thompson unwrapped the ribbon on the cake box and peeked inside.

Maria said, 'They are the best, from Batterbee's Bakery. I hope they will be to your liking, and yer wife enjoys them too.'

'There really was no need to go to this trouble. They look delicious, anything from Batterbee's is bound to be.'

'Good day, Sergeant. We shall now call on Mrs Willow.'

As they stepped towards the door, Jessie turned and asked, 'What about Miss Feathers? What's happened to her?'

'None of the girls she coerced for him are willing to speak about it, except one, and that may not be enough evidence. I believe she has family on the Isle of Wight and plans to spend time there while she decides on her future. I doubt she will show her face here again.'

'And the other man, Tobias Scott?' Maria asked.

The office replied, 'He's in the cells too and greatly regrets his involvement. He is assisting police, so the courts will look more kindly on him. Please pass on my sincerest wishes to

Mrs Willow. It is my intention to ensure the good citizens of King's Lynn can sleep well and venture out without having to look over their shoulders.'

'I'm glad to 'ear it. We'll be on our way then. Good day, Sergeant Thompson.'

Maria and Jessie stepped outside the station with a spring in their step. Jessie linked arms with Maria. 'If only Jack could be here, my happiness would be complete.'

'He will soon. You know he wants to be 'ere too,' Maria replied.

'If that's the case, why doesn't he do something about it? Beatrice has been acting strangely too and has stopped taking George's calls. What could be the reason for that?'

Within a few minutes they were outside Mr Bell's house. They stood back and admired the impressive three-storey town house with its ornate decorative doorway. Maria stepped forward and raised her hand to lift the knocker when a child's voice called their names.

'Maria? Jessie?'

'Rosie!'

Maria placed her parcel on the ground and stretched her arms out to sweep Rosie up as she ran excitedly towards her.

Kitty appeared red faced from around the corner and scolded, 'Rosie. What have I told you about running out of the house?'

'But I saw Maria and Jessie and was excited to see them.'

Kitty took Rosie's hand. 'I can't 'elp being overanxious, even though Mumbles is dead and his men can't harm us now. But it's so lovely to see you both.'

'That's perfectly understandable,' Maria agreed. 'I 'ope we 'aven't come at a bad time. I didn't 'ave time to write to you first.'

Jessie stepped forward to embrace Kitty, hugging her tightly. 'I've been so worried about you. How are you all? How is dear Victoria?'

'She's at school, she wanted to return as quickly as possible to put it all out of her mind. Would you like to come inside? Mr Bell won't mind.'

Maria said, 'That's kind, but I don't want to get yer into trouble.'

'Silly, of course it won't. I've been told by Mr Bell not to worry about the chores. I mainly sit with Mrs Bell, and that's no 'ardship. She's an interesting lady and a good listener.'

Maria handed Kitty the beautifully packaged box. 'These are for you.'

Rosie tugged at her mother's arm and leapt up and down. 'What is it, Ma? Can I look inside?'

Kitty's face lit up. 'They're from Batterbee's, I recognise the box. That is very kind of you, Maria.'

Maria and Jessie followed Kitty around the side of the house and entered through the back door into the kitchen. Miss Finchley was pouring from the kettle into a large teapot and Kitty introduced the housekeeper to Maria, placing the ribboned box on the table.

Miss Finchley welcomed them both with warmth. 'Kitty has spoken fondly of you, my dear. I am pleased to meet you. Will you excuse me for a moment while I take up some tea for Mrs Bell, and then I shall go out and leave you to catch up. There is an elderly lady I should like to visit in one of the alms houses who is almost blind and likes me to read to her.'

'It's a pleasure to meet you.' Maria smiled, her eyes scanning the comfortable surroundings and thinking how well Kitty had landed on her feet.

She pointed to a plate. 'Help yourself to a scone. They were freshly baked this morning. I am taking one now to Mrs Bell.'

After a few minutes Miss Finchley returned downstairs with her coat and hat, and walked to the back door. 'Just a word of warning, Mr Bell is occupied with some important paperwork in his office and asks not to be disturbed.'

As Maria, Jessie and Kitty bade farewell, Rosie knelt on a kitchen chair and untied the box's ribbon, ripping open the lid before they could stop her. 'Ma, look at these!'

Kitty reached out to remove them from Rosie's hands. Maria winked at Rosie. 'That's all right, Kitty, let her be. They're not just for looking at.'

Kitty shook her head. 'These look too good to eat. We always stop and admire the cakes in the window at Batterbee's when we pass.'

Jessie caught Maria's eyes feeling embarrassed by the thanks heaped upon them when she hadn't paid a farthing for the delicacies.

She owned up, 'We have a confession to make, Kitty. You see, Alice refused to take a farthing from us, even though we insisted, and fully intended to pay.'

'It's the thought that counts.' Kitty beamed. 'This is such a treat.'

Kitty counted the bakes, there was exactly one for each of her family. She refused to take first choice, but Maria insisted, and she selected the carrot cake, while Rosie plumped for the violet cupcake. Maria refused, saying they were intended for Kitty and the children to enjoy as a treat when they returned home later. Kitty and Rosie gleefully licked their lips and savoured every crumb, declaring they were the best cakes they had ever tasted. 'But don't tell Miss Finchley,' whispered Kitty.

Rosie picked up on the conversation. She teased, 'Do you think Miss Finchley could make me a cake like this?'

'There, she is only four and has a taste for fancy cakes. You've spoilt her,' laughed Kitty, rolling her eyes upwards.

The conversation turned to the Reverend Pierrepoint's meeting in Wolferton. When Rosie was out of earshot, Kitty confided, 'I listened to 'im, but he gave me no 'ope of my Frank ever coming home. I'd been putting it off, but Mr Perryman said it's time for me to apply for my widow's pension, he'll 'elp me with the form.'

Jessie inhaled a deep breath, her eyes narrowing. 'I'm so sorry that you have to go through this now, on top of everything that's happened. It just doesn't seem fair.'

Kitty sighed. 'Who says life is fair? War ain't fair. I could go mad thinking about all the unfairness in the world. But I also 'ave much to be grateful for, thanks to Mr Bell. We'll get along fine now.'

Maria exchanged her news and after an hour Jessie rose, indicating it was time to leave. A thought occurred to her.

'Are you free next Friday evening, Kitty? I wonder if you fancy coming to Aggie and Marcel's tea dance with me. It should cheer you up.'

'Me, dance? I'm not sure I'm in the mood for it,' replied Kitty.

Jessie spoke sympathetically. 'I understand, Kitty, but you have friends in Wolferton who care about you and would love to see you.'

Kitty pondered on it for a moment, and then nodded. 'Very well, if you are going too, but just for a short time. How will I get there? And what will I wear?'

Jessie raised a hand. 'I'll persuade George to go, he can bring you in his motor car. I have a feeling he would like to take Beatrice, even though he says he is not fond of dancing. It might be the right place for them to make up their tiff. I'll see if I can talk her into going.'

Kitty smiled. 'You are a wonderful matchmaker. But what about your Jack? Will he be there?'

Jessie shrugged her shoulders. 'I'm sure he would be if he could. Truth be told, I am getting tired of these long absences.'

Maria commented, 'I was in two minds about going so soon after Ma's passing, but Eddie persuaded me. 'E said Ma wouldn't want me to mope. What persuaded me is 'cause 'e says 'e wants to give it a try too. That's a big step for Eddie with his shell shock, and I don't want to discourage 'im if 'e feels 'e can cope with dance music.'

Kitty looked doubtful. 'I'll need to ask Miss Finchley if she doesn't mind keeping an eye on the children. And besides, I'm not sure Mr Perryman would want to be seen out in the evening with me, not if he's taking Beatrice there.'

Maria shook her head. 'You should know by now Mr Perryman doesn't 'ave airs and graces.'

When it was time to go, they waved farewell to Kitty, with Rosie clinging to her mother's skirt, and made their way back to the station, gesturing cheerily to Alice as they passed her shop.

On the journey back to Wolferton, Maria's mind turned to Eddie and his visit to Mrs Styles and wondered how it had gone. When they arrived, she waited a few minutes, knowing his train was due. When he stepped onto the platform her heart sank. His expression was downcast.

'How was Mrs Styles, Eddie? How did your visit go?'

Eddie clenched his fists. 'It was awful, Maria. Simon has a little 'un, a boy of three, he is the spitting image of his dad. It broke me 'eart to see 'im.'

'Oh Eddie, that's very sad. But it's not your fault, remember. How is his poor wife coping?'

'Sal, her name is. She ain't doing well. On paper Simon is a coward, which means she ain't entitled to a widow's pension. It ain't right. He weren't no coward. He was doing what he thought was best for his ma. Sal and her lad 'ave moved in with 'is ma, though the shock of this 'as made 'er give up the will to live.'

Maria shook her head. 'Poor woman, I know what it's like to feel an outcast. I can imagine the dirty looks she gets.'

'She does, and worse. She is spat at too and called names. She doesn't deserve that.'

Maria's face reddened and her eyes flashed. 'People are so quick to point the finger without knowing the truth. If you don't mind, Eddie, I should like to visit Sal and go out walking with 'er. If anyone tries to spit at her in my presence,

323

they'll have me to reckon with, they won't mess about with a Saward.'

Eddie asked, his eyes widening. 'Would you do that, Maria?'

'Of course I would, and more, anything I can to 'elp Simon and his family.'

Eddie's face brightened. 'I love that fire in yer belly and how you don't care what people think. I hope you won't be disappointed in me after we marry. Will you mind being Mrs Herring instead of a Saward?'

Maria grinned. 'Who says I'm gonna change me name? I might keep the Saward name, seeing it carries weight around here.'

Eddie's eyes dropped and he stared into his lap. Maria nudged him in the ribs. 'I'm only teasing you. Of course, I'll be proud to take yer name and be Mrs Eddie Herring.'

Eddie's eyes shone. 'I believed yer for a minute there. Come along, *Mrs Herring-to-be,* I'll walk yer 'ome.'

Chapter Twenty-Nine

Kitty and her family had settled well in Mr Bell's home, but she questioned how long she could be beholden to his kindness. She raised the subject once, but it was airily dismissed.

Mr Bell put her at ease by telling her that his household had benefited from her family's company too, with Mrs Bell senior getting immeasurable pleasure from her company, appearing brighter than she had for a very long time. Victoria was making a surprising recovery from her ordeal, which put Kitty's mind greatly at ease. Furthermore, Mr Bell's sister, Lucinda, was still away and had written to say she had no immediate plans to return. While Kitty relaxed into a steady routine, she was still conscious they could not remain there forever, despite Mr Bell's assurances.

Maria's and Jessie's recent visit had rekindled fond memories of her happy days living on the royal estate with Frank and the children. A part of her yearned to return there, but she accepted that was the past and she had to look forward to a new life.

Rosie still experienced moments of anxiety and wanted to be cuddled in her bed at night, clinging tightly onto her topsy-turvy doll or her mother's skirt. She enjoyed her new school in the town and had won the heart of a sympathetic teacher with her wide smile and angelic face.

Victoria dropped her off each morning, along with her other siblings who attended, with separate areas for younger and older children. There were separate classes too for boys and girls. Pip was no longer taunted by other lads or feared the cane. Kitty's heart sang when he returned home at the end of the school day with rosy cheeks and full of chatter about his new friends.

Although only twelve years old, Pip's aptitude for woodwork and his skill at carving greatly impressed his teacher and he spoke to Kitty about it. She readily agreed when the teacher offered to take Pip to see his father, a master furniture maker, one day after school. They hit it off immediately and Pip proudly accepted an offer to assist him with odd jobs at weekends and school holidays. How she wished her Frank could see how well Pip had turned out, following in his father's footsteps.

Laurie had grown in confidence and struck up a friendship with a fellow ten-year-old, a studious bespectacled boy he was seated next to in class by the name of Robin. The boy was cruelly teased for being a swot and Laurie became his protector. They spent hours after school with their heads locked together solving a complicated set of mathematical questions set by their teacher who was keen to encourage their enthusiasm. To Kitty's amazement, Laurie picked up Robin's love of maths and enjoyed being set challenging tests.

Billy was as mischievous as ever and could be heard several streets away playing his penny whistle as he skipped along the cobbles. He still played pranks and terrified Rosie by walking into her bedroom at night, a sheet over his head, the moon shining through the window, and standing over her bed making strange noises. Her shrieks filled the house, causing great alarm for the elderly Mrs Bell. Miss Finchley made it clear to him that such behaviour was unacceptable, and he quaked as she reprimanded him severely, making him fill the coal bucket every morning and night for the following week.

Iris was still a tomboy and a free spirit. As her brothers made new friends, she became more introverted. Mrs Bell heard about her woes and bribed Iris to spend time with her playing board games and she soon cheered up when she won a game of draughts or ludo, with Mrs Bell rewarding her with sweets or a penny or two, praising the seven-year-old girl on her good deed in keeping an elderly bedbound lady well amused. Iris became attached to her and enjoyed listening to Mrs Bell's stories from her young days, having to be shooed out of the room by her mother so Mrs Bell could rest.

Victoria was due to leave school in another year when she turned fourteen. She was considering Mrs Fairbairn's offer of a position as a teaching assistant at the workhouse school, but Kitty was unsure if Victoria should return there after her ordeal.

Victoria was determined to make her own decision, telling her mother, 'There are no bad men there any more, Ma. I should like to help. I know what it's like for the children there and if I can make them feel a teeny-weeny better, I shall feel very happy.'

Kitty's eyes shone . 'You 'ave a kind 'eart and the makings of a lovely lady. If that's what yer want to do, I won't stop you, Victoria.'

∞

A few days later, Kitty knocked lightly on Mr Bell's office door. She heard shuffling noises inside, but, getting no response, she opened the door slightly and peered inside.

She froze, staring in disbelief at Miss Finchley and Mr Bell who were in an embrace, and quickly pulled away from each other when they saw her.

Feeling deeply embarrassed, Kitty hastily dipped her knee, closed the door behind her and rushed into the kitchen. She couldn't believe what she had witnessed. How should she react when she saw them next?

A breath caught in her throat as she recalled two previous occasions when she noticed Miss Finchley and Mr Bell exchanging warm glances, his hand lingering on her arm once. She recalled too that the housekeeper's eyes seemed to follow Mr Bell's movements with a look of deep affection. She'd thought nothing of it at the time; after all, she was a housekeeper and in a lower social class, but putting the pieces together now, the thought occurred to her that there was an intimacy between them which she could no longer doubt.

She was still shaking and trying to make sense of what she had witnessed when the bell rang in Mrs Bell's room, connected to the kitchen. She paused as she passed the office door on her way to answer it, hearing raised voices from inside. Miss Finchley was protesting, 'No, Josiah, we can't say anything.'

Kitty drew away guiltily and stepped briskly up the stairs, her hands shaking. As she entered the room, Mrs Bell had pulled off the bedcovers and threw her legs over the side of the bed.

'I've had enough of staying put in that bed like an imbecile. Can you help me over to the chair please, Kitty?'

'Are you sure? What will Mr Bell say?'

'I couldn't care less. I've had enough of being treated like an invalid, even if I am one.'

Kitty placed a bedside jacket around Mrs Bell and folded it across her chest. Taking hold of her under her arm, Kitty helped Mrs Bell rise unsteadily, her feet wobbling, and she leant heavily against Kitty. She paused for a moment to steady herself and nodded to Kitty, who aided her towards the powder blue armchair in the corner of the room.

'That's better, much better,' gasped Mrs Bell, with relief. 'Talking of my son, could you please ask him to come up and see me?'

Kitty blurted, 'Oh no, I couldn't possibly . . .'

'What on earth do you mean?'

Kitty averted her eyes from Mrs Bell's prying gaze.

'Dammit, will you tell me what's happening in my household?'

Kitty stuttered, glancing shyly at her mistress. 'It's not that simple, seeing it's not my secret to share.'

'A secret, you say? We don't keep secrets from each other, do we? How about I be the judge of that?'

Kitty's shoulders slumped and she twisted her fingers in front of her, wondering what to do for the best. What she had seen left her feeling uneasy about her position in the house now and she couldn't hold back any longer.

'Very well. I saw Miss Finchley and Mr Bell together, his arms around her. Please don't tell them I told you.'

Kitty observed Mrs Bell's face for a reaction. She noticed her body stiffen and her lips press together.

'I see. Thank you for telling me, Kitty. I think the time has come for me to speak to my son about this.'

∽

By the time Kitty returned downstairs to pass on his mother's request to see him, George Perryman had made an appearance. He was hanging his coat in the hallway when Mr Bell put his head out of the office door. 'May I have a word please, George.'

Milly was back from the market and unpacking her shopping. She raised an eyebrow. 'Do yer know what's going on 'ere? I get the feeling something's going on. I opened me mouth to speak to Miss Finchley a moment ago, but she was really curt and said, "Not now, Milly. I have an important matter to discuss." She spoke so sharply I felt I'd been cut in 'arf. That ain't like 'er.'

Kitty's eyebrows met in the middle. She couldn't divulge what she had seen and began regretting that she had mentioned it to Mrs Bell.

'I'm sure she didn't mean to be harsh.'

Milly shrugged her shoulders. She stared at Kitty. 'You seem in a daze too. I dunno what's 'appened to everyone today.'

'I'm sure you're imagining it. Nothing is wrong.'

Milly placed her hands on her hips and threw her head back. 'Sorry I spoke.'

'I'm sorry, Milly,' spluttered Kitty. 'Read into it what you like. I really must get on.'

The bell from Mrs Bell's bedroom sounded downstairs again. When Kitty reached her, her mistress enquired, 'Is George here?'

'Yes, ma'am, he is. Mr Bell called him into his study and I didn't like to disturb him. Miss Finchley is with them. I think Milly has got wind of something. I didn't know what to say to her.'

Mrs Bell rose, a determined look etched across her face. 'Well, there's only one thing for it. Come on, I intend to go downstairs and get to the bottom of this.'

'But you can't. You're not strong enough!' exclaimed Kitty.

'With your help, I shall manage perfectly well. I've had enough of being wrapped up in cotton wool. I should like to wear my green dress with the white collar and cuffs. I've had enough of wearing nightgowns when I have a wardrobe full of the best clothing.'

Half an hour later, Mrs Bell was washed and dressed in her fine dress and her hair styled. She powdered her face and finished by rouging her lips.

Kitty stood back and admired her mistress. 'You do look lovely, ma'am. I've never seen you dressed so lovely before.'

Mrs Bell smiled, and Kitty added quickly, 'I mean, dressed in your day clothes. It's really something special. You look very elegant and smart. I can see you were a head-turner in yer young days.'

'That's very kind of you to say, Kitty. Will you pass me my pearl necklace, and then I shall be ready.'

331

Kitty's heart raced as she helped Mrs Bell to her feet. 'Just lean on me as much as you like. I'm strong enough to take it.'

They counted fourteen steps down to the hallway and each one was taken at a snail's pace, followed by Mrs Bell taking a deep inhale of breath, until they reached the bottom.

Mrs Bell paused to regain her breath, leaning against Kitty, whose hand supported her mistress under the crook of her arm.

'I'm going in now,' she declared, wobbling slightly against the doorframe, gripping the door handle and marching straight into the study.

'Mother!' exclaimed Josiah Bell, a shocked expression etched on his face. 'What are you doing here?'

'I think we should sit down and have a talk, don't you?'

Mr Bell rushed over to his mother to lend his arm for support, leading her to an armchair. He indicated to Kitty that she could go.

Once she was seated, Mrs Bell spoke authoritatively. 'That will do nicely, Josiah. Now, where shall we start?'

Chapter Thirty

Ruby laid out her favourite red dress to wear to Aggie and Marcel's tea dance. It had remained hanging in the wardrobe since she arrived in Wolferton. Every now and again she would take it out and stroke the silky fabric and wish she had somewhere special to wear it. Maria had encouraged her to put it on, warning it would only get eaten by moths if it didn't get a proper airing.

Mrs Rumbelow raised her eyebrows when she saw Ruby flounce down the stairs and the way the dress enhanced her womanly curves. It was low cut and a delicate white lace edging added some freshness and a little protection for her modesty.

'Piers bought it for me,' she said softly.

'My dear, you look most charming,' Jane said hesitantly.

'Do you like it? Only, I haven't been to a dance for so long. I don't know what to wear.'

'I wonder if it is a little risqué for Wolferton,' the vicar's wife replied with candour.

She disappeared for a moment and returned a moment later with her husband.

'You look lovely, my dear,' her husband complimented.

Mrs Rumbelow clutched a jewellery box embossed with mother of pearl. She lifted the lid and held out a necklace.

'Why don't you try this with it? It was a wedding present from Frederick, but I don't get the chance to wear it these days.'

Ruby's eyes widened as she gently lifted a pearl choker from box. It had a lustrous ruby set in the middle. She admired the thoughtful and generous gesture, the gem matching her name, but she replaced it in the box, laying it carefully on the pink satin lining, and closed the lid.

'I couldn't. It's far too good for the likes of me.'

Mrs Rumbelow insisted. 'Not at all. We want you to have it; you share the same name, after all. It would show people here that we have accepted you and our grandson into the family.'

Ruby stood her ground. 'I couldn't possibly wear your wedding present. It must mean so much to you and be worth a fortune. But thank yer for your kind offer. I am very touched by it.'

The vicar suggested, 'Maybe Ruby is right. Perhaps it might be too showy for a tea dance. But you do have a silver chain with a locket, the one with Piers's photograph inside and a lock of his hair from when he was a baby. Maybe she could borrow that instead?'

Mrs Rumbelow considered what her husband said, nodding in agreement. Ruby's face broke into a wide smile. 'That would be perfect, just perfect. I promise I will return it to you.'

Piers was playing on the floor with a wind-up musical toy. He glanced up when he heard his name being mentioned. 'Can I see the picture of me, Ma?'

She knelt down next to him and showed him the picture in the locket. 'It's not of you, but your pa, but it looks like you, doesn't it?'

'Why can't I have a new pa? Joey says his ma is getting married and he will have a new father.'

'I don't want to get married. Your pa was a very brave man, and a very clever man too. He would have loved you dearly.'

Joey clasped his arms around her neck.

She tied the clasp on the locket carefully around her neck and stroked it with her finger.

'This means more to me than all the fine jewels in the country. I feel Piers is close to me when wearing this.'

The vicar lay his hand around his wife's shoulder as they stood by the front door watching Ruby walk down the path. She had arranged to meet Maria and Eddie outside the station master's house.

Maria's eyes admired Ruby from head to toe. 'You look beautiful, Ruby. That dress is perfect. I have a feeling this is going to be a special night. Everyone's going. Beatrice, Ada and Alfie have gone ahead. Jessie is joining us later and has persuaded Lizzie Piper to come too. I believe Kitty is coming with Mr Perryman in his motor car. Word has spread around the estate how enjoyable these dances are, with more and more people coming from other villages.'

Ruby grinned. 'We'd best not waste a minute then, should we?'

As they crossed the road and passed the station, a train pulled in, but they were so engrossed with their thoughts of the dance that they barely glanced at it. A gathering of local people were swarmed around a male figure and appeared excited.

Curious, Maria strained her eyes to see who had caught their attention, but Eddie pulled her along.

'Do you realise this will be our first proper dance together?'

'The first of many,' she laughed.

∞

The meeting room was filling up when they entered the hall, with people jostling for seats. Maria led Eddie to a quiet corner while Ruby excused herself to talk to someone she recognised.

Once seated, Maria was confused to see Alfie standing and chatting to a group of friends while the sound of music filled the room, but was not played by him.

Ada approached Maria's table. She exclaimed, 'Isn't this new music wonderful. It means I get the chance to dance with my husband.'

'I don't understand. Where is the music coming from? Why isn't Alfie playing the piano?'

Ada pointed to the stage at the end of the room. Aggie and Marcel were hunched over a contraption she'd never seen before, with a large brass horn where the sound was coming from. It was placed over a box with a black disc spinning around. Marcel was taking some of the discs out of a sleeve and reading the writing in the middle.

'It's a gramophone. A clever modern contraption that plays the sounds of many instruments at the same time, and voices singing too. It's recorded in a special studio.'

Maria asked, 'What about Alfie? Doesn't he need the work?'

Before Ada could answer, Alfie came over and whispered in her ear and they moved towards the front of the hall. At

336

that moment Maria spotted George entering with Kitty and another young lady. He scanned the room for Beatrice and made a beeline for her. Maria invited Kitty and the other girl to join them.

Kitty introduced her, 'Thank you for inviting me, Maria, this looks fun. This is Fleur, she is a friend of George's and works at the hospital with Beatrice.'

'Pleased to meet you,' replied Maria, turning her head to look for Beatrice. She spotted her with a group of other nurses as George approached her, her appearance more elegant and stylish than her sensible clothing and usual nurse's attire.

Maria gawped. 'I never knew Beatrice was so pretty. Just look at her.'

George's mouth opened wide as he eyed the woman he adored wearing a smart black satin dress with white pearly buttons down the front, teamed with stylish black patent shoes with a shiny buckle. A string of pearls was draped down her chest and her hair was piled high with loose strands of curls hanging down the sides of her cheeks.

'Beatrice,' he whispered, his heart soaring as he walked towards her. He couldn't take his eyes off her, and when he reached her table, he gushed, 'You look utterly divine. You are the most beautiful woman in the room. Is there somewhere private we can talk?'

'I see you brought Fleur with you, and I was trying tonight to make an effort to make up with you, but there doesn't seem to be any point.'

George gasped. 'You surely don't think there is anything going on between Fleur and me?'

She glanced sideways at him. 'Isn't there?'

'No, you silly thing. Fleur is pretty, but it is you that has my heart. Please, let me explain. You see, she was brought up in the workhouse and was brave enough to speak to me about the things that happened there with Mumbles. That's what we were talking about when you saw us at the hospital. Only, of course, it was confidential. She felt ashamed of anyone knowing she was raised there. I introduced her to Kitty, and Kitty asked her along this evening.'

Beatrice's face turned crimson. 'I'm sorry, George. I should never have doubted you. What must you think of me?'

George's adoring gaze was the answer she needed as the sound of hands clapping broke out in the room, calling for everyone's attention. Alfie raised his hand and cleared his throat, with Ada at his side.

He spoke loudly. 'I have an announcement to make. Ada and I have some news we wanted to share with you.'

'News? What news?' asked George, his eyebrows raising.

'Ada and I are leaving Wolferton. Leslie too, of course. I've been asked to return to my old job at Cromer. It seems the person they appointed in my absence didn't fit in well and the congregation and choir petitioned for my return. As you can see, I am no longer needed here, now the gramophone has arrived in Wolferton. I believe it was Marcel's suggestion, and a most timely one.'

'What a surprise, I had no idea. Did you, Beatrice?' George asked.

'They mentioned it just before we came out. I shall miss them, we all will,' Beatrice replied.

'They won't be too far away, and we can always visit.' After a pause, he added, 'I've missed you too these past few weeks, darling Beatrice. I promise I won't let my work get in the way of seeing you again.'

'And I shall promise to curb my jealousy,' Beatrice replied. 'It shows how much I care for you.'

A romantic melodic tune began playing on the gramophone and people took to the dance floor.

'Shall we?' asked George, smiling, holding out his hand.

She accepted it and rose. 'How can I refuse the most handsome man in the room?'

George placed his arm around Beatrice's waist while her arm rested on his right shoulder. He led her around the room, his limp causing him to rise higher on one side. He missed some steps and winced.

'Are you tired?' Beatrice asked, her eyes showing concern.

'I'm afraid so. Do you mind if we sit awhile?'

George led her to an unoccupied table in a quiet part of the room.

Beatrice asked, 'What is it, George? You look serious all of a sudden.'

'There is something important I need to tell you, but first, my darling, I want you to know I truly love you. I cannot imagine spending the rest of my life with anyone else.'

'I love you too, George, you know it.'

'I only hope what I have to say now won't change the way you feel towards me.'

Beatrice pulled back. 'I'm feeling nervous now. It surely can't be so bad?'

'It's about my parentage. I have never spoken about it as I didn't know them. As you know I was brought up under Uncle Josiah's roof and he led me to believe that my father was his brother, Gilbert, a solicitor.

'Uncle Josiah told me my mother, Primrose, died in childbirth. My father, despite his shortcomings, adored her and was bereft after her death. He left me in Uncle Josiah's care and sailed to Australia where he intended to set up a legal practice and start afresh. He planned to return to England within a couple of years and take me back with him once he was established.

'However, it didn't go to plan. My father drowned the month before he was due to come for me. He was taking a pleasure trip on a boat when it was hit by an enormous wave and capsized.'

Beatrice rested her hand on his arm. 'I had no idea. I'm so sorry to hear this. Why the secrecy though?'

'Let me finish. You see, that is the story I was told by my uncle so I could have a respectable life, but it wasn't true, it was a cover-up. There's a twist in this sorry story.'

He paused and inhaled a breath. 'While it's true that Gilbert really existed and drowned on the other side of the world, he wasn't my father. He was my uncle.'

Beatrice stared at him, her eyes narrowing. 'I'm confused, George. So who is your father?'

'It's Uncle Josiah. I was his illegitimate love child and he kept it from me all these years to protect his reputation.'

Beatrice was aghast. 'None of this makes sense. So who was your mother?'

'That was the biggest surprise of all. It's Miss Finchley! Henrietta Finchley.'

Beatrice's eyes were unable to hide the shock she felt. 'You mean to say your housekeeper is really your mother?'

George rubbed his neck. 'As unfathomable as it sounds, that's correct. It turns out I do have a father and mother and have been living under the same roof as them all these years without realising. I'm still trying to make sense of it, though I've only just learnt of it after my grandmother said it was time for them to come clean.'

'I can hardly believe this. Could your uncle not have mentioned this to you before now?'

'Let me finish, there's more for you to hear. My father's business partner was Henrietta's father, Edward Finchley, who was a big gambler. He lost a fortune one night and couldn't pay his debt. He was threatened with violence unless he paid up within twenty-four hours, and, in desperation, he came up with the idea of giving away his share in the business to cover his debt. As you can imagine, Uncle Josiah, I mean, my father, was furious, and they begged and borrowed to repay the crooks, so he had sole ownership.

'However, Father was infatuated with Henrietta, and she returned his affections. Because of her father's disgrace, they kept their true feelings secret from his family. He hoped they would change their minds after they saw how happy they were together and they became secretly engaged to be married.'

'I'm not sure I understand,' Beatrice uttered.

George expostulated, 'My grandmother forced Father to give Henrietta up saying it would be a stain on their

341

business to still be associated with the Finchleys. He was told if he didn't do so, he would be disinherited. Unbeknown to Father, or herself at the time, Miss Finchley, my mother, was with child, with me. She was heartbroken when he broke off their engagement and went to Ireland to stay with a distant cousin.

'Father's mother tried in vain to introduce him to polite well-connected ladies in their social circles, but he wasn't interested. Two years later, Father discovered quite by chance that Henrietta had returned to King's Lynn following the death of her cousin. He also learnt she was living in the workhouse with a child. After her relative died, she could think of nowhere else to go and always hoped one day that she might see Father again as she never stopped loving him.'

Beatrice's jaw dropped. 'You mean . . . ?'

'Yes, Beatrice. I am a workhouse child, like Fleur, though I have no memory of it. Does that make you think any differently of me?'

Beatrice's eyes moistened. 'It doesn't matter to me. I love you for who you are. It's a sad story for both you and your parents.'

'Once Father tracked us down he demanded that my grandmother allow us to live with her so he could help me grow up into a gentleman. He threatened to leave the town with us if she didn't agree and Father never forgave himself for breaking off his engagement.

'Grandmother could see how determined Father was, so she suggested, to keep face, that my mother should be installed as their housekeeper and I was to be raised as his nephew.'

He paused, inhaling a deep breath. 'As you can imagine, hearing this came as a huge shock. If you need time to reconsider your feelings towards me, I will understand.'

Beatrice wiped a tear from her cheek. 'I don't know why I'm crying. I've already said I love you and I still do. You are still the same man I fell in love with. Thinking about it, what you say makes sense as I can see now why your father wants to do so much to improve conditions at the workhouse, and how you share his strong sense of justice for the underdog because it's in your blood.'

'That is true. Like my father, we believe in giving people a second chance, and not judging appearances or class.'

'I am curious on one matter. Where did your name come from, *Perryman*?'

'My father chose that name for me instead of Bell as part of his cover-up. I quite like it and shall keep it as it is on my birth certificate. It appears I genuinely have an uncle by that name on my mother's side who is a coroner. A *real* uncle, that is, called Sir Henry Perryman.'

'I'm lost for words. I never imagined what a dark horse you were, with so many secrets. If you're happy, my darling George, I'm happy too.'

'Thank you, darling Beatrice. I feel so much better for telling you.'

Beatrice raised her eyes to his and could only see tenderness staring back at her. She tilted his chin towards her face so their lips met. She felt a warm tingling sensation inside her.

Standing up, and then bending unsteadily on one leg George reached into his jacket pocket and produced a small box. He opened the lid and a sparkling diamond shimmered.

'Beatrice Saward, I am madly in love with you. Will you do me the honour of being my wife?'

Beatrice only had eyes for George. 'Yes, George, yes, I will marry you!'

Chapter Thirty-One

Word quickly spread about the engagement and a celebratory air filled the room. Ecstasy was written all over Beatrice and George's faces and Maria and Eddie congratulated them warmly, with Maria commenting, 'There are changes in the air, though I shall miss Ada when she moves away.'

Ruby joined in the congratulations, a warm glow rising within her at being part of a community that had suffered so much loss, but was now moving on. She had attracted admiring glances during the evening and was invited to dance by some of the single men there, but she declined out of loyalty to Piers and respect to his parents, while Fleur happily accepted and was seen being held closely by one young war veteran.

Jessie and Lizzie Piper partnered each other on the floor, whooping it up when they heard Beatrice and George's happy news.

Their energetic steps left them breathless as a pacy foxtrot came to an end. Jessie, mopping her brow, suggested they should sit the next dance out. She watched as people took their positions for a slow waltz. Within a few seconds, Jessie's ears pricked up. The tune sounded familiar and she strained her ears, her lips curling. 'I know this music, it's called, "A Rose for my Darling", isn't it?'

Maria confirmed it was. Jessie's eyes became misty. 'It's our special song, Jack and mine. It reminds me of when we dined in London last year and it was played by an orchestra. Jack asked me to dance. It was the most magical evening.'

'How romantic.' Ruby smiled. 'It is a beautiful piece of music.'

Maria noticed a man's figure walking towards them and inhaled a quick breath. Jessie's back was to him and he paused, catching Maria's eye, pressing his index finger against his lips to indicate she should remain quiet.

'Yes, it's a very beautiful song, Jessie,' Maria said, unable to conceal a big smile.

The man appeared at Jessie's side. 'It will always be our song, my darling. I brought it with me and asked Marcel to play it.'

Jessie's heart skipped a beat. 'Jack? I can't believe you're here.'

'Will you do me the honour of joining me for this dance, Jessie?'

Jessie stared at him, open mouthed. 'Jack! This is such a wonderful surprise, but why didn't you let me know you were coming?'

'I didn't want to let you down if my plans changed suddenly. Before we dance, I have something for you.'

Jack produced a single red rose with a flourish from behind his back and presented it to Jessie. 'That's the reason I'm late. I scoured all over London to find the right one. I wanted the song to be very special for us.'

Jessie's cheeks flushed as she took the flower, pressing it softly against her lips. She felt a fluttering feeling in her stomach and beamed. 'I'm lost for words at your thoughtful gesture. I feel foolish now for doubting you.'

Jack inhaled a breath and took her arm, placing the rose on the table. 'We can talk later. For now, let's savour every second of our tune.'

Jessie felt the warmth of his body as he placed his right arm around the small of her back and clutched her other palm high in his left hand. He pressed her gently towards him and she could feel their two hearts beating as one. A rippling sensation spread through her body and she felt deliriously happy.

She wished the dance could last forever and when it finished she returned to her table in a swoon where Beatrice and George, and Ada and Alfie were waiting for them.

Ruby turned to Maria. 'Well, what a night this has turned out to be. There's one thing left I reckon to make it the best night ever.'

'Oh yes, what's that?' she asked.

'It's time you and Eddie danced together.'

Maria retorted, 'He will ask in his own time I don't want to rush him.'

'Ruby is right. I've been plucking up the courage, but I'm willing to give it a go now,' Eddie asserted, with a twinkle in his eye. He stood up and extended his arm. 'Shall we, Maria, before I chicken out.'

Maria was up in a flash and Eddie wrapped his arm across her back. She moved closer towards him, feeling the warmth of his chest and the thumping beat from his heart. It was a quickstep, and as the tempo increased, they did their best to keep up, watching dancers around them for guidance, but in the end they danced around the floor not caring if they were out of step.

Eddie's face shone. 'I can't believe it. I'm dancing.'

Maria asked, 'What about the noise? Is it troubling you?'

'Not with you in my arms, my sweet Maria. I can't believe how much I'm enjoying meself.'

'You spoke too soon,' she teased, as he tripped up. 'Who cares? I'm happy you're doing it.'

'I'm happy to see the smile on your face too.'

When they returned to their seats, Eddie stroked Maria's cheek and turned her face towards his. 'How would you feel if we start planning our wedding, now I'm feeling much better?'

'I would like that, though we must wait a while for the mourning period to pass,' commented Maria as she rested her head on Eddie's shoulder. She wallowed in a warm blissful glow. She was deep in her own thoughts and didn't hear the door open or see the man's figure shuffle in leaning on a stick. He was wearing shabby clothing and appeared unkempt. Eddie jerked up and stared at the figure, pointing him out to Maria. She saw fingers pointing towards him, followed by shocked expressions on faces that appeared transfixed as he hobbled slowly, looking from side to side. The music began to fade and stopped.

Sensing something was amiss, Maria asked scrunching her eyes. 'What is it, Eddie? Who is he?'

The man shuffled closer in her direction. She stared harder and a sudden thought occurred – was this the man she had glimpsed in the distance on the station platform earlier that evening who had attracted so much attention?

His eyes darted across the room, as if he was looking for someone. He came to an abrupt halt, fixing his stare in their direction.

Maria swivelled her head as Kitty cried, 'No. It can't be him. It can't be.'

Kitty leapt up and walked cautiously through the startled gathering, stopping in front of him.

She took his face in his hands. 'Frank? No, it can't be.'

His eyes were moist and his voice unsteady. 'Aye, It's me, Kitty. I'm back.'

She pulled back, her voice cracking with emotion. 'But I thought you were dead. We all thought you were killed in Gallipoli.'

'I was left for dead, but I survived. I've prayed for this moment every day. And now it's happened'

He tossed his stick aside and held out his arms. Kitty fell into them and Frank wrapped her in a tight embrace, their bodies shaking. He buried his face in her hair and sobbed.

'I never thought I'd make it. Thinking of you and the children, that's what got me through.'

When she had no tears left, Kitty pulled away and tenderly stroked the growth that covered his face. Her husband was unrecognisable as the man who had left for war, but he was home. His return was a miracle!

Aware of the stares around her, she took Frank's hand in hers, held it high above their heads and cried, 'My Frank is alive. My husband is home.'

The room exploded into a loud applause and people gathered around to welcome him home.

Eddie placed his hand on Maria's shoulder. 'We should let them be.'

Maria nodded, staring at the couple. 'Turning up out of the blue like that is nothing short of a miracle. I can't believe Frank is alive, but you're right. This must be overwhelming for them. I wonder where he's been all this time, more than four years and with new news of him.'

'We'll find out all in good time, Maria.'

Maria's face glowed. 'You are right, my darling. The important thing is that Frank is back home. I am so happy for Kitty and the children. This has turned out to be the best day of me life.'

Eddie corrected her. 'The best day is yet to come, my darling Maria. It will be the day you become Mrs Herring.'

She teased. 'As long as we take the first dance together. But you need to brush up on yer steps first.'

Chapter Thirty-Two

Word spread quickly around Wolferton and beyond about Frank's sensational return home. Newspaper headlines screamed, 'Man Assumed Dead Returns Home After More Than Four Years!'

His remarkable story of survival against all the odds was marvelled at the length and breadth of the country. Though he sought no publicity and refused interview requests, he sensed his account of what happened was doubted by many, refusing to go into full details.

After a while the fuss died down and the guilt that consumed Frank for surviving while his friends died was too much. His moods darkened and he would disappear for hours, preferring solitude to company. Fingers pointed to him saying that he should have faced the Turks and died in Gallipoli as only a coward could have survived.

Kitty was distraught and confided in Mr Bell who had invited Frank to stay. 'It's not fair. It's not right. it breaks my 'eart to 'ear it and see him suffer so. I don't know what to say to him.'

The kindly benefactor responded by saying she must be patient, it would take time, and she should believe in her husband.

'There are no words that can ever show you the depth of our deep gratitude,' she thanked. 'But as soon as Frank is well enough to find a position with accommodation for us all, we'll be off. It ain't right to burden you with our troubles.'

Frank filled his time doing jobs around the house, fixing broken fencing and giving a lick of paint to the outside of the house.

Eddie offered to recommend Doctor Butterscotch's therapy to Frank, but he refused. Gradually, he began to open up. When the children were in bed one night and they were alone in the house, Frank told her the full story. Kitty listened incredulously as he described a fierce battle in Gallipoli, his friends and comrades killed all around him. He fell after taking a shot from a sniper and rolled into a ditch writhing in excruciating pain. He was unable to move and the sound of explosions and gunfire could be heard close by. He remembered a body rolling on top of him and then lost consciousness. When he opened his eyes again the fighting had stopped. All he could see was smoke and he could smell the dead bodies with shattered limbs around him. It took all the strength he could muster to push the body off him. As he did so, he heard footsteps coming in his direction. He froze, playing dead, afraid he would be captured by the enemy.

Suddenly the footsteps stopped and he was aware of a figure standing over him. He felt a sharp kick to his leg and yelped in pain. He opened his eyes and saw a Turkish soldier staring down at him.

Frank begged, 'In the name of the Lord, in the name of Allah, please don't shoot. I have a wife and six children. They need me.'

The soldier was young, only around seventeen years old. Without speaking he knelt down and picked up the bayonet at Frank's side and threw it out of reach. Frank pleaded again, his voice becoming weaker. 'Please, don't kill me, my family . . .'

The soldier helped him up and pressed his finger to his lips, whispering, 'Shhh.' After glancing around, and seeing nobody else was in sight, he helped Frank manoeuvre across the massacred remains, the shattered bodies and ripped-off limbs and faces on both sides. It was more than Frank could bear and he vomited. The Turk gave him a cloth to cover his face with and when they reached the edge of the killing fields, he saw a wagon pulled by a donkey. The captor lifted the cover and indicated he should get in.

Kitty interrupted, her eyes filled with fright. 'But surely this man was the enemy? Weren't you afraid to go off with him?'

'I was bloody petrified. I couldn't make out how he appeared out of the blue, but he didn't seem like the other Turks. I found out later he was collecting identification papers from the bodies of the Turks. I was ready to die, but he spared me life.'

'I shall forever be grateful to him. Who was he? Where did he take you?' Kitty pressed gently.

Frank stared down at the floor and remained silent. Kitty placed a consoling arm around his shoulder. She took his chin in her hand and tilted it towards her. 'Tell me, Frank. What happened next? What kept you from us all these years?'

He inhaled deeply. 'It's hard to believe how events turned out, but I swear every word is true. I lay on the floor of the cart and used the cleanest rag I could find around me leg. I closed me eyes, but I was haunted by the sight of those poor buggers, their bodies rotting; I can't imagine hell being worse. I 'ad no idea where we were going, I didn't 'ave the strength to run off. I must 'ave passed out 'cause the next time I opened me eye 'e was stopping outside an old stone hut.

'He lifted the cover and indicated to me to follow 'im. I was scared then, I admit it, thinking there might be a band of Turks inside who were going to do me in. I was hesitating when an old lady appeared with her arms stretched out. He kissed her on her cheeks and spoke in Turkish, addressing her as *Nine* – pronounced *neena,* which I know now means "grandmother". She was small and was dressed in black from head to toe and was really pleased to see him. She ushered him in, and she turned to me and said "Come", so I did.

'When we were inside the hut the soldier told me he was called Ali. He spoke some English and said his father is an Imam, a religious leader, and it was Ali's belief from his father's teachings that as I had been found alive, God had meant him to discover me and my life was in his hands, not as a soldier, but as a Muslim.

'He gave me a small cup of thick Turkish coffee which was bitter and said it was his wish to be a doctor one day. I wanted to ask if he could 'elp me to get 'ome, but he said I wasn't fit to travel. His words were, "It is the belief of our religion that Muslims will be held accountable for someone's death by God in the afterlife. *Nine* can treat your leg and you can stay here until it is safe for you to move on. In return,

I ask that you help my grandmother harvest her olives and make cheese from the goats.'

Kitty shook her head in disbelief. 'This is all so extraordinary.'

'I told you it would be. I had no choice but to stay. Ali told me, "My *Nine* says you can call her by her name, Nine Fatma. I think she likes you."

'I could scarcely believe what he said. I told him I was the enemy, and asked how he could trust me and leave me with his grandmother?

'Ali's reply made me feel ashamed. He said, "You and I are strangers thrown together, not during a battle, but when one is injured and needs help. We are human beings too. You have no need to worry. We are very remote here, very few people pass. You can let your hair grow and have a beard that covers your face. You will soon look Turkish and *Nine* has some old clothes from my grandfather you can wear. If anyone comes here, my grandmother will say you are deaf and dumb, you will ignore them and nobody will trouble you."

Kitty gulped and reached for a handkerchief. She dabbed her eyes. Frank paused and bit his lip. 'I'd no idea how long I was going to be there. Time passed and an unspoken affection grew between me and Ali's *Nine*. I had no money or papers or any idea where I was. I thought constantly of you, my darling Kitty, and the children. I told *Nine* all about you and she just smiled.'

Kitty gulped back tears. 'All those years we didn't know if you were dead or alive, we were thrown out of our 'ome and you were alive. Why didn't you get word to us that you were alive? We've suffered so much and ended up in the work-house. Couldn't you 'ave begged Ali to let us know you were alive?'

'I did ask, and hoped he would, but he was afraid if he passed on this information it would lead to my discovery. I even planned to escape. One day I walked for miles. I looked like a Turk and the peasants I passed didn't look twice at me, but I didn't 'ave any provisions or papers and knew I couldn't make it. I felt the best thing was to bide my time.'

Frank sniffled, taking Kitty's hand in his. 'I'm sorry to have put yer all through so much. You've every right to be angry. You should never 'ave been chucked out of yer 'ome. I promise I'll make it up to yer, if you give me a chance. We have Reverend Pierrepoint to thank that I'm back. If it weren't for him coming over and making enquiries about the Sandringham Company, I might still be there.'

Kitty stiffened. 'What's he got to do with this?'

Frank continued. 'One day Ali turned up at his grand-mother's and said, "It is time for you to go. Allah wills it."

'He said an English vicar was asking about the King's Men from Sandringham and this was my chance. I could hardly believe my ears. I left that day on the same donkey and cart and he dropped me off three hours later at a Red Cross centre. "These are good people, they will help you," he told me.

'They had heard about Reverend Pierrepont's visit to Gallipoli and informed Ali, who was acting as their Turkish intermediary.'

'Thank you for telling me, Frank. As Ali said, the Lord wished it.'

Kitty pressed her lips softly on her husband's mouth. Frank responded hungrily. 'It feels like a weight has been lifted now you know it all. It did cross me mind that yer might 'ave met another chap. Some women wouldn't have waited this long to find another man to father her children. I wouldn't have been able to take it.'

'You have the most faithful wife, Frank. What should we do now?'

'I'm thinking of trying for a job on a farm, somewhere that will include a roof over our heads?'

'As long as it's not on the royal estate, after the terrible way they treated us.'

∽

The children rejoiced at their father's return. Victoria was only nine when her father went to war, and she was now approaching fourteen. She was blossoming into a beauty and had a soft heart to match. She had eagerly accepted the offer of a full-time position at the workhouse as a teaching assistant in the new year when she turned fifteen.

Pip was eight when his father last set sight on him and Frank was thrilled to bits to learn a master furniture maker had spotted his talent and taken him under his wing.

Laurie and Billy, at six and four years old respectively when their father left for war, had hazier memories of him, but made up for lost time and bonded over long walks and games of hide and seek. Laurie continued to shine at school and impress teachers with his skill for numbers.

Frank affectionately teased Iris for her tomboy ways. She had been only three when he last saw her and she shied away from him for a few days, holding back until she saw her siblings go to him and chiding her for being unkind.

Rosie was just one year old when Frank left home and she playfully pulled at his beard. 'Are you really my papa?' Her childlike innocence melted his heart. Soon he was tickling her tummy and she was squealing and playing tag with him.

∽

The following day Kitty was processing everything Frank told her. Over their breakfast she recounted Frank's story to Miss Finchley and Milly and they listened agog, muttering words of shock and disbelief. Mr Bell and George walked through to enquire as to why their breakfast was delayed and when the reason was explained, they insisted on hearing the story from the beginning.

George rubbed the back of his neck. 'It really is the most extraordinary story. You must have been born under a lucky star, Frank Willow. I have good news for you'

Kitty and Frank exchanged puzzled glances. 'What do yer mean,' they asked.

'I was at the station master's house last night when Jessie mentioned that Lizzie Piper needs a new farm manager. Accommodation comes with the job. If it interests you, you should get in touch with her straightaway.'

Frank's face brightened. 'I think I will, without delay. What do yer say, Kitty?'

She flung her arms around his neck. 'Yes, it would be perfect for us.'

She drew back, her expression suddenly doubtful. 'But I want yer to promise me one thing, Frank.'

'What is that, my darling?'

'Promise me that we will save every farthing so we can one day have the key to our own front door and will have our own roof over our heads so nobody can throw us out.'

Frank instantly agreed. 'Too damned right I will.'

Chapter Thirty-Three

After the revelation about Mr Bell and Miss Finchley's relationship was revealed, they went out in society as a couple.

'We're too old to keep hiding under a bushel. It's time for the world to know my feelings for you,' he impassioned.

They received a mixed reception from different factions, with Mr Bell airily dismissing those who now gave him the cold shoulder, his spirits uplifted by those who shared their happiness and gave him their best wishes.

Two days before the Willow family were due to move into Blackbird Farm, Mr Bell announced, 'Miss Finchley and I would like to invite you to join us tomorrow, Sunday afternoon, for a slap-up tea at the Duke's Head. Our invitation is extended to everyone in this household, including Milly.'

The children were excited at the prospect of going to a smart hotel and dressed in their best clothes. When they arrived at the grand building, which overlooked the marketplace, they were led into the dining room and stared in awe at the ornate cornices in the high-ceilinged room. Works of art were pinned on the wall and giant aspidistra plants were placed appropriately. Sparkling glass chandeliers dipped down above their heads. They chatted excitedly as the food was laid in front of them.

Kitty warned them about their manners, but their excitement couldn't be contained and they licked their fingers after each morsel of the crustless ham sandwiches, meat pies and savoury flans, and dainty cakes piped exquisitely with icing. The scones melted in the mouth and every crumb was devoured.

'These are very delicious cakes,' Kitty praised the waitress. 'Do you make them here?'

She whispered behind her hand. 'I'm not supposed to say, but we have started ordering supplies from Batterbee's Bakery. Everyone knows they're the best.'

'Indeed they are, and are much in demand by the royal household.'

Kitty melted at she stared at Frank's smooth face. With his beard removed, he was the handsome husband of old that she had fallen in love with. He was relaxed and well dressed in a dark suit and a crisp white shirt and tie, thanks to the generosity of George who gave him the use of his wardrobe. Kitty couldn't recall seeing him so smart and she felt a warm swelling rising inside her.

She teased, 'Why, you look so handsome, I could marry you all over again.'

Frank eye's watered. 'How can I ever thank yer, Mr Bell, Mr Perryman, and everyone in yer 'ousehold, for all you've done for my Kitty and the little ones.'

'They're not so little now, are they, darling?' Kitty smiled, linking her arms through Frank's.

After their china cups had been replenished with steaming tea, and everyone declared they were so full they would burst if they ate another morsel, Mr Bell rose from his chair

361

and smiled affectionately at Miss Finchley, who was sitting on his right side.

All eyes fixed on him. 'These past few months have been extraordinary in many ways. Frank's story is a reminder to us that anything can happen when we least expect it and how we should never give up hope.'

'Hear, hear!' the group chorused, nodding their heads.

Mr Bell cleared his throat. 'You now all know of my deep friendship with Henrietta. I never thought the moment would come when she could hold on to my arm in public. I've longed for this moment, for the day when my beloved and I could share our affections openly and without shame, and our pride in letting the world know that George is our son.'

Mr Bell paused, overcome with emotion. He turned to Miss Finchley. 'We have some exciting news to share. You are the first to know. I am honoured to announce that Henrietta has agreed to be my wife.'

Mr Bell's smile stretched across his face as his eyes lingered lovingly on his future bride. 'After all this time, after all these wasted years, I cannot wait for us to be wed and live together as man and wife with the Lord's blessing.'

Miss Finchley blushed. 'It will just be a small wedding. We don't want a lot of fuss, not at our age.'

The happy couple beamed as Kitty, Mrs Bell senior, Frank and George congratulated them. Billy produced his penny whistle and played a happy tune, with the younger Willow children clapping their hands and giggling.

Mr Bell raised his hand. 'There's more good news to share. I can confirm that George is now an official partner in my law firm. One day he will take full charge and I know he will take on this responsibility with great diligence and continue our work representing those in most need.'

Rousing cheers and clapping followed and a joyful Mr Bell called the waiter over. He whispered in his ear, and the waiter returned a few moments later with a bottle of champagne and glasses for the adults.

'I believe this calls for a proper celebration,' he announced.

'I've never had champagne before,' muttered Kitty.

'Neither have I,' said Frank, 'but I intend to enjoy every drop.'

Diners from other tables approached and congratulated George and his father. Some recognised Frank's picture from the newspapers and shook his hand.

As they rose to leave, Miss Finchley turned to Kitty. 'I plan to train Milly to take over from me as housekeeper, she is more than capable. We shall employ a new maid from the workhouse to take her place.'

'Some good did come out of being sent to that godforsaken place.' Kitty beamed.

Kitty took her husband's arm as they left the hotel. Frank whispered in her ear, 'There is something I must do. I am here thanks to the kindness of Ali. I want to light a candle and pray for him. He and his grandmother saved my life.'

'I agree, my love. War has shown us that friendships are not bound by the country of your birth, but can be intertwined. Although it brings out the worst in men, it also shows us their best.'

Chapter Thirty-Four

Spring 1920

Maria stepped back from the mirror and stared at the reflection in front of her.

'You look beautiful, Maria. Eddie won't be able to take his eyes off yer,' Kitty extolled, smoothing the folds at the back of Maria's wedding dress. It was a cream cotton gown with a long pointed lace collar, long flowing sleeves and a matching lace hem that fell just above the knee. A pale blue satin bow around the waist completed the ensemble.

The reflection that stared back at Maria was a stranger, used to wearing dark clothes and practical attire; she felt for once like a princess.

There was a knock on the door and Beatrice pushed it open slightly. 'Are you ready? We just want a peep,' she said.

'I'm almost ready. You can come in,' Maria replied.

Beatrice, Jessie and Ada entered the room, their faces filled with admiration as their eyes fell on the beautiful bride standing before them.

Jessie drew in a deep breath. 'You really do look beautiful, Maria. Eddie will be in pieces when he sees you.'

'I 'ope he likes it. I'm feeling jittery inside.'

'That's a natural feeling.' Ada smiled.

'Although I'm yer step-aunt, we've been more like sisters since I arrived in Wolferton. I couldn't 'ave wished for a better family. Thank yer all, thank yer from the bottom of me 'eart.'

A tear trickled down Maria's cheek and she dabbed her eyes with the handkerchief that Kitty handed her.

'I wish ma could 'ave seen me on the happiest day of me life."

Ada dabbed her yes. 'She'll be looking down on you and smiling; she'll be happy for you. You look a picture and Eddie is a good man.'

'I feel so fortunate.' Maria nodded, while adjusting the long string of pearls that hung down her chest that had been lent to her by Aggie. Ada lent her a cream-coloured cloche hat that matched her dress perfectly, reminding her it was for luck – *something old, something new, something borrowed and something blue.*

Harry called upstairs, asking how they were getting on. He was giving Maria away and the station master's house was being used for the bridal party.

The bridesmaids were waiting downstairs: Victoria, Iris and Rosie, all angelic looking in their soft pink gowns and lavender satin waistbands, halos of fresh spring flowers sitting prettily on their heads. Joey was an attendant too and felt very grown up dressed in a smart pair of royal blue breeches and pale blue shirt. Harry and Sarah had stumped up the cost of the gowns and wedding breakfast, saying it's what their pa, William Saward, would have wanted. Mrs Watson arranged with the seamstress from the Big House to make all the dresses and declared they were as fine as any worn by the royal family.

'Are you sure Eddie will like it?' Maria asked Beatrice, tilting her head, and turning to her side.

Beatrice smiled. 'I don't think he'll like it. I know he'll love it, just as he loves you, though he'd love you just as much if you were dressed in a sack.'

Maria bit her lip. 'I'm nervous. I'm shaky inside.'

'It's natural on yer wedding day. Let's go down. We shouldn't keep them waiting any longer, otherwise Eddie will think he's been jilted.'

The sound of Maria's footsteps walking steadily down the stairs brought everyone rushing out. There was a chorus of gasps and words of admiration.

'Oh my dear, you look absolutely beautiful,' Harry told her, extending his arm.

'You look ever so pretty.' Victoria beamed.

Victoria passed Maria her scented bouquet of narcissi, white hyacinth and lily of the valley that was lying on the table.

Maria held her head high as she placed her hand on Harry's arm and stepped outside. The sky was pale grey, with flecks of pale yellow peeping between fluffy clouds. She paused for a moment, thinking to herself that this was the last moment she would be known as a Saward, that within the hour she would be addressed as Mrs Herring.

As she took a step forward, a robin fluttered overhead and perched on the garden fence. 'That's Ma's, it must be her,' she murmured with a smile. 'Thank you, Ma, for all you've done for me.'

She stepped into a chauffeured Daimler Queen Maud had given the use of for Maria and her bridesmaids. She felt like royalty climbing into the back of the shining limousine, with its soft red leather seats. The bridesmaids squeezed in alongside her. Rosie perched on Victoria's knee, while Harry and Joey sat in the front. Her brothers were already at the church and her heart pounded during the ride as she rested her back on the cushioned seat, staring out of the window, wondering which member of the royal family had sat there before her.

Jack was waiting in a car outside the house. He opened the front passenger door and Jessie slid in beside him, carefully hoisting up the pale pink fabric of her outfit. Beatrice and Ada sat in the back seat, their places in the front of the church reserved by George and Alfie.

As they drew alongside the lych gate, Maria drew in a breath. It had been decorated by Jessie with a lavish display of spring flowers that matched her bouquet, and the addition of white hellebores, daffodils and primroses. She stepped out to a rapturous cheer from a throng of well-wishers, staff she recognised from the royal estate. Her heart thumped as she walked through the lychgate with its sweet aroma.

'Ready, Maria?' Harry asked.

'I'm ready. I never thought I'd be nervous. I have butterflies and feel a bit wobbly.'

Harry patted her arm. 'You'll be just fine. It will be over in a flash and you'll wish you could do it all over again.'

Reverend Rumbelow was standing at the entrance to the church. He gave a sign inside for the music to start. As Alfie belted out 'The Wedding March' on the organ, Maria's tummy flipped and her legs wobbled as she walked up the aisle, leaning on Harry's arm.

She lifted her chin and relaxed, smiling at her husband-to-be, acknowledging his appreciative expression and the tender look in his eyes that moistened when she stood alongside him.

'I've never seen yer look so lovely,' he whispered.

The service passed in a blink and before she knew it Eddie slid a gold band on her finger and they were surrounded by cheering well wishers in the churchyard.

'There's one thing I must do,' Maria said, stepping carefully around the tombstones. She stopped when she reached her mother's grave and gently lay down her bouquet.

'Who would have thought it, Ma, the day you left me 'ere, that I would marry the best man in the world.'

Eddie knelt at the graveside. 'I promise yer I shall be the best husband and that Maria and Joey will want for nought. You can rest in peace knowing I shall take good care of them.'

Harry interjected. 'Come along, you two. Your wedding guests are waiting for you.'

They linked arms as they passed a throng of cheering friendly faces lining the path with handfuls of rose petals they threw at them, wishing the couple a happy life together. The meeting room was adorned with colourful bunting and flowers and rows of trestle tables laid out with white tablecloths in honour of the newlyweds. Batterbee's Bakery laid on a spread fit for a king, with delicious buffet food, including the best selection of desserts they could have wished for.

Harry and Sarah joined the happy couple at the top table. After they finished eating Harry rose, his face beaming, and proposed a toast as they were about to cut their wedding cake. 'Will you rise and please join me in wishing every happiness to my sister, Maria, and her husband Eddie. Maria's sudden arrival here four years ago was a shock for us all, but we all warmed to her ways and admire her determined spirit. Wolferton would not be the same without her now. Let's raise a glass to Maria and Eddie's future as Mr and Mrs Herring.'

Maria's throat tightened. She could barely believe the warm feelings and love that was bestowed on her as she glanced around at the cheering community. All her friends, staff from the Big House and Appleton House were there. Mabel and Abel were clapping their hands and Ruby and little Piers sat with the vicar and his wife.

Beautifully wrapped presents were piled high on a trestle table for them to open on the return from their honeymoon. She had never been given so many gifts in her life.

The Saward sisters were seated together with their partners and after the wedding breakfast had been eaten, Jack leaned towards Jessie. 'Can I speak to you alone. I have some good news. I can't wait to tell you.'

She followed him outside and he inhaled a breath. 'I've been offered a position in the royal household's treasurer's office. I wanted to let you know now before I leave on my next journey for the king as royal messenger. This will be my last mission. When I return, I will be based in England.'

'You'll be working in London, permanently?' That's wonderful news, Jack. Are you sure you won't tire of seeing me at weekends?'

'How could you think such a thing! These long partings show me how much I love you. I can't bear to be away from you anymore.'

Jessie's heart raced and her eyes shone. Jack produced a small box from his jacket pocket and knelt on one knee. 'I don't want to just see you at weekends, Jessie. I want to see you every day. I am asking if you will be my wife?'

She knelt down in front of Jack and pressed her lips against his, taking his face in her hands. When she drew away, she grinned. 'There's your answer, Jack Hawkins. I do.'

Jack flung his arms around her, lifting her off the ground and swinging her around. He told her, 'This is Maria and Eddie's day. Let's not say anything just yet.'

Jessie was bursting with joy to shout out her news to the whole world, and they were inseparable for the remainder of the wedding breakfast.

Aggie and Marcel set up their new gramophone. They removed a black disc from its sleeve and placed it down, with the needle in position. It was a waltz with romantic overtures.

Eddie took Maria's hand and led her to the dance floor.

'You did it, Eddie. You kept your word.'

'I did, Mrs Herring. I wish we could dance all night, but we 'ave to leave for our honeymoon shortly.'

Soon everyone was dancing. Harry and Sarah found they had a spring in their step, and all too soon, it was time for the happy couple to leave. Maria changed into a duck-egg blue dress with pearl buttons down the front. It had long sleeves finished with lace edging and Ada had lent Maria her best cream coat to wear over it. She pulled down a cloche hat in a darker blue, her hair pulled back behind her ears. Her face radiated pure joy and contentment. She hadn't expected to feel so happy so soon after her mother's death. Harry and Sarah were taking care of Joey while she was away, insisting she was not to worry about him.

'I had no idea what to pack. Eddie wouldn't tell me where we're going,' she told the wedding guests, throwing her hands in the air.

Eddie winked. 'It's going to be a surprise, Mrs Herring. We must go now, the train leaves in half an hour.'

Jessie, Beatrice and Ada followed behind them excitedly with rice to throw over the newlyweds. Just before they reached the station Beatrice paused. She addressed Jessie. 'Your cheeks seem flushed and your eyes are sparkling. You stare at Jack with a puppy love look on your face, more so than ever before. Is there something we should know?'

'Well,' she hesitated. 'Jack asked me not to say anything yet, but I can't keep a secret from my sisters. He asked me to marry him and I said yes.'

'This is just the best news.' The sisters beamed, congratulating Jessie.

Harry and Sarah overheard. Sarah suggested, 'I see no reason to delay the nuptials. How about a double wedding? And I shall speak to the vicar about it tomorrow.'

'Yes, a double wedding in the summer would be perfect,' Jessie and Beatrice agreed, glowing in anticipation.

The party arrived at the station just as a train was pulling in. Eddie took Maria's hand. She brimmed with excitement.

She turned to Harry. 'There's a red carpet laid out. Are you expecting a royal visitor?'

The station master leaned back and grinned. 'No, Maria. Today it is your turn to be royalty. Today you are the Queen of Wolferton.'

Author's Note

The men from the Sandringham Company who died during World War I live on in our minds today. Their names were engraved on a stone memorial that today stands in a prominent position close to the visitor's centre on the Sandringham Estate. Each name represents a story of heartache, their loss engraved on the hearts of those they left behind; their beloved wives, sweethearts, children, parents, siblings and their close knit community.

The memorial was unveiled by King George on 17 October 1920 and is a legendary landmark. Just a mile away, in the Church of St Peter and St Paul at West Newton, where the estate workers would regularly worship, there exists a stained glass window in memory of Captain Frank Beck and his men from the royal estate who died on 12 August 1915. Beneath the window is a brass plaque in memory of Frank's widow, Mary, who like many other wives and sweethearts of fallen servicemen, and those missing in action, refused to give up hope that their men miraculously might one day walk through the door, fling their kitbag down and rush into their arms.

The names of those left behind with their grief are never given any recognition. It is for that reason that I wanted to tell their story the best I could. These brave, stoic women, in spite of their immense suffering, carried the scars on their hearts with dignity and determination for the sake of their fatherless children.

More than one hundred years later, the Sandringham Estate is thriving. While Appleton House has since been demolished, the royal family's popular Norfolk residence at Sandringham attracts tens of thousands of visitors a year from all over the world and many of its staff continue to live in its pretty carstone cottages, their gardens filled with scented roses and hollyhocks.

Trains may no longer pull in at Wolferton Station, but some things never change.

Acknowledgements

As always, I would like to thank my brilliant editor, Claire Johnson-Creek, for sharing this journey with me and for her wise and insightful advice throughout.

I give huge thanks also to the talented team at Bonnier Books, with special mention to the cover designer and marketeers, and all those who have done a fantastic job for me behind the scenes.

This book would not have been possible without the kindness and support of Brian Heath who first told me of Harry Saward, royal station master extraordinaire, and was keen for me to share his great-grandfather's previously untold story; it has been a privilege getting to know him and his family.

I am grateful to Richard Brown and Ben Colson, who reside in their own suite of royal retiring rooms on opposite sides of the tracks at the royal Wolferton Station, near Sandringham, Norfolk and have kindly assisted me during my research.

Historian Neil Storey gives me peace of mind by fact checking my draft, I would be lost without him and appreciative his fine attention to detail.

I would also like to thank Kevin Hitchcock at King's Lynn library for sharing his love and knowledge of local history with me.

I thank my agent, Elizabeth Counsell, at Northbank Talent Agency, for her constant support.

This writing journey has been shared by my husband, Stephen, and family, David and Fiona, whose darling baby son, George, this book is dedicated to, and James and Beth; thank you for your patience and understanding when deadlines loom and my time with you is constrained.

Enormous thanks from my heart go to my readers for their interest in this series, it is always a joy hearing their comments. I very much hope they have enjoyed The Royal Station Master's Daughters trilogy.

Welcome to the world of Ellee Seymour

Keep reading for more from Ellee Seymour, to discover a recipe that features in this novel and to find out more about Ellee's upcoming books . . .

We'd also like to welcome you to Memory Lane, a place to discuss the very best saga stories from authors you know and love with other readers, plus get recommendations for new books we think you'll enjoy. Read on and join our club!

Dear Readers,

I would like to thank you for sharing my exciting author's journey, and what an adventure it has been for me as a debut fiction writer. It seems so long ago now, back in those dark Covid pandemic days, when *The Royal Station Master's Daughters* series was commissioned by Bonnier Zaffre, and I can still clearly recall the thrill I felt.

It was a dream come true to see the first book released in April 2022, followed a year later by *The Royal Station Master's Daughters at War*. Sadly, *The Royal Station Master's Daughters in Love* is the last in the trilogy, but I hope the books will continue to be read and give pleasure in future years.

I started writing this series to bring to life the untold story of a real royal station master, Harry Saward, his wife, Sarah, and three daughters, Jessie, Beatrice and Ada, staying true to their characters as described to me by Harry's great-grandson, Brian Heath. I also wanted to write about women's lives in this tight-knit community during World War I, these women with resilience who faced adversity and poverty, but somehow pulled through. Their lives were shattered following the disastrous Gallipoli campaign in 1915 when workers on the royal estate, the gardeners and groomsmen and others there who made up the Sandringham Company, perished on a Turkish battlefield. The agony for more than 120 families was prolonged when the bodies of their loved ones were not discovered until 1919; such unbearable suffering for them, which my last book describes.

Back to our station master. Harry was a one-off. He reigned over Wolferton Station for forty years, between 1884 and 1924, with great pride and dignity, decorum and courtesy, graciously welcoming royals when they set foot on the platform. The royal retiring rooms, where royalty and distinguished guests rested before travelling on to Sandringham House, or returning to London, are still in use today, as private accommodation, and remain the only ones in existence in the country; it was an unknown part of our royal history I wanted to write about and I hope my books have given Harry a measure of the recognition he deserves.

While researching and writing this series I was transported back into a bygone era that enthralled and exhilarated me. But it is my wonderful readers who contact me, who share their kind comments, who have made this the most memorable and pleasurable journey of my life. I thank you, and hope you will stay in touch.

· MEMORY LANE ·

You can read more about my books and the historical background on my website, https://www.elleeseymour. com/

With much love,
Ellee xxx

A Recipe for Lavender Cupcakes

Can you resist one of these heavenly lavender cupcakes with their delicate floral flavour as made by the Batterbee's Bakery? One bite, and they will become a favourite. If you do not have fresh lavender heads, you can buy it dried from supermarkets.

Ingredients

- 2 lavender heads (1 or 2 teaspoon dried lavender)
- 150g caster sugar
- 150g unsalted butter
- 150g self-raising flour
- 3 eggs
- ½ teaspoon baking power

Icing

- 200g fondant icing sugar
- 2 lavender heads, or dried equivalent
- purple food colouring

Method

- Heat the oven to 180°C (fan 160°C, gas mark 4).
- Line a cupcake tin with 12 paper cupcake cases.
- Place the butter and sugar in a mixing bowl and beat until light and fluffy.
- Beat in the eggs a little at a time until smooth, adding a little flour if the mixture curdles.
- Pull the seeds off the lavender heads and add to the mixture to give the desired flavour.
- Stir in the flour and baking powder and mix gently.
- Place heaped dessertspoon full in each cupcake case and bake for 20–25 minutes until just firm to the touch. Allow to cool on a wire rack.
- To decorate, make up the fondant icing as directed on the packet to a very thick pourable icing.
- Add a drop of colouring for a soft lilac colour. Pour over the cupcakes and leave to set, then top with sprinkles of lavender.

Don't miss the first two books in Ellee Seymour's Royal Station Master's Daughters series . . .

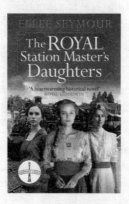

Roll out the red carpet. The royal train is due in half an hour and there's not a minute to be wasted.

It's 1915 and the country is at war. In the small Norfolk village of Wolferton, uncertainty plagues the daily lives of sisters Ada, Jessie and Beatrice Saward, as their men are dispatched to the frontlines of Gallipoli.

Harry, their father, is the station master at the local stop for the royal Sandringham Estate. With members of the royal family and their aristocratic guests passing through the station on their way to the palace, the Sawards' unique position gives them unrivalled access to the monarchy.

But when the Sawards' estranged and impoverished cousin Maria shows up out of the blue, everything the sisters thought they knew about their family is thrown into doubt.

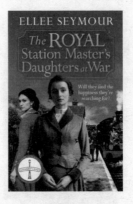

It is 1917 and Maria has adapted well to her new life on the royal
Sandringham estate where she works as a maid in the Big House for
Queen Alexandra and is in awe of the many treasures around her. It
is two years since she turned up at the royal station master's house
to escape her secret past, destitute and with nowhere else to turn.
Having proven herself to Harry Saward and his daughters, she is now
welcomed by them as one of the family. But when Nellie, a mysterious
relative turns up, on the run from the law, Maria's new-found
happiness could be under threat.

Meanwhile, the impact of World War I is felt deeply in the community
as the fate of missing men from the Sandringham Company, who fought
in Gallipoli, is still unknown. Harry's daughters pull together to support
each other and women on the royal estate as they face their sorrows and
challenges. Ada's husband, Alfie, is away fighting on the front line while
Beatrice is now a VAD nurse at a cottage hospital. Jessie has become a
land army girl, proudly doing a man's job, while pining for
her sweetheart Jack.

In a community torn apart by loss and tragedy, how will the
station master's family survive and find the happiness
they're all searching for?

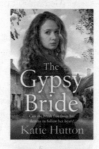